Her left arm throbbed.

Jennie stared down at her bloody jacket and remembered the stage bandits shooting at her from the second-story room. The bullet grazing her arm. The escape. She had to get out of Fillmore—now.

Mounting a horse, she headed for the road. The steady movement of the horse beneath her and the unrelenting pain in her arm lolled Jennie into a state of semiwakefulness. Ahead of her, she could see the angry faces of the thieves she'd robbed.

Then another image rose unbidden. The handsome features she'd grown to know so well. Unlike the others, Caleb regarded her with tenderness. But too quickly his expression changed to one of pain and anger.

He doesn't despise me now, but he will if he ever finds out what I've done. How would she explain her gunshot wound to Caleb and her family?

"Can't I have the ranch and Caleb, too?" she asked the heavens. The rumble of distant thunder was her only reply.

USA TODAY Bestselling Author

Stacy Henrie
and
Debra Ullrick

Lady Outlaw
&
The Unlikely Wife

LOVE INSPIRED
INSPIRATIONAL ROMANCE

LOVE INSPIRED®

INSPIRATIONAL ROMANCE

Recycling programs for this product may not exist in your area.

ISBN-13: 978-1-335-23989-1

Lady Outlaw & The Unlikely Wife

Copyright © 2020 by Harlequin Books S.A.

Lady Outlaw
First published in 2012. This edition published in 2020.
Copyright © 2012 by Stacy Henrie

The Unlikely Wife
First published in 2012. This edition published in 2020.
Copyright © 2012 by Debra Ullrick

This edition published by arrangement with Harlequin Books S.A.

For questions and comments about the quality of this book, please contact us at CustomerService@Harlequin.com.

Love Inspired
22 Adelaide St. West, 40th Floor
Toronto, Ontario M5H 4E3, Canada
www.Harlequin.com

Printed in U.S.A.

CONTENTS

Stacy Henrie has always had a love for history, fiction and chocolate. She earned her BA in public relations before turning her attention to raising a family and writing inspirational historical romances. The wife of an entrepreneur husband and a mother of three, Stacy loves to live out history through her fictional characters. In addition to being an author, she is also a reader, a road-trip enthusiast and a novice interior decorator.

Books by Stacy Henrie

Love Inspired Historical

Visit the Author Profile page
at Harlequin.com for more titles.

LADY OUTLAW

Stacy Henrie

For I the Lord thy God will hold thy right hand,
saying unto thee, Fear not; I will help thee.
—*Isaiah* 41:13

To Peter.
This story is as much ours as it is mine.
Thanks for never doubting.

Acknowledgments

First, foremost and always, thank you to my family—especially my husband, who read the manuscript about as many times as I did, who gave me the time I needed to revise and who never gave up on my dream, even when I wasn't so sure myself.

Thank you to my mom and grandma for instilling in me a love of reading, and to my dad for passing on his interest in history and helping me with the idea for Jennie's outlawing ways.

Thank you to my writer friends for their advice, encouragement, suggestions and laughter—especially Ali Cross, Elana Johnson, Jenn Wilks, Sara Olds, Becki Clayson and Rachel Nunes.

Thank you to the ladies in book club for their interest in my writing journey through the years. I hope this book gives you lots to talk about—after I leave the room.

Thank you to Jessica Alvarez for her vision and support, and to Elizabeth Mazer, who loved the story as much as I did and was willing to give me a second chance.

A final thank-you to my Father in Heaven for guiding my path, giving me this gift and teaching me to trust. Thankfully we don't always get what we want when we want it—typically the blessings are far greater than we could imagine when we least expect it.

Chapter One

Utah Territory—September 1869

"Regrettably, the answer is no, Miss Jones."

The bank president's apologetic tone might have fooled her, but Jennie caught a glint of satisfaction in Albert Dixon's gray eyes that contradicted his sympathetic words.

"I'm sure things have been more difficult on the ranch since your father's death, but you haven't made a payment on your mortgage in over a year." He cleared his throat. "That's eighteen hundred dollars you already owe us. We'll need to see five hundred of that before the end of the month, if you wish to keep your property. The full debt will be due next August—no exceptions."

Jennie gripped the handle of her purse so hard her fingers hurt. No matter the sum, she wouldn't give up the ranch. "And if I don't have the money…"

Mr. Dixon dropped a glance at the sheet of paper before him, then slid the document across the desk. Jennie read the words written in bold, black ink at the top—*Notice of Foreclosure.*

"If you can't produce the minimum amount, we'll have to terminate the loan." He shook his head and rose from his chair. "I wish there was more I could do. I'm deeply sorry."

"I'm sure you are." Jennie grabbed her small suitcase off the floor and came to her feet, eyeing him coldly. "But let me make something quite clear, Mr. Dixon. The only part of my father's cattle ranch you'll ever own is a steak dinner—and I hope it gives you a bad case of indigestion. Good day."

The bank president's round face and balding head turned a satisfying shade of red before Jennie headed for the door. She could hear him sputtering for a reply as she left the bank. She marched in the direction of the stage office, the heels of her boots stomping out a hard beat.

"I'd like to take a branding iron to that man," she muttered under her breath as she wound her way along Fillmore's storefronts.

She contemplated a number of other ways she might lower the bank president's arrogance before her fury changed to despair. As her anger ebbed so did her determined pace and finally Jennie came to a stop at the corner of the general mercantile.

Where would she find five hundred dollars to keep her ranch? She'd barely scraped together enough cash to finance her trip to Fillmore. She had no relatives to borrow money from and couldn't afford to sell any of their cattle, either. Since rustlers had cleaned them out of calves and half the herd in the spring, they had to keep every last cow in order to increase the number of cattle next year. *Besides, what good is a cattle ranch with no cows?*

A hat display in the window beside her caught Jennie's eye. *Latest Styles from the East,* a handwritten sign below the hats read. She loved hats—her father had always bought her a new one on his trips to Fillmore. The one she wore today, with a rounded brim and green braiding that accentuated her red hair, was the last one he'd purchased for her. That had been a little over a year ago, just before her twentieth birthday. On that occasion, he'd bought her a brooch, as well.

Jennie's fingers went to her throat, sliding over the simple but pretty cameo her father had said reminded him of her. She could just picture him in the store, happily chatting with the clerk as he picked out gifts to bring home. She fought back the tears that sprang to her eyes at the image.

Squaring her shoulders, she stepped toward the mercantile. She couldn't replace her father in so many ways, but at least she could look around for some small gift to bring home. The southbound stage wasn't likely to leave for another thirty minutes or so, and she needed a diversion from her depressing thoughts. Despite her limited funds, she hoped to spare one or two coins to buy Grandma Jones and Will some candy or a penny trinket instead of bringing back only bad news.

Caleb looked up at the tinkling sound of the sleigh bells hanging from the mercantile's doorknob and watched the young lady walk in. His time as a bounty hunter had honed his skills at taking the measure of a man—or woman—in a matter of moments, and it only took a glance for him to guess at the girl's story.

The clothes, neat and clean but worn, made it clear that money was tight at home. But she held her head

high, coffee-brown eyes sharp and keen, a nice con-
trast to her red hair. He read pride and determination
in her posture and expression. Times might be tough,
but clearly this lady wasn't one to give up.

He'd had that kind of determination, once. After the
death of his fiancée, he'd been filled with determination
to find the bandits involved, and see them all brought to
justice. But in the aftermath of the deadly confrontation
a year ago, his determination had fled. All he wanted
now was to earn enough money to start a small business
of his own—something far different from the farm life
he'd planned to share with Liza…and worlds away from
the bounty hunting business he'd left behind too late.

He watched as the woman nodded to the store clerk,
then headed toward the glass jars of brightly colored
candies that sat on the long counter. He felt a moment's
idle curiosity wondering what she'd choose before his
attention was snagged by the two men talking at the
end of the counter.

"Somebody wired the sheriff and told him the bandits were headed south," one of the men said. "He sent
out nearly twenty men looking for 'em, but I think they
must've slipped past."

At the word *bandits,* Caleb found himself straight-
ening up automatically, then he forced himself to relax.
He was done with bounty hunting—those bandits were
someone else's responsibility now.

"When did they rob the stage?" the other asked.

"Yesterday afternoon. They met up with the coach
about fifteen miles south of Nephi."

"How much money did they steal?"

"Two thousand dollars."

Two thousand dollars? Caleb was shocked…not just

by the amount, but by the loud crash that followed the announcement. He glanced over to see that the young lady had accidentally struck one of the candy jars with her suitcase. The container had toppled off the counter and smashed on the floor, spraying glass and peppermint sticks around everyone's feet. Caleb only caught a glimpse of her hotly embarrassed blush before she dropped to her knees and began picking up the candy with trembling hands.

Shaking hands and broken glass made for a dangerous combination so Caleb crouched down beside her to help. Reaching for one of the larger pieces of glass, his fingers almost brushed against hers. When she lifted her head to look at him, he was struck by just how pretty she was, with that fiery hair and warm brown eyes. *Nothing like Liza, of course,* Caleb thought to himself, heart twisting as it always did at the memory of Liza's dark hair and sweet smile, but very pretty all the same. Especially when she blushed like that.

"You don't have to help," she murmured.

"I'd like to." He slipped the glass from underneath her fingers and placed it to the side.

"No, that's all right. I can clean up the mess myself." Apparently he'd been right about the pride and determination. But he wasn't going to let that stop him. He continued to gather up the broken shards, acting as if he hadn't heard her. When the store clerk appeared with a broom, Caleb took hold of it and swept the glass into a pile while the young lady finished collecting the candy.

"I'm so sorry," she said to the clerk as she stood. She set the peppermint sticks on the counter. "I don't have enough to pay for the damage and purchase my ticket home, but…" She reached up to her collar, her hand covering the brooch pinned there. "Maybe I could trade—" Her fingers tightened over the piece of jewelry and Caleb could see that it hurt her to even think of giving it up. Maybe that was what prompted his next words.

"I'll pay for the candy." The hope of starting up a freighting business of his own had had Caleb saving every penny for the past year. As a result, he had plenty of cash on hand. The broken jar and candy shouldn't put him back by more than a dollar or two. He could spare that well enough. Digging around in his pocket, he extracted some cash, along with the letter he'd come into town to mail—yet another attempt to mend fences with his disapproving family. "I'd like to mail this letter, too," he said to the clerk. "So how much do I owe you?"

The girl shook her head. "I can't let you do that. I'd want to repay you, and I can't."

"I think two dollars oughta cover it," the store clerk said, seemingly in agreement with Caleb to ignore her protests.

Caleb handed over two bills along with his letter, then scooped up the candy. The clerk took the mail and money and returned to his post beside the cash register.

"You shouldn't have done that—paid for the candy, I mean." The lady frowned at Caleb as she collected her purse and suitcase. "I could have given him my brooch to make up the difference."

Certain any mention of how obviously she'd wanted to keep the brooch would just upset her, Caleb tried a different tactic. "Probably so, but I can think of a way to repay me," he said as he went to pick up another handful of peppermint sticks they'd missed near the door. When everything was gathered together, he turned to face her again.

"I can't eat all of these by myself. How about taking a few off my hands?" He offered her a fistful of candy.

The absurdity of the whole situation made her smile, just as he'd hoped. "All right," she said. "I'll take some."

She shifted her things to one arm and took the candy from him.

"I hope you enjoy them," he said, smiling back. "Always a pleasure to help a pretty girl."

For some reason, his compliment left her looking close to tears. Her reaction made him want to take her hand, ask her what was wrong. But if he tried, he was certain she'd tell him it was none of his concern. And she'd be right. Besides, now that he'd mailed his letter, it was time for him to be moving on. Tipping his hat, he gave her one more smile.

"Good day, miss," he said, then headed for the door.

Not until the stranger had disappeared did Jennie think to ask him his name. The unexpected kindness of this man almost made her forget Mr. Dixon and the debt, and she suddenly realized that she'd never even thanked him. Hurrying to the door, she tried to spot him, but he was already out of sight.

Oh, well, Jennie thought as she left the store. There wasn't really time to talk to him anyway. If she didn't hurry she might miss the stage that would take her home to Beaver and she certainly didn't have money to stay a second night in the boardinghouse.

She tucked the candy into her purse with her money and the four-shot, pepperbox pistol she always carried while still toting her suitcase, then she hurried to the booking office. The stagecoach stood out front, its six horses already hitched up. The man inside informed her that the driver would be along any minute.

Jennie purchased her ticket and sat outside on a nearby bench to wait. With nothing to read or do, except think over her mostly horrible morning, her mind soon filled with recollections of home. She pretended she was already riding her horse Dandy down the familiar wagon-rutted trail toward the ranch, past the corral fences and empty bunkhouse. Past the faded red barn where fourteen-year-old Will would be shoveling hay to the other pair of horses. Up to the two-story frame house with its front porch where Grandma Jones would be sitting in her rocker, mending clothes—the smell of her freshly baked bread mingling with the scent of meadow grass.

The possibility of losing everything she'd worked for and held so dear made her chest tighten. "What am I going to do?" She stared at her hands as if the gnawed fingernails and cracked knuckles held some kind of answer.

The sound of footsteps approaching brought up Jennie's chin. She watched as the stage driver made a thorough inspection of the coach before coming over to greet her.

"Afternoon, miss." He nodded, and Jennie forced a smile as she stood. He placed her suitcase on the top rack of the stage. "I hear it's just you and me today."

"Not a bad thing," she said, thinking of the crowded stagecoach she'd ridden in for two days before reaching Fillmore.

"Up you go then." He held her elbow in a gentle grip and helped her inside.

Being the only passenger, Jennie had her pick of one

of the three benches. She chose the one facing forward. She settled onto the lumpy, cracked leather next to the window and set her purse in her lap.

As the driver moved to close the small door, two gentlemen sprinted up to the stagecoach, each holding a piece of luggage. Jennie gathered they might be brothers with their matching dark hair, bushy eyebrows and brown suits.

"We got seats on this stage," the older-looking one said. He held up two stubs of paper.

From the window Jennie watched the driver inspect their tickets before nodding.

"I can place your bags on top, gentlemen."

The one with the tickets shook his head. "If it's all the same to you, we'll keep 'em with us."

The driver shot him a puzzled look, but he didn't insist they use the top rack. The men climbed into the stage and sat on the rear-facing seat. They squeezed their two bags in the narrow space beside their feet. Jennie noticed each man wore impeccable clothes, without a trace of dirt or signs of heavy wearing, and each carried a revolver in a holster beneath his jacket.

The younger and stockier brother eyed Jennie and grinned. "You traveling by yourself, little lady?"

Jennie responded with a simple nod as she slipped her hand into her purse and fingered the handle of the pistol. The young man likely didn't mean anything by his flirtatious manner, but she wanted to be prepared if things turned sour.

"Don't worry, miss," he continued. "Should we run across any Injuns or bandits…" He held open his jacket and tapped the butt of his revolver with a fat thumb. "We'll protect you."

"Shut up, Horace." The older brother drove an elbow into Horace's side. "You'll have to pardon my brother's rambling. Learned it from our ma."

With a scowl, Horace twisted in his seat to face his brother. "What you talking about, Clyde? We ain't seen Ma for eight years, so how do know what she did and didn't do? I told you, we oughta gone back home this winter, hole up before our next—"

"There he goes again." Clyde clapped a hand over Horace's mouth and smiled. "Can't help himself."

Jennie lifted her brows in amusement. The brothers' rough manners and speech didn't match their fancy clothes. What type of work did they do? Before she could ask, the stagecoach lurched forward. Jennie gripped the window ledge to keep from bouncing off her seat.

"Should've ridden those good horses we had, instead of takin' the stage." Horace righted himself and straightened his skewed hat.

"Here, have a drink," Clyde said. He pulled a silver flask from his jacket and wiggled it in the air. Horace seized the container and guzzled before wiping his mouth with the back of his hand.

This ought to be interesting. Jennie began chewing on her thumbnail. *They'll either drink themselves into a stupor or get fresh.* Given how her day had gone so far, she couldn't trust that they'd choose the option she'd prefer. She didn't feel like talking much—not after her long morning—but a little conversation might divert their attention from the alcohol.

"What exactly is your line of work, gentlemen?"

Horace chuckled again and glanced at Clyde. "I'd say we're in—"

"The money-making business," Clyde finished, a deadpan expression on his face.

Jennie waited for them to elaborate, but neither one did. Horace returned to his drinking, and Clyde stared out the window.

"Are you from around here?" she tried next.

Turning from the view, Clyde sized up Jennie as if trying to determine the reason for her questions. "Nope," he said after a long moment. "We're a ways from home."

"What sort of money-making business brought you to Fillmore then?"

Horace smiled. "She's a real talker, ain't she, Clyde? Not shy or silent like a lot of other girls."

"Give me that." Clyde snatched the flask from Horace. "That's enough talkin'." He gave Horace a stern look and took a long swig. Lowering the silver container from his mouth, he frowned at Jennie. "If it's all the same to you, miss, we'd prefer to do our drinking in peace and quiet."

"Suit yourself," Jennie muttered as she faced the window. Silence enveloped the inside of the stagecoach, except for the sound of the brothers passing the flask between them and gulping the liquor.

Jennie watched the sagebrush and distant hills moving past for a long time before she grew tired of the monotonous scenery. Leaning her head back against the seat, she shut her eyes. As rough as the ride could be, she preferred resting over watching two men become inebriated in front of her.

A headache began building at her temples and she tried to relax to keep it at bay. Thoughts of the bank president and her debt filled her head, but she chased them away with plans for what the ranch needed in preparation for colder weather.

A short time later, she heard loud whispering between Horace and Clyde. Curious, she pretended to still be sleeping and focused on their words.

"I told you wearing these fancy duds and takin' the stage would work," Clyde said in a slightly slurred voice.

"We sure showed 'em," Horace said, his speech thicker with intoxication than his brother's. "Slipped right past the sheriff. Bet he didn't think we'd be walkin' into town, all respectable." He snorted in obvious delight.

"Two thousand dollars, Horace! Now we can buy us some horses and land—whatever we want."

Horace murmured in agreement. "I'd like to go back to Wyoming soon and live by Ma, but I don't think she'd like knowin' we're bandits." He sighed heavily, then added in a brighter tone, "Maybe we could buy her somethin' real nice, so she ain't so mad. Whatdaya think she'd like?"

Jennie missed Clyde's response as her mind raced. *They're the bandits I heard about in the store—the ones who stole the two thousand dollars.*

Her first impulse was to jump out the door. She might not live through such a fall, but staying put could also mean death if the men realized what she'd overheard. That left her two choices: sit tight and pretend she hadn't heard a thing or try to disarm the men herself and hand them over to the stage driver.

At the pricking of her conscience, Jennie chose to act. But not just yet. Better to hold off until they were at their weakest. Perhaps all the alcohol they'd been drinking would work out in her favor in the end. She waited until their whispering turned to snores and opened her eyes. Both bandits were passed out on their respective sides of the stagecoach, mouths hanging open, their relaxed jaws bouncing with the stage's movement.

Jennie shifted her gaze from them to the luggage beside their feet. Which of the two bags held the money? *If only I had that cash...*

She shook her head, though she couldn't rid the wish completely from her thoughts. Slowly, the innocent desire for money became an idea—a bold, dangerous idea.

If she took the money, would it really be stealing? She'd only take what she needed to pay the bank at the end of the month and buy herself time to raise more funds. The ranch would be temporarily saved, and she and her family wouldn't lose everything. The brothers had already spent some of the money—their new clothes showed that. No one would expect the full two thousand to be recovered. *It's just my informal reward for turning in these men.*

Before she changed her mind, Jennie scooted to the edge of her seat. Her heart pounded loudly in her ears and her hands grew clammy. Sliding onto the middle seat, her back to the door, she leaned over to grab hold of the suitcase next to Clyde. She hefted it onto the bench and quietly cracked it open. Desperation surged through her at finding nothing but a faded bundle of sweat-and-campfire-scented clothes inside.

Jennie placed the bag back on the floor. She had to hurry before either man woke up. She scooted down the bench to reach Horace's bag and saw that one boot rested against it. With a sigh, Jennie pivoted on the bench to face Horace straight on. She bent down and gripped the boot with both hands. She gently slid his foot toward her. The drunken Horace didn't stir.

Exhaling with relief, she lifted the bag into her lap and unfastened the clasp. Peering inside, she sucked in a quick breath. She'd never seen so much cash in one place. She could pay the ranch's debt in full with that much money.

No, she told herself firmly. *Only what we need to buy more time.* Grabbing two bundles and hoping it was enough, she shoved the money into her purse.

"What are you doing there?" Clyde demanded.

Startled, Jennie pushed the money bag behind her. Thankfully the pounding of the horses' hooves and the creak of the wheels muffled the sound of the bag hitting the floor.

"I…uh…needed some air," she said, motioning to the window above the coach door.

"You sick?"

"Oh, no. I'm fine." She fanned her flushed face with her purse. "Just a tad warm."

"It can be dangerous sittin' in the middle there," Clyde said in a drowsy voice as he blinked heavily.

You have no idea. Jennie willed herself to smile as she took several calming breaths. She set aside her purse and busied herself arranging her skirts and examining her fingernails until Clyde fell back asleep. When she was certain he was unconscious, she retrieved the money bag, closed it up and put it back beside Horace's boots. Now she needed to get those guns and hand over these men to the stage driver.

Bending forward again, Jennie peeled back part of Horace's jacket to reach his revolver. As she inched her fingers toward the barrel, she heard a snort. She jerked her head up and found Horace watching her, a puzzled expression on his face.

"You had a bee on your knee," Jennie said, thinking fast. "I moved up to swat it away." She blushed as she straightened.

Horace cocked his head to one side and lifted his eyebrows. "Oh…um…thanks."

She hoped he'd join his brother in drunken slumber, but Horace stretched and sat up instead.

"How much farther we got to the next town?" he asked.

Jennie peered out the window at the afternoon sun. "We still have several hours until we stop for the night at Cove Fort. It's a way station for travelers." *Plenty of time to get those guns, but how?*

"You ever been to Wyoming?" Horace scratched at his hairy jaw.

"No," Jennie said curtly. She needed to formulate a plan, not waste more time chatting with Horace.

"That's where me and Clyde come from. I want to get back up there someday. Our ma's still there." Horace glanced out the window and exhaled a long sigh. "Sure do miss her cookin'. And my horse, Jasper."

Jennie tried to ignore his reminiscing, but he kept on.

"Clyde made me leave Jasper behind. Probably 'cause I ride better than he does. Can shoot better, too. Pa taught me to shoot anything with a trigger."

His words prompted similar memories in Jennie's mind—times when her father had shown her how to draw a gun and shoot straight.

That's it.

Jennie heaved a dramatic sigh and batted her eyelashes like she remembered her girlhood friends at church doing. "I don't know the first thing about guns. Why, I wouldn't know how to go about defending myself. I wish somebody would teach me."

"I'll show you." He hurried to sit beside her on the middle bench and pulled his gun from its holster. "This here's a .44 Remington revolver."

"Is that right? Well, imagine that," she said.

"Once it's loaded, you wanna pull the hammer back." Horace lifted his thumb and pantomimed the action, then aimed the gun out his window. "You point at your target, squeeze the trigger and shoot." He shrugged and passed the revolver to Jennie. "Nothin' to it."

Jennie pointed the gun out her window, hoping he didn't see her hands shaking with nervous energy. "Seems easy enough." Setting the gun on her right side, where Horace couldn't easily reach it, she smiled coyly. "What about your brother's gun?"

"Works the same." Horace leaned across her to pull out Clyde's revolver from beneath his jacket. Clyde twitched, peering at them through half-opened eyes. "I'm borrowin' your gun for a minute," Horace explained. His brother grunted, and to Jennie's relief, his eyelids shut again.

"Clyde's gun's a Colt revolver." Horace lifted it up for her to see. "His isn't as fast-loading as mine since he can't just slip a full cylinder in."

"How do you load it? Can you teach me that?"

Horace nodded. He pushed the revolver's cylinder to the left side and pointed to the six chambers. "The bullets go in there, but you see how you wanna leave one hole empty so the gun don't fire if it's dropped?"

"May I try?" Jennie asked, swallowing back the

panic rising in her throat. If Horace gave his brother back the gun, her plan wouldn't work.

He looked from her to the gun and over to Clyde. "I s'pose." He dumped out the bullets and extended the gun toward her. "Here you go."

She took the revolver and stuck out her hand for the bullets. Horace rolled them into her palm, but as she drew her hand back, she purposely let the bullets slip from her grip to the floor. "Oh, dear. How clumsy of me."

"I'll get them." Horace knelt in the tight space and tried to capture a bullet that rolled and jumped with the stage's movement.

Clyde sat up, rubbing his jaw. "What in tarnation are you doing, Horace?"

"Pickin' these up." He finally got a hold of a bullet and held it up for Clyde to see. "We dropped 'em."

Cursing softly, Clyde leaned down to help gather the ammunition.

Now's my chance. Keeping an eye on the two men, Jennie tossed both revolvers out her window. Her heart crashed against her rib cage as she reached inside her purse and cocked her pistol. She slowly removed the gun. Forcing herself to breathe evenly, she aimed the pistol at Horace and Clyde.

"What were ya doing with the bullets out of the gun anyway?" Clyde barked as he shoved bullets into his pocket. Neither of them paid any attention to Jennie, which gave her enough time to steady her hands and plaster a no-nonsense expression on her face. "Where's my gun? If you ruined it, so help me, Horace…" Clyde gave a vehement shake of his head.

The back of Horace's ears reddened with anger. "I

ain't done nothin' with your gun. I was just showin' the lady here how to use one." He turned to Jennie, and his eyes went wide as saucers at the sight of the pistol in her hand. "Where'd you get that?"

"Go sit by your brother," Jennie ordered in an even tone. Out of the corner of her eye, she saw Clyde's face blanch, then turn scarlet.

"You idiot." Clyde whopped Horace on the side of the head as he scrambled onto their seat. "Looks to me like she already knows how to use a gun. What'd you tell her while I was asleep?"

Horace blinked in obvious confusion. "I...uh...told her about home. I didn't say nothin' about us robbing the stage, honest, Clyde."

Clyde lifted his hand to strike his brother again, but Jennie pointed the gun in his direction. "Leave him alone. He didn't say anything. I learned all I needed to know from your drunken whispers earlier."

"Whatya goin' do with us now?" Horace asked, frowning.

Instead of answering, Jennie pointed the pistol at the floor and fired a bullet between the men's boots. Both of them yelped and jumped aside. "That's a warning," she explained. "I shoot even better at long-range, so I wouldn't suggest making a dash for it. You'd likely break every bone in your body if you tried to jump anyway."

The stagecoach came to an abrupt stop, as Jennie had hoped, and the driver soon appeared beside the door. He had a shotgun in his hand and a look of pure annoyance on his weathered face.

Throwing open the door, he glared at Horace and Clyde. "What do you mean firing a gun while we're moving? You'll scare the horses, or the lady here." He glanced over at Jennie, and seeing her pistol, his eyes widened.

"Forgive me. That shot was meant to alert you." Jennie smiled apologetically. "I overheard these men talking. I believe they're the bandits who robbed that stage yesterday."

"Well, I'll be." The driver scratched at his head beneath his hat, his gaze flitting from Jennie to the brothers and back again. "And the money?"

Swallowing the twinge of guilt that rose inside her, Jennie pointed her gun at the bag by Horace. "I believe it's in there."

The driver leaned into the stage and proceeded to grab the black bag, but Clyde snatched the other side of the handle and refused to let go. "You can't have it," he argued. "We worked and planned for months to get this cash."

"Let go, young man, or you'll be eatin' bullets." The stage driver trained the shotgun on Clyde. The two locked gazes before Clyde finally released his grip on the bag. The driver passed his shotgun to Jennie. "Hold this on 'em for a minute, miss, while I grab me some rope."

Jennie nodded and took the shotgun in hand. Shifting the pistol in Clyde's direction, she pointed the driver's gun at the sullen-looking Horace.

As soon as the driver disappeared from view, Clyde glowered at her. "You won't get away with this, missy," he hissed. "If you think I'm going to rot in jail and lose two thousand dollars 'cause some female has a hankering to be brave, you don't know me."

"Perhaps you ought to have considered that possibility before you robbed the stage," Jennie said, edging her pistol closer to him.

The stage driver returned and tied the men's hands and feet together. With Jennie holding both guns on them, neither one made an attempt to struggle.

"You might want to ride up with me, miss," the driver said when he'd finished.

"I believe I will." She handed him back his gun, but kept hers in her grip. The driver climbed out, and after gathering her purse, Jennie hurried to follow.

"We're goin' to find you," Clyde shouted as she descended the steps. "You're gonna wish you hadn't done this. Horace and I will—"

The stage driver slammed the door against Clyde's protests and led Jennie by the elbow to the front of the stage. "Don't pay him no mind, miss. You've done a brave thing. Nothing to be ashamed of." He helped her up onto the seat. "Afraid we'll have to turn back though, so we can turn those two rascals over to the law in Fillmore."

Jennie nodded in agreement as she tucked her pistol into her bag alongside the cash.

The stage driver joined her on the seat and gathered the reins. He turned the stagecoach around, heading north again. Jennie did her best to ignore Clyde's occasional shouts from below. She concentrated instead on the thrill she felt as she imagined marching into the bank tomorrow and slapping the five hundred dollars on Mr. Dixon's desk. Let him wonder how she came up with it so fast. At least the ranch would be safe from his greedy hands, for now.

Chapter Two

Seven months later

Caleb let his horse Saul pick its own way along the faint trail through the sagebrush while he sat in the saddle, finishing his cold supper of dry bread and jerky. He didn't have time to stop to eat if he was going to find lodging and a warm meal in Beaver by sundown.

He brushed the bits of bread from his chaps, and almost of its own accord, his hand rose to pat the pouch hidden beneath his shirt. Three hundred dollars sat inside—three hundred dollars his parents couldn't complain hadn't been earned through honest labor. Not that any amount of honest work would reconcile them to the fact that he wasn't coming home to the Salt Lake Valley. They hadn't liked it when he'd left, and they certainly hadn't been pleased when he'd become a bounty hunter. But the real divide had come when he'd stopped bounty hunting…and still refused to come home.

Didn't they understand how hard it was for him to think of returning to the place where he'd hoped to build a life with Liza? He'd settle down soon, but it would be someplace new—somewhere he could have a fresh start. And with God's help, he'd be ready for that soon. One more job, maybe two, and Caleb would have enough money to outfit his own freight business.

"We'll come back," he murmured to Saul as he gazed from beneath his hat at the juniper-covered hills and the distant mountain peaks. He'd come to love this rugged country. "Next time, though, it'll be with a wagon full of goods and a strong pair of horses." Saul's ears flicked back and the horse gave a long whinny. Caleb chuckled. "My apologies. But you wouldn't want to pull a loaded wag—"

The sound of a large animal crashing through the underbrush silenced Caleb's words. Reining Saul in, he twisted in the saddle, trying to discern which direction the noise came from. He gripped the butt of one of the revolvers in his holster. Neither gun was loaded, but Caleb figured whoever was headed his way wouldn't know that.

A moment later, a horse and rider burst from the trees a dozen yards up the trail. "Look out," a female voice yelled as the pair raced toward Caleb.

A woman? Out here? Caleb released his grip on the gun and wordlessly jerked his horse out of the way.

"You should leave," the woman added, thundering past him. Her dress flapped in the wind, revealing men's trousers under the skirt. Long red hair spilled out from beneath her cowboy hat.

Caleb peered after the retreating figure. Where would she be going in such a rush and why would she tell him to leave? Shaking his head in bewilderment, he faced forward again. Only this time he heard the faint but unmistakable sound of several horses riding hard in his direction. Someone was coming down the trail after the woman.

Out of instinct, Caleb scanned the area for a place of defense against those coming his way. To his right, on a small rise above the trail, a patch of trees provided both cover and a lookout position. He wouldn't take action—not yet, anyway. This wasn't his fight. He didn't know the circumstances and he didn't want to run the risk of being killed, or worse, having to kill a man—again. Still, from the sounds of it, there were several men coming after that woman. He'd stay out of the conflict for now, but if they appeared ready to hurt her, he'd be on hand to intervene.

He watched the woman rider until she disappeared behind a clump of trees and underbrush. She didn't reappear. If she stayed hidden, she might be all right. Maybe nothing would come of this after all.

Caleb guided Saul up the incline, behind the juniper trees, then he dropped from the saddle. He tied Saul's reins to a thick branch before lowering himself to his knees. He removed his bullet pouch just as five men rode into sight.

The riders' clothes were tattered and dirty, and each of them sported scruffy beards or mustaches beneath their dusty cowboy hats. All five had guns and wore the same hardened expressions he'd seen on the four stage robbers he'd hunted down, including the last one whose face was on the wanted poster he kept in his saddle bag.

The tallest of the five stopped within yards of the woman's hiding place and fired his rifle into the air. "Fun's over, missy," he sneered. "We know you're here, and we want what's ours."

Caleb quickly loaded one of his revolvers and crept

closer to the hill's edge, making certain to stay hidden behind the trees. Would the woman keep silent or make a stand? Either way, Caleb didn't plan on letting her be caught or shot by these ruffians.

"I'd watch it if I were you, Bart. You're surrounded," the woman called back. To her credit, Caleb didn't detect an ounce of fear in her voice. "I've got the sheriff with me and his posse's waiting down the trail for you."

Caleb scanned the nearby mountainside, but he saw no movement, no reinforcements. She had to be lying. A heavy silence followed her brave words. In the stillness, Caleb heard the distant trill of a bird. He tightened his grip on his gun, fully expecting a volley of shots in response to her bluff. But the quiet stretched on for nearly a minute.

"You're lying," Bart finally shouted back. "And you'll soon find out what we do with lying, thieving…"

Time to act. "Howdy, boys," Caleb hollered from behind the trees. All five men whipped their heads in his direction, disbelief radiating from more than one face. "Nice to see y'all are friends. Makes sharing a jail cell more enjoyable."

"It's the sheriff," a baby-faced fellow cried. "Let's split."

"Hold on. I still say she's bluffin' about him bringin' a whole posse," Bart said, scratching his motley beard. His narrowed gaze jumped from the hill, to the clump of trees beside the trail and back in Caleb's direction.

Before anyone could make a move, the woman fired a round of shots that hit the ground near one of the bandits. The man let out a loud yelp and jerked his horse away. Caleb aimed at a patch of sagebrush near another of the riders, hoping to spook the horse into bolting.

The riders attempted to return fire, but the bullets whizzing past them drove them into a tighter group on the exposed trail. Caleb could see the horses—and the riders—getting more agitated by the minute. Before long, one of them turned his horse and galloped away toward Caleb. Caleb let him ride past.

Another hurried after him. "We're outnumbered, Bart," the man screamed over his shoulder.

Bart fired once more before pointing his horse in the direction the other two had charged. "Let's go!" He threw an ugly look toward the trees, then up the hill as he retreated, the last two bandits behind him.

Caleb waited another minute to ensure they didn't double back. When the trail remained empty in either direction, he replaced his gun in its holster and untied Saul's reins.

The woman still hadn't emerged from the trees yet. Anxious to know if she'd fared well through the gunfight, Caleb led Saul down the incline and across the trail. Skirting the copse of trees, he entered the shelter they formed and found himself staring down the barrel of the woman's pistol.

"Whoa—don't shoot." He dropped the reins and lifted both hands in the air. Saul whinnied softly beside him.

"You're the one who pretended to be the sheriff." To his relief, she lowered her gun. "I thought I told you to leave."

"Are you all right? Why were those men chasing you? Have they…" He rubbed the back of his suddenly warm neck. "Have they laid their hands on you in any way?"

Her cheeks flushed. "No. Oh, no. They knew I had

some money with me—that's all." She pushed up her hat, revealing amused brown eyes—not the green he'd expected. "I'd say they got the worst of it."

He'd only ever seen one other girl with red hair and coffee-colored eyes, in a mercantile in Fillmore when he'd done some work up there last fall. He suspected that young lady, though, wouldn't go around fighting in shoot-outs or wearing men's trousers under her skirt.

"By the way, thanks for the help." She stuck her pistol into the holster tied around her skirt and reached for her horse's reins.

"What were you doing out on the trail by yourself?"

Her chin lifted a notch. "No one could be spared to come with me, and besides, I can handle myself just fine."

"Apparently, but what would you have done if I hadn't come along?"

"I would have figured something out," she said as she climbed into her saddle. "I usually do."

Caleb swung onto Saul's back. "Going up against a group of armed thugs is a regular pastime of yours?"

"Hardly." One corner of her mouth lifted in a half smile. "What about you? You play sheriff for hapless females on a regular basis?"

It was Caleb's turn to smile. "Not hapless in your case. But it is always a pleasure helping a pretty girl. Wouldn't mind that as a regular job."

Instead of blushing, a peculiar expression passed over the woman's face. She stared hard at him a moment before she visibly relaxed again. "Are you looking for work?"

"You hiring?"

"Maybe. What can you do?"

"Farming, freighting, a little carpentry." He purposely left bounty hunting off his list. That part of his life had ended abruptly a year and a half ago, and Caleb wanted to keep it that way.

She nudged her horse forward, in line with Saul. "Do you know anything about cattle ranching?"

"Can't say that I do." The question brought a twinge of disappointment. He'd never fancied himself living the life of a cowhand—a little too close to farming for his tastes. "The only cows I've handled in the past are ones that needed milking."

Her brow furrowed as she shook her head. "You don't milk these cows. What we need is some extra help on our ranch. It's only me, my grandmother and my younger brother. I've been doing most of the work myself for the past twenty months."

She set her hat on the saddle horn and rearranged her hair into a bun. "You could help with branding and looking after the few cattle we have. There are other chores around the ranch that need another set of hands. I can't pay you a lot—maybe twenty dollars a month." She stuck her hat back on and finally regarded him again. "I might be able to give you a little more when we sell the cows in the fall."

Twenty dollars wasn't much, especially when he'd heard of cowhands making closer to forty dollars in a month. Surely he could find another job—one where he could earn more money in less time.

Caleb fiddled with Saul's reins, ready to refuse her. But the words grew cold on his tongue. He hadn't missed the desperate tone behind her offer. Clearly she needed his help. He could work for a lower wage if it wasn't for long, couldn't he?

"I might consider working for you," he answered at last, "except I don't usually accept jobs from nameless employers."

A trace of a smile showed on her lips and then disappeared as quickly. "My name is Jennie. Jennie Jones."

"Miss Jones." Caleb pulled down the brim of his hat in greeting as if they'd met on the street and not in the middle of the desert—after a shoot-out. "Pleased to meet you. I'm Caleb Johnson."

"Will you accept the job then, Mr. Johnson?"

As had become his habit since he'd quit bounty hunting, Caleb searched inside himself for some inkling, some impression from God, that this course wasn't the one for him. None came.

Smiling, he waved her forward. "Lead the way, Miss Jones."

Through the blue twilight smearing the western sky, Jennie spotted the familiar outline of the corral fence. *Home.* "That's the ranch," she said, her first words during the long trip. Caleb had been equally as quiet.

She peered sideways at him, wondering why she hadn't recognized him before. His earlier comment about helping pretty girls had sparked her memory. The man from the general store who'd come to her aid last fall had said something similar and he, too, had deep blue eyes.

After nearly an hour riding beside him, Jennie was certain the two men were one and the same. He didn't seem to remember her, though, to her relief and slight disappointment. She wasn't the same woman she'd been that day when he had paid for the candy they'd shared.

What I am doing? she asked herself for the hundredth

time. She never should have pressed him into working for her. What if he said something to the family about Bart and his gang? What would he do if he knew this was her third time robbing stage bandits?

"Something wrong?"

Jennie jumped in the saddle, causing her horse Dandy to dance to the side. "No. Why?"

"'Cause you've been chewing that thumbnail of yours for the last five miles, and I'm wondering if there's any of it left."

Jerking her hand from her lips, Jennie stared at her thumb. All of her nails were worn from constant work, but the one on her thumb resembled the jagged edge of a saw blade. This fingernail always worked its way between her teeth when she was nervous or had a lot on her mind.

"I'm fine," she said, shrugging off his keen observation. She pretended to focus on the road ahead, though she knew every rut and bump from memory.

Her thoughts soon returned to the man beside her. Surely she could get along without help a little longer— she'd been doing things alone ever since her father had died. And having a stranger around the place might interfere with her plans to save the ranch.

Yanking back on Dandy's reins, she twisted around to face Caleb. He tweaked an eyebrow at her sudden movement, but he pulled his horse to a stop, as well.

"If you don't want to take this job, I'll understand. We can split company right here." Thankfully she couldn't see his face very well in the fading light. "I appreciate all you did for me today, but like you said, you don't know much about cattle ranching."

"Am I being let go?"

Jennie blinked in surprise. Was he teasing her? Her jaw tightened, and she drew herself up. "I didn't mean that. But you and I both know there are other better-paying jobs. You can stay the night with us, and then in the morning—"

"I'd like to at least have the job a full day, Miss Jones, before you decide anything."

She frowned at his amused tone. It was a risk to employ him after what he'd seen on the trail, and yet, she wanted him around. He was the first person in a long time to offer help without ulterior motive—first in the mercantile, then again today.

"All right." She rubbed the reins between her fingers. "You can try the job for six weeks. I'll pay you for your work then. If we're both not satisfied, you're free to move on."

"Fair enough."

They moved their horses forward a few steps before Jennie felt compelled to stop again. "I would appreciate it if you didn't say anything about the shoot-out with those men. I wouldn't want to worry my grandmother." For more reasons than one.

"I've found it's better sometimes to leave well enough alone," he said, his face turned toward something in the distance. "No need to drag the details into the light."

"Thank you." His compassion brought her a twinge of guilt when stacked against the truth, but Jennie easily pushed it aside.

She led him up the road, past the bunkhouse, to the barn where they both dismounted. The doors stood ajar, and through the opening, the soft glow of a lantern spilled out. Will had obviously anticipated her arrival.

With a grateful sigh, she pushed open the barn doors

and guided Dandy into his stall. She gave him an affectionate pat on the rump as she closed the pen door. "You can put your horse in that last stall," she told Caleb.

The other two ranch horses, Chief and Nellie, whinnied at the new company.

"Would you mind unsaddling them both?" Jennie removed the full saddlebag and flung it over her shoulder.

"You don't waste time putting your hired help to work, do you?"

"I need to take care of something," she said, ignoring his teasing. "There's hay in the stalls and the currycombs are over there." She waved a hand at the crude table littered with brushes. "I'll meet you back here to take you up to the house and introduce you."

Caleb tipped his hat. "Will do."

Jennie left the barn. She headed at an angle toward the house, then doubled back in the direction of the empty bunkhouse. She tried to force thoughts of hiring Caleb from her mind. There was one more task she needed to do, and she'd need all her wits about her. She'd been successful today in getting more money to save the ranch.

Now she had to pay the price.

Chapter Three

Jennie approached the bunkhouse from the back, pausing in the shadows. She set down the saddlebag and called in a low voice, "Nathan?"

The only sound was the chirp of crickets, but Jennie knew better. Brandishing her pistol, she managed one step forward before an arm wrapped itself tightly around her waist.

"Evening, love." Nathan's deep voice murmured in her ear. "Glad to see you're still in one piece."

The scent of alcohol and cigar smoke that typically accompanied him made Jennie wrinkle her nose. She pushed the barrel of her gun into his side. "Let go."

Nathan laughed, but he released her. "Were Bart and his gang where I said they'd be?"

"Yes. Everything went exactly as we planned." She decided not to mention Caleb's help. Though in her mind, the deal she had with Nathan Blaine was strictly business, she knew he wouldn't be pleased to hear about a new man in her life.

She stuck her gun back in place and knelt beside the saddlebag. Opening it, she rummaged through the supplies and drew out two thick wads of cash. She stood and handed him his money. She hated parting with half of the four hundred dollars she'd taken, but Nathan's help was worth every cent. His ability to mingle discreetly with outlaws had provided Jennie with the information she needed to accomplish her second and third robberies.

Nathan ran his thumb through the money and slipped it into a knapsack on his shoulder. "I knew you had pluck," he said, leaning too close, "the moment you walked into the saloon with your chin all stuck out and your eyes all determined."

Jennie cringed at the memory of standing in the noisy, suffocating saloon, searching the crowd of leering men for someone to help her. "Is that why you agreed to work with me?" she said in a teasing tone even as she took a deliberate step back, putting needed space between them.

"Maybe, maybe not." He grabbed her hand and placed it against his chest. Jennie squirmed, but Nathan wouldn't let go. Even in the dark, she could sense his ogling gaze. "Why not give up tryin' to save your ranch and come make some real money with me? With your beauty and the way you handle a gun, we could take on banks or trains. We'd live like royalty."

Pulling her hand free, Jennie stared past him at the barn and house. The moonlight shone down on the peeling paint of both buildings and the corral fence with holes large enough for a calf to squeeze through. There were other problems she couldn't see, but they were as apparent and real as the tattered ranch around her—the looming deadline from the bank and the two or three sets of bandits she'd still need to take from in order to meet it.

But I would never stoop to become a bandit myself.

"No, Nathan," she said, shaking her head. She wouldn't quit. She needed this land, and it needed her. "I'm going to make this place what it used to be."

He shrugged, but his disappointment hung in the air between them. "So long, love."

Jennie watched him swagger away before picking up her saddlebag. She slipped into the bunkhouse and knelt in the corner opposite the door. Pulling up the loose board, she placed her two hundred dollars inside the small space. She'd keep it hidden here until she could travel to Fillmore and give some of it to the horrid Mr. Dixon.

After replacing the board, Jennie stood and brushed off her skirt. A thin layer of dust typically covered the unused bunkhouse. It served as another reminder of the failing condition of the ranch. Even before her father had died, they'd been forced to let go of their three ranch hands. With so few cows, she and Will had managed to keep up, but the new group of calves meant more work now.

Thankfully the money she'd relieved Bart of would pay for Caleb's help and hopefully keep the ranch going a little longer. Maybe Bart and his thugs would even see the futility of robbing innocent people. At least she only took money from crooks and used it for far better purposes than drinking or gambling or immoral company. *Once my debt is paid in full, I'll be done with all of this.*

Leaving the bunkhouse, she walked quickly to the barn. She wanted to see her family, introduce them to Caleb and climb beneath clean sheets.

The barn doors were shut, though Jennie was certain she'd left them open when she went to meet Nathan. Shrugging off her forgetfulness, she entered the barn. The building stood dark. Jennie hurried back outside and scanned the yard. Where had Caleb gone? She glanced at the house. A light in the kitchen threw shadows against the curtains—three shadows.

"The nerve of that man!" she muttered as she marched toward the porch. Why had he gone to the house without her? What would he tell her family about fighting Bart and his thugs? She quickened her steps as anger rose inside her. Hiring Mr. Johnson might prove to be a bigger disaster than she'd imagined.

"Did you get enough to eat?" Jennie's grandmother, Grandma Jones as she'd introduced herself, asked from across the table.

Caleb finished up his last bite of rabbit stew and patted his stomach. "Yes, ma'am. Best meal I've had in months. Better than any boardinghouse, for sure."

He hadn't meant to come inside without Jennie, but the moment his boots had hit the porch steps, her brother and grandmother had come to the door. He'd hurried to explain his presence, choosing to voice just the basic facts, as Jennie had requested. He and Jennie had met outside of town, and she'd hired him when he had mentioned needing a job. Jennie's grandmother had welcomed him with a warm smile and invited him right in for supper.

"You could learn a thing or two about manners from Mr. Johnson, Will," she said to the boy seated on Caleb's right.

Will rolled his eyes as Grandma Jones took Caleb's

plate to the sideboard. The boy and his grandmother looked alike with the same green eyes and brown hair, though hers was streaked with gray.

The front door slammed shut, and a moment later, Jennie appeared in the kitchen doorway, a frantic look in her eye and a smear of dust across one cheek.

"There you are, Jennie." Grandma Jones walked over and wiped away the dust on Jennie's face with her apron. "I stalled supper as long as I could, but you know Will—always hungry."

Her brother paused long enough over his second helping of stew to smile at his sister.

"Would you like supper?" Grandma Jones asked Jennie.

"Yes, please." Jennie scowled at Caleb as her grandmother crossed to the stove to fix up a plate. "I thought we were coming in together, so I could properly introduce you."

Caleb didn't miss the tense quality to her voice. *She thinks I told them about the ruffians chasing after her.* He gave a quick shake of his head, trying to communicate that he hadn't broken his word, but she didn't seem to notice.

"No need for such formality." Grandma Jones smiled at Caleb over her shoulder. "We heard somebody outside and found this handsome, half-starved young man standing there." She set Jennie's supper on the table and sat down. "Did you have a good trip into town?"

Jennie nodded before frowning at Caleb. "I've hired Mr. Johnson to help us around the ranch."

"I told them why I was here," Caleb said, matching her level look with one of his own.

"You did?" Jennie sank into an empty chair, glancing at each of them in turn. The delicate muscles in her jaw tightened.

"What a blessing you two ran into each other," her grandmother said. "It'll be nice to have an extra pair of hands around here, what with all the new calves."

The tight lines in Jennie's face relaxed and she shot Caleb a grateful smile. "It will, won't it?"

"You a cowboy?" Will asked him.

"No. But I'm a fast learner."

Grandma Jones stood and lifted Will's empty plate. "Take the lamp from the parlor, Will, and show Mr. Johnson to your father's old room."

"I couldn't intrude like that," Caleb said. "I don't mind sleeping in the barn or the bunkhouse—"

"Nonsense." Grandma Jones waved away his protests. "As long as you're working here, you're welcome to the room. It's a bit dusty, but it's a far cry better than the bunkhouse or barn. And if there's anything else you need, Mr. Johnson, just holler. Breakfast is at dawn."

"Thank you. And please, call me Caleb." Smiling at her, he rose from his chair and gathered up his things from where he'd set them in the corner. "Good night to you both."

"Thank you," Jennie mouthed to him when Grandma Jones moved to the sink. Caleb doffed his hat to her, glad she knew he'd kept his word.

He met Will in the hallway and followed him up the stairs. At the first landing, Will opened a door on their left and stepped inside.

"This is Pa's old room." He set the lamp on the dresser near the door.

Caleb surveyed the small but tidy room. After sleeping in barns, out in the open, or in crowded boardinghouses for almost three years, the thought of having his own water basin and a real bed all to himself made him feel like a king. Perhaps the accommodations and the family's kindness would outweigh the low pay.

"Looks comfortable," Caleb said, dropping his pack onto the bed's faded patchwork quilt. "How long's it been since you had hired help?"

Will leaned his long body against the door frame. "Before our pa died. The only man that's come around recently just talks to Jennie."

"She hire him to help, too?"

The boy shook his head. "I thought that's what she was doing, but she's never introduced him or invited him up to the house. He seems a bit rough, though, you know?" He lifted one shoulder. "I haven't asked. I'm just glad you look a bit more…respectable."

"I appreciate that." Caleb placed his few belongings in the dresser.

Sounded to him like Jennie had a beau. Seemed like everyone his age did, though Caleb didn't mind so much. He wasn't sure if he'd ever care that deeply about a person again. Maybe his only chance for love and marriage had died when Liza did.

"I'm glad you took the job, even if you are a tenderfoot." Will grinned. "Jennie's been running things pretty much by herself since Pa passed. I try and help, but we need more than the two of us to make this place good again."

"Mind my asking what happened to your father?"

"No." Will put his hands in his pockets and stared at the floor. "Some Indians were rustling our cattle and Pa went after them. He was shot in the stomach with an arrow. He died before the doctor could get here."

"I'm sorry." Caleb hated how trite the expression sounded, conveying so little of the sympathy he felt at the family's loss.

Will lifted his head and offered another shrug. "It's all right. I just don't think Pa meant for Jennie to do so much by herself. That's why I'm glad you'll be helpin' us, Mr. Johnson. I mean, Caleb. Good night."

"Night, Will."

The boy left the room, shutting the door behind him. Caleb wandered over to the window and pulled back the thin curtains. Shadowed hills merged into mountains in the distance. He let the curtains drop back into place and removed his money pouch from his shirt. He set it on the dresser as he prepared for bed.

Before climbing beneath the covers, Caleb knelt on the hardwood floor. He thanked God for the new job, even with the low wages. Clearly he was needed here. "Help me be an instrument for good with this family," he prayed. "And grant me patience as I work toward my plans." He ended his prayer and slipped his pouch under the mattress before he got into bed.

Every dollar he earned put him one step closer to starting his freight business. One step closer to that new life he'd planned for, free from all reminders of his past. Compared to that, a few months being a cowhand was a small price to pay.

Chapter Four

Jennie scooped up a bite of stew, suddenly starved. She savored the taste of the rabbit meat and potatoes and smiled.

"He seems like a real gentleman." Grandma Jones sat down beside her. "Not to mention a face that could melt a girl's heart."

Jennie choked on the piece of potato in her mouth and hurried to wash it down with some water. "Grandma!"

Her grandmother chuckled, bringing her wrinkled hands to rest beneath her chin. "I still know a handsome man when I see one. Reminds me a bit of your grandfather. Quick to smile, a bit forthright. Your father didn't inherit his personality. He was more serious—a thinker, like you." She released a soft sigh, and Jennie wondered if she was thinking of all the people she'd lost in sixty-five years of life—her parents and sisters, a husband, two sons and a daughter-in-law. "Did you get the supplies we needed?" she asked, abruptly changing the subject.

Jennie pointed her spoon at her saddlebag by the door. She'd made sure to purchase the nails, leather straps and thread they needed in Beaver before encountering the bandits.

Her grandmother murmured approval. "I've got one other question and I don't want you gettin' all angry. How are you going to pay Mr. Johnson?"

"I have enough," Jennie said, trying to keep the defensiveness she felt out of her voice. "I only promised to pay him twenty dollars a month."

"And we have twenty dollars after buying all our supplies?" Grandma Jones raised her eyebrows.

"I sold some things." It wasn't a complete lie. Jennie had sold a number of the family's belongings last year to buy them a little more time on the ranch.

"Your mother's things, you mean?"

Jennie pushed her remaining stew around her plate. "Why does it matter? She isn't coming back for them."

Her grandmother's hand closed over hers, and the familiar warmth brought the sting of tears to Jennie's eyes. "You may not remember those first few years after we moved south to Parowan. Your mama and papa worked so hard to make a living there. Then she lost the baby." Grandma Jones increased the pressure on her hand until Jennie looked up. "I think her will just gave out after we moved to the ranch. Maybe she didn't feel like she could start all over. Maybe she was scared. I don't know. What I do know is she didn't love you and Will any less when she left."

Jennie gently removed her hand and set it in her lap. "Does that make it right then?" She hated how her voice wobbled with emotion. "To leave us to fend for ourselves?"

"Perhaps she thought we were more capable of adapting than she ever was." Grandma Jones stood and came around the side of the table to kiss the top of Jennie's head. "I think if she were here now, she'd tell you how well you've done under the circumstances, Jennie girl. I'm real proud of the way you and Will have turned out. But I'm even more proud of you for asking Mr. Johnson to help. Asking others for help was something your mother never quite learned to do."

A wave of shame ran through her as Jennie thought of the money hidden in the bunkhouse. She might have swallowed her pride enough to hire Caleb, but she hadn't bothered to include anyone else in solving the ranch's financial troubles.

Her grandmother and Will knew the ranch might go under, but Jennie had kept the seriousness of the situation and the bank deadline a secret. What else could she do? Telling them the truth would only worry them. And besides, she had the situation under control. She'd spent too many days working under the hot sun and too many nights dreaming of what the ranch could be to give up now.

"I'll see to the lamp," she said.

Grandma Jones patted her shoulder. "Good night, Jennie girl."

Jennie listened to her grandmother's footsteps shuffle down the hall. She remained in her chair, thinking back over the events of the day. She wasn't sure how long she'd sat there before she took the lamp and went upstairs to her bedroom, but the house echoed with silence.

She changed into her nightclothes, but instead of climbing into bed, she knelt beside the large trunk against the windowsill. She lifted the lid, breathing in the smell of cedar. It evoked happy memories of bringing out the thick quilts for winter and wrapping up in them to listen to her mother read.

Reaching inside Jennie lifted out two envelopes. The first had never been opened, addressed to her from her mother, Olivia Wilson Jones. From the second, she removed the telegram that had come two years before her father's death. She stared at the black, unemotional type, her chest constricting at the recollection. She could still picture the way her father's face had crumpled into tears when he'd read the few words.

OLIVIA DEAD STOP CONSUMPTION CITED AS CAUSE STOP

No other details from her mother's sister. No condolences for a grieving husband and children. Nothing.

Jennie felt moisture on her face and realized she'd started to cry. Rubbing away the tears with the back of one hand, she returned both envelopes to the trunk.

Twice she'd survived the heartache and pain of her mother leaving: first from the ranch and then in death. *I made it through then, and I can do it again. I won't give up like she did.*

After closing the trunk, Jennie extinguished the lamp and slipped into bed. Grandma Jones's words from earlier repeated in her mind: *I'm even more proud of you for asking Mr. Johnson to help. Asking others for help was something your mother never quite learned to do.*

"But I don't really need to ask others for help," she whispered into the dark. "Not really. Not when I can handle things myself."

Most of the time, she refused assistance, especially from those she loved. In that, perhaps she and her mother weren't so different after all. But her mother hadn't been able to handle things here. Jennie could. And *would*. With that resolution in mind, Jennie turned onto her side and tried to sleep.

Leaving the stuffiness of the barn, Caleb shut the double doors and breathed in the cool evening air. His first day on the ranch had mirrored those of his youth on his father's farm. He'd repaired the roofs on the house and barn and mended a hole in the loft. Jennie had told him at supper they would go round up the calves from off their range in two days. The delay before dealing with the herd suited Caleb just fine. Though he hadn't taken to farming, even with his own parcel of land, he preferred those familiar tasks over wrangling cattle.

A series of gunshots to his left made him spin around and reach for his holster out of habit before remembering he'd stowed his guns in his room. Then he saw Will, shooting at cans along the fence line.

Taking off his hat, Caleb wiped at the sweat on his forehead with his shirtsleeve and strode toward the boy. Four cans sat in a row on the top rail of the fence. The scene provoked memories of countless evenings spent shooting targets with his uncle.

"How many did you hit?" Caleb asked.

Will frowned. "None."

"Let's see."

The boy reloaded his revolver and aimed. He fired all six rounds at the cans, but every shot missed its mark.

"I can't even shoot one." Will growled in disgust and started for the house.

"Hold up, Will." Caleb motioned him back. "Try it

again, but this time remember to relax. If you're too stiff, you're going to jerk and that throws your aim off."

With a sigh, Will stalked over to him. He reloaded his gun and lifted his arm.

"You relaxed?"

"I guess so."

Caleb studied the boy's stance. "Let your shoulders drop a little more." Will obeyed. "Now make sure you bury your first sight in the second one when you aim."

Will stared down the barrel of the gun and adjusted the height of his arm.

"All right," Caleb said with a nod. "Take a nice even breath, and when you feel ready, go ahead."

Will fired the revolver and a can flew into the air. "I got one." He grinned at Caleb over his shoulder before shooting again. This time the bullet flew wild. "What'd I do wrong that time?"

Caleb chuckled. "You just gotta practice relaxing and getting your sights lined up. Then you'll be able to hit all four cans in seconds. May I?" He extended his hand toward Will's gun.

"Sure." The boy placed the gun in Caleb's grasp. "You wanna try all four?"

"You bet. I've got to show you how's it done."

Will slipped between the fence posts to retrieve the can he'd hit. He set it up beside the others and returned to Caleb's side.

Caleb aimed the gun at the first can, his eyes narrowing. His mind cleared and instinct replaced thoughts. He squeezed the trigger and shot the first can from the post with a satisfying crack of metal on metal. He dropped the second and third cans just as quickly.

He paused for a split second to readjust his aim and

squeezed the trigger, but the last can shot up into the air before he could hit it. His bullet sailed over the empty fence post. Turning his head, he saw Jennie lower her pistol to her side, a pleased smile on her face.

"Thought I needed some help?" he teased.

"No. I thought I'd join in the fun." She walked over to them.

"Caleb was helping me," Will said. "I even hit a can off myself."

"That's great, Will." Jennie glanced from him to Caleb. "Where'd you learn to shoot like that?" He liked the note of admiration he heard in her question.

"My uncle was a sheriff up north. Whenever he came to visit, he'd take me out back and make me target practice until we couldn't see the cans in the dark." Caleb passed the revolver back to Will. "Keep at it, Will, and you'll be a crack shot like your sister."

Will beamed and hurried back to the fence to set up the cans again. Caleb started for the house. Jennie fell into step beside him.

"Thanks…for teaching him," she said, her voice low.

Caleb turned to see Will taking aim. "Mind my asking why *you* haven't taught him?"

"I guess I didn't see the need. He's not quite fifteen."

"Every young man wants to learn to shoot." He allowed her to go ahead of him up the porch steps. "He'd probably prove to be a real good cowhand, too, if given the chance."

Jennie clenched her jaw. He'd made a mistake telling her what to do.

"Not that I want him taking over my job, mind you," Caleb quickly added with a smile.

Her face relaxed as she stepped through the front door. "You know anything about roping?"

"Sure. I roped stumps as a child. Even caught the family dog a time or two."

Jennie laughed as she shut the door behind them. Caleb liked the singsong inflection. He hadn't made a pretty girl laugh in a long time.

"I meant, have you ever roped something moving?" she asked.

"You should've seen how that dog ran."

She shook her head, her brown eyes still bright with amusement. "Have you used a lasso before?"

"Not exactly," he said, "but I can assure you, Miss Jones, I can handle any job you throw at me." Compared to bounty hunting, cattle ranching looked as simple as babysitting a bunch of cows.

Her eyebrows lifted. "Well, then. Let's see how well you do tomorrow. You can practice with a lasso and a sawhorse."

"Sounds easy enough."

The next morning he opened his door to find a bright bandanna, a lasso and a newer pair of boots waiting for him on the landing. Slipping back inside his room, he tied the bandanna around his neck and replaced his old shoes with the new ones. With a slight twist of apprehension in his gut at his boasting the night before, he swung the lasso over his shoulder and headed downstairs for breakfast.

The aroma of fried eggs and biscuits greeted him as he stepped into the kitchen. He joined the family at the table, hanging his hat and the lasso on the corner of his chair. "Smells delicious," he said. He ladled food onto his empty plate and began to eat.

"Have another." Grandma Jones pushed the platter of biscuits toward him. "It's going to be a long day."

Caleb heard the snickers and caught the meaningful glance that passed between Jennie and Will. "What's so funny?" he asked.

"Look, Will," Jennie said from behind her cup. "It's our very own mail-order cowboy."

"What's that?" Caleb stabbed another bite of eggs.

"A cowboy with all the right getup," Will volunteered, "but no experience."

Caleb wagged his fork at the boy. "I've got experience, boy. It just ain't in cow handling."

"Well, that will change in the next few days." Jennie stood and cleared away her dishes. Instead of a dress, she wore a billowy blouse and breeches. Caleb had never met a woman who liked wearing men's pants—his mother and sisters had always worn skirts or dresses, even to work around the farm.

"All right, you two." Grandma Jones frowned at her grandchildren but she couldn't keep it up for long. The twinkle in her eyes betrayed how much she enjoyed their bantering. "Go easy on him this week."

"Don't worry, Mrs. Jones." Caleb leaned back on his chair and crossed his arms, regarding Jennie. "I'm always game for a challenge."

After breakfast, lasso over his shoulder, he trailed Jennie outside, trying his best to appear unaffected by his new responsibilities. The apprehension in his stomach grew and he wished he'd declined his third biscuit.

Jennie easily vaulted the corral fence, dropping to her feet on the other side, and Caleb followed suit. She went to the sawhorse sitting on one side of the corral and dragged it into the center.

"Let me see your lasso," she said. He handed her the rope. "It's really quite simple. The trick is to keep your wrist relaxed as you swing and then extend your arm toward the sawhorse as you release."

She held the coils of rope in one hand as she spun the looped end over her head with the other. In one fluid motion, her wrist dropped and she thrust the lasso forward. The loop sailed through the air and around the neck of the sawhorse. She jerked the rope tight.

"Any questions?"

Caleb's jaw went slack with surprise. She made cattle roping appear as easy as walking. Embarrassed to ask her to repeat the lightning-speed lesson, he cleared his throat. "If I do have questions?"

"I'm going to start work on the fence down by the bunkhouse. You can find me there."

Caleb watched her walk away, her long braid swishing against her back, then he straightened his shoulders and marched over to the sawhorse. "I've tracked down wanted criminals before, how hard can this be?" he muttered as he unhooked the lasso.

He backed up a few feet, swung the end of the lasso like Jennie had, and released. The rope flew through the air and landed in the dirt, a good six feet from the sawhorse. His second and third throws landed closer, but the only thing hitting the "cow" square on was the dust.

Several more attempts had him working up a sweat— but with nothing to show for it. Blowing out his breath, Caleb admitted he'd met his match with cattle ranching. But he'd made a promise to Jennie to work this job for six weeks, and he intended to keep his word. Somehow, he needed to figure this out. And right now, it looked as if the only way was to admit he couldn't do this one on his own and ask for help.

He'd paid a heavy price in the past for his pride and vanity, and he wouldn't do it again. Climbing over the fence, he headed in Jennie's direction, hoping she wouldn't gloat too much.

Chapter Five

Jennie pushed down on the post in her hands and secured it into the hole she'd dug. Stepping back, she scrutinized her work. Another rail, and the fence would be nearly as good as new.

Hearing footsteps, she turned to see Caleb approaching. "Have you mastered it already?" she called to him.

"I came to ask for another lesson," he said, stopping a few feet from where she stood.

Jennie stared at him for a moment before deciding she could spare a few minutes. "One more," she finally said, wiping her grimy hands on her breeches.

"Show me what you're doing," she said when they arrived back at the corral.

Caleb demonstrated tossing the lasso, but he missed the sawhorse by a foot.

"You need to rotate your wrist a little more as you're spinning the rope, and make sure the loop is open to the sawhorse before you release." She picked up his rope and swung it over her head, feeling the motion, anticipating the release. At the right moment, she dropped her arm and sent the loop around the sawhorse. "Did you see that?"

Caleb's brow furrowed, but he dipped his head in answer.

"Here, we'll try one together." Jennie moved behind him and helped him position the coils correctly in his left hand. Stepping to his side, she placed her hand over his right wrist and let her other hand rest at the center of his back.

"Start to swing the loop," she directed, her hand moving with his. His gaze darted to hers, and she laughed. "Don't look at me, cowboy. Keep watching your target. On the range, that calf is going to move fast. You have to train your eye to follow the cow's moving feet." She waited for him to relax his wrist, then continued her instructions. "Using the forward momentum, when you're ready, drop your wrist in line with your shoulder and let go."

After a few more swings, Caleb lowered his wrist and released the lasso. Jennie watched with held breath as the rope flew through the air and circled the neck of the sawhorse.

"Wahoo!" Caleb threw his hat into the air.

"You're not done," Jennie said with a laugh. "You have to pull the rope tight or he'll get away from you."

He returned to her side and together they yanked back on the rope. Peering up at him, Jennie realized how close they stood, close enough to feel his warm breath against her cheek and smell the musky scent of his shaving cream. She tried to step away, but her hands were still holding the rope beneath his. Her heart began thudding loudly in her ears.

"Thanks for the help," he said with a grin.

Jennie managed a nod. She'd never met someone like Caleb Johnson—someone kind and good-looking and irritating all at the same time. She hadn't socialized with any young men in years—not since the family had stopped attending Sunday services. Occasionally on trips into town, she'd run across some boy she recognized from her time at church or school, but she'd been too embarrassed to strike up a conversation. She felt like an outsider, mostly because of her mother. Maybe that's why she hadn't found it hard to talk to Nathan that first time. Here was someone else on the cusp of society.

Nathan. Thoughts of him brought her traitorous pulse to almost normal speed.

Jerking her hands free, Jennie stumbled backward. "I think you have it," she said, her words still coming out shaky. She forced a cleansing breath. "Keep practicing until you can do it with ease. Then come help me with the fence." Without waiting for his response, she spun on her heel and hurried across the corral.

She couldn't like him—she wouldn't. Her focus had to remain on doing what she must to save her home. No charming, would-be cowboy was worth losing her ranch.

Muscles strained, Caleb held tight to the squirming calf while Jennie applied the branding iron near the animal's rump. The smell of burnt hair filled Caleb's nostrils, and sweat ran down his back from working close to the fire. It didn't help that the day was unusually warm for mid-April. His clothes were now damp, dirty and speckled with blood. He wished he'd worn his old boots for this messy work, instead of the newer ones he'd been given yesterday.

It's all for the freight business, he told himself. If he could survive the next few months, he'd never have to look at another cow rump again.

The calf bellowed and twisted in protest as Jennie put down the iron and took up her knife to cut a small notch in the animal's right ear.

"All right," she said, using the back of her hand to brush hair from her glistening forehead. "He's done."

Caleb untied the rope from the calf's feet and released it. He jumped out of the way as the animal scrambled through the brush in search of its mother. "How many have we done?"

Jennie blew out a long breath and plopped down in the dirt. "Twenty calves in all. We had twice that many last spring. It took me and Will three days to round them all up and brand them. We've lost quite a few since then."

"What happened?"

"A few died over the winter, but mostly it's been rustlers."

"You mean the Indians that shot your pa?" She looked up sharply at his words, so he quickly added, "Will told me what happened."

She nodded. "They took some, yes. But I think one of the other landowners around here might be stealing from us, too."

Caleb's eyebrows shot up. "Why would you think that?"

"The Indians might want a few head of cattle here and there, but since they don't have the setup to handle anything more, there's no cause for them to take very many. But the other landholders…they could add my calves to their stock with no problems at all, and have the bonus of driving us out at the same time. There are plenty of folks who think I can't handle this ranch on my own. I think someone's trying to prove it."

Her voice was strong and steady, but Caleb could see how tired she looked, how the responsibility for running and protecting the ranch wore away at her. A surge of protectiveness filled him and he promised himself that, for as long as he worked on the ranch, he'd help lift some of that load. But that brought up another question. Would his wages take away from the family's ability to survive? Could they support another mouth to feed? "Can you afford to pay me?"

He realized she'd misunderstood the motivation behind his question when her cheeks flamed red.

"That's not what I—"

"I said I would," she interjected. "It's going to take another set of hands to make this place what I want, what my father wanted." She climbed to her feet and threw him a haughty look. "I can afford to pay you when our agreement is up. Just as I promised. And I'll pay you for every month you stay after that."

"Then I'm not a mail-order cowboy anymore?" he teased, hoping to defuse her anger.

She scowled at him, but only for another few seconds, before she laughed. "I'll admit you've done well."

Will approached them carrying a calf, its ankles tied. "I think she's the last one."

"Caleb and I'll finish up," she said. "Why don't you go get some drinking water from the creek?"

Nodding, Will transferred the calf into Caleb's arms and headed off into the brush with one of the buckets.

As Caleb wrestled to keep the calf still, Jennie crouched beside the fire and pulled out the white-hot branding iron. When they were finished, Caleb let the calf go and stood to stretch his sore back. "You're good with that iron."

"I should be." She dropped the branding iron into a nearby bucket. The hot metal sizzled against the water inside. "My mother hated this part of ranching, but I found it fascinating. I was always getting in the way during branding season until my father finally agreed to teach me what to do. I've been branding cattle since I was twelve."

"Where's your mother now?"

Jennie eyed him with suspicion. "Why do you want to know?"

Caleb shrugged, unsure why the simple question had struck a wrong chord in her. "Just wondered, since she's not around."

Frowning, Jennie picked up a cloth and wiped off her knife. "My mother passed away two years before my father did. She wasn't living with us, though. She went to live with her sister when I was thirteen and Will was six."

The casualness of her words didn't disguise the pain Caleb heard behind them. He sat down on the ground and stretched out his legs, thinking of how to redeem himself. He hadn't meant to dredge up hurtful memories. Sometimes they were best left buried in the past.

"I'm sorry."

She stared off into the distance, the knife and cloth motionless in her hands. "You didn't know."

"That must've been tough."

"The next few years were difficult." She finished cleaning her knife and set it aside. "This is the point when you tell me it was all for the best. She couldn't care for us. She was obviously ill in mind and body. We were better off without her."

"Why would I say that?"

"Because that's what people said after she left." Jennie sat on the bare ground and wrapped her arms around her knees like a frightened child. Her vulnerability made Caleb want to put his arm along her stiff shoulders, but he didn't. She was his boss, after all.

"Maybe that's why my father stopped going to church," she said. "He couldn't stand people's feigned sympathy." Her eyes, dark with anguish, met his. "I couldn't stand it, either."

The urge to comfort her grew stronger, so he busied himself with opening the saddlebag that held their supper things. He unloaded the jerky, bread and dried fruit that Grandma Jones had packed for them. They'd stay tonight on the open range and return to the ranch tomorrow, once they'd doctored the few cows that needed it.

"I felt like that before," he finally said.

"What?" She spun her head around and blinked at him as if she'd forgotten his presence.

"There was a time I felt alone and angry, and couldn't stand it when people tried to sympathize."

"Why?"

Caleb took a long breath, steeling himself against the rush of memories. "It was right after my fiancée, Liza, died."

"Your fiancée?" Jennie brought her hand to her mouth. "What happened?"

"She…um…came down this way on the stage to visit her aunt, about a month before our wedding." He regarded a group of trees in the distance, embarrassed to see the pity he imagined he'd find on Jennie's face.

It had been more than a year since he'd last recounted the story, but the pain felt as fresh as ever as the words spilled from him. "There was…an accident with the stage, and she was killed instantly."

"I'm so sorry." She set her hand on his sleeve for a moment. "That must have been devastating."

"We attended the same church congregation with our families. I tried going a few times after Liza's death, but I couldn't take the pity I saw reflected in everyone's eyes, how they'd stop their whispered conversations when I came close. I quit going to any kind of church for a long time." He tore his gaze from the landscape back to hers, hoping to make his next point understood. "About a year ago, after making peace with God, I finally realized those people who knew Liza weren't being cruel or unkind on purpose. The real reason I'd quit going to church back then had nothing to with them, and everything to do with me."

With a shake of her head, Jennie scrambled to her feet. "You make it sound so easy, but it's not. You don't know what they said about my mother, the horrible rumors that they spread. Not that the truth was much better. Do you know she only wrote me once in those five years before we got the telegram about her death? Once."

Caleb couldn't fault her entirely for her reaction; he'd been stubborn about giving up his past hurts, too. "What'd your mother say in her letter?"

"I don't know." Her cheeks flushed red. "I never read it." She stalked away from him, calling over her shoulder, "I'm going to see what's keeping Will."

Breaking off a chunk of bread from the loaf at his side, Caleb opted to appease his growling stomach while he waited for Jennie and Will to return. He ripped off a smaller piece of bread and popped it into his mouth. He didn't regret telling Jennie about Liza, despite the sadness it still stirred inside him. Rather than pitying him, she'd shown sympathy. At least before she'd gotten mad and left.

Caleb ate another bite of bread as he thought over what Jennie had told him. He was honored she would share as much as she had about her own past, but it concerned him, too. He'd grown comfortable with only having to be responsible for himself, and he didn't like the idea of having people dependent on him again. It left too much potential for disappointment, and loss. Life was a whole lot simpler on his own.

Chapter Six

Caleb crept through the grayish mist of the nightmare, the voices of the two stage robbers arguing somewhere unseen ahead of him. He felt none of the anticipation he had that fateful day a year and a half ago when he'd discovered the final two members of the gang who'd robbed Liza's stage were together again. In the dream he felt only dread at what he knew was coming.

He moved toward the cabin and peered through the dirty window. The two men hunkered around the small fire, their weapons neglected on the nearby table. Brandishing his revolvers Caleb slipped silently to the door. He paused, the hatred he felt for these men thrumming as hard as his heartbeat. Lifting his boot, he kicked in the door and rushed inside.

"You're both under arrest!"

One of the men scrambled up and tossed his chair at Caleb. Caleb leaped out of the way but the split-second distraction allowed the man to lunge through the back window with a horrific crash of glass. Caleb fired a shot, hitting the man in the foot, but he still escaped.

"*Get down on the floor,*" *Caleb barked at the other bandit.*

"*Blaine,*" *he screamed as he lowered himself to his knees and put his hands in the air. "You gutless coward, get back here!*"

Keeping one gun trained on the man, Caleb stuck the other in his holster and reached for his rope. He approached the bandit. "Don't worry about your partner. I'll find him, too."

The man scowled, then hung his head.

Caleb tossed the loop in his rope over the man's head and waist, but just as he prepared to tighten it, the bandit leaped up, slashing at the air with a knife. The rope fell to the floor.

"*Put the knife down,*" *Caleb shouted as he jumped back to avoid the blade. "I don't want to take you in to the sheriff dead.*"

"*I ain't going no other way.*"

The man rushed him, his arm cocked. Caleb backed up and felt the wall hit his shoulders. He was cornered. He dropped to his knees as the man came at him, hoping to throw the bandit off balance, but Caleb found himself wrestled to the floor.

Caleb tried to work his gun free from the man's weight, but his arms were quickly growing tired from keeping the knife at bay. The blade inched nearer to his skin.

The bandit grinned, releasing foul breath into Caleb's sweaty face. "So long, sonny," he hissed.

Caleb put all his remaining strength into wrenching his arm loose. He angled his gun against the man's shirt and squeezed the trigger. The bandit's eyes flew open wide in shock before he crumpled onto Caleb's chest, dead.

At this point the dream whisked Caleb away from the horror of the cabin to the sheriff's crowded office.

"It was self-defense, Mr. Johnson," the sheriff said. "No judge would convict you otherwise."

"Self-defense," Caleb repeated, if only to convince himself. "Self-defense."

"Caleb? Caleb, wake up."

Grabbing his guns, Caleb jerked upright in his bedroll. In the moonlight he saw Jennie crouched next to him.

"It's all right," she said, drawing her coat tighter around herself. "I think you were having a dream. You kept muttering something."

"I—I'm sorry to wake you." He rubbed at his eyes to clear the sleep from them.

Her shoulders rose and fell. "I couldn't really sleep. I wanted to…" She ducked her head, her next words directed at the dirt. "I wanted to apologize for my… behavior earlier. I don't like talking about my mother leaving, but it wasn't right to lash out at you, either."

"Apology accepted." He steeled himself against the questions she would likely ask about his dream, but to his relief, she moved back to her makeshift bed. Caleb glanced at Will. The boy snored softly from his cocoon of blankets. At least he hadn't awakened him. "You going back to sleep?"

Jennie slipped into her bedroll, but she shook her head. "You?"

"Not yet." He needed to occupy his mind with something else, instead of the haunting images of his nightmare. Sometimes he'd had it twice in the same night. "You mind if I stoke the fire? It sure is chilly."

"Go ahead." Wrapping her arms around her blanketed knees, Jennie rested her chin on her legs as Caleb built the fire into a small but steady flame. "So does your family live around here?"

Caleb poked at the fire with a stick. "No. My folks live on a farm up north, in the Salt Lake Valley."

"What are you doing down here then?"

"Earning money. I want to have my own freight business."

She shifted closer to the fire. "Weren't there any jobs up north?"

"There were." He stared into the dancing flames. "I couldn't stay up there, though. Not with Liza gone."

"Were your parents sad to see you go?"

"Sad, yes, but more disappointed."

He sensed Jennie watching him. "Surely they understood your grief?"

"In a way." He let his stick grow black at the end and then pulled it out of the heat. "But I don't think they knew what to do about me. I quit farming the piece of land they'd given me—me and Liza. I quit going to church, like I told you. The memories of her were everywhere, and one day, I couldn't stand it anymore." A shadow of that desperation filled him and he clenched his jaw against it. "I went and told them I was leaving. Told them I knew I made a lousy farmer and I wanted to do something else with my life."

"Do they like the idea of you having your own freight business?"

"I think Pa's disappointed that I didn't stick with farming, but really I don't know if they care what I do as long as I'm working hard at something and helping others. What they really want is for me to come home. But that's not going to happen. It's time for me to make my own way."

Jennie bobbed her head in agreement. "I can relate to that—deciding to make your own way and not wanting others to step in. That's why I didn't want you paying for the candy I ruined in the mercantile seven months ago."

The candy? He studied her, her red hair brighter in the firelight, her brown eyes peering back at him. "You were the woman in the store?"

"I didn't want to feel beholden to you."

"I guess that's one way to look at it. But I'd say we're just about even, since you gave me a job. That was definitely worth the money to pay for the candy. And to see you smile."

She tucked her chin back down, but not before Caleb caught that same soft smile he'd seen in the store lifting her mouth for a moment.

"What were you doing up in Fillmore?" he asked.

"Meeting with the bank president about our loan." Her next question came quickly as if she couldn't change the subject fast enough. "When was the last time you saw your parents?"

"Three years ago, but I try to write every few weeks."

"It isn't the same, though, is it?"

"No." A feeling of loneliness swept over him. He hadn't realized until he had entered the close-knit circle of Jennie's family how much he missed his parents and siblings.

"I hope you get that freight business."

He cleared his throat to rid it of emotion. "Thanks.

It's a lot more exciting than farming. You get to travel, meet new people."

"Sometimes a life like that isn't so adventurous."

"What do you mean?"

"Nothing." Jennie released her hold around her knees. "I think I'm ready to sleep now. Good night, Caleb."

She stuck out her hand and Caleb shook it. He liked Jennie's firm but feminine grip. "Good night, Miss Jones. It was a pleasure talking with you."

Her cheeks colored, but he guessed it was from facing the fire. "You can call me Jennie."

"Jennie," he repeated. He banked the fire and moved back to his own bedroll. Tucking his arms behind his head, he shut his eyes and exhaled a long breath. His nightmare didn't come again. This time he dreamed of a girl in a green dress with a pretty smile and a pile of candy around her knees.

After a morning of doctoring the cattle that needed it, Jennie couldn't stand the smell of smoke and sweat in her hair any longer. She left Caleb and Will napping and walked to the creek to wash her hair, armed with soap, a cup, a blanket and her gun.

She removed her dusty boots and socks and dipped her feet into the water. The cool wetness on her bare toes brought a quick intake of breath, then a sigh of contentment.

When was the last time she'd taken a break in the middle of the week? She had Caleb to thank for that. For a farmer-freighter, he handled the cattle rather well, and she had to admit she was glad to have him around.

She had enjoyed talking with him the night before. Maybe too much. She didn't need him distracting her from her goal to save the ranch. Which meant she needed to keep their friendship professional—like Nathan's. But Nathan didn't cause butterflies in her stomach when he teased her or when he smiled, and she didn't care one whit what Nathan thought of her appearance.

"Is that why I'm doing this?" she murmured, glancing down at her washing things. To impress Caleb? She shook her head. "I just want to feel clean." Though she couldn't help recalling the few times he'd called her pretty.

Picking up the cup and soap, she hurried to wash her hair so the three of them could ride back to the ranch.

She shivered as she doused her head with the cold water and began scrubbing the dripping locks. If only she could wash away her silly romantic thoughts as easily.

Caleb yawned and sat up to stretch his arms. His muscles felt less sore today, evidence he was growing more used to his job as a cowboy.

"Where's your sister?" he called over to Will.

The boy jumped as though he'd been prodded with a pitchfork. "I...uh...don't know." He stuck the book he'd been reading behind his back. "Maybe she went to the creek."

"You reading somethin' interesting?"

Without answering, Will picked up his hat and rolled it between his hands.

"Care if I have a look?" Caleb asked, as he stood and approached Will.

Will studied him a moment before reaching for the

book. He plunked it into Caleb's outstretched hand. Caleb cocked an eyebrow when he saw it was the Bible.

"Is there a reason you're hiding it?"

"Maybe."

Caleb feigned a thoughtful nod as he handed back the book. "I guess you never know when those nonbeliever cows might demand you hand it over or they'll rough you up."

A smile replaced the frown on Will's face, then faded just as quickly. "I'm not worried about the cows." Setting the Bible on the grass, he ripped up a blade and twisted it between his fingers. "It's just that Jennie doesn't take too kindly to anything that smacks of religion."

"And that's the problem?"

Will nodded. "She won't go to church 'cause of stuff people said about our ma after she left us, but I'd like to go. Not just for the preaching, either." He broke the piece of grass in two and tossed them both aside. "I had to quit going to school after Pa died. So it'd be nice to be around people my own age again."

"I think that's real commendable," Caleb said, taking a seat on the ground. He admired Will's honest heart. "I don't know if I appreciated going when I was younger. Now, though, I realize how much I need it. It helps me be a better person." He studied Will's lowered head. "Maybe if you told Jennie it would help you meet new friends and be a better brother, she might let you go."

"Or she might just be mad at me for wanting the day off."

Caleb chuckled. "I don't think your sister's as hardhearted as that. Tell you what. I was going to ask her for some time off this Sunday to go to church myself. Why don't you come with me?"

"Really?" Will grinned, then he coughed and a look of nonchalance replaced his excited one. "I mean, that would be nice. If you don't mind."

"Not at all."

"So you'll ask for both of us?"

"Wait. What?" How'd the boy rope him into that arrangement?

"She's likely to tell me no but not you."

Caleb blew out his breath. He didn't want to ruffle Jennie's feathers by sticking his nose places it didn't belong. He needed this job. But Will looked so hopeful.

"All right," Caleb said, rising again to his feet. "I'll go talk to her, but you owe me some lousy ranch task in exchange."

"Deal."

Caleb put on his hat. "Where can I find her?"

"Since Dandy's still tethered here, she didn't go for a ride. I'd try the creek first." Will pointed southeast.

Caleb headed in that direction. He made his way around some scrub trees and found the creek, a greenish brown flow of water. He couldn't see Jennie, but he heard her soft humming from farther upstream.

He trudged along the bank, following the sound of her tune, before he caught a glimpse of her. She stood bent over, a cup in her hand. She appeared to be rinsing soap from her hair. The red color resembled wet copper, but it was the peaceful expression on her face that made him pause. No worry sharpened her face; no stubbornness tightened her full lips.

She really is beautiful, when she lets herself relax.

Clearing his throat, he circled a bush blocking his

path and stepped into the open. He might as well have fired one of his guns. Jennie jumped, her hair spraying water in all directions, and drew her pistol from its holster near her feet.

"Oh, it's you." She lowered the gun aimed at his chest. "Did Will tell you where to find me?"

"He said you might be here," Caleb said, walking to the water's edge.

Jennie stuck the pistol back in the holster and wrung out her hair. Rivulets ran into the dirt at their feet. "I'm almost done."

"I think you could use a second rinse." He wiped at some suds above her left ear.

Her face turned pink. "Oh, right." She bent and picked up her cup and filled it with water from the creek. After flipping her hair over again, she resumed rinsing, but she still missed half the soap.

Caleb chuckled. "Here, let me."

He held out his hand for the cup. Twisting her head, Jennie peered at him, uncertainty written on her face.

"I have four sisters," he explained. "I observed many hair-washings growing up."

She bit her lip, but she finally passed him the cup.

Caleb scooped some water and poured it over her hair, making sure to cover her ear. She sucked in a sharp breath. *From the cold water, no doubt*, he thought, as the chilly liquid ran over his hand. When he finished rinsing the suds, he set down the cup and squeezed the excess water from her hair.

"There you go." He stepped back. Jennie straightened, visibly shivering now. The sunlight shining against her wet hair and face enhanced her beauty even more. He lifted her blanket off the ground and wrapped it around her shoulders. Their hands met for a second as she grasped the ends of the rough material.

"Thank you—for washing my hair."

"Just consider it one of my ranching duties."

She gave a soft laugh. "Good at roping, cattle branding and washing hair? You're very versatile."

He meant to tease her back, but he got caught up staring into her eyes. He noticed for the first time the tiny green specks among the rich brown color. Of its own volition his gaze wandered down to her mouth. What would it be like to kiss a girl again, to feel the feminine softness of those lips?

The sudden noise of someone pushing through the undergrowth shattered his thoughts. His neck and face went hot, and Caleb hurried to turn away from Jennie. Thank goodness she hadn't known his thoughts. He could hardly believe them himself. He hadn't given any girl a second thought romantically since Liza. Surely he wasn't ready to care for anyone in that way again.

"Can I go? What did she say?" Will asked as he approached.

Jennie frowned at Caleb. "Go where?"

"To church." Will joined them beside the creek, glancing from one to the other. "Caleb said I could go with him, but I told him to ask you first."

"I see." Her knuckles whitened where they gripped the blanket and she glared at Caleb. "This was your idea?"

Caleb forced calmness into his voice. "I meant to ask you before Sunday if it would be all right if I went. I offered to take Will when I saw him reading the Bible just now."

"Why didn't you mention this to me?" Jennie turned her glare past him to direct it at her brother.

Will shuffled his feet and stared down at the dirt. "I knew you wouldn't like it. But I want to go with Caleb."

The crease on Jennie's brow deepened. "You want to go back, despite the horrible things people said about us and about Ma?"

Will lifted his chin. "Maybe those people aren't there anymore. Even if they are, that was a long time ago, Jennie." He shot a look at Caleb who nodded his agreement. The boy definitely had the makings of a mature young man.

Jennie exhaled a heavy sigh, her eyes focused on something in the distance before she drew herself up. "I suppose if that's how you feel, you're welcome to go on Sunday—both of you." She yanked the blanket off her shoulders and quickly gathered up her things. "You'll need to hurry back, no socializing for long afterward."

"Sure thing," Will said.

"Why don't you come with us?" Caleb offered. "Your grandmother could come, too."

Jennie was shaking her head before he even finished. "I'm not coming. More than one person judged our family and our mother with no real knowledge of the situation."

Caleb tried to swallow back the retort that popped into his head, but he couldn't. "Kind of like you're judging them now?" he asked in a low voice.

The air between them went deathly still. Jennie gaped at him for a moment before her face flushed with fury. "I told you he could go. I don't wish to discuss my church attendance or the absence of it any further, especially with you." She marched off through the trees, slashing at branches with her free hand and muttering under her breath.

Will blew out a sigh. "Sorry she got mad. Just like I said."

"I thought that went rather well," Caleb said with a smirk. "At least she's allowing us both to go. We can still ask your grandmother if she wants to join us."

"I bet she'd like that." Will's expression brightened. "I'll ask her first thing when we get back." He headed away from the creek.

Caleb followed at a slower pace. He wasn't thrilled about the ride back to the ranch. *So much for not ruffling feathers.* He'd even entertained the thought of kissing her a few moments ago.

Shaking his head at his folly, he reminded himself that he knew better than to allow another woman into his life right now. He hadn't completely let go of his feelings for Liza yet, and then there was the guilt he still had over his bounty-hunting days. He'd done things he wasn't proud of, things he'd done to avenge someone he loved.

No, love and courting were out of the question. They only made a man do foolish things.

Chapter Seven

Jennie watched from her bedroom window as Caleb drove the wagon away from the ranch Sunday morning. Her grandmother sat next to him on the seat and Will lounged in the back. Even from a distance, Jennie sensed their enthusiasm.

Dropping the curtains into place, she turned abruptly from the sight and folded her arms tight against her body.

It's all his *fault,* she thought, her thumbnail meeting her mouth. If Caleb hadn't showed up to "save" her from the stage bandits, if she hadn't foolishly hired him, everything would be the same. She wouldn't be so edgy and self-conscious all the time, and the family certainly wouldn't be trotting off to church.

He wouldn't have been staring at my lips yesterday, either. Try as she might the memory of Caleb rinsing her hair and watching her mouth, even for a moment, made her pulse speed up in a way that had nothing to do with her anger.

With everyone gone, she left her bedroom and tromped loudly down the stairs, her footsteps echoing in the empty house. Her irritation cooled a little when she found the plate of breakfast food Grandma Jones had set on the back of the stove for her.

Jennie ate slowly, trying to decide how to occupy the next several hours. There were numerous ranch chores to be done, but there was no rush. The family usually rested for a bit on Sunday anyway and she didn't see the need to change that habit now.

She washed her few dishes, grabbed a book from the parlor and went out on the porch to read in the sunshine. Though early still, the air already felt pleasant.

A single chapter took her much longer than it should have as her mind skipped back and forth from the story to what people at church might say about seeing her family come to services again for the first time in years. Finally Jennie tossed the book onto the rocker and walked to the barn. She could at least ride out to check on the cattle.

She had the saddle on Dandy and was cinching the straps tighter beneath the horse's belly when the barn door creaked. With quick fingers, Jennie reached for the pistol tucked into the waist of her breeches. Maybe the family had changed their minds about going to church, but she wasn't taking any chances.

"Going somewhere, love?"

Nathan stood at the barn entrance, his own horse crowding the doorway behind him.

"As a matter of fact I am," she said, frowning. She put away her gun, placed her foot in the stirrup and climbed into the saddle.

"Where to?" Nathan swung onto his horse and they fell in step beside her as she and Dandy rode from the barn.

"I'm off to see my cows." She smiled when Nathan gave a disdainful snort. "You're back sooner than I expected."

He nudged his horse close to hers and took her hand, rubbing it against the dark bristles of his face. "Missed me that much, huh?"

Jennie cringed at his touch and firmly removed her hand from his grip. She urged her horse into a trot, but Nathan kept pace.

"So why are you here?" she asked, hoping it wasn't just to make passes at her.

"Heard about a job last night. They'll be robbing the northbound stage a week from Friday."

"That soon?" Her second and third robberies had been several months apart. "How much?"

Nathan grinned, revealing his tobacco-stained teeth. "They think they'll collect five hundred greenbacks."

"I'll do it." As the words escaped her lips, Jennie clutched the reins harder between her fingers. Excitement, and a small dose of fear, coursed through her at the thought of besting another group of armed men.

"There's a problem, though." Nathan's expression changed from one of enthusiasm to soberness. "They know about you."

Jennie whirled around in the saddle. "How?"

"Seems you really made Bart mad last week. He got good and drunk the other night and spilled the story to all his friends about a redheaded spitfire who stole his stage money. They'll be watchin' for you."

"Should I pass up the job then?" She desperately needed the money, but she didn't want to wind up dead, either.

Nathan shook his head. "You'll be fine. Just be care-

ful. It's two men and this is their first time robbing a
stage."

"Thank you for the information, Nathan." She read
the silent question in his eyes and knew that he still
wanted her to run away with him. He liked her ability
with a gun and the adept way she handled bandits—
that's why he wanted her to leave with him. But he
didn't know the real Jennie Jones, the person she was
inside. That girl was much more than what he saw—
much more than what desperation had driven her to
become. She had to be.

"Always a pleasure, Jennie 'Spitfire' Jones." He
pulled his horse up short, and Jennie did the same. "I'll
be off—unless you got somethin' else in mind for us to
do besides stare at your pitiful cattle." He winked at her.

"No," she said with an emphatic shake of her head.
She still held to her morals when it came to some things.

"Of course not. You may be an outlaw, but you're a
prudish one at that." He laughed and wheeled his horse
around. "They'll attack the stage about ten miles south
of Cove Fort. Then they'll hole up for the rest of the
day in a cave, just west of there. You can overtake them
while they're hiding out, but you'll have a good, long
ride ahead of you. Make sure you get there in enough
time to steal the money before they split at dusk."

Jennie waved as he galloped away and renewed her
course. Her thoughts soon returned to Nathan calling
her an outlaw. She didn't think of herself in those terms.
She certainly wasn't a criminal like these thugs she
came up against.

A niggling doubt struggled to free itself, but Jennie
quickly silenced it by reviewing the week's tasks: finish

mending the fences, repair the chicken coop and decide what seeds they would plant in the garden.

Before long she located the bulk of the herd, resting in the shade of some juniper trees. She whistled loudly so they wouldn't be spooked and rode in a circle around the cattle. She observed each cow, checking for any sign of sickness or injury. They appeared to be in good health, besides being a bit skinnier than their cows in the past. She turned Dandy north and began a lazy search for the rest of the cattle.

After a mile or two, she realized she hadn't run across a single cow since leaving the main group, and she didn't remember seeing any calves back at the junipers, either. She headed east for a ways, then turned south again, pausing in confusion. Surely all the mother cows wouldn't have wandered off together.

She returned to the herd for a count. Thirty of the cows were missing, along with all the newborn calves. Which could only mean one thing. Someone had rustled her cows—again.

Jennie yanked Dandy to a stop, causing the horse to pull against the bit. The thieves couldn't be far away—the calves would slow them down and they'd want to stick near the prairie grass so the cows could feed. She scrutinized the ground, searching for any sign of the rustlers. She nudged her horse in one direction and then another. At last she saw what she'd hoped to, a few hundred yards to the west: patches of trampled grass.

She spurred Dandy forward to follow the tracks until reason caught up with her anger and she pulled back on the reins. Without knowing how many rustlers there were, she wouldn't know if she needed help or not. Even if she could overtake them and get the cows back, she would have a hard time driving the cattle back to the ranch alone. Yet the prospect of waiting until the others returned from church, allowing the thieves time to move the cattle farther away, made her groan with impatience. *If I went and got Caleb at the church, though...*

If she hurried, she could make it to the church in less than an hour. Then she and Caleb could fetch his horse and any supplies from the house and head back to the range without waiting for Will and Grandma Jones to come in the wagon.

Jennie pointed Dandy toward town. "Yaw," she cried, prodding the horse with her heels. Bending low across Dandy's back, she urged him into a full gallop.

Jennie found the churchyard empty, except for the waiting horses and wagons. The meeting wasn't over yet. She slid to the ground and tied Dandy to the nearby hitching post. She ascended the few steps and gripped the door handle, her heart pumping harder with more than fear about losing her cattle.

The memories of the last time she'd been to the little church washed over her and for a moment she couldn't move. All the things people had said about her mother whirled through her mind. Then she lifted her chin. She was only here to get Caleb and save her cattle.

Swallowing back her fear, she pulled open the door an inch. The murmur of a man's voice floated out from the church's main room. Though she meant to slip in quietly, inconspicuously, a sudden gust of wind jerked the door from Jennie's grasp and sent it crashing against the outside wall. Every person in the room spun around to stare at her.

Jennie nearly bolted back down the steps, but the

thought of losing her cows kept her rooted to the spot. She searched the faces of the crowd until she located the surprised but pleased ones of Grandma Jones, Will and Caleb.

"Caleb," she whispered, motioning for him to come to the door.

He furrowed his brow and tipped his head at the pastor who'd managed to keep to his sermon in spite of Jennie's interruption.

"Caleb," she tried again a little louder. But he'd turned forward again.

Someone to her left shushed her, bringing a blush to Jennie's cheeks. Humiliated but determined, she half crept down the aisle and wormed her way into the family's pew next to Caleb.

"If you were going for a big entrance, that was it," he said in a low voice. "I'm glad you changed your mind about coming."

"Do I look dressed for Sunday services?" She glared down at her trousers, then back up at Caleb. "You need to leave with me. Now."

Another person behind them said, "Shh." Jennie gripped the arm of the pew to keep from spinning around and glowering. The room felt too hot, the crowd too close.

"Someone's stolen my cows," she hissed into his ear. "I think we can catch them if we go now."

His eyebrows shot up. "We?" he said out of the corner of his mouth. "Why don't you get the sheriff?"

That was the last thing she wanted. Her association with stage thugs compelled her to stay far away from any lawman. "Not enough time," she whispered back. "We have to hurry. You can ride Dandy back with me."

Caleb exhaled loudly through his nose. "You sure you know what you're doing?"

"Yes." She held her breath. If he didn't help her, she wasn't sure what she would do.

"All right."

"Tell Will and Grandma Jones there's a problem with the herd. We can explain later. I don't want to worry them too much now."

Without waiting for him to follow through, Jennie rushed from the pew and toward the door. She couldn't leave fast enough—both for her cows and for herself. Outside she gulped in air.

She finished untying Dandy as Caleb emerged from the building. "What did they say?"

"Your grandmother said not to let you do anything impulsive." He walked over, concern evident on his face. "If she thinks I can stop you, then she doesn't know you well at all, does she? Are you sure you don't want to go get the sheriff and his men or maybe one of your neighbors here?"

Jennie gave an emphatic shake of her head. "I told you there isn't time. The tracks they left are still fairly fresh. I think we can catch up to the rustlers if we hurry. Now are you comin' or not, cowboy?"

Caleb frowned, but swung up into the saddle. "I didn't leave a perfectly good meeting just to chat." He leaned down and helped her climb onto Dandy's back.

Reluctantly, she wrapped her arms around Caleb's waist as he nudged Dandy into a full gallop and headed for home.

Jennie tried to distract herself from Caleb's nearness, from the knowledge of her hands encircling his strong back, by talking. But it sounded like nervous chatter, even to her ears.

"We'll ride to the house first. And then…then we need to get your horse and your guns. Probably something to eat. I found the cattle's tracks but didn't follow where they led completely."

"We'll find them," he reassured. "In the meantime, since you want my help, can I assume you've forgiven me for draggin' your family to church?"

Jennie's cheeks flamed. Thankfully he couldn't see her face. "I'm sorry." This was starting to become a pattern. "I guess I was…" She let her voice trail into silence as she tried to pinpoint why she'd been so angry with him about taking the family to church.

"Afraid?"

"Maybe." Was she really afraid of returning to church? Or was it something else, something deeper?

"What do you want to do once we find the rustlers?" Caleb asked, gratefully changing the subject.

Jennie resisted the urge to bite her thumbnail, knowing Caleb would only tease her if she did. She hadn't really formulated a plan. "We'll figure that out when we know how many there are."

"From what I saw the other week on the trail, fewer than six shouldn't be a problem."

She smiled at his back. "Are you saying I could have handled those men without your gallant assistance?"

To her surprise he didn't laugh. "We've got to figure out exactly how we're going to proceed once we track down these rustlers. We don't know who we're dealing with here, and things could go south mighty fast."

"All right. I'll think of something."

They rode on in silence as Jennie's thoughts raced

ahead to where the rustlers might be and how to go about stealing back her own cows. Hopefully with a little luck she and Caleb would be able to bring all of the cattle—and themselves—home safe and sound.

Chapter Eight

After collecting his revolvers from his room, Caleb saddled up Saul and met Jennie beside the corral. A lumpy saddlebag, probably holding food and lassos, straddled Dandy's back.

"You ready?" Jennie asked as she swung back up into her saddle.

Though apprehension had begun to unwind itself inside his stomach, Caleb nodded and climbed onto Saul. He reminded himself he wasn't operating in his old job as a bounty hunter, tracking down someone associated with Liza's death. He was simply going to help Jennie rescue her cattle. Without those cows he wouldn't have a job.

He kept Saul at a gallop, in step with Dandy, slowing his horse only when Jennie did hers. Before long, Caleb recognized the spot where they'd done the branding. Jennie signaled for him to stop.

"Those are the tracks the cows and calves made when they separated them from the herd." She pointed to a wobbly line of crushed grass that led west. "With all those new calves to slow them down, they can't be more than a few miles away. They'll have to stay near the prairie grass, too."

Caleb rode beside her as they followed the trail, but the tracks disappeared soon after in a thick patch of sagebrush.

"That can't be the end of the trail," Jennie said with a groan.

"We'll find them. Why don't you head that way?" He pointed due north. "I'll go this way."

Caleb led Saul to the right. Every few feet he stopped his horse and scrutinized the ground for signs the cows had passed this way. Soon he found what he wanted— several new hoofprints in a patch of sand among the brush. A little farther on he discovered some fresh cow dung.

"Jennie!" He stood in the stirrups and waved her over with his hat.

"Did you find something?"

"Here's their trail. The rustlers took them west, this way."

Jennie glanced from the ground to Caleb, respect evident in her eyes. "I didn't know you were a tracker."

"My uncle taught me more than just how to shoot a gun."

When the trail faded a second time, Jennie waited for him to find it again before they continued on. Caleb appreciated her trust in his skills, and for the first time since coming to the ranch, he felt useful, competent. Perhaps the abilities he'd honed as a bounty hunter could be put to good use and not just as triggers for memories he'd sooner forget.

They came to a small stream, and Jennie stopped him. Still in their saddles, they watered the horses and ate some of the jerky and bread she had brought along in her saddlebag. The setting sun changed the sky overhead to a dark blue and stole the warmth of the day.

Caleb paused and slipped on the coat he'd brought along when he caught the smell of smoke. "Can you smell that?"

Jennie drew Dandy to a stop and sniffed the air. "It's got to be a campfire. We must be close."

"If we are then we're also more likely to be seen, too," he cautioned.

Twisting in his saddle, Caleb surveyed the surrounding country. The scent of smoke came strongest toward his left, probably on the other side of the steep incline just ahead of them. Several patches of junipers stood nearby, and to the south, Caleb thought he spied a ravine.

"Let's tie the horses in those trees over there," he said, pointing, "then we'll move on foot up that ravine to see if we can get a better view of who we're dealing with."

"I was thinking the same thing." Jennie nudged Dandy toward the trees.

"I think that's a first."

She shook her head, a smile tugging at her lips. "Things are never dull with you around, are they, Caleb Johnson?"

"I could say the same for you, Jennie Jones."

Once the horses had been tied up, Caleb led Jennie toward the ravine. To his relief, she didn't put up a fuss about following. If she had, he might have refused to help her. He wasn't about to let her lead the way right through trouble's door, not if he could help it.

At the edge of the bank, he peered down. A trickle

of water ran between the rocks and bushes scattered along the bottom.

"I'll go first," he offered, jumping down and landing with a soft thud beside the stream. He turned back to assist Jennie, but she maneuvered the jump on her own. With an amused shake of his head, he watched her brush the dust from her trousers and fix her skewed hat.

With Jennie close behind him, Caleb stepped as softly as he could up the ravine. He figured they'd come about a hundred yards when he smelled the smoke even stronger. This time it was mingled with the scent of stewing meat. Caleb's stomach grumbled in response. Their cold supper hadn't been enough to fully satisfy his hunger.

Putting a finger to his lips, he motioned for Jennie to stop. "They've got to be right above us," he whispered. "We need to be able to see."

He pointed at a large rock that jutted out above the stream. Scaling the rock, he turned and offered his hand to Jennie. To his surprise, she accepted this time. He pulled her up beside him and lifted his head above the bank.

Three cowboys sat around the fire, their backs to the ravine. Beyond them to the north, the cattle milled about in the bushes. Caleb studied the cattle and the men. How would he and Jennie get her cows back without anybody getting killed?

"I know what we can do," Jennie whispered.

He indicated she should jump down from the rock, and he followed after her. In hushed tones, Jennie outlined her strategy for stealing back her cows. When she finished, she stepped back, her eyes bright with expectation.

Caleb regarded her with a frown. "Most of your plan hangs on my theatrical abilities?"

"You did so well playing the part of the sheriff when we met on the trail."

"That was different. We weren't trying to rustle fifty head of cattle then." He blew out his breath. He didn't like her idea, but he'd failed to come up with an acceptable one himself. Anything they did would be dangerous, but Jennie didn't have a ranch without those cows. "All right. I'll do it."

"Good. Let's go back for the horses, then you can ride into their camp."

Caleb forced a nod.

This time he allowed Jennie to take the lead as they hiked back up the streambed to the place where they'd entered the ravine. Using his hand as a cradle, he hoisted Jennie up and over the bank. Once she gained her footing, she turned and pulled on his arm with surprising strength, until Caleb managed to get himself out. When they returned to the horses, Jennie transferred the saddlebag to Saul.

"Are your revolvers loaded?" she asked as she readied her pistol.

"I've got them," he said, dodging her question. He tapped the butt of one of the guns beneath his coat.

"So they're already loaded?"

He frowned at her bent head. "No, they aren't."

Jennie shot him an impatient look. "How are you supposed to protect yourself riding around with unloaded guns? You'd better load them quick."

"I wasn't planning on it."

"What?" She returned her pistol to its place at the

waistband of her breeches. "These men are likely armed—"

"I'm aware of that, Jennie." The words came out harsher than he'd meant. "I don't usually keep them loaded," he added in a lower voice.

An expression of bewilderment settled onto her face. "Why ever not? You know how to handle a gun. I saw you."

"I have my reasons."

"And I have mine—for wanting you to load them. You're no good to me dead."

He growled, ready to argue with her—he wasn't likely to be the one who ended up dead in a gunfight against the rustlers—but he thought better of it. He could tell from her mulish expression that she wouldn't let him walk away without a loaded weapon. "If I load one, will that satisfy you?"

Her brow creased with irritation, but she nodded.

Caleb removed the bullets he'd brought along and hurried to load one of the revolvers before stowing it in his holster. He slipped the rest of the bullets into his coat pocket.

"You know the plan, right?" Jennie walked over to him.

"I divert their attention," he said, untying Saul's reins, "while you lead the cattle away. Then I catch up with you as soon as I can."

"I'll move fast."

"Right." The plan sounded easy enough, but carrying it out would likely prove to be much trickier. Caleb swallowed hard, hoping to push back the dread rising into his throat. He turned around to mount his horse, but Jennie stopped him with a hand to his arm.

"Wait."

He faced her again, raising his eyebrows in question. "Did you change your mind?" Part of him wished she would.

"No…" She still gripped his sleeve. "If you don't want to do this, I'll go on alone."

He forced a laugh. "You can't do this by yourself. You need those cows, and as your cowhand, so do I. That means it's my job to help. Let's just say assisting a pretty girl is becoming a weakness—"

Without warning, she went up on tiptoe and pressed her lips to his.

Too stunned to think, Caleb didn't draw away. Her kiss felt warm and wonderful. Then Liza's face appeared in his mind's eye, and he realized what he was doing. He'd sworn off love and courting. It only meant loss and pain and doing crazy things, like kissing his employer.

He stepped back. Jennie peered up at him, her face more vulnerable and open than he'd seen yet. But what was she doing?

"Jennie. I…"

She silenced him with a finger to his mouth. "Don't say anything. Not now. We need to get going."

He climbed into the saddle and cleared his throat. "I'll be watching for you," he said, more to the tree near her than to her face.

"Be careful," she said, grabbing Dandy's reins.

"I will."

Caleb pointed Saul toward the hill. He twisted around to see Jennie watching him from atop her horse. He felt the memory of her kiss, but he clenched his jaw to squash it. He could think more about it later. Right now he had to concentrate before he ended up doing something else foolish. He had a job to do.

He waved to her, hoping to inspire her with confidence he didn't quite feel, and she returned the gesture. As he guided Saul between the hill and the ravine, he let out a long breath that became a whispered prayer. *Please keep her safe, God. Help us be successful.*

The knot of nerves in his stomach didn't go away, but he felt a little better. Keeping his face pointed straight ahead, he braced himself for the moment when he would arrive at the thieves' camp.

Jennie watched him disappear behind the hill, half relieved after her blunder, half fearful for his life. Would Caleb be safe? What had she been thinking to kiss him? She hadn't, not clearly anyway. One remark about her being pretty and a moment of staring too long at those blue eyes and the arch in his lips, and she'd been lost.

She gripped Dandy's reins tighter, her cheeks hot. At least she'd managed to feign indifference when he'd stepped away. Inside, though, she felt her heart drop to her boots. She'd never kissed a man on the lips before. Had Caleb thought it a weak kiss? Could he tell it was her first? Or was there some other reason he'd looked almost frightened afterward? Jennie thought of what he'd said about his fiancée. What had she been like? Was she pretty? Did he mourn her death as much as the sadness behind his words implied?

Enough, she scolded herself. Caleb was riding into danger to help her and protect the ranch. She didn't want to imagine what she'd tell his parents if something happened to him. What would *she* do if he didn't make it back? What would her life be like without him in it? The thought left her feeling lonely, something she hadn't felt in a long time. Caleb wasn't just a good hired hand—he was the first friend she'd had in years.

Lowering her chin, hardly aware of the gesture, she shut her eyes and offered a quick prayer for his safety. The words felt awkward, even in her mind, but her fear eased a little as she finished. Wheeling Dandy around, she headed in the opposite direction. It was time to get her cattle back.

Chapter Nine

Quicker than he wanted, Caleb rounded the hill, placing him twenty yards from the thieves' campsite. He approached slowly, leisurely, but all three men jumped to their feet at the sound of his horse.

"Howdy, fellows," he called, lifting his arm in greeting.

They eyed him with plain suspicion, their hands already on the guns at their waists. One cowboy stood much shorter than the rest, but the other two—one skinny and one with a drooping mustache—regarded him as though he were the leader.

"Evening." He tipped his hat in Caleb's direction.

"Mind if I join you at your fire?" Caleb asked.

The short cowboy flicked his gaze to the others and nodded. "Sure thing. Have a seat."

Caleb dropped to the ground. He pulled a hobble from his saddlebag and put it on Saul's legs, purposely keeping his horse away from the others. He strode over to the three men, carrying the saddlebag with him. They'd resumed their seats.

"Care for some stew?" The short cowboy waved to a pot hung over the fire.

"Much obliged," Caleb said, though the smell wasn't as tantalizing as it had been before.

He sat in the dirt and accepted the full tin cup and a spoon. "You from around here?" he asked as he took a bite of food. Despite his earlier hunger, he wasn't sure how much he could stomach right now.

"We work not too far away," the leader said. "You?"

Caleb shook his head. "Naw. I'm from up north. I'm down here looking for a job."

Their tense postures relaxed, dispelling the strain in the air, though Caleb felt as edgy as ever.

"You might be able to get work with Marshall King," the skinny one said. "We work for him."

Caleb made a note of their employer's name for Jennie. "Maybe I'll do that. You roundin' up the calves for spring branding?" He was glad he'd learned a thing or two in the past week, enough to pass as a real cowboy.

The three exchanged a meaningful glance. "Just pickin' up the strays," the short one said toward the fire. His light tone sounded forced.

In the ensuing silence, Caleb watched the cattle milling about among the brush. He couldn't see Jennie yet, but she'd be coming soon. He had to get these men talking, distracted. "Name's Johnson, by the way."

"I'm Gunner," the short cowboy said. "That's Haws." He pointed at the skinny fellow. "The other fellow is Smith." The man with the mustache lifted a hand.

A movement out of the corner of his eye caught Caleb's attention, and he turned toward it. In the soft light of the evening, he could see the cattle starting to lumber through the brush. It was his signal.

"So," Caleb said, louder than he intended. He cleared his tight throat before continuing. "What's it like working for King?"

Haws shrugged. "Not bad. He pays better than anywhere else in these parts."

"How much?" Caleb feigned interest in Haws's lengthy answer. He only had another minute or two before the three noticed the moving cattle.

His mind raced for a way to distract the cowhands without having to shoot anyone, if he could help it. Caleb leaned forward, his elbows on his knees, and the heaviness in his right pocket reminded him of the bullets he'd stuck inside. They gave him an idea. He slipped one hand into his pocket and scooped up the bullets.

"Mind if I have a little more stew?" he asked as he stood.

Gunner took his cup, and while he filled it from the pot near the fire, Caleb edged closer and let the bullets slip from his hand into the flames.

Accepting the cup from Gunner, he took a few steps backward as if to sit back down, his muscles tensed.

Gunner glanced in the direction of the cattle and jumped to his feet. "Where'd the—"

Before he could finish his question, the bullets exploded in a terrific boom. The three cowhands tripped over themselves to get away from the fire and flying ash. Not waiting a second, Caleb dove at Smith. He wrestled the man's revolver from its holster and pointed it at the stunned cowhands.

"Sorry I can't stick around, boys," he said, enjoying the perplexity on their faces. Jennie's plan was going better than he'd expected. "Appreciate the supper, but

I think I'll just be takin' back these here cattle. 'Cause I know they don't belong to you. Now drop your guns."

Gunner and Haws obeyed, setting their guns in the dirt. Caleb kept the gun in his grip aimed at them as he walked over and knelt to collect the others. As he reached down to grab one of the guns, someone plowed into him from behind.

"Go get the cattle," Smith said from above him.

Caleb scrambled to get up off the ground, but Smith landed a punch to his lower jaw that knocked him back down. From the corner of his eye, he saw Haws and Gunner scoop up their guns and sprint toward their horses.

For one awful moment he froze—images from his nightmare flooding his thoughts and making his heart leap in fear. He couldn't—wouldn't—use his gun that way again.

But what about Jennie?

The possibility of the other two rustlers, who were armed again, reaching her first fueled Caleb's numb body with new energy. Pretending to be hurt, he waited for Smith to come at him again. When the cowhand approached, Caleb kicked out with his boot, connecting with the man's leg.

Smith cursed and stumbled backward, giving Caleb time to come to his feet. He lunged at Smith and planted a hard fist into the cowboy's belly. Groaning, Smith twisted away, but not before throwing a wild punch that connected with Caleb's right cheek.

Ignoring the taste of blood and the momentary ringing in his head, Caleb pounded a blow at the man's jaw. Smith fell back into the dirt, moaning loudly.

Caleb grabbed Smith's gun from where he'd dropped

it and ran to Saul. He threw off the horse's hobble and mounted.

"Yaw," he hollered, driving his heels into Saul's flanks.

When he rounded the hill, he saw the cattle running hard a quarter of a mile away. He couldn't spot Jennie, but the other two cowboys were racing to head off the herd.

Urging Saul faster, Caleb headed for Haws. The sound of pounding hooves matched his heartbeat as he drew closer.

Where's Jennie? Concern pulsed through him. Then he spied her to the left of the cattle, doing her best to turn the stampeding group in the direction of the ranch.

Caleb drew alongside Haws. The gap between them was less than thirty feet when the cowboy suddenly turned and fired his gun. Caleb bent in the saddle to avoid a direct hit from the shot, but a wave of pain and fire still pierced his right ear. He reached up and found to his relief that the bullet had only grazed the skin, tearing off a small piece of flesh.

He pushed his horse back toward the herd, leaning low in the saddle. It was time to put his gun skills to work. He aimed Smith's gun at Haws's hand and pulled the trigger. A second later, the cowboy screamed and dropped his own gun to the ground.

With two of the three thieves down, Caleb yanked his horse in the direction he'd last seen Gunner. The cows along the left side of the herd charged in closer to the others at his approach.

A quick glance at the front of the herd told him Jennie was still there, riding unharmed. Over his shoulder, he saw Gunner had given up the fight and was racing back toward the cowhands' camp. Haws, his injured arm cradled to his chest, rode hard behind him.

A surge of victory pushed Caleb up in the stirrups with a whoop. "We did it!" he yelled, with all the voice he could muster over the racket of pounding cattle hooves. He removed his hat and waved it in the air, hoping Jennie understood the signal.

He kept waving until Jennie saw him. Even from far away, he thought he saw a smile on her face as she lifted off her own hat and swung it in the air in answer.

Sitting once more, Caleb replaced his hat and stuck his newly acquired gun in the slot on his saddle. *Now to get these cows off the range.*

He and Jennie drove the cattle through the dimming light. When they reached the other half of the herd, they joined the two groups together and guided them toward the ranch.

Caleb's face and ear throbbed and his legs and back felt stiff from being in the saddle so long. He didn't let the complaints linger, though. He felt too exhilarated at their success. Perhaps cattle ranching wasn't so boring after all.

At last he spied the dark outline of the fence in the distance. As they drew closer, Jennie charged ahead and opened the corral. She helped him steer the cows inside, then she secured the gate.

"We'll give them something to eat in the morning," Jennie said in a weary voice as they dismounted and led their horses to the barn. "They should be fine for one night."

He followed her into the barn and put Saul away. The light of the moon coming through the open doors allowed enough light to see by. Caleb pulled off the saddle and gave Saul a quick brush over.

"Do you need a hand?" he asked when he finished.

Jennie shook her head, running a currycomb once more over Dandy's flanks. "I'm done for tonight."

Tossing the brush onto the table with the others, she joined him near the doors. A soft gasp escaped her lips as she took in the sight of his face. "What happened? You're covered in blood." She lifted her hand as if to touch him, but she clearly thought better of it.

A strange twinge of disappointment flared inside him and then disappeared. "One of the cowboys grazed my ear with his shot," Caleb answered. "I'm just glad he didn't take the whole thing off."

"I heard the gunfire, but I couldn't tell who was firing at whom. When I saw you waving your silly hat, I knew you were all right." A faint smile lifted her mouth. "Let's get you patched up inside."

She closed the barn doors and fell into step beside him as he started for the house. He shot a glance at her and saw her quickly look away. Now that the excitement of rustling back her cattle had faded, Caleb felt awkwardness between them.

"About that…um…" He coughed, suddenly unsure how to proceed.

"You mean the kiss?" Jennie stopped walking and turned to face him, her arms folded.

Caleb ran a hand over his stubbled chin. "Yes, that. If I've been too casual in my teasing…"

"If you're worried about your job, you shouldn't. I won't…do that again." She stared down at her boots and shrugged. "I don't know what I was thinking. I suppose

I was just caught up in the moment and the possibility of something happening to either of us."

"Jennie."

He touched her sleeve, but he wished he hadn't done it when the gesture made her peer up at him. Even the dim light couldn't erase the hurt he saw reflected in those dark eyes. He wanted to say something to take the pain away...but then the front door flew open and the moment was lost.

Jennie looked up as Will came out onto the porch. "We thought we heard you," he said. "What happened?"

Jennie seized the opportunity to distance herself from Caleb and hurried toward her brother. "We're fine, Will. The cattle are fine, too."

Grandma Jones appeared in the doorway. "We've been sick with worry."

Caleb trailed the family into the kitchen, and Jennie heard Grandma Jones and Will gasp at the sight of the blood trickling down his neck and into the collar of his shirt.

"Oh, my! You're bleeding. What happened?" Grandma Jones asked Caleb, fussing around the kitchen for medical supplies.

"We went after the cattle, Grandma." Jennie sank into a chair. "Someone stole them."

"What?" Will exclaimed.

"For goodness' sake. And you went after them yourselves?" Grandma Jones stopped midway through cleaning Caleb's injury with a damp cloth. "Good thing I didn't know. Why didn't you go for the sheriff?"

Jennie placed her elbows on the table and massaged at her forehead. Her head ached and she felt weighed down with weariness. "There wasn't time. I tracked their trail before I came to the church. I figured if Caleb and I hurried, we could find the cattle."

Will flipped around a chair and sat down, his arms resting against the back. "How'd you get 'em?"

"Caleb pretended to be traveling in the area." She looked over at Caleb, careful to guard her expression. "While he distracted the three cowhands, I drove off the cattle."

Grandma Jones shook her gray head in disbelief. "No one was hurt?"

"Just Caleb's ear," Jennie said. Perhaps God had heard her awkward prayer for his safety, after all. "He didn't duck quite fast enough to dodge a bullet."

All three turned toward him.

"I'll be all right." Their attention brought a flush to his neck. "I just need some sleep."

Grandma Jones clucked her tongue. "You need a good deal more than that. The alcohol may sting some, but it'll help." Jennie's grandmother dabbed the liquid onto her rag and pressed it to his ear. Once she seemed certain the wound wouldn't get infected, Grandma Jones bandaged his ear with quick fingers and stood back.

"You're all done." She smiled.

Caleb gingerly touched the bandage. "Thank you." He climbed to his feet, then paused, seeming to remember something. "By the way, I found out who those cowhands were working for."

"Who?" Jennie questioned.

"A Mr. King."

Anger was Jennie's first reaction—one that was shared by Will, if the way he slapped his fist against his chair was any indication. Grandma Jones just looked shocked.

"You know him?" Caleb asked.

Grandma Jones nodded. "He's practically our neighbor."

"I should have known it was him," Jennie said, her voice strained from trying to hold in the fury she felt. "Whenever we see him in town, he's always asking how things are now that Pa's gone. He might even be the one who stole our calves last spring." At the time, she'd thought he was just another rancher who thought she couldn't handle it—couldn't run things now that her father was gone. Now she wondered if he was the one arranging things so that she *couldn't* hold them together, sabotaging her deliberately to make her fail, no matter how hard she tried.

"Now, Jennie." Her grandmother shook her head. "We don't know that for certain. Besides, Mr. King was here just the other day asking to talk to you about sharing water. Why would he come over if he planned to steal our cattle?"

"I don't know, but I still don't trust him."

"We ought to go to the sheriff," Caleb suggested. "Have the man arrested, or at least questioned, for cattle rustling."

"No," she said, more adamantly than she intended. All three of them stared in surprise at her. Involving the law would only make things worse, Jennie was sure of that. "I don't think that's wise." She made her voice more even. "We only have the word of his cowhands, since King wasn't actually a part of the theft. It would be our story against theirs." She scraped back her chair and stood. "And for that matter, they could have been lying. They said they worked for Mr. King, but they didn't have any proof, did they?"

"We shouldn't let him off." Will scowled.

Caleb nodded. "I agree with Will."

"Either course has its repercussions," Grandma Jones interjected. "By not going to the law, we're running the risk that it could happen again, which means we'll have to keep a better watch on the cattle. But accusing the man of something as serious as cattle rustling would definitely stir up trouble."

"Mr. King's a powerful man. If we accuse him without any proof, he could make this difficult for us. And we've got difficulties enough already. No real harm was done," Jennie added. "Well, except to Caleb."

"Thanks," Caleb muttered. He didn't seem pleased, but at least he didn't try to change her mind.

"I think we should be grateful we found the cattle," Jennie said, "and leave it at that."

"I agree with Jennie. The cows are back and we don't want to go ruffling feathers." Grandma Jones moved about the kitchen, putting away the supplies she'd used to mend Caleb's ear. "Now it's time for this old woman to turn in."

She ushered Caleb and the others from the kitchen and up the stairs. Jennie let out a sigh of relief that the day was nearly over. It was one of the most frightening, exhilarating and, ultimately, disheartening days she'd ever known. She would be very glad to put it behind her. But she tensed when she saw that Caleb had paused outside his room.

Was he going to make her talk about what had happened between them after all?

* * *

Caleb knew he couldn't go to sleep until he'd at least tried to make things right with Jennie. He hated the idea that he'd hurt her, however unintentionally. He hadn't been the one to instigate their kiss, but he hadn't refused her at first, either. Little wonder she felt hurt and confused by his behavior after their return. How could he make this right?

"Jennie?" he said as she passed by him.

She stopped, her attention on the floorboards. Grandma Jones threw them a questioning look and then disappeared into her room. Will continued on up the stairs to his room in the attic.

"Jennie, I didn't mean to—"

"Please, Caleb." Her voice wavered until she lifted her chin. The steeliness had returned to her eyes. "It was my mistake. I appreciate all your help, I really do. I'll be fine. Good night."

She crossed the landing and went into her room. Caleb stared at the shut door. He thought less of Liza the more time he spent with Jennie and he'd come to prize her friendship. It was nice talking to a woman again, making her smile. But that didn't mean he was ready for a more serious relationship. He couldn't risk caring that much for someone else. Not yet. Jennie would be fine, just like she'd told him. But somehow he still felt like he'd made the wrong move.

Chapter Ten

Jennie tucked bean seeds into the small holes in the dirt Caleb had made with his stick. Pushing up her hat, she watched him working farther down the garden row. They'd both been quieter since rustling back her cattle, twelve days ago, less teasing, fewer smiles.

If only I hadn't kissed him out on the range, she told herself yet again. She had talked herself through the different reasons he'd spurned her. She was after all his employer, and he was still grieving the loss of his fiancée. Yet his rejection stung just the same.

Her poor grandmother had interpreted the awkwardness between Jennie and Caleb as something different—a sign they felt something more for each other but were too shy to act on it. The woman had been making not-so-subtle attempts to matchmake by having Jennie and Caleb work alone—like planting the garden. Will could have helped, but Grandma Jones had insisted he give her a hand in making a new batch of soap, a task he loathed.

If only life were different. She bent and pressed another seed into the ground with a sigh. If she had met

Caleb at church, if she didn't have the bank debt looming over her, maybe then they might have made something more of their friendship.

Thoughts of the debt reminded Jennie of the stage
robbery tomorrow. She'd nearly forgotten about it in all
the excitement of rustling back her cattle. She needed to
contrive a way to get to town. Sitting back on her heels,
she stared unseeing across the garden.

"Something wrong?"

Startled from her thoughts, Jennie glanced up. Caleb
watched her closely, one elbow resting on the top of
his stick.

"No." She lowered her chin and placed the seeds into
the next hole. "Just thinking."

"About?" he prodded. Out of the corner of her eye,
Jennie saw him return to his job, stamping his stick
into the soft dirt.

"I think I'm going to town tomorrow." She did her
best to keep her voice nonchalant, even bored. "We need
more seeds, and perhaps I'll see about finding something new to wear…to church."

The words were out before she could stop them, but
did she really want to go again? Her grandmother and
Will had shared with her how kind everyone had been,
and their acceptance back into the congregation had
stirred wants inside Jennie—a longing to be a part of
something normal and inclusive.

Caleb's face brightened into a genuine smile—the
first she'd seen in days. "You'll come with us on Sunday?"

"Not this week, but soon," she hedged. Her stomach
still twisted at the thought of being inside the building

for more than a few minutes. Not even a new hair ribbon or comb would cure that.

"You still worried about what people will think?"

"They weren't exactly welcoming the other week."

"No one knew what was going on with your cattle—they were just trying to listen." Caleb set down his stick and removed his hat to wipe his brow with his sleeve. "What do you say to taking a rest? A short one?" he added, a teasing glint to his blue eyes.

Jennie nodded, grateful to see him acting more like he had his first week at the ranch. She missed having him around as a friend, not just hired help. She followed him to the shade beside the barn where they sat with their backs against the weathered wood. Jennie took off her hat and used it to fan her flushed cheeks. The coolness of the shadows brought relief from the hot sun.

Caleb fiddled with his hat brim. "What do you think people are gonna say if you come with us some Sunday?"

"You don't beat around the bush, do you?"

"Don't usually see a reason to." He smiled, but the reaction was short. "It might help to share what's on your mind."

Setting her hat beside her, she stared at the hills in the distance. Would it help to share her burden or would reopening the wound be too much to bear?

"It isn't what they'll say now, but what they said right after my mother left." She swallowed hard, hoping to dislodge the lump sprouting in her throat. "Looking back I realize she was unhappy. There were days I'd find her on the porch, staring at nothing. I took over more of her responsibilities, like caring for Will and helping my father. But nothing seemed to make her happier."

Jennie sniffed back the tears that stung in her eyes, afraid they might spill over anyway. "One day, I went out on the porch and she wasn't alone. A neighbor and his wife were waiting in front of the house in their wagon. My mother's suitcase was sitting on the steps beside her."

A traitorous drop of moisture slid down her cheek. Caleb lifted his hand and wiped the tear away with his thumb.

"What happened next?" he asked.

Jennie exhaled a long breath. "She apologized half a dozen times, kissed us all goodbye and left. Later we found a note that said she'd gone to her sister's back East." She studied a smudge of dirt on her trousers. "None of us really understood why she left, especially Will. Grandma Jones kept telling us that she wasn't well and maybe she'd come back once she got better. But she never did.

"After the shock wore off a little, we went to church again. I wanted to see my friends, return to something normal. But someone had already spread nasty rumors." She cringed as the ugly insinuations leaped to her mind. The passing of eight years hadn't dulled the memory one bit. "My friends told me they'd heard my mother had some secret lover and my father had been cruel to her. Apparently everyone believed that those were her reasons for leaving."

"And you believed them?" The question held only curiosity, not accusation.

"Not at first."

Jennie tightened her hands into fists. She dug her

nails into the flesh of her palms to keep her emotions from boiling over into greater resentment, or worse, more tears.

"I never questioned my father's love for her—you could see it in his eyes whenever she came into the room. And yet, after a while I started to wonder if she really had a secret life. I even asked my father about it." She shook her head, tasting the regret in her mouth. "I can't imagine what pain my question caused him, but his response shocked me even more. 'I wish that were the reason, Jennie girl. That would be easier to swallow than the truth.' But he never told me what the truth was."

Slowly she uncurled her fists and peered down at the tiny marks from her nails. They were raw and tinged with blood but so small when compared to the marks left on her heart.

"Over time I forced myself to believe the nasty lies about her." Her voice rose in pitch as the pain washed over her anew. "It made things easier, gave me the anger I needed to survive. If I believed what they'd said, then I didn't have to face what I suspected was the truth."

"Which is?"

"That she left because of me." Jennie choked on a sob. "Maybe I didn't help her enough or maybe I helped her too much. Either way, I must have made it hard for her to…to…love me." Turning her face, she swiped at her tears with the back of her hand, but they were coming too fast. A strong arm wrapped around her shoulders, drawing her to him, and she buried her face in Caleb's shirt as she wept.

When she had no more tears, she lifted her head. Her eyes were dry, but her cheeks were warm with embarrassment. She scooted away from Caleb's protective arm. "That's why I haven't been back to church and why I worry about going again." She'd never told anyone the truth about her mother before.

"I'm sorry, Jennie. I can't imagine going through something like that at a young age." Caleb set his hat on his raised knee, his brow furrowed. "I do have to disagree with one thing, though."

Unsure she'd heard him right, she gaped in shock. "I'm not asking if you agreed. You wanted to know what I was worried about, and I told you."

Jennie scrambled to her feet, but he grasped her arm and pulled her gently back down beside him. "Hold on. Hear me out. I only meant to say I think you're wrong about being hard to love."

She struggled against his grip, but his hand stayed firm. "How would you know?"

"Because your grandmother cares about you and your brother cares about you..." Had his face gone a bit red? "And well... I care about you, too."

He released her arm and locked gazes with her, freeing butterflies in her middle, despite the somber topic. "Your mother's leaving likely had nothing to do with you. You were just a child, Jennie. Don't let her mistakes dictate who you are or what you do."

"Maybe you're right."

"About time you admitted that out loud." He stood and offered her his hand. She allowed him to help her up. "You're strong and caring. Don't let anyone make you think otherwise."

"Thank you... Caleb."

With a nod, he put on his hat. "Back to work."

She walked beside him to the garden and resumed

planting the seeds they had on hand, but she couldn't help shooting glances at Caleb as he worked.

Could he feel a bit more than friendship for her, something more than obligation as her cowhand, even after rejecting her kiss? Deep down she hoped so, though her practical self argued with her heart. His friendship, however comforting and exciting, wouldn't save her ranch or clear her debt. Only she could do that.

Jennie encountered little opposition about making the trip to Beaver alone. She had assigned enough tasks to Caleb and Will to keep them busy and Grandma Jones had begged off coming, saying she wanted to start sewing a new skirt.

She arrived in town with enough time to buy the seeds they needed before starting on her long ride to the bandits' hideout. Turning onto Main Street, Jennie slowed Dandy to a casual gait as she observed the activity on the street. Shopkeepers swept their front stoops, men called greetings to one another from the wagons and horses shuffling past, women hung laundry on bushes or lines and young children played about their feet.

She guided Dandy toward the general store and dismounted. Before she could tie up her horse, Jennie's neck prickled with the unsettling sensation she was being watched—intently. She peered over her shoulder at a group of women bustling down the street, but they seemed to be ignoring her. Thankfully she'd worn a dress instead of her breeches to be less conspicuous.

Turning in the opposite direction, she saw a cowboy hitching his palomino pony to the post outside the saloon. His short stature drew her attention. When he darted a quick glance at her, Jennie looked away, embarrassed to be caught staring. Perhaps she'd given too much weight to Nathan's warning that the bandits would be watching for her today.

She tied Dandy to the hitching post and entered the coolness of the mercantile. She maneuvered her way through the assortment of home goods and tools to the far end of the counter where seeds of all kinds were displayed.

"Can I help you, miss?" A man wearing a long white apron and wire spectacles smiled as Jennie approached.

She pointed at the seed display. "I'll take two packets each of cucumbers, carrots, beets and potatoes."

"Certainly." The storekeeper began pulling the seeds off the shelf.

Lifting the flap of her saddlebag, Jennie reached inside for her money. Her fingers grasped a folded piece of paper, and she pulled it into the light. A single word was scribbled across the front in unfamiliar handwriting: *Jennie*. It had to be from Caleb.

She set her bag on the counter, her pulse racing. What would he possibly need to say in writing that he couldn't say in person? Would he say something more about her stolen kiss? Would he confess he liked her?

She opened the paper with trembling fingers and three dollars slipped onto the counter. Picking them up, Jennie stared wide-eyed at the cash, then she read the words scrawled on the page.

This money is for you to buy a new dress for church. I don't want you to repay me. Find something you like.
Caleb

"I say, miss, are you feeling all right?"

Jennie blinked. She'd forgotten the storekeeper was even there.

"Oh, yes. I'm fine," she said. A feeling of light-headedness washed over her and she gripped the counter. "Actually, I think I could use a chair and a glass of water."

He bobbed his head and hurried around the counter to her side. Jennie held on to his arm as he led her toward the back of the store. Several chairs crowded the black stove. Jennie sank into the closest one, the money and letter still clutched in her hand.

"I'll get you some water."

Jennie nodded and shut her eyes, hoping to clear her head. *I can handle swindling armed robbers of their stolen loot and I can practically run the ranch single-handed. But I get faint over the generosity of one handsome young man.*

Releasing a mirthless laugh, she opened her eyes and read the letter a second time. Caleb's thoughtfulness and the idea of something new to wear left her stomach fluttering with anticipation.

She didn't have time to order a new dress, not if she planned to be at the bandits' hideout before they left. Then again, the money in her hand might be put to better use for the ranch. If she returned home empty-handed, though, she would have to either lie about her reasons for not buying something or divulge her financial troubles to Caleb. She didn't want to do either, fearing he would read the truth on her face.

Resting her elbows on her knees, she dropped her head into her palms and groaned. What could she do?

She felt like a horse being jerked one way and then another by a lead rope.

What if I simply pass on this job?

Jennie sat straight up in the chair, some of the tension and light-headedness disappearing with the thought. Her loan wasn't due in full for another four months— plenty of time to get the $850 she still owed before she lost the ranch. Nathan could easily find two lucrative jobs before August. Besides, if she was being watched, a simple trip to town for supplies and a new dress might convince the bandits she'd given up her thieving ways.

"Here you go, miss." The storekeeper handed her a cup. "You look like you're feeling better."

"I am." Jennie swallowed the cool well water. Handing back the cup, she stood. "I'll pay for those seeds now."

"Of course."

The man followed her to the main part of the store. He placed her seeds beside the cash register. Jennie lifted her neglected saddlebag and placed the money and note into one of the interior pockets. After purchasing her seeds, she left the general store.

Outside, she paused to locate a suitable dressmaker's shop along the street. To her surprise, the short cowboy she'd been staring at earlier sat in one of the rocking chairs outside the saloon, watching her. The moment their eyes locked, he yanked his hat over his eyes and appeared to be sleeping.

Was it just coincidence? Shrugging off the unsettled feeling creeping up her spine, Jennie darted into the roadway between two wagons and onto the opposite side of the street. A whitewashed sign over one of the buildings read Miss Felicity's Tailoring Shop. A tremor of girlish excitement leaped inside Jennie at the thought of something to wear besides faded dresses and men's trousers.

Inside the shop, bolts of fabric—deep blues, mint-greens and butter-yellows—spread over chairs, a table and several dress dummies. A smartly attired woman met her at the door, a tape measure hanging about her neck.

"What can I do for you, miss?" She sized up Jennie.

Jennie flushed, conscious of the patched calico she wore. She'd never ordered a dress before. "I need a new dress." She lifted her chin. "Something suitable for church and special occasions."

The woman smiled. "I think I have just the thing to go with those beautiful brown eyes of yours." She waved Jennie into a vacant chair and headed into a small room at the rear of the shop. A moment later, the seamstress returned holding a dress of rich brown draped over her arm. "I finished this last week, but the woman who wanted it changed her mind."

Reaching out, Jennie touched a corner of the silk material. The brown dress was edged in cream-colored ruffles. "It's gorgeous," she murmured, wondering if she had enough to pay for it.

"See how it forms a slight bustle in back? Very stylish." The woman spun the dress around to show Jennie. "It might be a little big for you in the waist, but I can take it in." She reverently laid the gown over a nearby dressing screen, calling over her shoulder, "Come try it on, honey, so we can see how it fits."

Jennie ducked behind the screen to change. She gladly slipped off her own dress and pulled the smooth silk over her head and shoulders. Glancing down at her figure, she could tell the woman had been right about the size. She swished the skirt like a bell.

"How does it fit?" the seamstress asked.

Jennie stepped around the screen and curtsied. "Rather well, I think."

The woman laughed. "Ah, you've fallen in love with it." She adjusted the seams at Jennie's waist and arms and fastened some pins into the proper places. "I'll take a little in here…and here. Then it ought to fit like a glove. You can come for it this afternoon."

"How much will it cost?" Jennie held her breath, her fingers toying with one of the cream cuffs.

The dressmaker pursed her lips in thought. "With the adjustments I'd say $2.75."

Jennie exhaled, her shoulders drooping slightly. She'd hoped for a new hat, too. Running a hand over the dress, she knew she'd never find anything so lovely.

"I'll take it."

She stepped behind the screen and changed back into her drab gown. This time she didn't care quite so much about the state of her appearance. She would have a beautiful dress before the day was over.

She handed the dress to the woman with a promise to return. Once outside, Jennie surveyed the other shops. She was rarely in town long enough to study the options. Down the way stood the saloon where the cowboy in the chair still appeared to be napping.

Relieved, Jennie decided to cross the street so she wouldn't have to walk past him. She hurried at her usual pace until she remembered she had the whole day to wander. When she spotted a millinery shop, she stopped and lingered in front of the window. She thought of Caleb's words: *Find something you like.* And that something was a new hat for her dress. With a little money left over after buying the seeds, she hoped she might find a nice, simple one for less than a dollar.

Determined, she walked into the shop and viewed the stunning creations bursting with flowers and feathers. She breathed in the smell of straw and new cloth. Tears came to her eyes at the memory of the stylish hats her father had purchased for her. How many times had he come into a shop like this, excited to find a millinery treasure for her?

One of several customers, Jennie had time to browse uninterrupted among the shop's wares. A green velvet hat captivated her interest, and she reached out to stroke the luxurious fabric. Upon seeing the price card, she forced herself to peruse the modest straw bonnets. When she discovered she couldn't afford any of them either, she headed to the box of leftover trimmings.

Jennie rifled through the contents and found a long piece of gold ribbon and three tiny brown flowers. She could use them to make over one of her old bonnets into something new and no one need know differently.

She took the trimmings to the counter.

"Twenty-five cents," the young female clerk said.

She waited while the girl wrapped her purchases in brown paper. Tucking the package under her arm, Jennie left the shop. Her stomach rumbled with hunger. She'd brought along jerky and bread for her trip, but the nearby hotel advertised fresh pie.

With her remaining coins from the mercantile, she purchased a glass of milk and a slice of pie for twenty cents. Jennie gobbled up the sweet treat as she watched the passersby through the window.

She hadn't been sitting long when the cowboy from

the saloon strolled past the window. Jennie thought nothing of it until he turned and saw her through the glass. He stopped and his eyes widened with recognition at the same moment hers did. From the brief glance she'd had of the men who rustled her cattle and Caleb's description of them later, she knew this man was the short cowhand who worked for Mr. King.

Jennie jumped up from her chair, prepared to go outside and confront him, but the cowboy sprinted down the street away from the hotel. Unnerved, she sat down and forced herself to finish the last few bites of her pie. This time the treat tasted less scrumptious.

Why would Mr. King's cowhand be following her? Why did her neighbor care how she spent her time? Was he waiting for her to be away from home so that he could go after her cattle again? For a moment, she considered leaving the dress behind and heading straight back to the ranch, but she forced herself to sit still. She trusted Caleb and Will to look after everything in her absence.

When she left the hotel, she searched the street for any sign of the cowboy. She couldn't see him anywhere. Hoping the whole incident had been some bizarre coincidence, she returned to the dress shop. Inside, the woman was spreading a large sheet of wrapping paper on a table.

"It will fit better now." She smiled and lifted the gown for Jennie to see.

"Thank you. Your work is amazing."

The dressmaker beamed as she wrapped up the dress and handed it to Jennie. "Do you have a beau?" she asked after Jennie paid for the gown. "He'll be dreamy-eyed for days after he sees you wearing this. See if I am right." She laughed.

"I'll count on it," Jennie said, smiling. She moved slowly back up the street toward her horse. She imagined the admiration she hoped to see on Caleb's face when she modeled the dress for him and her family. She frowned a little and reminded herself that Caleb didn't see her that way. He was kind to her, protective, even generous. But loving her was clearly something he had never even considered.

Just as she reached her horse, she remembered with all the excitement of the new dress she'd forgotten to post the letter Caleb had given her for his family. She'd nearly given in to the temptation to open it, curious if he'd written anything about her, but she didn't feel right about prying into his personal affairs.

"I'll be right back, Dandy," she muttered, shifting the parcels in her arms to give the horse a reassuring pat on the nose. "I won't be long."

She walked back to the hotel.

"Back so soon?" the proprietress asked. "Would you like more pie?"

Jennie blushed. "No, thank you. I forgot to post a letter." She handed Caleb's letter to the woman, along with the money for postage.

"Would you like me to see if any mail has come for you?"

She nodded, though she didn't expect anything. Her grandmother occasionally received a letter, but Jennie rarely did. "It would be for Jennie or Aurelia Jones."

"One moment." The woman entered a small room off the main entryway.

As Jennie waited, she hugged the bundle in her arms

to her chest. A new dress and new trimmings for a hat. Much better than dealing with foolhardy bandits. In spite of the strange encounter with the cowboy, she'd thoroughly enjoyed her outing to town and almost wished she had a reason to stay longer.

"There are two letters for you, miss." The hotel proprietress handed them to Jennie.

She thanked her, added the letters to her pile and stepped out of the hotel. When she reached Dandy's side again, she stuck the letters between her teeth as she stowed away her other purchases for the ride home.

Once her hands were free, she studied the letters. The first was for Grandma Jones. Jennie recognized the name of a long-time friend written on the back. The other was addressed to her. Curious, she turned over the envelope. The words *Albert Dixon* brought a deep frown.

What does he want now? She tore open the letter and drew out the paper, forcing herself to take a steadying breath. Perhaps the bank president had come to his senses and forgiven her debt—or at least extended the deadline.

Hoping for good news, Jennie unfolded the letter. To her surprise, the date at the top read only two days earlier.

Dear Miss Jones,
In light of circumstances both difficult and unforeseen for our banking establishment, I regret that I must change the date for which the total balance of your debt is required. Your debt must now be paid in full by the first of June in the year

of our Lord 1870 or we will be forced to foreclose
on your loan.
Regrettably,
Albert Dixon, bank president

"No, no!" Jennie crushed the letter in her fist. The
new deadline gave her less than five weeks. Five weeks
to come up with nearly a thousand dollars—an impossible task.

"What do I do? What do I do?" she moaned, pressing
her head against the worn leather of her saddle. Panic
brought the taste of bile to her throat and she clapped a
hand over her mouth to keep from retching.

She'd been a fool to buy the dress and a meal in town
instead of going after the bandits' stolen money. Even if
another robbery came along, it wasn't likely to pay what
she needed, especially after she gave Nathan his half.

Nathan. Whirling around, Jennie hurried in the direction of the saloon, forgetting her horse and bags for
the moment. She had to get another robbery job as soon
as possible.

Jennie pushed her way through the saloon doors and
paused, allowing her eyes to adjust to the smoky, dim
light. Though midmorning, the place still held a large
crowd of patrons. Men sat at tables, drinking and playing cards, or lounged at the bar beside one of several
saloon girls. The stench of alcohol and unwashed bodies made her cover her nose and reminded her all too
well of the last time she'd been here, when she'd hired
Nathan.

"Where is he?" Jennie hissed under her breath as she
searched the room, trying to identify the faces beneath
the assortment of hats. In one corner, a man and a girl

with too much rouge sat close, a bottle of something between them. The girl whispered something in his ear, and the man threw back his head in uproarious laughter. Jennie recognized Nathan at once and frowned. *So he fancies whichever pretty face is in front of him.*

Ignoring the catcalls and attention she drew from the other men as she crossed the room, she strode purposely to Nathan's table, determined to speak with him. He lifted his head as she approached his table.

"Done already?" He set down his shot glass and leaned back in his chair, chuckling. "You get faster every time."

Jennie shook her head. "I didn't go. That's why I need to talk to you." She threw a pointed glance at the saloon girl who was scowling at her. "Alone," she added.

Nathan's thick eyebrows drew together in annoyance and possible anger, but he nodded. "Excuse me," he said to the girl.

He took Jennie's elbow firmly in his hand and propelled her down a narrow hallway off the saloon's main room. Releasing her arm, he regarded her with a surly expression in his dark eyes. "What's so blasted important you skipped out on a perfectly good job? I needed that money, too, Jennie. You goin' soft on me?"

"No." She stared at her hands. "It doesn't matter why I didn't go. I came to see you because… I need another job." She lifted her head, silently pleading for his help. "The bank sent me a notice—they're calling my loan due. I have five weeks, Nathan. Five weeks to come up with the rest of the money or I lose my ranch."

He cursed beneath his breath. "Those rich folks think they can run other people's lives. That's why I say forget 'em, forget the cattle and come away with me."

Jennie bit back a comment about his lady friend waiting in the saloon. "Can you find me another job? I'll take anything."

"I'll try to hunt up something new. But there might not be another robbery for weeks. The job today came sooner than I'd expected."

He fingered a lock of her hair, but instead of exciting butterflies in her middle like Caleb's touch, Jennie felt only tension. She crossed her arms and stepped back.

"You sure you want to go to all this trouble to keep that dying ranch?" he asked.

Jennie's hands tightened into fists, but she forced herself to stay calm. She needed his support. "I won't let it go without a good fight."

Nathan laughed. "Well I'll give you credit for that, love."

"I don't need credit. I need money."

"Money's not the only reason I'm risking my hide for you, you know."

Jennie feigned interest in the wall beside her. Would he refuse to help her this time if she didn't agree to run away with him? Without Nathan's help she would have to hang around the saloon again, weaseling information about upcoming stage robberies from drunk and leering men. The thought made her stomach ache. What choice did she have, though? She wouldn't go with him.

"I'm sorry, Nathan." She drew herself up. "We want different things. So if you don't wish to help me anymore—"

"Our business ain't over yet. I'm makin' too good of money with you, Jennie Jones, to quit now. At least when you follow through."

She released her held breath. "Thank you, Nathan."

He sauntered past her into the main part of the saloon, a sure sign their conversation had ended. "I'll come as soon as I've found something," he said in a low voice before he resumed his seat beside the pouting bar girl.

Without making eye contact with anyone, Jennie wove her way through the maze of tables and out the saloon. She blinked as she stepped into the street, telling herself it was the bright sunlight and not threatening tears. She walked in a daze back to Dandy.

Untying his reins, she noticed her forgotten purchases hadn't been disturbed in her absence. Somewhere inside she felt relief, but the feeling quickly disappeared beneath numbing apathy. A new dress meant nothing when she faced the reality of losing everything she'd worked and fought for over the past seven months. She settled herself into the saddle and guided Dandy down the street toward home—and her impending fate.

Chapter Eleven

Seated in the saddle, Caleb rolled up his shirtsleeves and gave Saul a pat. "Sure is warm today, huh, boy?"

Most of the cattle rested in patches of shade, except for one that Caleb had rounded up twice already for straying too far. He removed his hat and used it to create a breeze. Out of the corner of his eye, he spied movement and turned toward the ranch a quarter mile away. Will rode toward him.

"Is it your turn?" Caleb called.

Will stopped his horse beside Saul. "Slow morning?"

"Mostly. Watch that one, though." Caleb pointed at the wandering cow with a glare. "Old cuss has made a bolt for it twice."

Will chuckled. "You're just too slow, old man. I'm gonna take a nap." He slouched in the saddle and pulled his hat low, feigning sleep.

"Then I'll come to your funeral once your sister gets finished with you." Caleb put his hat back on and pointed Saul in the direction of the ranch. "Did she say what she wanted me to do this afternoon?"

"Nope," Will said, tipping up his hat. "She's washing clothes in the yard, if you want to ask her."

Nodding, Caleb rode back to the ranch. He was pleased Jennie had started giving Will more responsibility. The boy had a knack with the cattle and he'd be a great help to his sister once Caleb left to start his business.

After giving Saul his feed and water, Caleb went in search of Jennie to ask what task she wanted him to start on next. He found her in the yard between the house and the barn, hanging wash on the clothesline. She stood with her back to him, her red hair falling loose past her shoulders today. Not for the first time, he wondered what her hair would feel like to the touch.

"Jennie," he said as he stepped closer.

She whirled around, her hand to her throat. "Caleb, you scared me."

"Sorry."

She'd been more distracted the past week and a half, ever since her trip into town. Instead of visiting with him and her family after supper, she would excuse herself and go outside alone. He'd gone to the door once and saw her leaning against the corral fence, her chin on her hands.

"Will's watching the cattle. What would you like me to do next?"

She shook her head as if to clear her thoughts. "Did you get lunch?"

"Your grandmother packed me something to eat."

"We could use some more wood."

"Chopping wood it is then." Caleb started to walk away, but he changed his mind and turned back. "Are you all right, Jennie? Not feeling sick or anything, are you?"

"No, no." She reached for one of Will's shirts and pinned it to the line. "I'm fine, really. Just a lot on my mind. Things will be better soon, I'm sure of it."

With a nod, he left, unsure what more to say. Her words sounded positive, but he sensed the hope missing from them. Maybe her concerns were money related. He knew the ranch wasn't anywhere near thriving like it once had been. Not for the first time, he considered giving Jennie the money he'd saved so far. Then she could buy more cattle and food and hired help.

He dismissed the thought almost as quickly as it came. Jennie wouldn't accept his help. He'd been surprised she'd used the money he had given her for a new dress. No, it was better that he kept that money. He needed it for his business, for the chance to start fresh somewhere and build a life for himself.

Caleb located an ax in the barn and went to the dwindling woodpile. He placed a piece of wood on top of the nearby chopping block and swung down the ax. The log split in half and he tossed the pieces onto the pile.

Sweat soon dripped down his neck and chest, but he reveled in the hard labor, something he missed when he was just sitting on his horse watching over the cattle.

At the sound of an approaching horse, Caleb lowered his ax. Was there a problem with the herd? But it wasn't Will riding toward the ranch. The rider was taller and Caleb didn't recognize the horse.

Should he move closer to Jennie? In all the weeks he'd been here, the family had never had a visitor. Will's words from Caleb's first night at the ranch repeated in his mind: *The only man that's come around recently just talks to Jennie...he seems a bit rough, though.* Could this be the stranger Will had been talking about?

Frowning, Caleb took a defensive step toward the horse and rider. "Howdy," he said, keeping his voice light, friendly.

"Afternoon." The stranger tipped his hat at Caleb, but he nudged his horse past him.

Something about the man's black eyes and square face sparked familiarity in Caleb's memory, but he couldn't think where he would have met him. Certainly not in the saloons the stranger likely frequented.

"Is there something *we* can do for you?" Caleb called after him, annoyed at the man's presumptuous attitude.

He pulled back on the reins and twisted in the saddle to peer down at Caleb. "You are..."

"The family's hired help. And you'd be?"

"Here to carry out some business with Miss Jones." The stranger turned and resumed riding toward the house.

Fighting the urge to follow, Caleb forced himself to pick up his ax and the next piece of wood. He kept watch, though, from the corner of his eye.

The man dismounted at the house and walked toward Jennie. When she saw him, her face registered surprise and something else. Relief, delight? She led him around to the back of the house, out of sight. Caleb frowned. It wasn't his business who the stranger was or what his dealings were with Jennie, and yet, he couldn't squelch the protectiveness he felt for her and her family.

Is she kissing him, too? he wondered. The possibility brought a twinge of jealousy, something he hadn't felt in years. He shook his head at his foolishness. Jennie wasn't his girl. Maybe he'd been working too long in the sun.

He reached into his pocket to pull out his bandanna. His fingers brushed the slip of paper he'd used to practice writing his note to Jennie. It reminded him of another paper he'd kept in his pocket for months until he gave up bounty hunting. Now it resided in his saddlebag up in his room. He'd memorized the wanted-poster's contents long ago—the bearded face and dark eyes, the names *Otis Nathan Blaine* or *Black-Eyed Blaine*.

Caleb stared at the corner of the house where the stranger and Jennie had disappeared. The two men had some similarities, like their dark eyes and rough appearance. Should he be worried? But no, how could they be the same person? This man was clearly someone Jennie knew, and surely she wouldn't be associating with a wanted stage thief.

Removing his bandanna, Caleb wiped his face and neck, then resumed his work. His shirtfront was wet with perspiration by the time the stranger returned to his horse and rode away.

Caleb kept chopping wood, though curiosity nearly drove him to find Jennie and ask her what was going on. He refrained, though, not wanting to get her ire up again for treading where he shouldn't. She'd been unusually quiet the past week, but he preferred that to having her fired-up angry at him.

"Would you like a drink?"

He looked up to see Jennie holding a water bucket and ladle. "That'd be nice. Thank you."

He accepted the ladle and drank the entire thing. The water felt delicious on his dry throat. He passed back the ladle and she filled it again.

"You've got quite the pile of wood already. You're faster at that than I am at the washing."

Caleb dumped the water over his head and shook it from his hair. "It helped that I didn't have a visitor," he said dropping the ladle into her bucket. He regretted the words at once, but she didn't lash back at him. Instead she blushed.

"Yes, well, that was unexpected."

He waited for her to say more, but she didn't. "Just be careful, Jennie."

"What do you mean?" Her brown eyes narrowed, and the old expression of mistrust flitted across her pink cheeks.

"Be sure he treats you right. You deserve that."

Now her face went crimson. "Not that it's any of your business, but that man is not my beau. He's helping me with a financial venture. It should pull the ranch out of its poverty, if all goes well."

Relief filled his gut at her words, despite exciting her temper again. "What is it?"

"I'd like to see if it works out before I say anything—to anyone."

Caleb respected that. "I'm glad to hear you might be able to make this place great again. It would be something to see."

"Do I detect a fondness for cattle ranching?" she asked, her question full of amusement. She hadn't bantered with him like this in days and he'd missed it.

"Not a chance. I'd rather take bounty on a bunch of smelly bandits than a branding iron to a bunch of cows."

She laughed. "What do you know about taking bounty?"

Too late Caleb realized his slip. "Thanks for the water. I ought to finish up with this wood."

"Caleb?" The merriment on her face died at once. "What do you know about taking bounty?" she repeated.

Running a hand through his damp hair, he blew out his breath in frustration. He didn't want to recall those days. "It doesn't matter now. That job's over."

"Y-you were a bounty hunter?" She matched his steps back to the woodpile, the bucket still in hand. "You didn't tell me this when I asked about your other jobs."

Why did she sound so upset?

"I didn't see the need. I quit that job long before we met." He picked up another piece of wood and set it on the chopping block.

"How come?"

"Does it really matter?" He didn't bother hiding his frustration as he grabbed up the ax. Jennie stood rooted to her spot near his elbow, her chin lifted in stubbornness. Apparently she wasn't going anywhere. Had he really admired her tenacity earlier? "I shot someone, all right?"

"Don't you have to do that sometimes as a bounty hunter?"

"Not necessarily. A good bounty hunter should never have to kill anyone. You're just supposed to bring the crooks in." The images of that day rolled over him again and he pushed aside his piece of wood to sit on the chopping block. He stared at the ax in his grip. "I killed a man. It was ruled self-defense by the sheriff, but I stopped after that. I never want to be in that position again. That's why I keep my guns unloaded in my holster. It might seem foolish, but it's to remind me never to rob another man of his life, however ill spent. I still relive that day in my nightmares."

Jennie set down her bucket and knelt in front of him. She looked as though she might touch his arm, but she lowered her hand back to her side just as quickly.

"Is that what you were dreaming about—that night on the range?" she asked.

He nodded. Her eyes were almost on the same level as his and he found himself gazing into those dark depths. He hadn't told anyone his reason for quitting his job as a bounty hunter, not even his parents. What was it about Jennie that made him share it with her?

"You're a good man, Caleb."

He shrugged off her compliment. If he'd truly been a good man back then, he wouldn't have let hatred and vengeance rule his life so completely. The death of that bandit had brought him up short and helped him find God again, find greater peace with Liza's death.

"I'm trying—just like all of us. Going to church helps a lot."

Jennie stood and hoisted the water bucket. "In that case, maybe I'd better go with you this Sunday," she said in a rush, her eyes focused on the dirt at her feet.

His eyebrows shot up. "Really?"

She banged his leg with the bucket, sloshing water onto his boot. "Don't act so surprised or I might change my mind."

Climbing to his feet, Caleb smiled. "So you coming or not?"

"I'll go," she said, returning his smile. "I'm always up for a challenge."

He laughed at hearing his own words turned against

him. Jennie walked away and Caleb placed his wood back on the block. He whistled a tune as he added to the woodpile, feeling happier than he'd been in a long time.

After dressing with care in her new brown silk, Jennie stepped out of the house Sunday morning to go to church with the family. The nerves in her stomach nearly made her bolt upstairs and hide in her room, but Caleb was sure to drag her back outside, even kicking and screaming.

She fiddled with her hands, her skirt, her fingernails the entire ride into town, her anxiety too great to make conversation with Caleb and her family. Thankfully the others seemed to understand the source of her quiet and didn't press her to talk.

Would the people at church remember her—or worse, her mother? Would they accept Jennie as readily as they'd accepted her brother and grandmother? As the church came into sight, Jennie struggled to breathe normally.

"You look real nice in your dress," Caleb said when he helped her down from the wagon. He extended his elbow to her, and after a brief hesitation, she linked her arm through his.

She kept her chin up in feigned confidence as she took a seat beside Caleb and the family in one of the middle pews. The meeting started soon after, and Jennie found her jitters returning full force. Could she make it through the entire meeting? She chewed her thumbnail as the opening hymn started. Caleb nudged her with his shoulder and pointed at her mouth. She flushed and dropped her hand to her lap, but she was still too filled with nervous energy to sing.

When it was time for the pastor to speak, Jennie sat up straight and tried to concentrate. But as he entreated the congregation to love their neighbors, she felt a flash of irritation. As if any of the people here had showed any love or concern for her family in the past few years. They'd all but forgotten the Joneses.

Turning her head, she stole glances at those across the aisle from her. Several of the families were familiar. A few stared back, suspicion plain on their faces. Most of those who met her eye, though, did so with curious but friendly expressions.

At last the pastor finished his sermon and announced the final hymn, one of her father's favorites. The throaty tones of the small organ filled the room as a middle-aged woman rose to lead the group in song. Caleb extended an open hymnal toward her, and Jennie took the other end. Their fingers touched beneath the book before they both scooted their hands to the outside edges.

This time she sang along with the rest of the congregation, enjoying Caleb's deep baritone and her grandmother's sweet soprano. The music and the singing rose in volume with each verse, and something inside Jennie responded.

A feeling of love and warmth began at her heart and spread outward, reminding her of the way she'd felt when her father would sing or play his harmonica for them at night. How she missed him and his music. If she could see him, talk to him, would he praise her efforts to save the ranch he loved or would he lament her decisions?

Tears of regret blurred the words on the page, and her throat could no longer sing out the notes. Jennie passed the hymnal to Caleb and clasped her hands together as she pushed at the worn, wood floor with the toe of her boot. She was a hypocrite, judging her neighbors for their past actions when her present ones were perhaps just as erroneous.

The pressure of Caleb's hand on top of hers caused her to look up.

"I'm glad you came," he said softly. To her disappointment, he released his gentle grip.

His words brought the blossom of hope inside her. She could still make things right—once the ranch was safe. Maybe then she could find a way to pay the rightful owners what she'd taken from the bandits.

When the song ended, the chorister took her seat and the congregation bowed their heads for prayer. Jennie wished they could sing again. She wanted to keep the warm feeling inside her a little longer.

Once the meeting ended, Jennie headed for the door, the other three following behind. She tried to push her way gently through the throng, but more than one hand reached out to stop her progress.

"Jennie Jones. It's so good to see you." Jennie recognized the young woman but couldn't remember her name. She held a baby on her hip and wore a smile.

"How you and your brother have grown," an older woman added.

"We're glad you joined your family at meeting this week."

Jennie peered into the friendly faces, too overwhelmed to speak.

"We hoped you'd come back to us."

"Who is this fine-looking young man?"

A hand closed over her elbow. "I'm Caleb Johnson. I work at the ranch."

With a smile to the crowd, Caleb guided Jennie out of the church and down the front steps. "I'm sorry if you wanted to stay. You just looked like you could use some air." Only when they reached the wagon did he let go of her arm.

He had been more solicitous the past while—first with the money for her dress and now the way he held her arm or touched her hand. Did he regret his rejection of her kiss? Did she want him to? The more she came to know Caleb, the more she admired and cared about him. She hated to think of him leaving the ranch for good in a few months. But she also knew that a man who valued his faith as strongly as Caleb could never understand or forgive the things she'd done to hold on to the ranch. The thing she'd do again, if she could.

"Thank you, for your help back there," she said, leaning against the side of the wagon.

"Was the meeting as bad as you'd imagined?"

She shook her head as she watched Will and Grandma Jones standing in different groups talking with what appeared to be new friends. "Everyone seems happy to see us."

"You may still find one or two who insist on dredging up the past, but those are the ones you just ignore."

Jennie opened her mouth to protest. She'd told Caleb what horrible things members of the congregation had said. How could she ignore people like that? The memory that he, too, had wrestled with hurts in the past stilled her anger.

"It took courage to come today, Jennie." He reached up to brush a strand of hair back beneath her bonnet, his blue eyes dark with intensity. Jennie reminded herself to breathe. "Just remember the only person whose opinion really matters is God's. I don't doubt He cares a great deal for you."

"How can you be so sure?" The question came out demanding, unbelieving and broke the intimacy of the moment. But she was glad she'd asked it. Did God really care what happened to her and her family? God hadn't stopped her from losing her mother—twice—or her father. How could she believe that a God who allowed all that to happen wanted her to be happy?

Caleb turned around and rested his arms on the rim of the wagon bed. His answer came so softly that Jennie had to step closer to be sure she heard him. "It's like that song—I was lost and now I'm found." He gave a self-deprecating laugh. "That was me, three years ago. I was lost in grief and anger, but after killing that bandit, I woke up, so to speak. I realized God hadn't gone anywhere after Liza's death—I was the one who'd put the distance between us. When I was ready, He was waiting, ready to take my burden away if I let Him." He twisted to look at her. "He can do the same for you."

The sincerity of his declaration had the same effect as the song, bringing hope to Jennie's troubled heart. Maybe he was right. There were still too many complications to figure out such things for herself right then, but Jennie could admit the morning hadn't been as bad as she'd anticipated. For once she had made the right decision.

Now if only she could save the ranch. It was all she had left—she couldn't lose it. Not if there was any way to hold on. And when she'd done whatever needed to be done, she could only hope that God, and Caleb, would forgive her.

Chapter Twelve

Though supper had been over for some time, Caleb wasn't ready to head to bed. For now, he just wanted to sit around the table with the family and relish the end of a very good day. The church service had been edifying, even more so with Jennie there, and he'd enjoyed two slices of Grandma Jones's delicious spice cake. Jennie, Will and their grandmother didn't seem in a hurry to leave the kitchen, either.

"I'd like to go to Fillmore—tomorrow," Jennie announced during a lull in the conversation about the warmer weather and the cattle.

"What for?" Grandma Jones asked.

Jennie's cheeks tinged pink, though Caleb wasn't sure why. "About finances for the ranch."

Caleb leaned forward and rested his arms on the table. "Are you going alone?"

"We can't spare you or Will," Jennie said. "Not when the cattle need watching during the day and rounding up into the corral at night. I've gone up there alone before. I'll be all right."

He wanted to remind her about their encounter with

the thugs on the trail before he'd come to the ranch, but he couldn't, not in front of her family. He didn't doubt Jennie's abilities to handle herself, though he wasn't keen on the idea of her traveling alone. But what could he say? He was only their hired hand.

Grandma Jones patted Jennie's hand. "Promise me you'll be careful, Jennie girl."

"I will, Grandma." Uneasiness flitted over Jennie's face, but Caleb shook off the observation. Likely her nervousness stemmed from whatever financial meeting she had planned. "I'll be back in four days. Can you get along without me until then?"

Caleb gave a deep sigh and eyed Will. "Whatdaya think, Will? Think we'll manage for a couple days without your sister?"

The boy grinned, then feigned a frown. "I don't know. I think those cows are plottin' a revolt."

Caleb smothered a laugh with a hand to his mouth. His sarcastic wit was clearly rubbing off on Jennie's brother.

Jennie glared at them both. "Very funny, you two. Just try not to get the cows rustled again in my absence."

"I take offense at that," Caleb said, arranging his face into a deadpan expression. "I lost a piece of my ear for those lousy cows. You think I'm gonna stand by and let them get stolen again—just to lose some limb this time? I don't think so."

Grandma Jones and Will chuckled, and finally Jennie's mouth broke into a smile. "You're impossible."

"I'll take that as a compliment." Caleb tipped his head. "What I don't understand is how Will here can get those cows to stay still. I'm always having to ride after one or two that get it in their thick heads to run for the hills."

"I play my harmonica." Will unearthed the instrument from his pocket.

"Play something for us," Grandma Jones requested. "It's been ages since we've heard any music."

Will put the harmonica to his lips and began to play a jaunty tune. Caleb tapped his feet in time to the music and Grandma Jones clapped her hands. After a minute, Caleb couldn't remain seated anymore. He pushed back his chair and stood.

"Would you care to dance, Mrs. Jones?"

Smiling, Grandma Jones nodded. Caleb led her around the table in a slow polka as Will continued to play.

A few turns later, Grandma Jones begged off. Will lowered the harmonica. "I'm not as young as I used to be, but thank you for the dance, young man. Why don't you join him, Jennie? Play another, Will."

Caleb threw Jennie a questioning glance. Would she dance with him or make up an excuse so she wouldn't have to? She had been more receptive to him today, taking his arm in hers before and after church. Holding his breath, Caleb held out his hand to her.

Jennie stood, her expression unreadable, but she allowed him to pull her into dancing position. Caleb exhaled as Will started another catchy song.

"You ready?" he asked Jennie.

She gave a wordless nod and he led her in a circle around the kitchen. He liked the feel of her small waist beneath his hand and the way her hair smelled of perfumed soap.

"It seems you can dance as well as you can shoot,"

she said, turning her head to look up at him with those big, brown eyes.

Time and sound seemed to slow. Caleb peered into her face and then at her parted lips. What would it be like to kiss her, not in a moment of fear or as her hired hand, but because they both cared for the other? The thought made his heart pound as hard and fast as their feet because he knew he *did* care for her. He'd never expected to want to love again after losing Liza, but then nearly everything about Jennie took him by surprise. There was nothing he could have done to prepare himself for her or the way she made him feel. Her beauty, her loyalty, her stubborn pride and fierce determination, her wonderful family, even her annoying cows had somehow won him over. But was he truly prepared to give love another try?

Without warning, his boot caught the corner of his chair as they rounded the table again and Caleb stumbled forward. He nearly dropped Jennie, but she managed to fall against the table with a laugh.

"Guess I'm still better at shooting." He rubbed the back of his warm neck. "Thank you for the dance, ladies. I think I'll step outside for a bit."

He hurried to the door. Behind him he heard light footsteps start to follow, but they stopped when Grandma Jones whispered, "Let him go."

Caleb welcomed the baptism of cold night air on his face as he walked outside and to the corral. The notes of another song could be heard from the direction of the kitchen. Placing one foot on the bottom rung of the fence, he rested his arms against the top and stared at the milling cattle.

Unbidden, Liza's face, framed in dark hair, appeared

in his mind. She and Jennie were as different in personality as they were in coloring.

Liza had always been drawn to people and get-togethers, while Jennie had struck Caleb as quiet and reserved, at least until he'd gotten to know her. Now he knew she could be as witty and teasing as him. And that rock-hard strength—that was what he respected the most. When she put her mind to something, she wouldn't give up.

Had she given up on the idea of them together? Part of him hoped not, but the other part cringed at the thought of caring for someone so deeply again. It had been three years. Could he open his heart to the possibility of pain and loss and love a second time?

He reached into his pocket and pulled out the wanted notice he'd fished from his saddlebag the other day. It was too dark now to see the face or type, but he'd memorized every detail anyway. He stared unseeing at the paper, feeling as though he held the last surviving shadow of his past. The notice represented all the grief and hate and vengeance that had driven him to be a bounty hunter. He'd made his peace with God about his actions, and yet, he'd kept this final reminder of all he'd lost—a love, a marriage, a family.

Shutting his eyes for a moment, Caleb opened them and blew out a long breath. Something deep inside him whispered it was time. He ripped the notice in half and then half again. When all that remained were tiny scraps of paper, he left the corral and walked north, past the house and barn. In the dark, he lifted his hand and let the pieces go. The wind whipped them into the air and scattered them like bits of snow over the sagebrush. The remnants of his past were gone.

Caleb headed back to the house, one of Will's songs rising to his lips. He whistled as he strode through the yard and up the porch. Music still came from inside, which meant maybe he could get another dance with Jennie.

After the stage rolled to a stop in Fillmore, much later than Jennie had anticipated, she rushed down the steps and in the direction of the saloon. According to Nathan's information, that was where the bandits would be lying low until midnight. She pulled her short jacket tighter around her body to keep out the chill of the evening air. The drop in temperature and the dark clouds smearing the sky signaled a good storm and made it seem much later than suppertime.

With her fingers gripped tightly around her purse, her pistol inside, she pushed through the saloon doors. Her entrance went largely unnoticed in the crowded room except for the men at the closest tables who grinned lewdly at her over their mugs of beer.

Ignoring them, Jennie headed toward the bar, scanning the room in both directions as she walked. Nathan had told her to search for a tall, redheaded fellow and a dark one with a scar on his cheek. No one in the mass of cowboys and businessmen matched his descriptions, but Jennie hadn't expected to find them down here. Men who'd robbed six hundred from a stagecoach yesterday wouldn't be openly mingling with the saloon crowd.

"Excuse me," she said to the man behind the counter.

He glanced up from the shot glass he'd been cleaning with a rag. A look of surprise settled on his face. "Do you need something, miss?"

Jennie nodded. "I believe some friends of mine are

staying with you tonight." She gave the bartender the false names Nathan had provided. "Could you tell me which room they're in?"

The man lifted a bushy eyebrow, still clearly puzzled by her presence. "Up the stairs, third door." He waved a thumb at the nearby staircase.

"Thank you." Jennie made her way across the room. Instead of ascending the stairs, though, she walked toward a group of saloon girls milling about a large table where a poker game was in full swing. She stopped a few feet away to observe them, scrutinizing the faces and behavior of each girl. She needed the cleverest and the prettiest to help her.

Once she decided, she strode forward and tapped the bare shoulder of a shapely blonde. The girl spun around, the smile on her face freezing into place at the sight of Jennie.

"What do ya want?" Her painted face scrunched in annoyance.

"I need your help with a couple of men upstairs." Jennie pulled four five-dollar bills from her purse and showed the girl. "I'm willing to pay you and your friend there—" she pointed to a dark-eyed young lady loitering nearby "—twenty dollars to split between you."

"Ten dollars apiece?" the girl exclaimed.

"Shh." Jennie glanced around the room, relieved no one appeared to be listening to them.

"For ten dollars, I'd kiss the Pope."

Jennie chuckled. "Not necessary. I only need you and your friend to get these two men to leave their room and come downstairs with you without any luggage. Then I need them detained for at least half an hour. Can you do that?"

"Consider it done, sweetheart." The girl waved a hand at her friend. "Nellie. Come here." The other girl frowned and wandered over.

"We got ourselves a more profitable job," the blonde whispered to her, "that beats waitin' around for these cowboys to finish up."

Jennie led the girls to the stairs where she repeated her instructions, emphasizing the part about no luggage coming downstairs.

"Here's your money." She handed each girl two bills, which they tucked into their boots. She knew it might be foolish to give them all of the money up-front, but she was already behind schedule. "Whatever you do, don't tell them about me."

"Don't worry. Your secret's safe with us." The blonde one sniffed, her hands on her hips. "We'll have 'em down here in five minutes or you can have your money back."

Jennie smiled at her confidence. "I appreciate the help."

"Anytime," the dark-eyed girl said over her shoulder as they sauntered up the stairs.

Jennie watched them until they reached the upstairs hall, then she slipped into the shadows beside the staircase. She'd carefully constructed her plan during the tedious stage ride, and yet, she couldn't help but worry. Everything hinged on the girls' ability to get the bandits downstairs—without their money—and hold them long enough for Jennie to do her job.

With nothing to do except wait, she gnawed on her thumbnail, her stomach churning with nerves. The nervous action reminded her of all the times Caleb had noticed it and she lowered her hand to her side. She didn't want to think about Caleb now, not in the middle of a saloon about to take money from thugs.

To clear her mind, she reached into her purse for her pistol. She checked her gun again, even though she'd loaded it before leaving home.

The sound of footsteps at the top of the stairs made her press against the wall. Holding her breath, Jennie trained her gaze on the last few steps. High-pitched giggles and the murmur of male voices moved closer.

At last, she saw them. The tall redhead had his arm draped around the shoulders of the dark-eyed girl and the bearded man with the scar clasped the waist of the blonde.

"Why don't we buy you ladies a drink?" the taller one said.

As the group walked to the bar, Jennie slipped out of the shadows. She put her gun back into the purse dangling from her wrist. She forced her feet to take slow, measured steps up the stairs, so as not to draw attention. When she reached the upstairs hall, she allowed herself a long, full breath at having made it this far.

She counted the doors as she walked, stopping in front of the third one. She turned the knob and found it locked. Expecting as much, she knelt on the worn carpet and removed a hairpin from inside her hat. Like she'd learned, she stuck the makeshift key into the lock and jiggled it until she heard a soft click. She turned the handle and the door opened.

Smiling at the relative ease of it all, Jennie rose to her feet and walked into the room. The sound of snoring brought her footsteps to a halt and made her heart leap painfully in panic. Nathan had told her there would only be two robbers. Did she have the wrong room?

She leaned out the doorway and counted the doors off the main hallway. She had the right room. *But who's inside?* She hesitated, unsure whether to proceed or leave, until the memory of Mr. Dixon's notice with the ugly word *foreclosure* on top entered her mind. *I'm not giving up yet.*

Squaring her shoulders, Jennie crept back through the open door. She shut it softly behind her. The room was modestly furnished with a dresser, a wash basin, a table and chairs and a bed.

A large man lay facedown across the bed, his massive back rising with deep snores, his hand still gripping a bottle. Two more bottles and several dirty glasses sat on the table. The stench of alcohol hung in the stale air.

Jennie made a slow canvas around the room, searching for the bag of money and keeping her steps mere whispers against the floor. The man on the bed continued his drunken slumber. She found two saddlebags dumped into one corner, but neither of them held the cash.

Frowning, she set the bags back into place and surveyed her surroundings once more. Nothing appeared odd or out of place except a lumpy blanket wadded up beside the man's feet. She tiptoed forward and knelt at the foot of the bed. Lifting a corner of the blanket, she pushed her hand under the fabric. Her fingers touched something smooth and hard—a bag.

Squelching the urge to laugh, Jennie inched the bag toward her. A muffled groan made her freeze, her hand caught beneath the blanket. The bed shook as the man shifted his weight. Once more the room filled with the sound of heavy breathing.

Jennie waited another half minute before resuming

her task. At last the bag bumped softly against the footboard. In one quick movement, she lifted the edge of the blanket and pulled the bag onto the floor. She untwisted the metal clasp and peered inside. Neat stacks of cash brought a smile to her face.

Jennie stowed her purse and gun inside the bag before taking it with her to the door. She needed to hurry; it had taken her more time than she'd intended to find the money.

With a last look at the sleeping bandit, she walked out the door and closed it. She headed down the hall, hoping to slip out the saloon's main doors unnoticed, but a short man blocked the way to the stairs. She stopped, and their eyes met.

"I know you." She pointed an accusing finger at him. "You're one of the cowboys who stole my cattle for Mr. King. You were in Beaver the other week. Have you been following me?"

She knew the answer even before his face blanched.

"Why are you here?" She took a defensive step forward, the money and the bandits momentarily forgotten in the wake of her anger.

Frowning, the cowhand hurried down the stairs, plowing into the tall redhead and the scarred darkhaired man coming up. Too late, Jennie realized her time had run out. She spun around, away from the bandits, searching for some way to escape.

"Whataya got there, missy?" one of them asked.

Jennie ignored him and sprinted toward the closest room. She prayed it wasn't locked. She grabbed the knob and pushed against the door, throwing a glance at the men coming after her.

"Hey, that's our money," the man with the scar on his face said.

"It's the little imp who's been stealing everybody's dough," the tall one replied as Jennie bolted into the room and slammed the door behind her.

Twisting the lock into place, Jennie frantically searched the empty apartment for a way to escape. There was only one choice.

She crossed to the window, listening to the sound of the men's boots smacking the floor outside the door. Soon they were pounding their fists against the wood. Shouted profanities and threats seeped into the room from the hallway.

Visibly shaking, Jennie pushed up the window and stuck out her head. Crates of empty bottles and several old barrels were scattered along the outer wall, about ten feet below. She could probably jump and survive.

Realizing the pounding had ceased, Jennie pulled back inside the room and stared at the door. Had they given up? The blast of a bullet through the door and into the nearby dresser told her otherwise. She considered firing back with her pistol, but that might end her chance for escape.

She tossed the money bag out the window and crawled through the opening. Clinging to the casing with both hands, Jennie tried to determine the best position to drop.

Another shot fired inside the room. Even if the men didn't break the door soon, they'd be racing down the stairs and around the building to get her before long. Shutting her eyes, Jennie let go.

For a brief moment, she felt the strange panic of free-falling until she crumpled to the dirt below. The impact knocked the wind from her, forcing her to lie still until she could breathe again. From above came the sound of the bandits crashing into the room.

Come on. Get up. Thirty feet away, Jennie spied an alley between the saloon and the next building.

She grabbed the bag and ran as hard as she could toward the alley. *Twenty more feet.*

A shout shattered the air behind her. "Don't let her get away!"

Ten more feet.

A gun exploded behind her.

Five more feet.

She stumbled on a bottle but righted herself. Then something hot and piercing bit through the side of her shoulder. Gasping at the pain, Jennie hurried into the alley and slumped to the ground. Pricks of light danced before her eyes. She reached up and gingerly touched her arm. When she let go, blood covered her fingers.

"This isn't happening," she said with a moan. She pressed a fist to her forehead, hoping to clear the haze filling her brain. She had to get out of the alley and out of Fillmore, fast.

Using a barrel as leverage, Jennie climbed to her feet. The men would expect her to exit the alley near the front of the saloon. She'd have to make her escape elsewhere.

She held the money bag with her good arm as she searched along the back side of the next building for a suitable place to hide. At last she spied the rear entrance of a livery stable.

Sucking air between clenched teeth, she reached the outer door, but it was locked. Jennie braced herself against the wall and removed another hairpin. After some fiddling, the padlock fell open on the ground.

She pushed her way inside and shut the door. She could make out the odd shapes of half a dozen carriages and buggies and heard the restless shifting of the horses in their stalls.

Jennie hauled herself into the bed of the nearest buggy. She set her bag between her feet and removed her jacket, pressing it against her wound to slow the bleeding. Her near escape and throbbing arm brought the dizzy feeling back, stronger this time. She rested her head against the cool leather seat and gratefully passed out.

Chapter Thirteen

Jennie forced open her eyes and blinked at the strange shadows around her. Why was she lying in a buggy indoors? Confused, she sat up. Her left arm throbbed. She stared down at the bloody jacket next to her on the seat and remembrance flooded her aching head. The stage bandits shooting at her from the second-story room. The bullet grazing her arm. The escape into the livery stable.

She pressed her back against the seat, her muscles tensing as she waited for someone to materialize beside the buggy and snatch the money. No one appeared, though.

Careful to put little strain on her injured arm, she climbed out of the buggy and picked up the money bag. She had to get out of Fillmore—now.

Enough moonlight came through the high windows that she was able to locate the horse tack in one corner of the livery. Gathering what she needed, she walked down the line of horse stalls, assessing each animal. She needed a strong horse, one that could get her to Cove Fort and then to Beaver as fast as possible. Once there she'd make arrangements for returning the horse.

Jennie opted for a black thoroughbred mare about sixteen hands tall that stood alert and awake in its stall. Sliding her hand along the horse's nose, she let the animal nuzzle her to get used to her smell and presence before she entered the stall. She saddled the horse and tucked the cash, her purse and pistol into a saddlebag she'd found with the tack. After hiding the empty money bag beneath the straw in a corner of the stall, she looped the reins around her good hand. The horse whinnied softly as Jennie led her out of the livery.

Outside, she used a broken crate to hoist herself into the saddle and tied herself to the saddle horn, in case she fainted. A wave of nausea from jostling her wound made her bend over the side of the horse and retch on the ground.

Jennie drew a shaky hand over her mouth. She needed medical help and soon, but first she wanted to be as far away from Fillmore and the bandits as she could. Once she reached Cove Fort, she'd only be a day's ride from home.

She held the horse to a trot, hoping to avoid any undue attention, as they rode down the quiet street. Most of the windows still had lamps shining in them, which told Jennie that she hadn't been unconscious for too long.

A quarter mile outside of the city, she pushed the mare into a full gallop. The moon disappeared at intervals as the storm clouds moved across the evening sky. Jennie hoped the dark night and the horse's black color would keep her from becoming a target for other thugs or Indians.

The steady movement of the horse beneath her and the unrelenting pain in her arm lulled Jennie into a state of semi-wakefulness. Ahead of her, she could see the faces of the thieves she'd robbed. They watched her with hard, ugly eyes, their lips pulled back in angry sneers.

Knowing she was half dreaming, Jennie tried to force the images from her mind, but another rose unbidden. The blond hair, the firm jaw, the handsome features she'd grown to know so well. Unlike the others, Caleb regarded her with tenderness as he had two nights before while they were dancing. But too quickly his expression changed to one of pain and anger.

Jennie buried her head in the horse's mane and squeezed her eyes shut against the apparition. *He doesn't despise me now, but he will if he ever finds out what I've done.* How would she explain her gunshot wound to Caleb and her family?

"Can't I have the ranch and Caleb, too?" she asked the heavens. The rumble of distant thunder was her only reply, and yet, the answer pounded in her ears as if someone had spoken it aloud.

She couldn't hope to save the ranch this way and expect to win Caleb's affection. Sooner or later she'd have to make a choice, between this man she realized she loved and the land she'd fought—honorably or not—to save.

Moaning as much from the pain in her mind as the pain in her arm, Jennie allowed the blackness to overcome her senses again. Occasionally she startled awake when the mare slowed her step. Jennie would search for water and let the horse rest and drink, checking to make certain they were headed in the right direction, before urging the animal into a canter again and drifting back into unconsciousness.

The pictures in her dreams ran together like the images in the kaleidoscope her father had brought home years ago. Happy pictures of the family before her mother had left, meeting Caleb in the store, kissing him out on the range. Then the vision would whirl and change into the frightening imageries of her other robberies and Mr. Dixon shoving the foreclosure notice at her again and again.

She awoke, cold with sweat, when a crash of thunder rolled above. The horse responded with a nervous whinny. Rain began to fall, and a flash of lightning illuminated the landscape. In the sudden light, Jennie spotted the fort's sturdy stone walls half a mile away.

By the time Jennie reached the massive door, the rain was pummeling the ground in large, angry drops. She slid off the horse and landed in a heap in the mud. Her legs didn't want to move. She half crawled the few feet to the fort's west entrance and pounded a fist against the wood.

"Open up," she cried as loud as she could. "Please, open up."

Only the sounds of rain and thunder pulsed in her ears.

"Please," she repeated. She leaned her forehead against the door, giving in to the tears building behind her eyes.

"Who's there?" someone finally called out.

Jennie choked back a sob of relief. "My name is Jennie Jones. I was here yesterday with the northbound stage. I've been attacked and I need some help."

The door jerked opened and a man hurried out, a lantern held high in his hand. "Let's get you and your horse inside, Miss Jones."

* * *

Warm sunlight shone on her face, and the smell of fried corn cakes and ham filled her nose. She'd over-slept. Jennie opened her eyes and stared in panic at the door. Had the bandits come for her? Had Mr. King's cowhand followed her to the fort?

A knock at the door sent her heart racing. Were they here for her? She sat up, her injured arm protesting the movement, and searched the room for her gun. Then she remembered she'd put the pistol in the saddlebag.

Before she could scramble out of bed, a woman with a kind smile poked her head into the room. "You're awake."

Jennie released her held breath in relief. "Yes, come in." She recognized the woman as the fort owner's wife, Adelaide, who Jennie had seen before on her trips to and from Fillmore. The woman had bandaged Jennie's arm upon her arrival and given her a nightgown to wear. "What time is it?"

"About eleven o'clock. I'm afraid you missed break-fast, but there are some leftovers. Are you hungry?"

"A little." Jennie's stomach rumbled, making them both laugh. "Maybe more than a little."

Adelaide approached the bed and set a folded piece of calico cloth next to Jennie on the quilt. "I thought you could use a new dress to replace your other one. I believe we're about the same height."

"You don't have to do that. I'm already indebted to you."

She lifted her shoulders in a shrug. "No trouble." She leaned in as if imparting a secret. "Would it ease your mind, if you knew the dress has never been one of my favorites?"

Jennie gave a soft laugh. "That does make it easier."

"Good." She pointed at Jennie's left arm. "May I re-wrap that for you?"

"Yes. Thank you."

Adelaide gathered some supplies from the bureau and sat on the edge of the bed. Jennie pushed the night-gown over her shoulder and watched as Adelaide gently removed the bandage.

"The bleeding's stopped."

"It actually feels better this morning," Jennie said, grateful she wouldn't sustain any permanent damage, beyond a scar.

Adelaide rewrapped her arm and stood. "How did you get such a wound in the first place?"

Biting her lip, Jennie mentally scrambled for a simple explanation. "A saloon brawl."

It's half true, she told herself, her body stiffening as she waited for Adelaide's judgment. *What was she doing in a saloon anyway?* she could imagine this proper woman thinking. But Adelaide's green eyes shone with compassion.

"I'm sorry to hear that. The good news is the wound isn't too deep, and I think your arm will heal quickly." She smiled. "Would you like some help getting up?"

"I can manage."

Adelaide bent and patted her hand in a way that reminded Jennie of her grandmother. A sudden longing to be home brought the sting of tears to Jennie's eyes. No matter the befuddled mess she'd made of things, she wanted to see Will and Grandma Jones. And Caleb.

"Do you remember where to find the kitchen?" Adelaide asked, moving to the door.

Jennie nodded. "Um… Adelaide…has anyone come

asking for me?" She bit her lip, fearful of the answer, but the woman shook her head.

"We haven't had any new travelers since you came in early this morning."

Relieved, Jennie gave her a genuine smile. She waited until Adelaide shut the door before she swung her legs over the side of the bed to get dressed. Her sore arm made putting on the borrowed long-sleeved gown more difficult than she'd anticipated. When Jennie finally had all the buttons done up and her shoes laced, her breath came quicker and her arm ached worse.

Running her fingers through her hair, Jennie stepped to the chair where her hat and saddlebag waited. She opened the bag with the money and started to recount the number of bundles when a wave of guilt washed over her. The fort owners had been more than gracious to her; they wouldn't steal her money. Why did she always feel suspicious of others?

Too weary to determine the answer, Jennie pushed the plaguing question to the back of her mind and left the room, her things in tow. She crossed the courtyard, past two girls playing with their dolls, and entered the dining room and adjoining kitchen. Adelaide looked up from stirring something in a bowl at the sideboard and smiled.

"I hope you enjoy the food and the quiet, now that all our travelers are gone."

Smiling back, Jennie slipped into the chair in front of the single place setting and began to eat. Usually the room was crowded with people, all talking and eating at once. She was relieved to not have to make conversation or answer questions, though her long sleeves hid any sign of her bandage. No one but Adelaide and her husband had to know the state in which Jennie had shown up to the fort in the wee hours of the morning.

The hot food tasted delicious, and Jennie ate every morsel. When she finished, she rose from the table and cleared her dishes.

"If anyone from Fillmore should come looking for me," Jennie said in a low voice, though no one else but Adelaide was about, "please, don't give them my name."

Adelaide stopped cooking and peered intently at Jennie. "Are you in trouble, Miss Jones? Is there something we can do for you?"

Jennie blushed at the sincere concern. "No, no. It's just… I would rather return home knowing I don't have some angry, drunken man on my heels."

Adelaide gave a decisive nod. "I think I understand. We'll not share what you wish to keep secret."

"Thank you." Jennie realized she'd been holding her breath. "For the wonderful meal, too." She took a step toward the door. "I should probably be going."

"Are you sure? You don't want to rest one more day?" Adelaide glanced purposely at Jennie's arm.

Jennie shook her head. Right now the only place she wanted to be was home.

"Very well." Adelaide wiped her hands on her apron. "Let's rummage up some food for your journey and then we'll get your horse."

With some bread and cheese tied up in a handkerchief, Jennie followed Adelaide to the stable where they found Adelaide's husband, Ira, attending to the horses.

"Morning, Miss Jones," he said cheerfully. "It's good to see you up and moving. You were a bit worse for wear this morning."

"She's ready to go, Ira," Adelaide announced.

Ira's face registered the same surprise Adelaide had shown in the kitchen, but he nodded. "I'll get your horse ready."

While he saddled up the mare, Jennie discreetly withdrew a wad of cash to pay the couple for their care. "Here, please take this." She held out the money to Ira. "I would have been in a bad spot without your kindness. And it wasn't like I was traveling with the stagecoach this morning."

Ira shook his head and gently pushed back her hand. "We're glad we could help. We'll leave it at that."

Jennie blinked in open curiosity at him. With all the people they had coming through their fort and eating their food, surely they felt justified in accepting a little reward now and then.

As if reading her thoughts, Adelaide spoke. "That's what we were asked to do here—help folks like yourself on this lonely stretch of road. Every time we do, we find we're more than compensated by God's bounty."

"I'll help you onto your horse," Ira said, smiling.

A growing lump in her throat prevented Jennie from responding. She put one foot into the stirrups and allowed Ira to help her onto the saddle. Why was she so touched? *Probably because this place reminds me of home.*

Instead of an image of the ranch filling her mind, she pictured the scene in the kitchen the night before she'd left for Fillmore. Will playing their father's old harmonica and her and Caleb dancing. She could still recall the warmth and love she'd felt, surrounded by the people she cared for most.

Forcing her thoughts back to the present, Jennie thanked Ira and Adelaide once more. They walked her to the fort's main entrance, and Ira opened the giant doors. Jennie rode through, pointing her horse south. Twisting in the saddle, she waved goodbye to the two figures framed inside the doorway.

Jennie alternated the mare's gait from a canter to a walk and back. If she hurried, she might reach the livery stable in Beaver before dark to collect Dandy—a day ahead of schedule.

She located a stream a few hours into her ride where she watered and rested the horse and ate her lunch. A nearby rock helped her maneuver again into the saddle without reinjuring her arm.

More than once, her mind returned to her experience at the fort and Ira and Adelaide's selfless service. Jennie might have sacrificed quite a bit—even risking her life—yesterday to save the ranch. Was all her sacrifice really worth it?

"We need it to survive," she argued out loud. The mare's ears flicked back at the break in the silence. "How would we ever make it without the ranch?"

She tried to convince herself that everything would work out for the best. Nathan could surely find her another job in the next two weeks without garnering suspicion. Then she could pay the bank and keep her home. She'd never take from another stage thief again. No one would ever have to know how she pulled her family out of their current poverty. They would be safe, provided for and happy on the land she valued so dearly.

These thoughts brought her some measure of comfort, but one nagging question remained. What was King's man doing in Fillmore? Had it merely been coincidence she saw him there, like their encounter in Beaver, or was he really following her? What did he want? Jennie hated that she didn't have the answers. Hopefully the cowhand didn't know what she'd been doing at the saloon and her confrontation with him in the hallway would deter him from coming around again.

She reached Beaver a short time after sunset and led the mare to the livery. Taking some bills from her saddlebag, she paid for Dandy's stay and made arrangements with the livery owner to have the mare go with the next stage to Fillmore and the livery stable there.

Exhaustion seeped from every muscle, but she still had to find Nathan at the saloon. Thankfully he was waiting outside for her. She gave him his half of the money and quickly related her experience in Fillmore, leaving out the part about being shot. If he thought she couldn't handle another job soon, he might pass one up.

Jennie let Dandy set the pace for home. She was too sore to care about speed. Once she worked out a plausible explanation for her borrowed dress and injury, she began to breathe a little easier. The real details of her trip to Fillmore could remain a secret.

She would ride up, hug her brother and grandmother, talk with Caleb, and everything would stay the same. *Nothing has to change.*

Chapter Fourteen

Caleb pitched the last bits of hay into the corral troughs before taking his pitchfork and lantern to the barn to feed the horses. His gaze shot to the road in front of the ranch, though he knew Jennie wouldn't be home for another day. He'd started missing her about an hour after she'd left three days earlier. Things weren't the same at the ranch without her around to talk to or tease.

Was she safe and well? Ladies typically had no trouble traveling alone on a stagecoach. Or so he'd thought before Liza's accident.

He closed his mind to the memories by concentrating his thoughts on his next task. He lit into the horses' hay with a vengeance, tossing it faster than he ever had. He had one last horse to feed, minus Dandy, when he heard a noise at the barn doors.

Jennie walked inside, leading Dandy by the reins. Caleb's heart quickened with relief and happiness.

"You're home early. We didn't expect you until tomorrow night."

"It's a long story." In the lamplight her pretty face was etched with weariness.

"I'm glad you're safe," he said with practiced nonchalance, embarrassed by his earlier worry. "I'll take care of Dandy. You sit down and rest."

For once Jennie didn't protest. Instead she handed him the reins and sank down on a nearby bale of hay. "Feels good to be on something that isn't moving," she muttered, setting her hat beside her.

Caleb led Dandy into his stall and removed the saddle and blanket. "If you don't mind my asking, how'd your financial meeting go?"

"It went fine." Her exhausted tone made the words less convincing, but Caleb refrained from saying so. "I can't borrow any more money, but I hope to pay the loan off soon. Once the bank isn't breathing down our necks, we can turn this place around."

"How are you gonna pay off the debt?" he asked as he put the tack away.

Jennie didn't answer right away. Caleb lifted his head to see a look of trepidation on her face. Had he said something wrong?

"We'll be fine."

He grabbed a currycomb and returned to Dandy's stall. He gave the horse a few strokes with the brush before stopping. "I know I've said it before, Jennie, but I meant it. You don't have to pay me my wages just yet."

"It'll all work out," she said, her chin lifted in her determined stance. She released a deep yawn.

"Why don't you go on up to the house? Will and Grandma Jones will be excited to see you."

"Yes, but first I need to hear how things went with me gone."

Caleb chuckled. "Is that the reason you're home a

day early? You wanted to make sure we hadn't run the place into the ground yet?"

"Very funny," she murmured. "Did you get the garden finished?"

"Yes, and the cattle are all fine. I thought I'd start on the hay fields tomorrow."

When she remained silent, he twisted around. Her eyes were closed and her head rested against one of the stall posts. Nervousness churned his stomach, but he forced himself to walk to her side. He'd decided the night before to tell her how he felt when she returned. He was still anxious about starting a courtship, but he was willing to try—on the condition that they would take it slow, see where things went.

Crouching down beside the bale of hay, Caleb took hold of one of her hands. Jennie's eyes flew open and her gaze jumped from his face to his hand and back again.

"Wh-what is it? Are you headed into the house?"

"Not yet." Caleb stared down at her hand, caressing the lines of it with his thumb. Her skin felt warm and soft beneath his touch. "There's something I need to tell you."

"Oh?" The word came out a squeak. He quickly choked back a laugh. She was clearly as nervous as him.

"I need to admit I was wrong about something."

"What is that?"

"I should've kissed you all those weeks ago, out on the range." He forced his gaze upward, but only for a moment. "I… I…care about you, Jennie. A lot. When I think about you, my heart just wants to jump right out of my chest. I haven't felt that in a long, long time.

I know I work for you and that's a bit awkward, but if you think—"

Her lips silenced the rest of his words. He drank in their warmth, and his heart ricocheted with emotion like one of Will's bullets. He hadn't felt so alive and wonderful since courting Liza. He deepened the kiss, his hands rising to her shoulders to pull her closer, but she suddenly cried out.

Caleb jerked away. "Are you all right? Did I hurt you?"

"No, no." Jennie shook her head, but the muscles in her jaw tightened. "It's nothing—really. I hurt my arm, that's all."

"How hurt are you?"

"I'll be fine, honest."

"What happened to your arm?"

Jennie's lips pressed together in a tight line. "I cut my arm on the window casing when the stagecoach broke a wheel near Cove Fort. That's why I'm back early. I didn't want to wait around for the stage to be fixed, so I borrowed a horse and rode home today. The fort owner's wife patched me up before I left and gave me this dress since my other had a rip on the sleeve." Her face softened a little as she added, "There's nothing to be concerned about."

Caleb nodded, though he couldn't help wondering how bad the wound was if she'd needed a new dress. He decided not to press her, though, since she was so tired. Rest was probably what she needed most. Another kiss would have to wait.

Swallowing his disappointment, he carefully swept her up into his arms. "Let's get you off to bed then, young lady."

"Caleb, put me down. I can walk."

"Nope. You're going to let someone else help you for a change. Which means no work for you tomorrow."

She gave a soft laugh and wound her arms around his neck. "Fine. I promise to rest, if you promise to finish that kiss soon."

"Aha. So you admit you do like me back?"

"Who kissed you first?"

"Good point." He smiled down at her, enjoying the feel of holding her against his chest. "Let's get you fixed up."

He carried her out of the barn and toward the house, but he wasn't sure his boots actually hit the ground. He didn't know how this new relationship with Jennie would change things, but he refused to dwell on it. Tonight he simply wanted to revel in the knowledge that the spunky woman with her head on his shoulder was his to love.

Jennie lifted her arms and stretched, careful of her healing wound. She had to admit her whole body felt better after a day of resting. But if she didn't get up and do something productive today she might go mad from inactivity.

In the early-morning light, she put on a blouse and trousers and moved to the door. Only silence sounded outside on the landing.

Good. They must all be at breakfast. If she could show her grandmother and Caleb she was well enough to join them in the kitchen, then perhaps they'd let her do more than mending or drying dishes.

Caleb had been right, though. The time in bed yesterday had made her wound heal much faster than if she'd gotten her way and started right back into the work.

The memory of his admission in the barn two nights earlier brought a smile to her lips as she crept out her door.

"Good morning, Jennie. And where do you think you're going?"

Jennie squealed with fright as Caleb stepped out from the shadows by the stairs.

"I knew you couldn't rest for more than a day."

"I'm only coming down for breakfast," she said, tilting her chin with all the haughtiness she could muster.

"How's the arm?"

"Much better." She carefully rotated her shoulder as proof. "I can work today, honest."

"You're easier to boss when you're injured."

Jennie rolled her eyes. "I can't stand another day of confinement to the house or the porch. Besides, who is working for who on this ranch?"

He ignored her. "I'll strike a deal with you. You go back to bed after breakfast and then you can come into town with me this afternoon."

"You're no fun," she said with a pout.

Chuckling, Caleb leaned forward and pressed a kiss to her forehead. Though not as exciting as kissing him on the mouth, his touch still released flurries in her stomach. "May I escort you downstairs?"

"Yes." She linked her arm through his and they moved down the stairs.

He's so good to me. Her cheeks warmed as Caleb glanced at her, his blue eyes bright with tenderness. *I want to be the same to him.*

From the back of her mind, a thought marched forward: *Then give up taking money from stage bandits.* Jennie frowned.

"Something wrong?"

She shook her head, forcing a smile. "Perhaps I'm a little more tired than I thought."

After breakfast, Jennie returned upstairs. She lay down on her bed and shut her eyes, but she couldn't sleep. There were too many things to think about. She still needed one, maybe two more jobs from Nathan to eliminate her debt to the bank. And she only had two weeks to do it.

With a sigh, she sat up and stared at the walls. Fretting about the money wouldn't accomplish anything. What would she do until lunch? She reached out to finger her brown and cream dress, rubbing the fine material over her fingertips. What a lovely wedding dress it would make. Her cheeks warmed at the thought—Caleb had only confessed his feelings for her, not proposed—but she would've accepted him without hesitation if he had asked for her hand in marriage the other night. She imagined herself in the gown, her hair done up fancy, standing next to Caleb who would look so dashing in a suit.

It was just an idle fantasy for now. She needed to finish with the mortgage, and leave her shameful actions in the past. Only then would she truly be ready to be the wife that Caleb deserved. But surely that day would come soon—the day when she'd be clear of the debt and could leave the whole messy business behind her. She could hardly wait. Once that day came, if Caleb didn't propose soon, she might just ask him herself!

The dream of her own wedding made her think of her parents. Had they truly been in love when they had married? Did her mother regret the promises she'd broken by leaving? A fierce longing to speak with her mother about love and marriage brought the sting of tears to Jennie's eyes.

A knock sounded at the door, jerking Jennie back to the present.

"Just a minute," she croaked over the lump in her throat. She straightened her blouse and opened the door. Her grandmother stood there, frowning.

"You have a visitor."

"Who?" Jennie peered past her toward the stairs.

"A Mr. Blaine. He's in the parlor."

Nathan? That could only mean one thing; he'd found a job. Jennie rushed out the door and started down the stairs, but her grandmother called after her.

"I've never said a word about that man coming around or the fact that you've never introduced him." Grandma Jones gave her a stern look that made Jennie squirm. "Whatever your past relationship, I think he needs to know where your feelings now lie."

Jennie's cheeks burned with embarrassment. She wasn't trying to string Nathan along. After today, she hoped she wouldn't have to worry about him coming around anymore. "I'll tell him," she answered quietly.

Before her grandmother could chastise her further, Jennie hurried downstairs to the parlor. She pushed through the partially opened door, hoping Nathan hadn't overheard her grandmother's warning. He stood, hat in hand, appearing out of place even in the humble parlor.

"Did you find me a job?" she blurted out.

"Good morning to you, too."

"Have you found something?" She sat down in a nearby chair.

Nathan tossed his hat onto the sofa and took a seat for himself. "You are one lucky lady, Jennie Jones." He grinned. "Some fellow talked to me in the saloon yesterday, tipped me off to a big job tomorrow. Four men will be robbing the stage heading east from Nevada to Beaver."

"How much?"

Nathan leaned forward, his dark eyes sparkling. "How's five thousand dollars sound to you?"

Jennie's mouth dropped open. She'd never taken so much money before. Even after giving Nathan his half, she'd still have more than enough left over to pay off her loan and buy herself more cattle. The idea of being so close to freedom made her light-headed. "You're certain that's the amount?"

"I asked the man three times. Some mining company is transferring funds to a bank up north." He leaned back, stretching his arm along the top of the sofa. "It's gonna be a bit dicey for those robbers, though. The mining company's sending the cash with an armed guard and a seasoned stage driver. That means those four men aren't likely to be partial to you waltzing in and taking that cash away from 'em."

"I'll do just fine."

"*We'll* do just fine."

She lifted her eyebrows. "What do you mean?"

"If these gentlemen suspect you're coming, like those other ones did, you might do better with some help."

She could see his point, and his assistance would come in handy with her injured arm. She didn't need to get herself shot again. "All right."

"Now here's my idea of how we're goin' pull this off...."

* * *

Half an hour later, she and Nathan had devised a detailed plan to steal back the bank money. *A rather good plan,* Jennie thought, crossing her arms loosely. Only one thing troubled her, nibbling at the edges of her excitement—having to lie to Caleb and her family, again.

"I'm off, love." Nathan put on his hat and stood. "I'll meet you west of Beaver tomorrow."

He crossed to her chair and held out his hand to help her up. She ignored him and stood on her own, but Nathan stepped closer. Jennie wanted to move back, but the chair stood directly behind her.

"My offers still stands, Jennie," he said, his voice low. "We could finish this job and slip away. Leave enough money for your granny and brother to get on just fine, then we'd set our sights for bigger and better things."

Jennie bit her lip, afraid how to respond. If she told him how she felt about Caleb, would he refuse to help her? Or worse, would he work against her? She couldn't very well carry out their plan alone, but she had to be forthright. She loved Caleb, and once this job was through, she hoped to bury any connection to this part of her life, including her association with Nathan Blaine.

"I'm indebted to you, Nathan, for all you've done." She forced herself to look him straight in the eye. "But as I've said before, I can't accept your offer, for many reasons."

"Would it have something to do with that hired hand of yours?"

She blushed. "Yes."

"That explains the ugly scowl he gave me when I

rode up." He took a step backward, giving her room to breathe again. "Choosing the settled life, huh?"

"We haven't talked about all that." She studied her hands.

"Well, since I probably won't be around to give you my congratulations then…" He grabbed her good arm, yanked her close and roughly kissed her mouth. Jennie shoved hard against his chest, pushing him away. What would Caleb think if he saw them?

Chuckling, Nathan let her go. "I've wanted to do that for a long time."

"Get out of here, you scoundrel." Jennie darted a quick glance at the open door.

"No one saw, if that's what you're worried about." He walked out of the room before turning back. "But you should tell him about it yourself. It'll remind that fellow of yours what a lucky man he is."

Jennie's anger softened a little at the compliment. "Good day, Nathan."

"Goodbye, Jennie." Tipping his hat, he headed out the front door, whistling to himself.

Jennie followed, pausing on the porch. She watched Nathan stride arrogantly down the front steps to his waiting horse and shook her head. Even if Nathan's kiss was meant to inspire grateful jealousy in Caleb, Jennie still didn't plan to tell him. She had enough explaining to do about Nathan's visit in general, and then, more lies regarding her plans for tomorrow. Things were looking up, though. Surely her luck would hold out one more time—it had to.

Chapter Fifteen

Caleb finished hitching the horses to the wagon and headed to the house to collect Jennie. He paused in the kitchen doorway to observe her unnoticed. She sat at the table, a bit of pencil motionless in one hand, her chin resting on the other. She was supposed to be making a list of the things they needed to pick up in town, but she appeared deep in thought instead. She'd been that way since that stranger came by earlier.

Caleb's jaw tightened at the memory of the man strutting onto the porch as if he had a right to be there. Taking a deep breath, he calmed his jealous irritation. Jennie's description of their visit had sounded harmless enough.

"We met for the last time," she'd told Caleb, "about our plan to pull the ranch out of debt."

He hoped she succeeded in keeping the ranch going, though secretly he was relieved to hear that man wouldn't be coming around anymore.

Jennie lifted her head and a smile broke across her face. "You ready?"

He nodded.

"I'm just about finished with my list."

"Go ahead. I can just stand here and stare." He leaned his shoulder against the door frame, taking in the sight of her. He grinned when she rolled her eyes.

"How am I supposed to concentrate with you doing that?" She ducked her head and scrawled something onto her scrap of paper.

"Maybe you're not supposed to."

Her cheeks flamed red, and he chuckled.

"I'm finished," she said a minute later, pushing back her chair. She started past him, but Caleb caught her elbow and pulled her close.

"Did I tell you good morning today?"

"Hmm." She scrunched her face in mock contemplation. "Yes, I believe you told me good morning."

"Have I told you today how pretty you are?"

"In not so many words."

"You're beautiful, Jennie."

She lowered her chin, but not before Caleb saw the love and adoration she hadn't yet voiced shining in her eyes.

"Have I told you how happy this tenderfooted cowhand is to be with you?"

She laughed softly and stepped closer to him. "I don't see any tenderfoot here."

He bent down to kiss her, but Grandma Jones stepped into the hallway. Caleb's face and neck went warm.

"Sorry to interrupt," she said, smiling openly at them, "but I wanted to remind you to get me some dark blue thread, Jennie."

Her cheeks pink as well, Jennie nodded. "We're leaving now."

Caleb followed Jennie outside. He helped her onto the

wagon seat and climbed up beside her. Lifting the reins, he gently slapped the backs of the team and guided the wagon toward Beaver.

The sky shone bright blue above them, not a cloud to be seen. The day hadn't been too hot either, and a pleasant breeze blew across Caleb's face. He liked working down here, but starting his business in the north, close to the railroad, made the most sense. Maybe he could convince Jennie and her family to come with him in a few months.

"You ever thought of selling the ranch? Starting over up north?"

"Sell the ranch?" Her eyes went dark with anger. "You think I ought to sell the ranch?"

"It's an idea…"

She angled away from him, her shoulders hunched as if to ward off a blow. "I don't want to sell the ranch, even if things are bad. This is all Will and I have from our parents. I haven't worked so hard for so long to hand it over to someone else."

Caleb reached for her hand. She flinched at his touch, but she didn't pull away. "Jennie?" He waited until she shot him a glance before he went on. "I thought it might help things if you sold the place to the bank. Then you'd be free from your debt, free to do what you want. That's all."

"The ranch is what I want."

Her chin lifted stubbornly, and Caleb decided to drop the subject. He'd pushed his suggestion far enough. He gave her hand a gentle squeeze to let her know he hadn't meant to upset her. Though she kept her face pointed forward, she squeezed his hand back. He understood the silent acceptance of his apology.

Once they reached town, Caleb tied the horses to the post in front of the general store and helped Jennie down. Inside, he relinquished the lead to her, following her around the full barrels and shelves while she placed needed objects into his outstretched arms.

"Is that everything we need?" She studied her list. "We can ask for the hayseed and then—" Jennie sucked in a sharp breath.

"What is it?" Caleb leaned forward as best he could with his arms full. Was she sick?

Without answering, Jennie bolted toward the back of the store. Caleb strode after her, trying to keep from dropping the goods he held. He peered at her in concern. She looked more angry than ill, her mouth set into a tight line. "What's wrong?"

"We have to leave—now."

"But we didn't get the thread yet that your grandmother asked for."

"It doesn't matter." She gave a frantic shake of her head. "Marshall King is here, in the store."

"Really?" Caleb glanced surreptitiously over his shoulder. He didn't have to guess which customer was King. A man in a worn leather vest with dark hair falling over his collar stood watching the two of them from his place in line. A rascally smile graced his weather-beaten face.

"Please, Caleb, let's just leave. If I so much as go near him, I'll start shouting."

"You won't need to, and we don't have to leave, either. I'll stand in line. You wait here." He nodded at one of the wooden chairs arranged around the cold stove.

"Caleb, I don't think—"

"It'll be fine. I can handle him."

She released a heavy sigh. "All right. Thank you." She slipped several bills into his hand so he could pay the clerk.

He gave her a grim smile. "I might have to put a fist in the man's stomach myself." He slowly spun around and started for the short line.

If King had been smiling before, his face lit up even more as Caleb approached. His lack of contrition for stealing Jennie's cattle sent flashes of hot anger through Caleb, and he had to force himself to breathe deeply.

Unfortunately, King stood at the back of the line, so Caleb had no choice except to take his place behind him. He didn't have to give the man the pleasure of his company, though. Caleb stared in the direction of the front door and tried to think of other things than smashing the man's ample jaw.

"You must be Miss Jones's hired help."

Caleb eyed King, annoyed and surprised at the man's attempt to make casual conversation. "I am."

"I've been meaning to ride over and make you an offer."

"An offer for what?"

"I'd like to give you a job. My sources say you're a good, hard worker." Mr. King folded his arms across his meaty chest. "You come work for me, and I'll pay you a lot more money than you're earning now."

For a moment, Caleb was too stunned to reply. After allowing his cowhands to rustle Jennie's cattle, did King honestly think Caleb would join up with him? *Don't give him the satisfaction of seeing your anger,* he told himself as he lifted his head and looked the man square in the eye. *He's only trying to goad you.*

"If you were the last employer on earth, Mr. King,

I wouldn't accept a job with you." In a low, hard voice, he added, "I don't work for thieves."

The rancher grinned in a dangerous way. "Oh, I wouldn't be too sure about that."

"What're you talking about?"

"Why don't you ask Miss Jones?" King scoffed, his gaze flicking toward the back of the store.

Caleb turned and regarded Jennie. Even from a distance, he could see her pale face and troubled expression. "I don't know what you're getting at, old man."

"Why don't you ask her how she's managed to keep her ranch going for so long?" His words hissed like water hitting hot flames. "Why don't you ask her the real reason she takes off for town or Fillmore all alone? Or why she meets with that fellow from the saloon?"

How could King know any of those things unless he'd been spying on Jennie? His hands clenched into fists as Caleb considered dropping his load to the floor and pounding the conceit out of this man. "How dare—"

"She's robbin' stage thieves, you fool." King brought his sneering face within inches of Caleb's. "She waits 'til the bandits steal the money, then steals it back. She's using it to keep that sorry ranch of hers alive."

Something deep inside Caleb went cold at King's words. Jennie—robbing stage thieves? The same type of criminals he'd hunted down as a bounty hunter? *Impossible.*

He surveyed her beautiful face and tried desperately to erase the suggestion of her carrying out such a deceitful deed. His heart rebelled at the thought, but his head argued that King's story made some sense. It would explain the thugs chasing after Jennie when Caleb had helped her on the trail, the "financial" meetings with the rough-looking stranger, the excuses to leave the ranch unaccompanied.

"Changes things a bit, don't it?" King said, his affable manner returning. "My offer still stands—whenever you decide to quit the place."

Caleb shook his head, forcing his mind to concentrate on the present and nothing beyond that, for the moment. "Whether I leave or stay, I'd never work for you."

"A pleasure meetin' you all the same." Tipping his hat, King took his place at the cash register to purchase some feed.

Caleb's jaw and neck muscles tensed as he glared at the man's back. Maybe he should have punched King straight away—then he wouldn't have heard the man's accusations about Jennie, accusations that brought too many unanswered questions. Finally, King left and it was Caleb's turn to step up to the counter.

Numbly, he set down the load of goods and paid the clerk. As he started for the back of the store, he felt an almost tangible weight pulling at his feet, slowing each step. How could he face Jennie with King's words still ringing in his ears, especially when a part of him wondered if they held any truth?

"Caleb, are you all right?" Jennie leaped up and grabbed his arm. "What did King say?"

Swallowing hard, Caleb made himself meet her gaze. "He offered me a job."

"He didn't!"

"I refused, of course." He shifted his pile carefully into the crook of one arm, so he could hold her hand. Just the feel of her fingers intertwined with his helped alleviate some of his growing fear.

"Is that all he said? You looked more upset than I've

ever seen you before." She peered intently at him as they headed for the door.

"He's a scoundrel," Caleb said, avoiding her question. He hid his conflicting emotions with ease, another skill he'd learned as a bounty hunter. "Let's go home."

We'll talk about it sometime this evening, he told himself. *I'm sure there's a logical explanation for King's wild assertions.*

A voice inside Caleb, growing more insistent by the minute, claimed otherwise, warning him that his conversation with Jennie might very well rob him of the happiness he'd felt the past few days and steal his second chance at love.

Jennie volunteered to care for the horses when they returned from the trip to town. To her surprise, Caleb didn't offer to help. Instead he told her that he'd take over watching the cattle for Will and left the barn.

Why had Caleb been so quiet on the way home? she wondered as she brushed the horses until they gleamed. Was there something more to his conversation with King? She didn't believe a job offer would provoke the kind of shock she'd seen on Caleb's face.

Could he know my secret?

King might have learned the truth from his cowhand, the one she'd seen at the saloon in Fillmore and who'd trailed her in town a few weeks earlier. The rancher might have told Caleb what the cowboy had observed.

"But Caleb would've mentioned it," she said, trying to reassure herself. "Wouldn't he?"

She didn't see him again the rest of the afternoon. She and Will continued the work on the spring planting that Caleb had already started, and by suppertime,

Jennie was so tired she'd almost forgotten the encounter with King in town. Almost.

She told Will to go help Caleb bring the cattle into the corral while she fed and watered the horses. For some reason she felt reluctant to face Caleb. When she finished with the horses, she surveyed the barn, desperate for something else to do. The place was immaculate. It had been ever since Caleb had come to the ranch.

The memory of seeing him come through the brush, handsome and confident, after helping her against Bart and his thugs made her heart swell with pride. She loved him and couldn't stand the thought of losing him. Why couldn't things be simpler? No financial burdens, no stage bandits. Just her and Caleb and her family, living happily.

Blowing out a deep sigh, she left the barn and secured the doors behind her. A hand on her arm made her cry out in surprise.

"Caleb. You scared me."

"Maybe you need scaring," he muttered so softly she wasn't sure she'd heard him correctly. To her disappointment, he released her arm, his hand dropping to his side. "We need to go somewhere and talk."

"I think Grandma Jones is expecting us for supper," she hedged. The anxiety in his blue eyes set off warning bells inside her head.

"She'll understand if we don't come in for a while."

If she went with him, something told her things would never be the same. But she didn't usually back down from hard things and she wouldn't now.

"All right."

Jennie licked her lips and followed him past the house. She tried to breathe evenly as she forced her steps to keep up with his. Maybe he wanted to talk about his wages or his earlier suggestion for her to sell the ranch. And yet, if it were either of those wouldn't he hold her hand? Fear knotted her stomach and the distance between them felt much wider than a few feet.

Caleb stopped at the far end of the corral. Jennie swallowed hard and waited for him to speak, feeling lost and unsure. At any other time, she would have had the comfort of his warm smile or his shoulder resting against hers to calm her nerves and give her strength. Now he stood away from her, his brow furrowed, his shoulders stiff.

"I need to ask you something."

The tightness in his voice frightened her almost as much as his words. She gave a silent nod and clasped her trembling hands together.

"However strange or absurd it might sound, I want you to answer the question."

"What is it?" she forced herself to ask, wishing she could run to the house and hide.

"Why were those bandits chasing you that day on the trail?"

Jennie stumbled backward, his question knocking the breath from her as if she'd been punched in the stomach. She reached out and grabbed the fence to steady herself. "I…" She bit her lip and tasted blood. "I…told you already. They were after my money."

"Was it your money?"

"What do you mean?" She twisted around to look at the fence, the milling cattle, the distant mountains— anything but Caleb.

"Just answer the question, Jennie. Was the money they were after rightfully yours?"

"W-why are you asking me this?" A spark of anger ignited inside her and she stoked it with defensive thoughts—afraid if she wasn't angry, she might drown in his displeasure. Did he have to go and ruin everything when she was so close to winning the ranch back? Couldn't he leave well enough alone? "I wouldn't do anything I didn't feel was best for my family."

Caleb slammed his fist against the fence, making her jump. "You're avoiding the question. Was that your money or not?"

"No, it wasn't." She folded her arms and pressed them together, trying to hold in the ache beginning in her chest. "I took it from them, all right? But the money was already taken from its original owners, and the men who had it would have spent the money on drinks or worse. I used it for something good and decent."

"Decent?" He blew out his breath. "The money was stolen. It doesn't matter what they would've spent it on. It belonged to someone else."

"Why are you asking me this?" she repeated, her voice rising in pitch as anger and fear battled inside her. "Why now? Why today?"

"Because Mr. King," Caleb said, his jaw clenching, "was kind enough to share your exploits with me during our conversation at the store."

"Now who's being dishonest?" she lashed out in defense. "You said he only talked to you about working for him."

"I said he offered me a job and that he is a scoundrel. All of that is true. I wasn't trying to keep the rest of our conversation from you, but I needed time to…to think."

"And what have you decided?" Her voiced sounded as small as she felt.

Instead of answering, Caleb countered with a question of his own. "That wasn't the first robbery was it?"

She hazarded a glance at him and regretted it at once. The hurt and betrayal on his face nearly stopped her heart altogether.

"How many stage robberies have you committed, Jennie?"

"None," she whispered to the ground. "I never robbed a stage. I only robbed stage thieves."

Caleb's harsh laugh brought up her head. "My mistake. How many times have you taken money from thieves like the ones shooting at us that day on the trail? Like the ones I spent more than a year of my life tracking down?"

She swallowed, trying to bring moisture to her dry mouth. "Four."

"Four?" Caleb echoed before sweeping off his hat and whacking it against his leg. "Only four, huh? Well, that's good to know, I suppose. 'Cause I was worried it might've been more." She glanced away, stung by his sarcasm. "Do you know why I became a bounty hunter?"

His question caught her off guard but she welcomed the change in subject. "No. You didn't say the other day."

"It's because of Liza." When he paused, Jennie peered up at him. Fresh pain etched his face. "The stage she'd taken was robbed by four men. When they shot the driver, the stage flipped and she was killed."

Fresh guilt washed over her. She knew she wasn't responsible for those hurt by the stage thugs she took from. Still, she'd never thought about those people's lives.

"I spent over a year tracking down three of those men. The fourth got away…after I killed his partner. But to think those are the type of people you've been dealing with…" He shook his head, his voice strangled. "I'm not sure I can stay here any longer."

Did he mean a few days or forever? Jennie hadn't fooled herself into thinking he wouldn't be mad. But leaving? She didn't want to think about him going away for good. She had to make him see, make him understand. "I'll tell you the whole story, just please…" She sniffed back the threatening tears, her chin wobbling with the effort. "Don't leave—not until I've explained."

He frowned, but stood still.

"The day we met in the store when you helped me with the spilled candy, I…" She exhaled, forcing out the words with her next breath. "I'd just come from the bank. The bank president told me that if I didn't pay five hundred dollars of my loan before the end of the month—and the other thirteen hundred by this August—he'd foreclose. I was on the stagecoach back home, desperately trying to think of a way to get the money, when I met my first bandits. They got drunk during the ride and it loosened their tongues. From what they had said, and from what I'd overheard about the robbery in the mercantile earlier, I realized they were the ones responsible, and that they had two thousand dollars with them."

"Wait a minute," Caleb interjected with a shake of his head. "I heard about that robbery. The sheriff got his hands on the thieves and the stolen money."

"Not all of the money. I took the five hundred I needed. Then I got rid of the men's guns and alerted the stage driver by firing my pistol. We tied up the thieves and turned back for Fillmore. I made it onto another stage before the sheriff arrived."

"So that's how it's been with all of them?" His bitter tone made her cringe inwardly. "You pit yourself against dangerous men and walk away without a scratch?"

"No." She gave a helpless shrug but didn't say anything more, afraid to tell him about the bullet graze to her arm.

He ran a hand through his hair as he angrily paced away from her and then returned. "What were you thinking? Why would you put your life at risk to do something so morally wrong?"

His words seeped like poison into her heart, igniting fresh resentment. "That's not how I see it. This place is my life, Caleb. It's all we have. I couldn't bear the thought of losing what my father had worked so hard to keep. I had to fight for it, in whatever way I could. That's why I've only taken money from criminals— money that's already been stolen."

"Is that what these meetings with that ruffian were all about? The robberies? Or whatever you want to call them?"

"You still think it's some kind of affair, don't you?" Jennie didn't wait for his reply. "Nathan Blaine is a business partner, nothing more. He spends enough time in the saloons to learn who'll be robbing what stage and when. I pay him for his help with half the money I take."

Caleb's face went pale and he grabbed her arm, hard. "Did you say that man's name is *Nathan Blaine*? Is his first name Otis?"

His reaction made her pulse race with new fear, though she wasn't sure why. "I don't know. He only told me he was called Nathan Blaine."

"Did he used to rob stages?"

"I—I don't know for sure."

He let go of her arm and marched past her, then seemed to change his mind. He spun back, his eyes dark blue with barely controlled anger. "You said the other day that you wouldn't be meeting with him again. Does that mean you're done robbing stage thieves?"

The roar of her heartbeat in her ears nearly drowned out his question. How could she tell him no? "Caleb..." She lifted her thumbnail to her mouth and then dropped her hand. "The bank called my loan due in twelve days. I still owe five hundred and fifty dollars. There's another stage robbery planned for tomorrow—"

"What? No." The muscles in his jaw tightened again. "No." He stalked toward the house.

Jennie raced after him. "Caleb, wait."

She gripped his sleeve, but released it when he spun around. The pain in his eyes eerily matched the pain in another pair of eyes, ones Jennie hadn't seen in eight years. Her mother had looked as troubled and hollow the day she'd left as Caleb did now.

"Where are you going?" she asked, her voice rising with alarm.

"I'm not going to stay here and watch you ride off to do something illegal—something dangerous. If you were caught, you'd go to *jail,* Jennie. Jail. For a long time. What would happen to your family then? What would Will and Grandma Jones do?"

"What I am supposed to do? Say goodbye to all of this?" She swept her arm in an arc, taking in the house and barn with the motion. "I've worked for years to make this place beautiful and profitable like my father wanted. But I can't..." She stifled the sob rising in her throat with a fist to her mouth. "How can I do that if I lose the place? Are we just supposed to start over with nothing?"

Caleb reached to hold her hand for the first time all evening. His touch sent a jolt of hope through her until he spoke. "You could walk away from it. Start over, like I suggested this morning."

Abandon the ranch? "I can't—not yet." That couldn't be the only answer. "Maybe we could sell the cattle to hold the bank off a little longer. I could go see Mr. Dixon and beg him to reconsider." She realized her mistake the moment the words were out.

"Isn't that who you went to see in Fillmore?"

Jennie flushed.

"You didn't go, did you? It was just another ruse for a robbery, wasn't it?"

"I could talk to him, for real this time. Maybe he'd extend the loan." She squeezed his hand, hoping he'd understand. "Please, Caleb. I can't give up—not like my mother."

"Is that what this is really all about?" He yanked his hand from her grasp. "Not giving up like your mother?"

"You don't know anything about it." She wrapped her arms around herself to ward off the sudden cold inside her.

His answering gaze seemed to pierce into the hidden corners of her soul. "Maybe not. But I know this. Your mother was too scared or stubborn to ask for help when she needed it most, and that's your problem, too. You judged all those people at church, while you sat out here with your nose in the air, not willing to ask anything from anybody."

"They wouldn't have helped us anyway." She no longer cared about keeping the tears back; they slid hot down her face, creating the only warmth in her body.

"How do you know? There are a lot of decent people in this world who would've gladly lent a hand until you could get back on your feet. And what about God? Did you ask Him what to do?" Caleb rubbed a tired hand over his face. "No. You just went ahead and solved the problem your own way—by robbing bandits."

Before she could reply, he took another step toward the house.

"I'm falling in love with you, Jennie," he said, his back to her. "Even knowing all of this, my feelings haven't changed. But I think it's best if I leave."

"Wh-what are you saying?" His words resurrected the painful thumping of her heart. Why did everyone have to leave? First her mother, then her father and now Caleb.

"How can I stay?" Caleb turned slowly to face her, his expression full of grief. "I can't live here. Not when I know my wages and the ranch are paid for with stolen money."

Jennie jabbed at the tears on her cheeks with the back of her hand. "There's nothing that'll change your mind?"

He hesitated, causing Jennie to hope again, then he lowered his head. "You've made your choice clear. I'll leave in the morning. Don't worry about my pay." With that, he walked away, not looking back.

Jennie hurried to the bunkhouse, grateful for once that they didn't have any other ranch hands. She slumped to the floor, her chin resting on her knees. Her unrestrained sobs echoed off the walls.

When her shoulders stopped shaking, she twisted

her head to study the loose board that concealed most of the stolen money. For the first time in eight months, she questioned the course she'd taken that day in the stage with Horace and Clyde. She hadn't meant to do anything wrong or hurt the people she loved.

Was it too late to make things right? Or was she in too deep to turn back now? The stillness of the room held no answers.

Chapter Sixteen

Grandma Jones served Caleb's favorite dish for supper—flapjacks and fried potatoes. But despite the delicious smells and the sweet taste of the molasses he drizzled over everything, he could barely choke down the meal.

"You haven't touched much of your food, Caleb," Grandma Jones said, giving him a long look.

Caleb ate another bite and swallowed. "Not because it isn't excellent. I guess I'm just a bit tuckered out."

"You aren't the only one." She nodded at Will who'd fallen asleep in his chair, his head resting beside his plate on the table.

Caleb didn't want to say goodbye to Will or Grandma Jones tomorrow. They'd become like family the past six weeks and he hated the idea of them being hurt by Jennie's foolish choices.

Should he turn Jennie in to the law? No, he couldn't do that. But he did know someone who deserved to be brought in. He stood abruptly and took his half-full plate to the sideboard.

"I think Saul and I are gonna go for a ride. Will you

tell Jennie?" he asked Grandma Jones. "I'm not sure where she went."

Grandma Jones lifted an eyebrow. "I'll tell her when she comes in. You going to be gone long?"

"We'll be back in a few hours."

He left the kitchen and went to his room. Inside, he loaded his revolvers and placed them in the holster he buckled around his waist. He slipped outside and headed to the barn. He hadn't seen Jennie since before supper. Thankfully she wasn't in the barn. He needed to complete his plan before he saw her again.

After saddling Saul, Caleb led the horse toward town. With sunset coming later in the evening, he would have plenty of time to do what he had to and be back at the ranch before too late.

His earlier anger and hurt at Jennie's confession rolled through him again as he rode. How could she have lied to him and her family? How could she have participated in something so wrong? And then to throw in lots with the likes of Black-Eyed Blaine.

Thoughts of Nathan led to thoughts of Liza and her unfair death. This man had never paid for robbing Caleb of his fiancée and his dreams of marriage and family; he had escaped any consequence. *Well, that ends tonight.* Caleb clenched the reins tight as seeds of hate and revenge sprouted anew inside him.

This time Caleb wouldn't let him go. This time Nathan would see justice served for all his misdeeds, starting with robbing Liza's stage. Vengeance burned hot through his veins and he urged Saul into a gallop. He would finally bring in his last man.

Caleb rode straight to the saloon, certain from Jennie's story that Nathan would be there. He pulled his hat low and entered the crowded establishment. Raucous laughter and the smell of booze filled the air. Taking a seat at an empty table at the back, Caleb searched the room for Nathan. He didn't see him.

Tasting bitter disappointment, he started to stand when a couple coming down the stairs caught his eye. He sat back down when he realized it was Nathan and a saloon girl. Fresh loathing for this man washed over Caleb, and he grit his teeth to keep from leaping up and shooting him at once. Instead he slipped one of his guns from his holster and concealed it beneath his jacket as he waited for Nathan and the girl to find a table.

Once they were seated, Caleb rose to his feet and ambled in their direction. He paused at a table where a poker game was in full swing, feigning interest so he would appear to be just one of the crowd. He didn't want Nathan to see him coming until too late.

Caleb angled his way across the room to come in at Nathan's back. The stage robber had obviously gone soft in the three years since robbing Liza's stage to sit in the open with his back to most of the room. Bringing him in would be easier than Caleb had thought.

He approached the two who were whispering, keeping his footsteps light. Someone on the other side of the room shouted something and Nathan turned in that direction. Caleb quickly dropped into a seat at the table next to theirs. He held still as Nathan returned to his conversation with the saloon girl.

Scooting his chair out from the table, Caleb twisted in his seat and brought the gun from beneath his jacket. His heart lurched with familiar anticipation, just as it had when he'd brought in Nathan's three partners—two alive, one dead.

One dead, his mind repeated.

Caleb froze, his fingers gripped so tight around his gun that they started to ache. He wasn't wrong to bring this criminal to justice—was he? *No, but you made a promise.*

Remorse every bit as sharp as his hatred cut through him and he had to gulp in several deep breaths. He might have killed Nathan's partner in self-defense, but Caleb's dreams of revenge had brought him to that fateful situation. After that, he'd promised God he would give up bounty hunting, he would give up his thirst for retribution. Neither one would bring back Liza or restore peace to his life.

So how can I go through with this? he asked himself, glancing over his shoulder at Nathan's bent head. *Help me do right, Lord.*

A new idea emerged from his troubled thoughts—a way to keep his promise, but also keep the man from implicating Jennie if Caleb turned him over to the sheriff. As much as Caleb disliked Jennie's choices, he hated even more the thought of her being put away behind bars and leaving her grandmother and Will to fend for themselves. Standing, he stuck his gun against Nathan's back and leaned forward over the man's shoulder.

"Howdy, Mr. Blaine."

Nathan lifted his chin slowly and shot a glance up at Caleb. "Howdy. You're Jennie's hired hand." He turned to the girl beside him whose face had gone white. Even if she couldn't see the gun in Caleb's hand, she clearly sensed he wasn't being friendly. "Is this some jealous rampage?"

"No." Caleb allowed a mirthless laugh. "This is actually your lucky day…" He bent toward Nathan's ear and whispered, "Black-Eyed Blaine."

The color drained from Nathan's face and he frowned. "Will you excuse us, Bette? No need to look so alarmed, love. This here's a business meeting."

The girl eyed them both before climbing to her feet. She walked away, throwing them one last glance over her shoulder. When she was out of earshot, Nathan demanded, "What do you want?"

Caleb shifted the gun barrel to the man's side and slid into the seat next to him. "The way I see it is I've got enough information on you to see you jailed for life. Not just for robbing my fiancée's stage three years ago and indirectly killing her." Caleb paused as Nathan visibly swallowed hard. "But also working with Miss Jones to rob a lot of good people of their money."

"How's this my lucky day then?"

"Because I'm gonna let you go."

Nathan's brow furrowed. "I don't understand."

"Then I'll make it real clear, Mr. Blaine." Caleb pressed the gun farther into Nathan's side to show he meant business. "You are going to leave this saloon in sixty seconds or less and then you are going to hightail it out of town. I don't care where you go or what you do. But if I ever hear the name Nathan Blaine around here again or learn you've been mixing with stage thugs, I'll have you arrested so fast you won't have time to grab your boots. Is that clear enough?"

Nathan gave a slow nod.

Caleb rose to his feet and slipped his gun beneath his jacket again. "Now get up and walk out that door."

Nathan stood, his eyes meeting Caleb's. "You were the one in that cabin, weren't you?"

"Yes."

"Why'd you let me go twice?"

Caleb frowned, fighting the urge to change his mind. "I guess you could say it has to do with redemption."

"Then I suppose you'd offer some to another?"

Caleb didn't know what he meant.

"Miss Jones," Nathan said, his voice thoughtful. "She's not a criminal—not like me. Just desperate to hold on to the only thing she's got left."

Caleb frowned. He didn't care to discuss the matter with Nathan Blaine.

"Much obliged." Nathan gathered up his hat from off the table and put it on. With another nod to Caleb, he headed for the door.

Blowing out his breath, Caleb sank back down in his chair. He'd come so close to breaking his vow, to giving in to the hate again. His limbs felt shaky. He allowed himself a few minutes to gather his strength again before he left the saloon. Nathan was nowhere to be seen, but his last words stayed with Caleb. Did Jennie really think the ranch was the only thing she had left? When he let himself think about it, he realized that she probably did. The ranch was her home, her legacy from her father and her opportunity to give her brother and grandmother a safe haven.

Had he ever had anything in his life that mattered that much? Not until recently, Caleb realized. In fact, he'd spent the past three years running from everything that he used to consider valuable and important—his home, his family, the places that reminded him of the life he'd wanted to have. It was as if he'd thought by cutting all ties to the people and places that mattered to him, he could keep from getting hurt again.

He'd been wrong—and so had Jennie. Running from any type of connection the way he had wasn't the answer, and neither was clinging to the past, like Jennie. Maybe the best choice was to hold on to the things that really mattered—the *people* who really mattered. And for him, that was Jennie. But could he truly see past what she'd done—what she planned to do *again?*

Caleb climbed onto Saul and started back for the ranch. Nathan's words echoed in his mind about redemption for Jennie. Did she deserve it? *Did I deserve it after letting vengeance rule my life?*

The question made him hang his head with sudden shame. If he had obtained forgiveness for his mistakes, then surely Jennie could, too. Somehow there had to be a way out of the mess things had become, for both of them.

The house stood dark, except for a light in the kitchen. Had Grandma Jones left a lamp on for him or was someone still up? He slipped inside and down the hallway to the kitchen. He froze when he saw Jennie seated at the table, a plate of untouched food before her. Should he talk with her or go to bed?

Something prodded him forward and he stepped into the room. Jennie looked up, her eyes red-rimmed. "I thought you'd gone to sleep."

"Same." He considered telling her about Nathan, but decided against it. She might be angry at him for sending Nathan away. "I went on a ride."

"Oh." She pushed the food around her plate with her fork. "Are you still leaving in the morning?"

"I guess that depends—on what you choose to do."

The hope in her countenance added to his own. Maybe they could set things right after all.

"I'm sorry, Caleb. I still… I mean… I don't expect you to understand. You probably don't know what it's like lying there at night, wondering how your family's going to eat…" She stopped and took a deep breath as if to steady her voice. "How you're going to survive the winter."

"I didn't exactly grow up with great wealth, Jennie. My parents came here from Nebraska with only the few things they could cram into a wagon. They worked hard to make our farm what it is, and we worked right along beside them."

"I know. But I don't have my parents to help or all those siblings like you. It's just…me." The sight of her lovely face etched with concern still made his heart pound, made him want to protect her—especially from herself.

"It doesn't have to be that way. You have your brother and your grandmother. And me." He crossed to the table and took a seat. "I'll always be your friend, Jennie. Always."

"Just a friend, huh?" Tears swam in her deep brown eyes.

"You don't have to go through with this robbery tomorrow. There has to be another way. We can still make a life together."

"I told you before. I can't leave this ranch behind—not yet. Mr. Dixon will have to drag me off the property before I'll abandon everything I've sacrificed for."

"Is that what this is about? Making sacrifices?" He leaned forward. "A sacrifice is only worth something if it's right. Sacrificing your integrity, your happiness, your freedom—that won't bring you anything but misery. I know, because I tried."

She rubbed at her temples. "Maybe you're right. But haven't you ever loved something so much you thought you might die if it was taken away?"

"Yes," he said. He stopped to swallow the lump in his throat. "You."

A soft cry escaped her lips before her face crumpled and she covered it with her hands. Caleb watched, helpless, for a minute as she cried, then he reached out and placed his hand on her shoulder. He could feel the quiet sobs shaking through her.

In that moment of shared grief, Caleb knew with certainty that he loved her and he always would. His future would be bleak indeed without this redhead by his side.

"Jennie, please look at me."

Slowly she lifted her head, agony burning in every feature.

"I love you, despite everything you've told me." He brushed a piece of hair from her damp cheek, her skin warm and soft beneath his touch. "Your friendship is dearer to me than anything I possess right now or hope to one day have. To show you I mean it, I have something to give you. Wait here."

Caleb hurried out of the kitchen and up the stairs. The wound from Jennie's betrayal would take time to fully heal, but he was confident it would.

He entered his room and pulled the leather pouch from underneath his mattress. Three hundred dollars wouldn't be everything Jennie needed, but it would be a start. A start toward a future together.

Chapter Seventeen

A thud of footsteps brought up Jennie's head. Grandma Jones pulled a shawl around her long nightgown and entered the kitchen.

"I wanted to make sure you'd come in and gotten supper. Is Caleb back from his ride?"

"Yes." Jennie brushed at the tears on her face. "Thank you for saving me some flapjacks."

"You two have a fight?"

Blushing, Jennie stuffed some food into her mouth and swallowed before answering, "I'm not sure what you mean."

Grandma Jones gave an amused snort. "Come on, Jennie girl, I know a lovers' quarrel when I see one. First off, you two didn't come into supper together like you usually do, and Caleb didn't know where you were earlier. Second, your eyes are red from crying, no matter how hard you try to hide it." She folded her arms over her nightgown. "You want to talk about it?"

"No…maybe."

Her grandmother took the seat beside her, but Jennie was unsure where to start. Caleb's tender words still rang in her ears—*I love you. Your friendship is dearer to me than anything I possess right now or hope to one day have.* Did she believe him? After all she'd confessed, would he really stay?

Caleb reentered the kitchen before she could voice any of her confusing thoughts to Grandma Jones. His blue eyes appeared especially bright and he held something in one hand.

"This is for you, Jennie." He lifted a leather pouch.

"What is it?"

"Two hundred and ninety seven dollars."

"What?" Jennie choked out. Grandma Jones gave a soft gasp.

Caleb pulled a thick wad of bills from the pouch. "I want you to use this to pay some of your debt against the ranch." He set the cash on the table. "It won't be enough to cover everything, but I'm sure we can come up with a way to earn the rest."

"But…" She brought her hands to her mouth as she stared in shock at the money. The money meant to fund Caleb's freight business. She remembered the way his face had lit up when he talked about his plans. "But this is for your business. So you can have a fresh start."

"Not anymore." He knelt in front of her. "Think about what you want, but remember we can do this— together."

She couldn't form a reply. Red-hot shame burned her throat at his selfless offer.

He stood, regarding her with a level look. "I'll see you in the morning." His words were full of confidence that she'd make the right decision. "Good night, ladies."

"Good night, Caleb," Grandma Jones called after him. Jennie watched Caleb leave and felt a piece of her going with him. She stared down at the stack of money before her.

Almost three hundred dollars.

She couldn't quite believe the answer to most of her troubles sat in front of her. She imagined walking into the bank, head held high as she plunked the cash onto Mr. Dixon's desk. Where would they get the rest to pay off her loan in time, though?

There was more cash in the bunkhouse that she could combine with Caleb's money, but Jennie quickly pushed the idea from her mind. She had to do things right this time if she wanted Caleb to stay, which meant giving back the stolen money to the rightful owners. She would have to find some other way to make up the difference.

For the first time in months, Jennie allowed herself to imagine being free of her debt. No more robberies, no more lies, no more being alone. Yet her freedom wouldn't come without a price. Her ranch, for Caleb's dream.

Happy memories from the past six weeks flitted through her mind: Caleb helping her on the trail, watching him learn to be a cowboy, making him laugh, kissing him for the first time, talking of their lives and their feelings for each other.

"You ready to talk?" Grandma Jones asked.

Jennie had almost forgotten her grandmother sitting there. She pushed aside her plate, her stomach too wound in knots to eat. She fingered one of the bills. "I think I've made a terrible mistake, Grandma."

"Oh, honey." Grandma Jones tipped up Jennie's chin, her eyes warm and caring. "That's what life's about. You start down one path and realize you should have taken another. The important thing is recognizing when you need to switch."

Jennie set down the bills and took a steadying breath.

"Did you ever make any big mistakes?" she asked as she stood and took her plate to the sink.

Grandma Jones laughed. "I've made hundreds and hundreds of little ones—like we all do. Made my share of big ones, too—like leaving home so young and writing only sporadically. I didn't even make it back to Illinois after my mother's death. I don't know if my father and sisters ever quite forgave me that." She clasped her hands together and rested them on the table. "But there's one decision I still shudder to think I almost got wrong."

"What was it?"

"I almost didn't marry your grandfather."

Jennie whirled around. "What happened?"

"That's a long story." Her grandmother smiled and nodded at Jennie's vacant chair. Jennie returned to her seat. Anticipation tingled through her, nearly erasing her worries—this wasn't a story she'd heard before. "I met your grandpa when I was finishing up my third year of teaching. We courted some, and I liked him very much. But I decided to accept my aunt's offer to spend the summer traveling with her.

"I'd always wanted to go to Europe and New York City. Then your grandfather started talking marriage and settling down. I didn't know what to do. I wanted to marry him, but I also felt this was my one and only chance to see the world. So I told him he'd have to wait until I came home to marry me."

"Did you go and see all those places?" Jennie tried to picture seeing the ocean or a castle, things she'd only read about in her grandmother's collection of books.

Grandma Jones shook her head, her gaze distant. "I never went. When I climbed aboard the steamboat to leave, I had the strongest feeling I needed to get right back off, find Matthew Jones and accept his hand in marriage." She shrugged her thin shoulders. "That's what I did. We were married a week later. He was such a faith-filled man—always sharing his love of the Lord with others. I don't know if I would have grown as close to God as I have if I hadn't married your grandfather." She traced a grain in the tabletop. When she spoke again, her voice sounded full of unshed tears, "Not a day goes by that I don't thank God for nudging me hard enough to get off that boat."

"Didn't you regret not seeing all those lovely places, though?"

Her grandmother lifted her chin. "Sometimes. The only places I've seen since then have been mostly wilderness." She chuckled. "But usually the hardest thing to do is the right one. I know now that the people and the God I love are far more important to me than seeing Paris or London."

Jennie rested her chin on her hands. She hadn't put God and the people in her life ahead of material things, like the ranch. A new wave of remorse ran through her.

"I'm sorry, Grandma."

"Whatever for?" Grandma Jones reached over and gave Jennie's arm a gentle squeeze.

"You must have missed going to church all these years."

"Yes, but I knew it'd be hard for you to return—at least until you were ready."

"It's not that I stopped believing in God. I just didn't want to hear the rumors about my mother. I didn't want to face seeing the possible truth in the eyes of all those people whispering about her." Jennie lowered her hands to the table. "I couldn't face feeling responsible for her leaving."

"Now, Jennie girl. Nothing they said is true. And you certainly weren't at fault for your mama leaving." She rubbed Jennie's arm. "Your mother left because she couldn't handle life out here anymore. She loved your father, but she didn't share his dream of building a home out here in the West. She went along with it, moved from one place to another, starting over again and again without complaining, but she couldn't be truly happy that way." Grandma Jones released a sigh. "She wasn't used to that kind of life, not after growing up in a wealthy house with everything she needed in easy reach. She still loved you and Will and your father, though. She told me so the night before she left. She just had to figure out what she truly needed to be happy. I think if she hadn't taken ill, she might have come back and done just fine."

Jennie sniffed back fresh tears. "I'd like to think so."

Grandma Jones pulled Jennie onto her knees and gave her a fierce hug. Jennie embraced her and then rested her head in her grandmother's lap. "Your mother did have a backbone on her. Don't think she didn't. To start over like that, you have to have something in you. You've gotten that from both your parents." She stroked Jennie's hair. "You're strong, Jennie. But don't make the mistake of being so strong you forget to let others help you. We all need that."

Jennie swiped at her runny nose with her hand and nodded. She'd tried to be strong for so long, but she'd done it alone. Now she needed help, and surely she could be humble enough to ask.

Lifting her head, Jennie forced herself to meet her grandmother's eyes. "This is one of those times I need help, Grandma. But first, I have to tell you something. Something I'm ashamed to admit…"

Jennie slipped into her room and softly shut the door behind her. She guessed it must be after midnight, but strangely, she felt more awake than she had this morning.

After changing into her nightdress, she started to climb into bed. The trunk beneath the windowsill drew her notice. A longing to bridge the gap of misunderstanding between her and her mother pushed Jennie to her feet.

Kneeling before the trunk, she opened the lid and drew out the unopened letter. She stared at the wrinkled surface, imagining her mother's hands—those soft, delicate hands—sealing her words inside.

Jennie swallowed the anxiety pulsing through her as she tore open the envelope and removed two sheets of paper, filled with the faded but familiar handwriting of her mother.

Using the trunk as a seat, she pulled back the curtains and read her letter by moonlight.

August 10, 1863
Dearest Jennie,
I hope this finds you well and happy. Your father wrote and told me what a great help you've been to him, and I thank you for it. He also says you've

grown taller this past year. I can hardly imagine my little girl a grown woman now.

Your hair has probably darkened, though I imagine it will always stay that rich red color that you inherited from my side of the family. With your pretty brown eyes, I cannot help but think what a beauty you must be. I wish so badly I could see and hold you. Are you too old, daughter, to sit again on your mother's lap, resting your head against my shoulder as you used to?

How are Will and Grandma Jones? Be certain to listen to your grandmother; she is a wise woman. Are the cattle faring well? And your father? He seems content enough, but I often wonder what heartache I have inflicted on him and you children.

Every day I live with the guilt of running away, but I no longer felt capable of being a good mother. I thought returning to my home would heal my heart, but now I've found I left it out West with you.

Never be ashamed, my dear girl, to stumble about sometimes, but also find the courage to ask for help when you need it most. I pray to God each day for forgiveness. I know now I cannot move through life without His help. Remember that, Jennie.

I have often packed my things with plans to return before I unpack them again. Perhaps it is cowardice of me, but I fear your rejection. Maybe one day I will be able to forgive myself and come home at last. Until then, know I love you. You will be an extraordinary woman, stronger and more capable in that wilderness than I ever was. But leave room in your heart for love and softness too, Jennie. Without both strength and tenderness, you may find life much more difficult.

Please write, if you wish to. I long for any word from my family. I shall write again soon if I am able. I seem to have left my good health at the ranch, but do not worry. I am to see the doctor here soon, and everything shall be fine.

All my love,

Your mother, Olivia Wilson Jones.

Jennie could hardly make out her mother's signature through the tears spilling down her face. She'd never wept so much in her life.

Leaning her head against the cool windowpane, she allowed her anguish to flow uninhibited. She cried for her mother's pain and for her own, for her selfishness in not reading the letter years earlier, when she could have written back. For so long, she had concentrated only on the hurt she felt, never thinking of the shame and suffering her mother might have experienced.

"I'm sorry, Mama," she whispered into the dark, hoping and praying her mother could somehow hear her words, even in heaven. "I should have written. I should have tried to see you, at least once before you died. I'm so very sorry."

Jennie covered her mouth with her hand to muffle the sound of her sobs. She didn't want to wake the rest of the family. When she could breathe normally again, she read the letter through once more, then tucked it again inside the envelope. Instead of putting it in the trunk, she returned to her bed and slipped the precious pages beneath her pillow. *To read often.*

She climbed beneath the covers, but a thought made her sit up. Her mother had told her to remember God. That meant voicing to Him the truth she'd told her grandmother and Caleb tonight. His help was the real one she needed in the days ahead. Feeling a bit awkward, she knelt beside her bed, unable to remember the last time she'd gotten down on her knees to pray.

Perhaps if I'd prayed earlier I wouldn't be in such a mess. The realization both surprised and humbled her. Bowing her head, she silently reviewed everything she'd done the past eight months, starting with the day she had left the bank, overwhelmed with despair at possibly losing the ranch. When she finished cataloging all her wrongdoings, she tentatively pled for forgiveness.

Once she ran out of things to say, Jennie ended her prayer and sat on the bed. She felt nothing at first, then slowly a feeling of peace began to spread throughout her body. A feeling similar to the one she'd felt during the singing at church. A feeling almost like an embrace.

She kept still for a few minutes, hugging her knees to her chest, as she relished the emotion. When it faded, she got into bed, feeling hope for the first time in months.

Chapter Eighteen

Caleb woke the next morning feeling like he hadn't slept much at all. He hadn't been able to find a comfortable position, and when he had finally drifted to sleep, he had a disturbing dream. It wasn't his usual nightmare. This time when he burst into the cabin, he found Jennie there with Nathan, wearing a bandanna over her face and carting her pistol.

She's given all that up, he reassured himself as he climbed out of bed and got dressed. No matter how troubling his dreams, he'd seen the remorse in Jennie's eyes last night and felt confident she'd accept his money to help the ranch. Besides, without Nathan around to help her, she'd be forced to give up robbing stage thieves.

Relieved he wouldn't have to say goodbye to the family, Caleb hurried down the stairs, eager to see Jennie. He planned to take her into his arms and give her a good, long kiss, even in the company of her brother and grandmother.

Caleb skidded to a stop inside the kitchen doorway. Grandma Jones and Will were moving about the kitchen getting breakfast onto the table, but Jennie wasn't there. Alarm began to worm its way up his throat.

Maybe she's in the barn, getting an early start on chores.

"Morning," he said, relieving the stack of plates from Grandma Jones. As he placed them around the table, he noted there were only three, not four. "Did Jennie eat already?" He kept his voice as casual as he could, despite the sudden pounding of his heart.

"She left about half an hour ago." Grandma Jones took a seat and motioned for Will and Caleb to join her. "Said she had some business to take care of in town this morning."

Caleb gripped the plate in his hand so hard he thought it might snap. She didn't still plan to go through with the robbery, did she? No, she wouldn't. Not after their talk last night, not after he'd given her his hard-earned money. "Will she be long?"

"Probably most of the day, but she said not to worry."

Something in the woman's green eyes told Caleb that Grandma Jones knew more than she was saying. But she wouldn't know about Jennie robbing stage thieves, so it didn't matter what lie her granddaughter had told in order to go to town alone.

"Sit down, Caleb. Have some biscuits." It sounded more like a command than a suggestion.

He shook his head. "I'm not hungry this morning. I think I'll go out to the barn." Turning away, he prayed they hadn't seen the pain seeping into his face.

Instead of heading outside, Caleb stepped quietly up the stairs to his room. He removed his pack from beside the bureau and opened the top drawer.

All the betrayal and frustration he'd felt the day before rushed back full force and he had to stop and take several deep breaths to calm himself. He had forgiven Jennie's past deeds, but that was when he'd thought she was willing to change her ways. He refused to be a witness to her deceitful and dangerous actions—no matter how much he still cared for her.

Distance and time would eventually heal his heart—again—though he vowed to be done with love. Too much pain, not to mention the loss of all the money he'd saved. Bitter disappointment cut through him at the thought of having to find another job and putting off his dream of a freight business another year, maybe two.

Once packed, Caleb shouldered his bag and grabbed his guns. He managed to slip outdoors without Will and Grandma Jones noticing. He planned to saddle up Saul and come back to the house to say goodbye. The waiting horse would show the family he meant to leave—now. He needed to be long gone before Jennie came back. Seeing her again would be too painful.

He strode with heavy steps to the barn and entered the building. Inside, he set his pack on the ground and grabbed the horse's tack. Saul pawed at the straw as if sensing Caleb's eagerness to leave.

The sound of pounding horse hooves brought up Caleb's head in time to see a horse and rider rush past. Caleb hurried out of the barn. *Who would come to the house this early unless something's happened?* Anxiety for Jennie's safety filled him.

"Hello there," he called to the rider, who'd dismounted near the porch. "Can I help you?"

The man came around the side of the horse. He didn't even reach the top of the saddle. Grabbing the lead rope, he led his horse toward Caleb.

"Do I know you?" Caleb asked. The man didn't answer, but as he drew closer, Caleb recognized him as one of King's cowboys—the one called Gunner. "Hold up there a minute. I told Mr. King I wasn't working for him, and that hasn't changed. You can hop right back on that horse and leave." Turning his back to him, Caleb started for the barn.

"Wait. You're Miss Jones's hired hand. There's somethin' I need to tell ya."

I was more than that to her, at least until yesterday, Caleb thought. "What do you want?"

Gunner stepped closer as he spoke. "The thieves she's planning to rob today aren't really thieves."

Caleb's eyes narrowed with suspicion. "How'd you know about that?"

"Because Mr. King and three of his men are gonna rob that stage. It's a trap for Miss Jones."

Caleb scowled at the cowhand. How he'd like to maim that arrogant rancher. "What does King have against Jennie?"

Gunner licked his lips and studied the ground. "He wants her land. That's why he paid off the bank president to call her loan due, why he's rustled her cattle and why he had me follow her all over town and up to Fillmore." He threw a guilty glance at Caleb. "When he found out she's kept her ranch going by robbing stage thieves, King set a trap for her. He knew she couldn't resist five thousand dollars. He's gonna rob the stage first and wait for Jennie to come rob him."

"Then what?" Caleb's pulse thundered in his ears as the weight of the cowboy's confession hit him.

"He'll likely shoot her and claim self-defense."

Mistrust and worry battled inside Caleb. "Why should I believe you? You're a cattle thief and a spy."

"Even so, I don't condone murder." Gunner re-mounted his horse with surprising ease despite his lack of height. "I gotta go before someone at King's ranch notices I'm gone."

"What stage are they robbing?" Caleb asked. His lingering doubts had disappeared. The cowhand wouldn't risk his job—and possibly his life—to ride over and tell anything less than the truth.

"It's the stage coming east from Pioche, Nevada. King'll overtake it in Milford Valley before the stage reaches the Mineral Mountains. Good luck to you, cowboy." With that, he thrust his spurs into his mount's side and took off at a gallop.

Caleb sprinted to the house, but he slowed his steps before he entered the kitchen where Will and Grandma Jones lingered at the table.

"I realized I've got some things I need to do in town today myself," Caleb said, keeping his voice light, despite the urgency pulsing through him.

"Can I come?" Will's face lit up with excitement.

"Not today, Will. With Jennie and I both gone, someone needs to watch the cattle this morning."

Will blew out his breath in obvious disappointment, but he nodded acceptance.

"I shouldn't be too long." Caleb moved to the door. "I'll try to find Jennie, and we can ride back together."

Grandma Jones gave him a questioning look, but Caleb simply forced a smile. "Save some supper for us," he said as walked out the front door.

Once outside, he let the smile drop from his face as he ran to the barn. Having his horse already saddled saved him time. However much he didn't agree with Jennie's actions, he wouldn't stand back and let her walk into mortal danger.

I only hope I'm not too late, he thought as he urged Saul toward the distant mountains.

Jennie tied Dandy to the hitching post outside the sheriff's office. She brushed away the dust sticking to her brown and cream dress and made sure the breeches she had on underneath didn't show. Her work pants would give her more mobility for the hard ride ahead, but for now, she needed to look the part of a proper young lady.

Resolved she'd made the right decision, Jennie inhaled a deep breath, tugged her kid gloves into place, and forced her feet in the direction of the door. Anticipation and worry pulled equally at her heart as she turned the handle and stepped into the building.

A young deputy sat with his boots resting on top of an empty table, one hand drawing his revolver and spinning it back into its holster. When he saw her, he immediately put his gun away, jerked his feet to the floor and sat up straight.

"Can I help you, miss?"

Jennie nodded. "I need to speak to the sheriff."

The deputy arched an eyebrow in open curiosity as he studied Jennie. "One moment."

He rose from his seat and knocked on the inner door situated at his right. After a moment a muffled response came from the other side. The deputy opened the door and stuck his head inside. Jennie could easily hear his words, however quiet.

"A lady to see you, sir... No, she didn't say what it's

about… All right. I'll send her in." He stepped back into the main office and motioned Jennie forward. "He'll see you."

Jennie thanked him and strode purposefully into the tiny room. A man with a drooping, sandy-colored mustache and a silver star attached to his waistcoat stood up from his desk.

"Come in, miss. Let me get you a seat."

The sheriff plucked a hardback chair from the corner and positioned it in front of his desk. He motioned for Jennie to sit down while he shut the door.

"Now what can I do for you?" he asked, taking his seat behind the desk again.

Jennie swallowed hard—there was no going back now that she was here.

"I've come to inform you about a stage robbery taking place today."

The lines on the man's forehead bunched together in consternation as he eased back into his chair. "A stage robbery? Today?"

"That's correct." Jennie kept her gaze steady on his blue-gray eyes.

He studied her, the corners of his mouth lifting in hidden amusement. "You mind sharing a few more details with me, Miss…"

"Jones," she finished. "I'm afraid that's all the information I can give you at the moment, sheriff, unless you agree to help me with something."

"Is that right?" He joined his hands to form a steeple and tapped his index fingers against his chin.

Bestowing a ladylike smile, she leaned forward. "I am more than happy to share everything you need to apprehend the bandits and keep a very large sum of money safe if…" She paused long enough to secure his full attention. "If you'll agree not to press charges against me."

This time the sheriff did laugh, but it trailed off when she didn't join in. "You're serious, aren't you?"

"Very serious."

He shook his head, a smile still peeking out beneath his mustache. "And what sort of fiendish behavior are we talking about, Miss Jones? Selling whiskey to the Indians? Sneaking milk from a neighbor's cow?"

Jennie tried not to appear offended. He certainly underestimated what she was capable of, but he also held the key—or the lock—to her freedom.

"No, sir." She lowered her head, staring hard at a particularly large knot in the wood of the desk. *You can do this,* she told herself. *It's the right thing to do, no matter what he chooses to do afterward.* She thought of Caleb and the admiration on his face once she told him about coming to the sheriff, even if it was from behind bars. The thought of his reaction gave her the courage to lift her chin.

"I've been robbing stage thieves."

When she'd finished telling the sheriff the particulars of her financial troubles and the different robberies, purposely leaving off mention of Nathan, Jennie slumped back into her chair and waited for the man to cast his judgment. He sat quiet for almost a minute. Jennie fiddled with her gloves as she waited, her heart thumping louder in the ensuing silence.

"Very interesting account, Miss Jones." The sheriff bent forward and plucked at the end of his mustache.

"We don't take stealing lightly around here. I could throw you in one of our jail cells right now."

Jennie swallowed hard, pushing the words out of her throat with effort, "Yes, sir."

"But I understand you're in a hard way and I don't want to see your kid brother and grandmother suffer any more." His face relaxed. "I also admire your gumption for wantin' to make things right."

A tiny puff of air escaped Jennie's lips, and she realized she'd been holding her breath.

"My concern now," he said, drumming his fingers on the desk, "is that you repay all that cash you stole. It needs to be to the rightful owners in a month's time. If you can do that, then I see nothin' wrong with keeping a lady like yourself from spending time behind bars."

"Really?" A month wasn't much time, but Jennie had entertained only a glimmer of hope that he'd go along with her plan.

"Now I'd like you to tell me everything I need to know to keep that stage safe and you a free woman."

Jennie lifted her mouth in a genuine smile. "The stage from Pioche, Nevada, has five thousand dollars on it for a bank up north. It will be attacked by bandits as it crosses Milford Valley in about two hours. Once they steal the money, the thieves will seek refuge in an abandoned shack north of the trail."

"Incredible," the sheriff murmured.

Jennie didn't know if he meant the bandits' scheme or her knowledge of it, but she nodded anyway, hoping it was enough to buy her freedom. He paused, long enough to make her squirm again with worry.

"If you're right, Miss Jones," he said at last, "and we're able to keep that stage and the money safe, I'll agree not to press charges against you. However, in light of your past actions, if something goes wrong and that money gets away, I'm going to assume it ended up in your pockets. Is that clear?"

"Yes, sir. You can trust me on this."

"Good. I'll round up the rest of my deputies and we'll head out there." As he pushed away from the desk and stood, Jennie rushed to her feet.

"I'd like to go, too, sheriff." When the man started to shake his head, Jennie hurried to finish. "I know you'll say it's too dangerous, but I've been living with that sort of danger for eight months. Besides, you need someone along who knows how these bandits operate."

The sheriff frowned hard at her before giving a curt nod of his head. "Perhaps you're—"

The door to the office flew open, and the deputy burst in. "I'm sorry, sir. Amos just rode up and said Old Man Lackerdey is causing a big fuss over at the saloon. He's breakin' chairs and threatenin' to shoot anybody that comes near him."

"Most likely inebriated." The sheriff cursed softly. "Miss Jones, you wait here. I'll quickly take care of Lackerdey and gather up the rest of my men. They're not gonna like having a woman with us, but I think your skills might come in handy."

Jennie graciously inclined her head. "Thank you, sir."

Nodding in return, the sheriff left his office. "See that she's comfortable, Daniels," he barked to the deputy as he headed out the door.

"Can I get you anything, miss?" Daniels grinned, making Jennie glad she had something else to do be-

sides wait in the cramped space with the overly attentive deputy.

"Actually, I have an errand to run first." She moved
past him toward the door. "I'll be back."

She escaped the building, making her way down the
street to the boardinghouse where Nathan stayed. Inside, she inquired after him. A rotund housekeeper with
a tight bun told her that he hadn't come in last night.
Probably too drunk, no doubt.

Jennie asked for a pencil and paper and scrawled
a quick note, telling him she couldn't meet him today
and apologizing for changing her mind. She felt certain
Nathan would understand the cryptic message and the
housekeeper would not.

Satisfied, she left the boardinghouse and turned in
the direction of the sheriff's office. She walked slowly,
reluctant to face the deputy again. What was Caleb
doing at the moment? *Feeding the animals most likely,*
she concluded, squinting up at the sun. She hoped the
sheriff hurried, so they could warn the stage in time.

Daniels jumped up as she entered the office again
and offered her a chair by the window. After thanking
him, Jennie sat down and turned her shoulder to him.
Undaunted by her coolness, he tried making small talk
with her.

When he finally fell silent, Jennie gratefully stared
out the window at the comings and goings of the towns-
people on the other side of the glass. What were the
towns like farther north? Could she and her family be
happy there? Knowing she couldn't keep the ranch from
being foreclosed on, she had to consider the possibility
of moving somewhere. If she could just stay near Caleb.

A sense of loss filled her at leaving Beaver. She'd

miss the town and its people, despite her choice to live so isolated on the ranch these past few years. Still, there were likely to be kind neighbors wherever they went, and if they headed north, she would finally be able to see Salt Lake City, something she'd always wanted.

But right now, we need to get to that stage.

Jennie spun away from the window and released an impatient sigh. Any longer, and the sheriff and his men would be too late to save the money and catch the bandits. Then she'd have to forfeit her freedom.

"Do you know the time?" she asked Daniels.

His face lit up at her sudden attention, and he made a show of removing a fancy pocket watch from his waistcoat. "About half past nine, miss. Are you hungry? Can I buy you something to eat from the hotel?"

She gave an emphatic shake of her head, mentally calculating the distance to Milford Valley. If the sheriff came now, they would have just over an hour to meet the stage before the bandits did. Jennie stood up. That might be too late. If she didn't ensure the safety of that stage and its valuable freight, she would lose her bargaining chip.

"Listen," she said, stepping to the table. "A stage coming here from Nevada is going to be robbed very soon. I need you to go get the sheriff—now. Or we'll be too late."

Daniels climbed to his feet. "I'll go down there, miss. But sometimes Lackerdey takes time to calm down."

"I don't have time." She whirled around to face the door, calling over her shoulder, "Tell the sheriff I'll meet him and his men in Milford Valley."

"B-but, miss. He told you to wait—"

"I can't. It'll be easier to protect that money than

steal it back." Jennie hurried out the door, not bothering to close it.

"Miss?" he called, coming outside.

Ignoring him, Jennie untied Dandy, made certain her gun was still inside the holster on her saddle and swung onto her horse. She had a stage to catch.

Chapter Nineteen

By the time she broke free from the mountains and descended onto the sagebrush plain of Milford Valley, Jennie was glad she'd eaten very little for breakfast that morning. She'd never been so nervous to deal with stage robbers—but then, she'd always been fairly certain of the outcome. Shifting the reins from one hand to the other, Jennie wiped her sweaty palms against her dress and took a long, shaky breath.

She urged Dandy into a faster gait as she cautiously searched the valley for any sign of the bandits. Without knowing where the robbers would ambush the stage, she focused her attention on reaching the western chain of mountains and the stagecoach before they did.

A flash of movement caught Jennie's eye, and she turned northward to determine the source. A quarter of a mile away a lone rider raced in the same westerly direction as she was moving. It couldn't be one of the bandits—there were supposed to be four of them.

Twisting in the saddle, she scrutinized the landscape again, but the rider appeared to be the only other person on the prairie besides herself.

Jennie urged Dandy a little faster and focused on the mountains ahead. From the corner of her eye, she saw the rider change directions, riding straight toward her now. She immediately reached for her pistol, keeping the weapon out of sight at her left side. She reined in her horse and searched the area for some place to hide. The nearest juniper trees weren't thick or tall enough to hide behind.

Panic pulsed through her. What should she do? Whipping around to look at the rider again, she frowned in confusion. The horse could almost be Saul. But that was impossible. Caleb and his horse were at the ranch.

Lifting her pistol, she aimed to miss, wanting only to warn the man she wasn't defenseless. Before she could squeeze the trigger, a familiar voice shouted, "Jennie!"

Jennie wheeled her horse around and charged toward Caleb, her heart racing with surprise and anticipation. How had he found her? She hadn't even told her grandmother the details of her plan, afraid of worrying her.

"Caleb," she yelled as she waved her hat in the air. She couldn't wait to tell him her plan for staying out of jail.

She jerked Dandy to a stop and dismounted at the same time Caleb dropped to the ground beside Saul. Spinning around, Jennie rushed forward to hug Caleb, but she froze when she saw his stiff stance and pain-filled gaze. His disappointment washed over her, scorching her happiness.

He thinks I'm going through with the robbery.

The horrid realization made her stomach sink to her shoes. "No. It's not what you think, Caleb. You don't under—"

"I'm here to warn you," he said, his voice tight.

"About what?"

"King's going to rob the stage. It's a setup. He plans to steal the money, and then when you come get it, he'll shoot you."

She sucked in her breath. "But why?"

"One of his cowhands rode over this morning and confessed the whole story." He wouldn't quite look at her. "King wants your land. He bought off the bank president in Fillmore to call your loan due, so he could claim the ranch sooner. When that didn't go like he'd planned, he tried stealing your cattle and then decided to lure you in with this stage robbery."

"You rode all this way to tell me?" Her voice quavered as unshed tears filled her throat. Even betrayed and upset, he'd still come to her aid—again.

A tortured expression contorted his handsome features. "I couldn't leave without warning you that your life is in danger. And now I need to go."

"Wait." She grabbed his sleeve before he could mount his horse.

"There's nothing more to say, Jennie. I hold no malice toward you, but I think it's better if I—"

"I'm not here to rob the bandits, Caleb."

The look on his face slowly changed from anguish to surprise. "You're not?"

Jennie shook her head.

"Then what are you doing?"

"I have to warn the stage about the attack." She forced her fingers to release his shirt, though she feared if she let go he might leave. "I've got to keep that money safe, so the sheriff won't bring charges against me."

Confusion furrowed his brow. "I don't understand."

"I struck a deal with the sheriff. I gave him the information about today's stage robbery, and if I help keep the money safe, he agreed not to press charges for the other robberies. I have to figure out a way to pay back all that money in a mon—"

He robbed her of her words when he pulled her close and pressed his lips firmly to hers. It was the first time he'd initiated a kiss between them. Jennie's heart leaped at his strong but tender touch and she threw her arms around his neck. She never wanted to let go. The thought that he might have said goodbye for good without hearing her explanation made her cling to him even tighter. He was largely the reason she was attempting to set things right today.

After a long minute, he released her, one hand cradling the side of her face. "Why didn't you wait to tell me what you were doing or leave a note? You could've got yourself killed."

"I'm sorry I didn't tell you before I left, but I wanted to be sure everything worked out with the sheriff first."

"I'm sorry I doubted you."

Jennie blushed and stared at the weeds by her boots. "I haven't given you much reason to trust me."

"I still love and believe in you," he said, tipping up her chin with his finger. "Especially now."

The rumble of distant horse hooves and wheels filled her ears and she turned toward the sound. "The stage. I have to go."

"Not by yourself, you're not." Caleb helped her into the saddle.

"The sheriff and his men are coming," she said, throwing a hopeless glance over her shoulder. "He was held up at the saloon by some drunk. I can't wait,

Caleb. I have to keep that money away from King or I'll go to jail."

Caleb grasped her hand where it held the reins. "That's exactly why I'm coming with you."

Jennie smiled down at him. "Then mount up, cowboy. It's time to ride."

"What is it?" Caleb asked moments later, jerking back on the reins when he realized Jennie had come to a stop beside him.

"Something's wrong with the stage."

He studied the stagecoach moving fast over the sagebrush less than a quarter of a mile away. Instead of traveling in an easterly course toward Beaver, the stage appeared to be racing south.

As Caleb watched, the coach dropped sharply to the left, a wheel slipping into some unseen crevice, before the whole thing bounced wildly back out. Screams carried through the morning air and Caleb cringed at the frightened sound.

He couldn't see anyone sitting on the high seat. "Something's happened to the driver."

"Then we're too late," Jennie said, bitterness coating her voice. "King must have beaten us to the stage. He probably shot the driver and took the money." She threw a glance in the direction of the stage, then northward where she'd told him the bandits would be, and finally back at Caleb. "I can't lose that cash, Caleb, or the sheriff isn't going to help me. You go save the stage, and I'll go—"

"No," he interrupted. "I'm not letting you go against King alone."

"I'll just scout things out. I won't do anything rash."

She threw him a pleading look. "If they decide to leave, I can follow them and then come back for help."

He scowled at her, hating the idea of being separated, but he could see her point. "All right. But you'd better be in one piece when I find you. Promise?"

Jennie nodded, a hint of a smile on her lips. "Ride straight north, about three miles. There should be an abandoned cabin there. That's where they'll be hiding out." With that, she and Dandy took off, heading north.

Caleb didn't waste time staring after her. He raced west toward the careening coach. He had a job to do, too, and the sooner he finished, the sooner he could re-unite with Jennie.

The thundering of horse hooves and the cries of the panicked passengers grew louder as he drew closer to the stage. Caleb's mouth went dry with nerves. Could he really save these people?

For one horrid moment he felt as though he were chasing down Liza's stage, before it flipped. He'd done that in his dreams right after her death. He imagined her black hair flapping through the open window, her dark eyes wide with fear as she stared at him.

This isn't Liza's stage, Caleb told himself, shaking his head to clear the image. He hadn't been able to save Liza, hadn't even been there. If he had, he might have been killed himself instead of being the hero. *But I can save these people.*

He scanned the terrain ahead and noticed a slight ra-vine in the direct path of the runaway stage. Gauging the distance between the stage and the ravine, Caleb knew he'd have to hurry to keep the coach from smash-ing apart in the gully and killing the horses and pas-sengers.

"Let's go," he said, urging Saul even faster. As they came even with the back of the stage, one of the leather curtains over the windows swooshed back and a feminine boot poked out. A moment later it was joined by a dark curly head.

"What are you doing?" Caleb hollered above the racket. The crazy woman was going to climb out. "You're going to kill yourself. Get back inside! I'm going to try and stop the stage."

The girl retreated most of the way back through the window. She pointed toward the front of the stagecoach and shouted, "I think our driver's been shot."

Just as Jennie had predicted. Caleb hoped the man hadn't been killed. "You stay put. I'm going to slow the horses."

He nudged Saul as close to the runaway stage as the horse could get and stretched out his hands. Finally his fingers clasped the side of the luggage rack. He wished for a better position to jump, but there wasn't time. Too many lives depended on his speed.

Making certain he had a good grip, Caleb lunged toward the stage. His stomach lurched as he flew through the air, then he crashed into the side of the coach. He groaned with the momentary pain, but he couldn't stop now.

Dust and dirt plowed into his face and gritted teeth as he clung tightly to the bouncing stage. Slowly he slid his hands down the luggage rack. The driver's seat was in sight. He worked one arm as far down the rack as he dared stretch.

A sudden drop in the wheels brought Caleb's head against the side of the stagecoach with a horrible crack. His left hand slipped off the rack as his vision blurred.

He hung on with his right hand, his arm straining, pulsing with pain. His body smacked against the stage as it hit another bump. Would it end here? he wondered. Before he could save the stage, before he and Jennie could finally be together?

Thoughts of Jennie, alone with King, fueled his body with new energy. Ignoring his burning muscles, Caleb lifted his left arm and gripped the rack again with both hands. He inched toward the seat again, and at last, his fingers touched the side. He swung himself upward and onto the seat, only to be greeted by the barrel of a shotgun. A haggard face stared at him from the other end.

"Don't shoot," Caleb said in between gulps of air. He attempted to raise his aching arms to show he meant no harm, but he couldn't. "Hold on, I'm just tryin' to get you stopped."

"Please, help. The reins are caught on my boot." The stranger lowered his gun and collapsed against the seat.

Caleb hurried to untangle the reins from the man's foot. He noticed a dark patch of blood on the man's thigh, but they'd have to deal with the injury later.

He pulled back on the reins, using all his weight, and shouted at the two horse teams, "Whoa, whoa!"

The taut leather burned against his palms as he tested his strength against the frightened horses. Instead of slowing, they ran faster, leaning into the bits in their mouths. Fighting panic, Caleb gripped the reins even harder. His heart pounded loud in his ears. The gully loomed closer. Perhaps his fate was to be the same as Liza's. He had no other solutions. Except…

A memory propelled itself forward in his mind—something his father had said to him once. "If you've lost control of your horse, turn him in a nice, tight circle. Horses can't bolt when they're turning."

With no other choice, Caleb all but dropped the left rein and pulled the right with every last ounce of strength. *Please, God, let this work. Let me see Jennie again. Let these people be safe.*

"Come on, horses," he muttered, sweat forming beneath his hat.

The coach swung around sharply, one wheel teetering on the brink of the gully before righting itself. Then the stage shuddered to an abrupt stop.

Caleb pried open his hands and released the reins. He collapsed onto the seat behind him. *We did it, You and me, Lord.* He released a huge rush of air from his lungs. "That was for you, Liza," he whispered to the blue sky above him.

A groan from the injured man brought Caleb's attention back to the task at hand. "How badly are you hurt?"

"I was shot…in the leg." The man's face turned a shade whiter. "We were…ambushed… Ol' Phil was shot, too…he fell off."

Caleb figured Ol' Phil must be the stage driver and this wounded fellow was the shotgun messenger, sent to guard the money.

He assessed the man's wound and removed the bandanna from around his own neck. "I'm no doctor, but it looks like the bullet went straight through. I'll tie it up for you until you can get to town." Caleb secured the cloth around the bloodied leg. "There you are. Now I'd better go check on the others."

The shotgun rider nodded as Caleb lowered himself to the ground, a much simpler task now that the stage wasn't moving.

"So glad you came along, stranger," the dark-haired girl said as she exited the stage. She could almost be Liza, minus the curly hair and saloon gown. "You maneuvered that climb easier than I would've in this dress." She lifted the ruffled bottom and laughed.

"Is everyone all right?" Caleb tried to see inside the stage.

A blond girl hopped down the steps. "Thanks to you, we're right as rain. Don't know about Mr. Fulman though." She gave an indignant sniff. "He sat there the whole time, screamin' and shakin' like a leaf. Apparently he's got no stomach for adventure or danger, not like Ellen and me."

As if on cue, a tall, bony man bent his way out of the stage, his face pale. "Are they gone?"

Caleb whistled for his horse. A minute passed before Saul trotted up, appearing no worse for their adventure. "How many bandits were there?"

"Four," Mr. Fulman said, sinking to the ground next to the stage. "They stole the cash box. All five thousand dollars." He covered his face with his hands and moaned.

"The sheriff should be along soon to help you," Caleb said, mounting his horse. Now that his head and arms were no longer throbbing, he was impatient to get going. A nagging worry at the back of his mind was growing more insistent by the minute. If he knew Jennie, she might not wait for the sheriff. "I'm sorry I can't stay."

"Where you off to in such a hurry?" Ellen asked.

"I'm going to help my…girl. She already followed after the bandits to see about getting the money back."

The blonde laughed. "No offense, but every one of

them men were armed. How are you and your girl gonna take them all?"

Before Caleb could answer, the shotgun messenger called down, "Name's Amos. With this busted-up leg, I can't do much, but I'd like to help just the same."

"Thanks, Amos," Caleb said, admiring the man's determination to be of assistance despite his injury, "but—"

"Clara and I want to help, too," Ellen interjected. "We both know how to throw a hard punch."

Caleb frowned at the motley group. He didn't think the shotgun messenger would be of much help, but the girls might prove to be useful. "All right. Load back up then." He turned to the depressed bank man. "What about you, Mr. Fulman? You comin' with us or waitin' here for the sheriff?"

Mr. Fulman peered nervously around the prairie, then his face hardened. "I want my money back."

"You know how to drive a team?"

The bank man nodded.

"Then get up there and follow me."

Mr. Fulman scrambled up next to Amos on the seat and maneuvered the stage around. Caleb pointed Saul north and nudged the horse's flanks with his heels. The stage had better keep up. He and Jennie had been apart long enough. It was time to beat Mr. King at his own game.

Chapter Twenty

Jennie tied Dandy to a tree, a safe distance from the ramshackle cabin. Four horses were tethered out front, but she saw no sign of King or his men. Licking her lips, Jennie drew in several deep breaths.

I'm only going to check out the situation, she reassured herself as she removed her pistol from the holster on her saddle. *Nothing foolish.* Keeping low to the ground, she sneaked across the yard toward the back of the cabin, diving to the ground at any little noise from inside.

When she drew alongside the back wall, she crouched near the window and listened. She could hear the scuffling of boots and a labored sigh from someone inside. Scooting onto her knees, she tried to peek over the window ledge.

"She should've come by now," King bellowed.

Startled, Jennie dropped flat to the ground. Her nose filled with the acrid smell of rotting wood as she lay facing the cabin's lowest logs.

"She'll be here, boss," someone said. Jennie heard a disgusted snort and guessed this came from King.

"Gunner said that Nathan fellow was real excited about the robbery. Asked him lots of questions."

"Excitement and questions don't mean she's coming for certain," King replied. The sound of a fist pounding the wall carried on the air. "She'd better take the bait."

A moment of quiet followed King's words before another voice said, "I thought you were just gonna claim the place after she lost it."

"I am. But I need to make certain Jones and her family don't try to stop me."

Jennie felt the color drain from her face. What did he mean? Would he shoot her like Caleb had said and then go after her family?

I won't let that happen. Her jaw clenched with anger. *We'll stop them somehow.*

Turning to look at the log closest to her, Jennie discovered a chink in the wood. Several more littered the back of the cabin. She crawled to one and then another, but both were too small to get a good view of the room. At last she found a hole smaller than her fist, but not so big she'd be seen by those inside.

Positioning herself in front of the hole, Jennie peered into the cabin's interior. A chair leg and a box obscured most of her view, but by craning her head, she was able to locate three of the men. Two sat against the far wall, their guns held close. Jennie thought she recognized them as the rustlers who'd stolen her cattle, though she'd only had a brief look at them that night. The third man appeared to be standing by the door. She couldn't see King, but she guessed he had to be sitting on the chair, judging by the nearness of his voice when he talked.

If I could just see him... She considered moving farther down the wall to find another chink until she realized what had been blocking her view. *The cash box*.

The five thousand dollars, the ticket to her freedom, sat beneath Mr. King's chair, less than six inches from her face. She tried to reach through the hole to touch the box, but her hand wouldn't fit. She swapped her pistol for the knife she'd hidden in her boot and silently whittled away at the soft wood. When she could maneuver her hand through the hole, ignoring the scrape of splinters, Jennie let her fingers explore the metal surface of the cash box. Thankfully the lock had been broken.

She couldn't leave now—not when the money was literally within reach. It was her ticket out of jail, and she had to try to get it, even without Caleb's help.

Sliding her hand back out of the hole, Jennie stuck her knife into her boot and pressed her forehead against her fist to think. If she could open the box, the lid would help hide her movements as she removed the money. Then no matter what happened, the cash would be safe and she'd have her freedom payment.

Gritting her teeth in determination, she pushed her hand through the hole and grasped the lid of the cash box. When she lifted it, one of the hinges creaked. Jennie froze.

"Did you hear something, boss?" one of the cowhands said.

Jennie's heart jumped into her throat, beating so loud she feared they'd hear it, too. She bit her lip, trying not to breathe.

After a long pause, King laughed. "I don't hear a thing, Haws. How you ever became a cowhand, I still don't know. You're the jumpiest son-of-a-gun I ever met."

Haws grumbled in response, his words inaudible.

Exhaling, Jennie slipped her hand inside the box and touched the bundles of money, feeling their size. She'd have to be extra careful to keep the lid from slamming and giving away her position. She grasped one of the bundles and slid it slowly up and out of the box. Sweat beaded on her upper lip as she pulled the cash through the hole. A rush of euphoria swept through her as she reached in for the second wad of cash.

She emptied the cashbox of all five bundles, stopping once more when she heard King shifting his weight on the chair above her. Once all five thousand dollars sat outside the cabin wall, she softly pushed the box's lid into place, withdrew her hand and rolled onto her back in the grass.

Making certain to keep out of sight, Jennie climbed to her knees and placed the bundles and her gun onto her lap. She lifted the hem of her skirt, cradling the cash and weapon inside, and crept away from the cabin. By the time she reached Dandy, her whole body was damp with sweat.

She stuffed the money into her saddlebag. How she'd love to see the look on King's face when he realized she'd fooled him. She smiled, ready to climb onto her horse, but the other mounts tethered in front of the cabin caught her eye. If she let the animals go, King and his cowhand thugs wouldn't be able to make their escape— or worse, ride to the ranch and hurt her family—before the sheriff arrived.

She spun around and struck out for the cabin again. She inched along, keeping behind the taller brush when possible. As she drew parallel to the building, she went down on hands and knees and crawled along the ground.

Wish I hadn't worn my best dress now. She could only imagine what condition the brown silk would be in after today.

To keep from scaring the horses and alerting King, Jennie gave the animals a wide berth before approaching slowly from the north. She walked half-crouched over, her free hand extended toward the nearest horse until she touched its velvety nose.

After rubbing the horse's muzzle, she untied him from the tree where he'd been tethered. She looped the reins around her hand and guided him toward the next horse. After she'd freed all four animals, she led them a little ways from the cabin. She released all four sets of reins and slapped the rump of the horse next to her. "Go on."

The horse loped through the brush, snapping branches, while the others followed. A shout came from inside the cabin. "Someone's out there, boss. I really heard somethin' this time."

Whirling around, Jennie sprinted south toward her own horse. If she could reach Dandy before the men reached her, she'd be fine. She kept her eyes on the ground as she ran, but she could plainly hear the commotion behind her as the men exited the cabin.

"The horses. They're gone," someone shouted.

King swore loudly. "It's Jennie Jones's doing, I know it."

"Look there, boss," another cowhand yelled. "There she is. Running toward those trees."

Jennie pushed her legs faster, her lungs burning. *Just a little farther.* She ran down a slight incline, but instead of finding her feet back on flat ground, her boot caught on the hem of her dress. She crashed to the ground, her pistol slipping from her grasp. For one horrible moment, she couldn't breathe. Gulping air, she scrambled to her knees and frantically searched the dirt for her gun. Two sets of ironlike hands stopped her.

"You're comin' with us," a cowhand said, his tobacco-stained teeth showing through his cocky smile. The other, one of the two she recognized, picked up her pistol from off the ground and nodded.

"No." Jennie fought their hold, kicking at their legs with her boots and pulling back as hard as she could against their hands. But she wasn't much of a match for men used to wrestling thousand-pound cattle.

As they half dragged, half carried her toward the cabin, she glanced up to see King standing out front, grinning. *At least he won't have his money,* she told herself as she stared at the Colt revolver in his hand.

Tears of regret stung her eyes, and she willed herself to hold them back. She wouldn't give these men the satisfaction of seeing her cry. If only she'd left after taking back the money or waited for Caleb in the first place, she wouldn't be facing the possibility of her own death. Why did she insist on doing everything on her own? Even she—strong and independent as she liked to think of herself—needed help now and then.

"Surprised to see us, Miss Jones?" King asked as she and her captors came closer to the cabin. "We've been waitin' for you." Even at a distance, she saw the cold triumph blazing in his dark eyes.

She craned her neck to see past the man holding her left arm, hoping Caleb or the sheriff would ride up at that moment. The sagebrush plain stood empty, but there was still One she could petition for help. Not caring what King thought, she dropped her chin to her chest and silently prayed.

God, I'm trying to make things right. But I need Thy help. Please give me strength and let me live to see Caleb and my family again....

Jennie fought back the panic that threatened to overwhelm her as the men dragged her toward the cabin door where King waited.

"Do come in." He grabbed her roughly from his cowhands and shoved her inside. The others filed in behind them. "I knew you couldn't resist the lure of five thousand dollars to save your little ranch."

King pushed her down onto the floor in a corner of the room. Jennie hit the hard-packed dirt with a muffled groan. She watched helpless as the cowboy with her pistol stuck it in his holster.

"I've heard all about your robberies," King bragged, "so I planned this little get-together myself. Had my man Gunner drop hints about today's robbery to your partner, Nathan. Then we rode out here first thing this morning and robbed that stage." He waved his revolver in the direction of the cash box before pointing it at her.

Jennie wanted to smile, pleased she'd stolen the five thousand dollars right out from under his nose, but she could hardly swallow, and her head had begun to pound with fear.

She kept a steady eye on his gun as he went on talking. "As soon as I can get to Fillmore, I'll claim your ranch and join it with mine. I reckon you won't object— seeing how you ain't got a cent for that bank president."

Jennie feigned surprise at the mention of Mr. Dixon,

deciding to play along. She even managed a soft gasp from her dry throat.

King grinned, pushing his face so close to hers that Jennie could smell the bacon he'd eaten for breakfast.

"That's right, missy. Mr. Dixon and I are good friends. We worked out a nice little arrangement for speeding things up for me to get what I want." He drew back and ran a finger over the barrel of his revolver. "'Course, in the end, he still moved too slowly for me."

"Did you kill him, too?" she asked, not bothering to hide the bitterness from her voice.

With a laugh, King cocked his gun. "No, Miss Jones. He ain't standing in my way of having the largest cattle operation in the territory. You are." He pressed the cold metal against her throbbing temple. "You understand, don't you? I can't have you tryin' to win the place back again."

"Boss…" one of the cowhands interjected.

"What is it, Smith?" King shot a glance at his men while keeping the gun against Jennie's head.

The man didn't respond right away, and in the long pause, Jennie managed a quick sideways glance in his direction. With a pained expression on his face, the cowboy stared at the dirt floor. Jennie noticed the other two were also looking everywhere but at her and King.

"Well, boss," Smith answered, "I—I know you said you might have to shoot her, but can't we just rough her up a bit instead?" Murmurs of agreement sounded from the other cowboys, apparently giving Smith the courage to continue. "I don't mind wounding stage drivers," he said, his voice stronger, "but killin' women?"

Jennie hardly dared believe his words. Hope beat sharply in her chest. Could she somehow turn these men against King and escape? They could easily gain the upper hand in number and weapons.

Turning slowly, King brandished his gun at his men. "You wanna repeat your pretty little speech, Smith?" The venom in his tone made even Jennie shiver, blotting out all hope.

Smith lowered his head. They were clearly too afraid to go against their boss.

"Good," King snarled. "'Cause if any of you liver-bellied boys think you can bail out now, you're wrong. If you try, I'll keep the small fortunes I promised ya, and you'll be lucky if I don't plant a bullet in your backsides, too. Is that understood?" All three men nodded.

"All right, then." King turned to Jennie. "Now we can get on—"

The cabin door flung open, banging against the opposite wall and sending a tremor through the old building. King whirled around, his eyes wide with surprise. His men scrambled to draw their guns. A man with a dirty bandanna over his mouth and nose appeared in the doorway, a shotgun in his hand.

Jennie recognized his dusty clothes and blue eyes at once. *Caleb.* Relief flooded through her, calming the frantic beating of her heart. Two young women Jennie didn't know, one blonde and one dark-haired, cowered behind him, their hands tied. Who were they and what was Caleb doing with them?

She leveled a gaze on his partially covered face, trying to communicate that she recognized him. But he ignored her. Something in his rigid stance told her to keep quiet, let things play out without her interference.

"Who in tarnation are you?" King demanded, aiming his revolver at Caleb's head. Jennie swallowed hard.

She hoped Caleb's plan—whatever it might be—would work.

Caleb lowered his shotgun, but only a little. "I'd ask you the same question. This here's my hideout and I don't take kindly to strangers using it for their hostages." The girls' crying rose in volume. "Silence," he barked at them before turning back to King. "Seeing how you've got me outnumbered, though, I'd be willing to share it with you gentlemen."

"We're conductin' a little business meeting." King trained his gun on Jennie again. "So if you don't mind steppin' outside, I'd like to finish up."

Caleb lifted a hand in surrender. "Fine by me." Pushing the girls ahead of him, he headed out of the cabin. Jennie watched numbly as the door swung shut. She rushed to her feet, but King pushed her back to her knees.

"Sit down, Miss Jones."

Caleb, she wanted to scream. *Come back.*

As if he'd heard her thoughts, the door opened again and Caleb stuck his head inside. "Could you show me the spot where you hid your horses? I need to get mine out of sight, too."

King exhaled loudly. "They ain't hidden—this young lady let 'em go." He pressed the gun harder against Jennie's temple. She swallowed, trying to ignore the ache behind her eyes and praying Caleb had a good plan.

"That little slip of a thing released your horses?" Caleb chuckled. Jennie scowled at him. This was no time for jokes.

"Is that funny to you, boy?" King growled, swinging his gun from Jennie to Caleb.

"Nope." Caleb sobered immediately. "If you do need

some horses, I've got a few extras." He straightened up, his tall frame filling the doorway. "I'll sell 'em to you cheap. Send one or two of your men out here to pick what you want."

His gun still pointed at Caleb, King narrowed his eyes. Was he really considering Caleb's proposal? Jennie held her breath. She had no idea how Caleb meant to rescue her.

"All right." King motioned with his gun at Smith and the cowhand with Jennie's pistol. "Haws and Smith, you go check out the horses. Make sure they ain't old or feeble."

The two men followed Caleb outside and the door closed behind them. Jennie released her breath in a soft rush and contemplated her chances of escape. Two men would be easier to handle than four, but she still didn't have a weapon.

King frowned. "Let's get this over with."

Jennie eyed the window. Perhaps she could make it before King shot her. Just as she tensed to move, a loud cry followed by a heavy thud sounded outside the cabin. All three of them turned in the direction of the door.

Please, come back, Caleb, Jennie silently cried to the walls. Had King's men done something to him?

"What was that, boss?" the remaining cowboy asked.

"Don't know," King snapped, his face turning red with irritation. "Go find out what's goin' on. I'll tie her up." Glaring down at Jennie, he gripped her wrist hard and added in a low hiss, "I don't need no more interruptions."

The cowhand hurried through the door. Before it swung shut again, Jennie strained to see outside as King pulled a rope from his belt. She hesitated too long in her decision to stay put or run, and the rancher had her wrists tied before she could move.

Another shout floated in through the gaps in the logs. King cursed and slammed his fist against the nearest wall.

"Time to end this." He aimed the revolver at Jennie again. His jaw tightened in deadly resolve, and his lips lifted in a sneer. "Who's got the upper hand now, Miss Jones? You got no friends or guns to help you this time. It's just you and me."

Jennie licked her lips, keeping her chin held high even as she prepared for the inevitable shot.

"Any last words before I pull the trigger?"

"Yeah. Step away from my girl!"

Sucking in a sharp breath, Jennie felt her whole body sag at Caleb's words. She'd been so focused on the gun barrel trained at her head, she hadn't heard him enter. Now he stood in the doorway, appearing every bit as strong and capable and handsome as the day they'd met on the trail. The bandanna around his face had been removed, and he pointed his shotgun straight at King.

Still facing Jennie, King didn't move a muscle. But Jennie detected the glint in his eye just before he swung around toward Caleb.

"Caleb, look out," she shouted.

Jumping to her feet, she plowed her shoulder into the lower back of the giant rancher. King's gun blasted above their heads, bringing bits of wood and dirt from the ceiling raining down on them. Jennie hit the floor hard enough to crush the breath from her lungs a second time and cause the room to spin around her. When her vision cleared, she scrambled to sit up in time to see King kick Caleb's shotgun away. Caleb lunged toward him and drove a fist into King's gut. The man grunted, but connected a punch to Caleb's lower jaw, sending Caleb backward.

As the two wrestled each other, Jennie brought her boot to her bound hands and managed to pull out her knife. She twisted her hand and sawed at the rope. A loud groan brought her head up. In horror, she watched Caleb curl into a ball and roll away from King.

"Caleb!" she screamed.

Spinning on his heel, King lumbered toward her, his eyes wild and dangerous. Jennie dropped the knife and tried to crawl away, but she couldn't move fast enough with her bound hands. King grabbed her foot and yanked her back. She shut her eyes, fear turning her blood to ice in her veins. A grunt made her open her eyes. Caleb had pulled King back to the floor, but she could see the weariness on Caleb's face. She had to help.

With renewed energy, Jennie found the knife again and cut at the rope until it slipped off. Finally free, she searched the floor for King's revolver. She located his gun on the floor and picked it up. Standing, she crossed to King and Caleb, still locked in a battle of strength.

She offered a rushed prayer for help and lifted the gun in the air. She waited until King rocked back on his heels, breaking from the flurry of swinging fists and feet. Seeing her chance, she brought the revolver down as hard as she could against the man's head. The rancher roared with pain. Caleb seized the pause in momentum and plowed a fist into King's jaw. This time the rancher crumpled to the ground and lay unmoving.

Jennie sank to the floor with a cry and set down the gun. Her hands were shaking too badly to hold it anymore. She bit her lip, hard enough to taste blood, to keep from crying.

Caleb crawled over to her. His nose and lip were bleeding and one arm cradled his stomach. He pulled her to him with his free hand. "Thanks for the help." He released her to pick up the rope near her feet. "We need to tie him up."

"I'll do it," she said, knowing he was in pain. She looped the rope around King's wrists and attempted to tie a knot, but she had to pause until she stopped trembling. Finally she secured his hands. "How long do you think he'll be unconscious?" she whispered, peering into the man's battered face.

"It might be a while," Caleb said. "The sheriff can deal with him—if he and his men ever show up."

He sat on the ground beside her and wrapped her protectively in his arms again. Jennie pressed her ear to his chest, more grateful than she could ever say to hear his heart beating beneath his dusty, blood-stained shirt.

Releasing her, Caleb pushed her sweaty hair off her face. "I thought you weren't going to do anything foolish."

Jennie managed a laugh. "I didn't plan to, until I found the money. I got it out of the cash box without King knowing." She pointed in the direction of the box, still sitting underneath the chair. "I meant to leave after that, but I thought I should get rid of their horses first…" She let her voice trail off; he could guess the rest.

Caleb pulled her close again and rested his chin against her hair. "You crazy girl. I'm glad you're safe."

"Mr. Johnson?" A feminine voice hollered.

Jennie eased back. "Who's that?"

Caleb managed half a smile. "Come meet your other rescuers."

They emerged from the cabin, and the two young women Jennie had seen earlier hurried over. They didn't appear helpless now. From their lavish dresses and dark rouge, Jennie suspected they'd worked in a saloon.

"You all right, Miss Jones?" the dark-haired one asked.

"This is Ellen," Caleb said, motioning to the girl who'd spoken. "And this is Clara." He pointed to the blonde. "They were passengers on the stage. After today's performance, I think they ought to join an acting troupe."

Before Jennie could respond, a thin gentleman rushed up to them. "Did you find the cash box?" he asked.

"Mr. Fulman is the bank man from Nevada," Caleb explained.

Jennie smiled, grateful for both her sake and the bank man's that she had the cash. "Your money is safe, Mr. Fulman—all of it. I'll get it for you just as soon as someone tells me how all of you managed to get rid of King's men."

"It was Amos's idea to have them come out to see the horses," Caleb said. He pointed north to where the stagecoach sat behind some trees. "That's him on the driver's seat. He's the shotgun messenger. Took a bullet in the thigh, so he's acting as guard."

"When those thugs left the cabin," Clara interjected, "we knocked 'em out and tied 'em up. We just finished putting them all inside the stage."

"Best time of my life." Mr. Fulman brushed at the

front of his dirty suit and chuckled. "Beats sittin' behind a desk all day. Maybe I should become a deputy."

Jennie joined his laughter. "Thank you, each of you,
for your help. I'll get your money, Mr. Fulman."

She headed for the tree where she'd tied Dandy, but
she hadn't gone far when a hand gripped hers. Turning,
she found Caleb beside her, his face somber despite the
twinkle in his blue eyes.

"You coming, too?" she teased.

He nodded and squeezed her hand. "I plan on stickin'
extra close from now on, Jennie Jones. I don't need any
more bandits or lawmen or cattle spiriting you away.
Deal?"

Laughing, Jennie gently kissed the corner of his
mouth that wasn't bleeding. "It's a deal, cowboy."

Chapter Twenty-One

Jennie collected the money from her saddlebag and untied Dandy, recounting for Caleb how she'd managed to pilfer the cash out of the box. Only then did she notice the state of her brown dress. It was dirty, sweaty and torn at the hem. She felt bad for ruining the dress Caleb had paid for, but she consoled herself with the possibility that Grandma Jones might be able to salvage it.

She and Dandy followed Caleb back to the cabin and she gave Mr. Fulman the money. The bank man sat right down on the ground to thumb through it. He placed the bills inside the cash box he'd removed from the cabin.

"We ought to check on King again," Jennie said, not wanting to give the man a chance to escape.

"He was starting to moan when I crept in there," Mr. Fulman said. He shut the lid to the cash box and stood. "The money appears to be all there—thank you."

"Better load King into the stage while he's fairly unconscious," Caleb said. "Will you help us, Mr. Fulman?"

Jennie tied Dandy near the stage before trailing Caleb and Mr. Fulman into the cabin. Sure enough audible groans came from King's split mouth, but his eyes remained shut. Caleb hefted his shoulders while Jennie and the bank man each took hold of a leg. They lifted King and started slowly from the cabin.

Halfway to the stagecoach, Jennie heard the sound of approaching horses. She glanced toward the east and saw four men riding at a gallop toward them. "I think the sheriff has finally arrived."

"Miss Jones?" someone shouted as the riders drew closer. Jennie recognized the sheriff's voice.

Shifting the weight of King's leg, she gave a quick wave. "I'm here, sheriff."

The sheriff and his deputies came to an abrupt halt beside her. "Miss Jones." The man's eyebrows rose sharply as he took in the scene before him and the nearby stage filled with groaning captives. "What in the world happened?" he asked as he dismounted.

Jennie met Caleb's amused look over her shoulder. "It's a rather long story, sheriff."

"I'm anxious to hear it." He waved a hand to include the rest of the stage passengers who had gathered around. "All of you will need to come to my office for questioning."

He barked orders for his men to carry King to the stagecoach. Jennie relinquished her post gladly—her head and muscles had begun to ache again from all the drama. Once the rancher had been placed inside the stage, the sheriff walked up to her, his face somber. For one dreadful moment, Jennie worried he'd changed his mind about not pressing charges. Then his face broke into a smile.

"My apologies, Miss Jones, for my delay. I hadn't the foggiest idea what you were going to do when I heard you'd come out here alone. I wondered at first if you were taking the money for yourself. But I couldn't quite believe that. So I figured you had to be either crazy or extremely stubborn." The sheriff shook his head and chuckled. "Now I see it's a bit of both."

"I couldn't agree more, sir." Caleb took her hand in his. She pretended offense at his words, but inside she felt only deep gratitude and love for him.

The sheriff sized up Caleb. "Who might you be?"

"The man I love," Jennie answered with a smile at Caleb. "Mr. Johnson's also our hired hand and the finest cowboy around."

The sheriff's gaze sparked with pleasure at her confession before he turned and swung onto his horse. "I want to get these men to the jail, so let's load up."

Jennie climbed onto Dandy, grateful to be heading closer to home, and waited as Caleb mounted Saul. Mr. Fulman volunteered to drive the stage again, and Ellen and Clara piled on the back of two of the deputies' horses.

With everyone situated, the sheriff waved the stagecoach forward. He and his deputies took up positions on either side while Jennie and Caleb rode at the back. They hadn't gone far when Caleb yelled for the sheriff to stop.

"What's wrong?" Jennie asked.

"We forgot Ol' Phil, the stage driver."

Caleb rode ahead to tell the sheriff. The entourage headed southwest under Amos's directions until someone spied the stage driver near a patch of sagebrush.

The sheriff and his men, along with Caleb, went to assess the body while Jennie sat in the saddle, chewing on her thumbnail and praying the man wasn't dead.

Somehow she felt it would be her fault if he was, since she hadn't intercepted the stage sooner.

Was this the sort of weighty guilt Caleb had carried after Liza's death? The knowledge he'd tried to fix things—even if he believed it was the wrong way—struck her as ironic. Perhaps his past had made it easier for him to forgive hers. That thought brought a measure of peace to her troubled mind.

When two of the deputies hoisted the man, Jennie saw his lined face contort into a grimace. Gratitude coursed through her. The sheriff made one of the cowhands ride on top of the stage so the driver could be placed inside.

Jennie nudged Dandy next to Caleb and Saul as the whole group started their trek eastward again. "Will the driver be all right?"

"I think so. He got a bullet in the hip and one to the shoulder, but they think the doctor can fix him up. He ought to be driving again before too long, though he may end up with a limp."

Jennie gave a quick nod and turned away from him. Now that the whole ordeal was almost over, she couldn't restrain her tears anymore.

"What's wrong?"

"I've been a fool." Her voice cracked on a sob, and she had to clear her throat to continue. "I realized that as King's men were dragging me back to the cabin and I saw him standing there with his gun. I jeopardized my life, your life and the lives of all these people…" She waved her hand to include those on the stage and those riding beside it. "All because of my stubborn insistence on doing everything myself."

"Jennie, look at me."

She regarded his kind face, now furrowed with concern. "Everything's going to be fine. Amos is going to heal, the stage driver will, too, and you got the bank's money back. You're free to live your life, to do and be whatever you want now."

Jennie sniffled and rubbed her nose with the back of her hand. "I'm still going to lose the ranch." She hated how the words tasted on her tongue—full of defeat and pain.

"I love you, Jennie," he said, prodding his horse closer to hers. "I'm proud of you for doing the right thing."

She smiled at him through her tears. "Now I just have to find a way to pay back the money I stole by the end of the month."

"You can start with the money I gave you. Then we'll just do the best we can to come up with the rest until all of it's paid back."

Jennie murmured agreement, grateful he wanted to help, but she didn't want to use Caleb's hard-earned money to pay for her mistakes. She hated to think he wouldn't be able to have his freight business because of her.

"King told me he planned to lay claim to the property once I lost it. I suppose he still can." Jennie frowned at the thought of such a horrid man taking over her beloved home.

Caleb shook his head. "I think he's going to be locked up for quite a while."

"One of his men could still do it for him." She studied the prairie and the green-flecked mountains on both sides. "Maybe Grandma Jones, Will and I should go up north with you."

"You mean that?" The hope was unmistakable in his voice.

The events of the past twenty-four hours made the idea of starting over in a new place very appealing. Especially if it meant being close to Caleb. "Do you think you could stand to have us nearby, after today?"

He chuckled. The tenderness in his eyes set her heart racing. "Life would be mighty dull without you around, Jennie. I've sort of gotten used to it."

Jennie held her breath, hoping he'd say more. Maybe ask for her hand in marriage, even though they weren't alone. Caleb glanced away, but not before Jennie caught a mischievous smile on his lips. *He's thinking the very same thing.* The possibility of being engaged to Caleb soon tempered her impatience and increased her excitement at the prospect of heading north.

Would she and Caleb start another ranch? Jennie didn't think so. It would take more capital than she'd have at the end of the month and Caleb was looking forward to owning his freight business. She tried to picture a life without cattle and branding and doing more around her home than caring for farm animals and tending a garden, but she couldn't.

Despite her enthusiasm to follow Caleb north, hopefully as his fiancée, she couldn't ignore the misgivings whispering at the back of her mind. Worries about the cash she had to pay back, about leaving the ranch. Acquiring the stage money today had been harder than she'd thought, and she suspected the sacrifices in her future would be every bit as difficult.

But when she looked over to see Caleb riding at her side, she knew that any struggle would all be worth it to have his love and respect. Grandma Jones had said that the hardest things to do were usually the right ones. And as Caleb caught her eye and grinned, she knew that nothing could ever be more right than this.

When the group reached town, the sheriff directed his men to unload the prisoners and lock them up in the jail. Jennie and the others were directed into the sheriff's office next door for questioning. King had woken up on the ride to Beaver, and as two of the deputies dragged him inside, Jennie plainly heard his cursing—most of which he directed at her.

"All right, Miss Jones," the sheriff said, taking a seat at the table where Daniels had been practicing his gun work earlier. "Why don't we start with you? Would you kindly explain what happened from the time you left my office to the time we found you at the old cabin?"

Jennie stood straight; she had nothing to hide this time. "I would be glad to, sir."

With Caleb's hand resting reassuringly on the small of her back, Jennie recounted all that had gone on after she met Caleb in the valley, and how he and the others had rescued her. When she finished, Caleb and the stage passengers added their stories to hers.

"Thank you for your help," the sheriff said, rising from his chair. "Those of you from the stage are free to go. Miss Jones, if you and Mr. Johnson would remain behind, please."

Before Jennie could step toward him, she and Caleb were surrounded by Amos, Mr. Fulman and the two girls. They talked over each other, repeating their thanks for the help and wishing her and Caleb good luck. Jennie hugged each one and offered her own thanks. If they hadn't come to her aid, she might not be standing here alive. With a mixture of gratitude and sadness, she watched them file out of the jail.

"Now, Miss Jones." The sheriff resumed his seat and folded his arms. She and Caleb stepped closer to the table. "Since you met the terms of our arrangement, I'm happy to inform you that I will not be pressing charges of theft." Leaning forward, he wagged a finger at her. "But you'd better have that money paid back by the end of the month or our agreement is null and void. Is that clear?"

"You have my word, sir." Jennie wanted to laugh and cry and shout all at the same time. She didn't know yet how she'd pay back all that money, but she was almost free.

The sheriff nodded. "Based on your accounts, I am going to hold Mr. King and his men here until their trial, on charges of theft and attempted murder. Is that all?"

Jennie exchanged a long look with Caleb. She knew what he was thinking. "There has been at least once incidence of him and his men cattle rustling, sir. I don't want to see the man hung, especially since we took my cows back this last time, but I thought you should know."

"Cattle rustling?" The sheriff pounded his fist against the table, his eyes blazing. "Why that no-account…" He shook his head. "Are you sure you don't wish to add that charge to the list, Miss Jones? We don't take cattle rustling lightly around here."

"I only wanted you to know, so you could be on the lookout once Mr. King and his men are allowed to go."

The sheriff stared at her, his face thoughtful. "I've got a better idea. Would you come with me please, Miss Jones?" He stood and went to the door.

"Where are we going?" Jennie asked.

"To visit Mr. King."

Caleb wrapped a protective arm around her waist. "Is that wise, sheriff?"

"She'll be perfectly fine in my company, Mr. Johnson. We'll be back in a few moments. Please wait here." He held open the door for Jennie.

"It'll be fine," she murmured to Caleb before stepping outside. Still, apprehension twisted her stomach as she followed the sheriff next door to the jail.

The two deputies seated at the room's only table stood up, their faces registering their surprise at seeing her and the sheriff. The animated conversation between King's cowhands stopped and they peered suspiciously at them from their shared cell.

"I need to see Mr. King," the sheriff announced. Taking Jennie gently by the elbow, he led her past the deputies to the last of the three cells.

"Mr. King?" the sheriff called out to the dozing figure on the cot.

King lifted his head and blinked. When his saw the sheriff, his face turned a shade pale. "What do you want?"

"I have a proposition for you, Mr. King." The sheriff threw Jennie a conspiratorial grin. Baffled at what his plan could be, she didn't return the gesture.

King's eyes narrowed with suspicion as he stood and crossed to the cell door. "What is it?"

Turning to Jennie, the sheriff asked in her a low voice, "How much money do you need to repay, Miss Jones?"

Jennie shot King a quick look before whispering, "Thirty-eight-hundred dollars."

If the amount shocked him, the sheriff didn't show it. Instead he spoke to Mr. King in a firm voice. "I want you to buy Miss Jones's ranch—for thirty-eight-hundred dollars."

Jennie wasn't sure who looked the most surprised at the request—her or Mr. King.

"Buy it?" the rancher said with a smirk. "Why would I do that? It ain't worth that."

"From what Miss Jones has told me, you're probably right." The sheriff appeared thoughtful, but with his next words, his face hardened. "But that's the asking price for your life."

King frowned. "Whatdaya mean? The bank man on that stage got his money back and she ain't dead. I won't be in here long."

The sheriff leaned forward as if imparting a great secret. "Yes, but the penalty for cattle rustling is hanging. Isn't that true, Miss Jones?"

Jennie bit back a smile herself. "Yes, yes it is, sheriff."

"Cattle rustling," King repeated in a strained voice. He rubbed a hand over his stubbled jaw, the fight visibly draining from him. He glanced at Jennie and then back at the sheriff. "If I buy her ranch, you won't press that…uh…other charge?"

"You have my word, but Miss Jones will need the money before the end of the month."

"If I don't have it?"

Unable to resist, Jennie stepped forward. "I know an excellent banker in Fillmore who might make you a loan."

King glowered at her. "Fine. I'll have my man Gunner ride over with it next week."

"I thought you said you didn't have it," Jennie said, folding her arms.

"Guess we all have our secrets, don't we?" King sneered.

The sheriff touched Jennie's arm. "You now have a buyer for your ranch, Miss Jones. Shall we go?"

Almost dizzy with excitement, Jennie trailed him down the line of cells and past the deputies. "Thank you," she said, pausing in front of the door.

The sheriff tipped his hat to her. "My pleasure."

Though she'd still lose the ranch, she would be able to repay the money she'd stolen. She'd be free, and Caleb would be able to keep his hard-earned cash.

"Thank You," she murmured again, this time with a meaningful glance toward the ceiling as she and the sheriff stepped outside. She couldn't wait to give Caleb back his money.

Chapter Twenty-Two

Caleb stared into the orange flames flickering in the fireplace, his arm around Jennie as they sat on the sofa. He couldn't recall ever feeling so exhausted. *But then again,* he thought with a smirk, *I've never stopped a runaway stage, rescued the girl I love from being shot and told the same story a dozen times, all in one day.*

"What's so funny?" Jennie said, poking him in the side. She'd been lost in thought, too, ever since her grandmother had shooed them off to the parlor to rest after supper.

"I was thinking I definitely earned my keep today." He smiled when she rolled her eyes. "In fact, I think I've earned my keep for a lifetime, which means you're heavily in my debt."

"In that case, how can I repay you?" she asked, warming up to his game.

Caleb rubbed his chin in mock contemplation. "You could start with a kiss." Jennie pushed up from the couch and kissed him. He loved the way her lips fit against his. He was so grateful she was here beside him, alive.

"Next," he said, easing back, "I think you could take over some of my cattle watching times."

"I think I can manage that. Anything else?"

Caleb peered down at her pretty face. His pulse skipped faster. He knew what he wanted to ask—had known ever since this morning when he learned Jennie's plan for setting things straight. But would she say yes?

Taking a deep breath, he reached for her hand. "How about marrying me?"

Her eyes widened and her free hand rose to her mouth. "You mean that?"

With a nod, he slid off the couch and knelt in front of her. "Jennie Aurelia Jones, will you agree to be my wife?"

"Yes, cowboy," she half whispered before throwing her arms around him. He nearly toppled over but managed to keep them both upright.

He loosened her arms from around his neck so he could kiss her, but she squirmed out of his embrace and stood up.

"Did I miss something?" he protested. "Doesn't a man deserve another kiss after proposing?"

"Yes, but I just remembered something I wanted to give you." She gave him an impish smile. "I'll be right back."

Caleb returned to his seat on the sofa. In the kitchen, Grandma Jones was washing dishes and singing to herself. The front door creaked open, and Caleb guessed Will had finished tending to the animals.

"Good night, Grandma," the young man called out before he appeared in the parlor doorway. "Where's Jennie?" he asked Caleb.

"Getting something upstairs, I think."

"I still can't believe what you two did today." Will leaned against the door frame. "The only things I did were watch those boring cows and muck stalls. Saving runaway stages sounds a lot more exciting."

Caleb chuckled. "I used to think so, too, but after today, I think I'll stick with tending animals."

"Did Jennie really rob all those bandits like she said?"

"Crazy, isn't it?" Caleb couldn't describe the relief he felt to have Jennie done with robbing thieves. "But remember what she said if she ever finds out you've done something like that."

"I know, I know." Will held up his hands as if in surrender. "She'd tan my hide within an inch of my life. I got it." He ducked out the door. "Good night."

"'Night, Will."

"Thanks," he said, pausing in the hallway.

"For what?"

His shoulders lifted in his characteristic shrug. "For helping Jennie…and our family."

A strange lump formed in Caleb's throat, and he had to swallow hard to loosen it. "You're my family, too. Your sister just agreed to marry me."

"About time," Will said with a grin before he turned and bounded up the stairs.

Caleb glanced at the fire again, realizing how much he meant what he'd said to Will. Jennie's family had become as dear to him as his own. And now that he'd decided to stop running from his past, he was ready to reconnect with his family again. He couldn't wait to show Jennie the Salt Lake Valley. God had blessed him so much in the past six weeks, in ways he'd never imagined. He offered a prayer of thanks, finishing just as Jennie entered the room, her hands hidden behind her back.

"Are you ready?" she asked.

When he nodded, she lifted a small bundle of cash for him to see.

"What's this?"

Jennie's eyes glistened in the firelight with unshed tears. "It's yours, Caleb. It's the money you gave me."

"But…" He shook his head, not understanding. "I thought you were going to use it to pay back the money you still owe from the robberies."

"I was." She handed him the money and sat down. "Then the sheriff forced King to buy the ranch for thirty-eight-hundred dollars. More than enough to pay back the robberies and the bank."

Caleb stared at the cash in his hands, then back up at Jennie. "Are you crazy?"

"Crazy in love with you."

"I meant crazy to let someone like Marshall King buy your ranch."

Jennie wiped at her wet eyes. "Maybe. But I didn't feel right about using your money to pay for my wrong-doings. It would take us months, or even longer, to earn it back."

"You're sure King will pay up?"

"Yes." She wriggled under his arm and rested her head against his shoulder again. He liked holding her this way. "The sheriff told King if he didn't buy the ranch he'd be charged with cattle rustling. King agreed to buy the place and said he'd have one of his men bring the money over next week."

"Is that what happened when you and the sheriff went to the jail? You did seem rather pleased when you came back." He playfully tapped the end of her nose with his finger.

They fell into comfortable silence until Caleb remembered he hadn't yet told her about Nathan Blaine. If they were to marry, he didn't want any more secrets between them.

"Remember how I asked you yesterday about Nathan—being a stage robber or not?"

Jennie's brow furrowed. "Yes, why?"

Caleb cleared his throat, expecting the old anger and urge for revenge to fill him as he recalled the events of the past. This time he felt only peace, which gave him the courage to continue. He twisted around on the sofa so he could face Jennie. "Nathan Blaine was the fourth man involved in the robbery of Liza's stage."

"Oh, Caleb." Her face went pale. "I—I had no idea."

He pressed his finger to her mouth to silence her worry. "I know you didn't. But you need to know that part of my story before I tell you where I went last night."

"I didn't know you'd gone anywhere."

"I went to town, to the saloon, actually. I found Nathan there, but…" He interlocked his hand with hers. "I'd planned on the ride over to haul him into the sheriff. When I went to arrest him, though, I couldn't do it. I realized I was letting my old hate and need for vengeance drive me again. So I persuaded him to leave town."

"How?"

"I detailed the charges against him and said if he didn't leave town right then, that I'd turn him over to the law. I also let him know I didn't ever want to hear his name associated with stage robbing again." Caleb let out the breath he'd been holding. "I knew it was the right thing to do, but I also hoped it would prevent you from dealing with anymore stage thieves yourself or winding up in jail, if Nathan implicated you."

Jennie squeezed his hand. When he looked at her, she reached up to touch his cheek. "Thank you. For telling me and for being merciful to Nathan. No wonder he wasn't around this morning when I went to the boardinghouse to tell him not to help me." She snuggled back under Caleb's arm.

Relieved to have this last confession off his chest, he stroked her hair, liking the softness slipping through his fingers.

Jennie yawned. "Aren't you sleepy?"

"Not after a day like this one." He smiled down at her. "How do Will and Grandma Jones feel about you selling the ranch?"

"I haven't told them yet. I figured they've heard an earful already today. They knew we were going to lose the ranch anyway." She shut her eyes. "I'll tell them tomorrow. Along with the news that we're engaged. Maybe that will make things easier."

"I already told Will."

"What did he say about it?"

"His exact words were 'about time.'"

Jennie released a soft laugh. "I imagine Grandma Jones will say something similar. Should I tell them we'll be heading north with you after the sale of the ranch?"

Caleb pulled her closer to his side. "I'm not going anywhere, Jennie, not without you."

"What will your parents say when you show up with three extra mouths to feed?"

"They'll love you, just like I do."

She cracked open her eyes, tenderness shining in their brown depths. "When do you think we should marry?"

"Yesterday," he said, grinning. "But since that didn't work out, how about in a month?"

"Sounds good, cowboy," she murmured as she shut her eyes again.

Caleb pressed a kiss to her forehead, soliciting a murmur of contentment from Jennie. He understood the feeling. Despite the events of the day, he felt joy and hope for the future. Soon he'd be returning home, with more than he could've hoped for when he'd left three years before.

Another lump formed in his throat as he gazed down at his sleeping bride-to-be. *That's the second time I've almost cried in less than an hour.* To cover his own embarrassment, he let his mind fill with plans.

Tomorrow he'd write his parents and tell them about Jennie and her family. He was glad she would be living near them during his absences with his freight business. Eventually he could have others do the traveling for him, but to begin, he would have to make the treks southward himself. The thought of being away from Jennie so much brought a tangible ache.

Would she adapt to life up north without her ranch? Caleb couldn't picture her wearing a dress and apron every day like his mother or sisters. She needed her men's breeches and old hat, a rope in one hand.

He stared down at her sleeping form again, her beautiful features soft and relaxed. Out of love for him, Jennie would become a freighter's wife, with some land to farm to get them by. But he knew instinctively how much she'd miss this place. The ranch had been her lifeblood.

Tears formed in his eyes, and Caleb let them leak out as he tightened his arm around her shoulders. He couldn't give Jennie back her ranch, but he had an idea of what he could do to keep that vibrant light in her eyes.

Chapter Twenty-Three

Four weeks later

Jennie woke to semidarkness outside her window. Sitting up in bed, she stretched and wondered what her grandmother was making for breakfast. Then she remembered. She wasn't at the ranch; she and Will and Grandma Jones were now living with Caleb's family. And today she would become Mrs. Caleb Johnson.

The one day I was told I should sleep in, she thought, shaking her head with amusement, *and I'm up at dawn as usual.*

Hugging her knees to her chest, Jennie smiled as a tremor of excitement ran up her spine. Her life had changed so much in the past four weeks that her memories of the ranch felt as hazy as if months had gone by instead of days.

Of course she'd been too busy to dwell for long on saying goodbye to her home. Gunner had come with the money as promised, and Jennie managed to keep her tears in check as she relinquished the key to the house. By then, she'd learned of the man's daring visit to warn Caleb about Mr. King's plot. In gratitude, she told him to take two of her best heifers to start his own herd before she sold the rest.

The trip northward had been long, but thankfully, uneventful. The morning after they stopped in Fillmore—the very day her loan was due—Jennie had insisted on going inside the bank alone to present her money to Mr. Dixon. The man's balding head and clean-shaven face had paled as he'd listened to Jennie explain about the robberies and the sale of her ranch.

"There's enough money here to absolve my full debt and repay what was stolen." She slid the overstuffed bag of money across the tidy desk. "I have a note here outlining the dates of the various robberies and amounts. I also have a letter from the sheriff in Beaver, requesting your help in seeing that this money is returned to its rightful owners." She handed him both papers. "The sheriff and I agreed this would be a suitable way to redeem yourself, Mr. Dixon, for becoming involved with Mr. King."

Mr. Dixon wiped away the sweat glistening on his head with a handkerchief, his face turning from white to red. "I…uh…don't know what to say, Miss Jones. Other than I appreciate your willingness to work with me." He swallowed, and Jennie couldn't help a smile.

"It's all right, Mr. Dixon." She rose and tugged her hat more securely on her head. She hadn't bothered to change out of her breeches. "As someone recently informed me, we all have our secrets."

The bank president was still sputtering for a response as Jennie left the bank, chin held high with real victory this time.

They'd pulled into the Salt Lake Valley a week later,

sore and tired. Jennie, Will and Grandma Jones were immediately taken in by the Johnson family with as much warmth and kindness as if they'd known each other for years.

They all attended church together that first Sunday in the valley, with Jennie clutching tightly to Caleb's hand. After a while she relaxed and even spoke with a few of the neighbors when the services ended. She still feared being accepted into the church community, but she wouldn't quit going. She knew the price she and her family had paid during their years of absence, and she was determined never to repeat that mistake again. She needed God, and as Caleb kept reminding her, He needed her, too.

A knock on the door scattered Jennie's thoughts. "Come in." She pulled the covers up to her chin, though no one could see much of her in the unlit room.

Caleb stuck his head around the door, a lamp in his hand. "I thought you might be up."

Jennie pretended to scowl at him. "Isn't it bad luck to see the bride before the wedding?"

He lifted the lamp and scrutinized her. "I think that only applies to seeing your wedding dress. How fast can you get ready?"

She blinked at him. The most important day of their lives and he wanted her to rush? "I didn't think we had to go for another couple hours. I still need to iron my new dress, and your sisters are coming over to do my hair…" She let her voice fade out when he shook his head.

"No. I meant how quickly can you dress for an outing?"

"An outing? Where are we going?"

He wouldn't answer her question, and Jennie imagined the playful glint in his eyes. "Ma put together some breakfast for us to take along. Get dressed, and I'll go hitch up the wagon."

"All right. Give me five minutes."

He set the lamp on the bureau and shut the door behind him. Throwing off the covers, Jennie jumped out of bed. She quickly scrubbed her face with the ice-cold water in the washbasin, put on one of her old dresses and pulled a brush through her hair. Though it was now June, the mornings could be cool, so she threw a shawl over her shoulders and blew out the lamp. The house stood quiet around her as she hurried down the stairs.

As she made her way down the hall, she heard Caleb and his mother, Rachel, in conversation. She didn't mean to eavesdrop, but their words floated easily through the quiet house.

"You think she'll like it?" Rachel asked. *What could she mean?* Jennie wondered, pausing just outside the door in hopes of unearthing the secret behind Caleb's outing.

"I know she will."

Jennie heard the rustle of a skirt. "I'm so proud of you, Caleb. Your decisions these last two months have made us so happy. We worried about you when you left here three years ago. We still loved you then and understood your grief, but it pleases me so much to see you finally at peace."

"You really are proud?" Jennie heard the hope and relief in Caleb's voice.

"Very much so. Jennie is so good for you and I think you'll be good for her."

"I couldn't agree more." Footsteps headed for the back door. "I'm gonna hitch up the wagon."

Jennie remained where she stood a moment more, resisting the urge to run after him and kiss him soundly in front of his mother. The knowledge that she could be a help to him as he had so many times to her made her heart nearly burst with love.

She smoothed the front of her dress and stepped into the kitchen. Warm air wrapped itself around her.

Rachel glanced up and smiled before returning to her task of kneading dough in the light of another lamp. "Your breakfast is in that basket by the door."

Jennie thanked her as she crossed the room and picked up the basket. With her hand on the doorknob, she turned back to Rachel. "Is this improper, an outing with the bride before the wedding?"

The older woman laughed, reminding Jennie so much of Caleb. "For other grooms perhaps, but not for my Caleb."

Jennie slipped out the door. She waited as Caleb hooked up the team of horses to the wagon. When he finished, he helped her onto the seat and placed a blanket over her lap. He stowed the breakfast basket beneath their seat.

"Ready?" he asked.

"I suppose," she said with a laugh.

They drove away from the rising sun, toward the dark sky in the west. Jennie could see a few stars still twinkling above them. Caleb put his arm around her, and she snuggled into his warmth, completely content. They spoke quietly of their plans for the day, and Jennie successfully thwarted Caleb's attempts to wiggle information out of her about her dress or how she planned to do her hair.

"I have to maintain some surprise," she teased.

Before long, the sky began to lighten, and soon the chain of western mountains stood out more clearly. Fewer farms occupied this side of the valley.

"Where are we going?"

"This is it," Caleb said, pulling on the reins. "We're here."

Jennie glanced more closely at the landscape. Sagebrush and wild grass swayed in the breeze, and from a stand of nearby trees, some birds chirped their morning calls. "What is this place?"

Instead of answering, Caleb jumped to the ground and hurried around the wagon to help her down. He kept her hand in his and led her a few yards from the horses. "This," he said, sweeping his arm in an arc in front of them, "will be our new home."

"Oh, Caleb, it's perfect." *This is where we will live and raise our family.* She went up on tiptoe and kissed his cheek.

"I bought it two days ago, but I wanted you to see it before the wedding."

Jennie smiled, the love she felt for him washing over her anew. "We'll still need to purchase a place in town for your freighting office."

Caleb led her around, pointing in different directions as they walked. "Here is where I thought we'd build the house, so we'd have a nice view of the mountains to the east and a place for a vegetable garden."

Jennie found herself growing more excited as he voiced his plans.

"Over there, we can build the barn and an icehouse

one day." Caleb drew her farther away from the wagon. "The property goes all the way to the foothills, so we can plant a few crops and then the rest of the land will be for the cattle."

She'd been nodding as he inventoried the possibilities, but when she heard him say "cattle," she stopped bobbing her head. "We won't need so much space for a milk cow or two."

"I didn't say they'd be milk cows."

"But what kind—"

"I figure if we're going to have a ranch we better have a lot of range for our cattle."

"You mean…" She grasped his arm, afraid she hadn't heard him right. "You mean, you're not going to be a freighter? We're going to have a ranch instead?"

At his nod, a lump formed in Jennie's throat, making any more words impossible. Caleb pulled her into his embrace, and she rested her head against his shirt.

"What is it they say?" he whispered into her ear. "You can take the woman from the ranch, but you can't take the ranch from the woman?"

Jennie sniffled. "Is that what they say?"

"Whether they do or not, it's true. You need a ranch, Jennie Jones, and I need you. So I guess my cattle days aren't numbered."

Reaching up, Jennie placed a hand against his cheek, loving the smoothness of his freshly shaved jaw. "Thank you, Caleb. Thank you today, and tomorrow and forever. Next to having you as my husband, I can't think of a better gift."

"Seeing your smile every day will be thanks enough," he said as he pressed his forehead to hers.

A new round of tears temporarily blurred her vision.

"Are you sure you knew what you were doing that day you accepted my job offer?"

"No, but God did."

Jennie smiled, then easing back, she gave him a serious look. "You don't wish you were marrying someone else? Another girl might cause you a lot less trouble."

Caleb shook his head, his blue eyes devoid of teasing. "I've known for a while that you're the girl for me. Even with your men's clothes and your stubborn ways, I love you, Jennie. And I always will."

Jennie threw her arms around his neck. "Does that mean you won't mind sleeping next to me and my pistol?"

"As long as you aren't pointin' it at me."

Her heart thudded wildly in her chest as Caleb bent down and kissed her. She felt breathless and filled to bursting with joy. Whatever lay ahead, she and Caleb would face it together.

"You ready to head back?" he asked as they ended their kiss.

Nodding, Jennie reached for his hand and gave it a squeeze. "Let's go get married, cowboy."

* * * * *

Debra Ullrick is an award-winning author who is happily married to her husband of over thirty-five years. For more than twenty-five years, she and her husband and their only daughter lived and worked on cattle ranches in the Colorado mountains. The last ranch Debra lived on was also where a famous movie star and her screenwriter husband chose to purchase property. She now lives in the flatlands, where she's dealing with cultural whiplash. Debra loves animals, classic cars, mud-bog racing and monster trucks.

Debra loves hearing from her readers. You can contact her through her website, www.debraullrick.com.

Books by Debra Ullrick

Love Inspired Historical

The Unexpected Bride
The Unlikely Wife
Groom Wanted
The Unintended Groom

Visit the Author Profile page
at Harlequin.com for more titles.

THE UNLIKELY WIFE

Debra Ullrick

For the Lord does not see as man sees;
for man looks at the outward appearance,
but the Lord looks at the heart.
—*1 Samuel* 16:7

This book is dedicated to my dear sister,
Marlene Baylor.

Every time I've needed a friend, or a listening ear,
or encouragement, or lifting up, you've been there
for me. Thank you so much! You'll never know how
much that means to me. How much YOU mean to me.
I luv ya high as the sky, Marlene.

God bless you.

Chapter One

❧

Paradise Haven, Idaho Territory
1885

This has to be a nightmare.

Standing in front of Michael Bowen at Paradise Haven's train station was the woman who claimed to be his wife. His eyes traveled up and down the length of her. Instead of a dress, she wore a red scarf draped around her neck, a black cowboy hat with a stampede string, black cowboy boots and brown loose-fitting trousers. In her hands she held a Long Tom black powder rifle.

A rifle? The woman was holding a rifle. No matter how hard he tried he couldn't pull his gaze away from the weapon that was nearly as long as she was tall.

Michael bore down on his teeth until he thought his jaw would snap. Even with her heart-shaped face, stunning smile and beautiful brown eyes, the person standing before him looked more like a female outlaw on a wanted poster than the genteel lady he had been corresponding with for the past five months. The woman he had fallen deeply and passionately in love with. The woman he had legally married sight unseen.

This woman was nothing like what he'd expected. Nothing. There had to be some mistake. There just had to be.

Suddenly, she lunged toward him and threw her arms around his neck. He stiffened and struggled to draw in even the smallest amount of air because she squeezed him so tightly. *Dear God, have mercy on me.*

"Oh, Michael! It's so nice to finally meet ya." Selina Farleigh Bowen pulled back and stared into her new husband's face. She knew Michael would be handsome—no one who wrote letters that sweet could not be. But even if he were uglier than a Kentucky toad, she'd still love him.

She took a second to study his face. Jaw, nice and square. Nose, straight. Eyes, breathtaking and smiling, the color of a sapphire necklace her ma once had when days were better. Lips, bow shaped. The man was so handsome. And he was all hers. "I just can't believe I'm finally here."

Michael stared down at her with wide eyes.

Her husband wasn't smiling, and he looked like he'd just swallowed a giant cricket. Her joy evaporated.

She took a step back and dipped her head sideways, wondering if she'd done something wrong or if he was disappointed in her looks. Maybe she shouldn't have grabbed him and hugged him like she had. After all, that was a mighty bold thing to do, but she couldn't help herself. She'd waited five long months for this day.

Still, maybe her boldness had upset him. She reckoned she'd better apologize. "I'm sorry, Michael. I oughta not tossed my arms about you like that. Forgive me iffen that was outta line."

He continued to stare, saying nothing.

"Bear got your tongue or somethin'?"

"You—you can't be Selina."

Whoa. She wasn't expecting that. "What do ya mean I can't be Selina? Of course I'm Selina."

He tugged his gray cowboy hat off his head and ran the back of his hand over his sweaty forehead, then settled the hat back into place. "You can't be. The Selina who wrote me was…" His eyelids lowered to the wood planks under his feet, but Selina still caught sight of the hurt in his eyes.

Quicksand plopped into her belly. "Michael." She waited until he looked at her. His expression was blank. "You said the Selina who wrote you was… Was what, Michael?"

"She was…"

She was what?

The longer he stood there not saying anything the more skittish her insides got. "Tell me, Michael. She was… I mean, I was what?"

"Well, will you look at her? That's repulsive." Disgust oozed from a woman's voice as she passed by them.

Selina swung her attention to two young women standing about five yards away with their fancy dresses and matching hats with long feathers sticking out of them.

"Are you sure it's a she? Looks more like a man to me."

Selina caught sight of their faces.

They looked her up and down with a snarl on their

faces. *Jumpin' crickets.* Did those women have their corsets in a twist or what?

"I can't believe she would be seen in public like that."

Selina had dealt with their type all her life. People who thought they were better than her just because they had money and could afford fancy clothes.

Selina narrowed her eyes, pursed her lips and gave them her meanest stare while patting her rifle.

Their eyes widened. They linked arms and scurried off like a herd of scared mice stuck in a shack filled with cats. Worked every time.

Selina turned back to Michael.

His eyes followed the women until they disappeared around the train depot building. She wondered what was going through his mind. "Michael, would you mind iffen we found someplace over yonder so we can talk? I need you to tell me what was in them letters."

"What do you mean you need me to tell you what was in the letters? You wrote them." A frown pulled at his face. "What's going on here, Selina?" His voice was harsh and loud enough that people stopped what they were doing to stare at them.

"Whoa." She held up her hand to ward off the roughness of his words. "Just back up your horses, cowboy, and I'll explain everything. But not here. Come on." She tugged on his shirt sleeve. He balked like a stubborn mule, and she had to practically drag him all the way to the edge of the trees out of the earshot of others.

She sat down on a log and hoped Michael would do the same, but he just stood there, towering over her.

"Won't you please sit a spell? I'll have a crick in my neck iffen I have to keep lookin' up at you like this."

He lowered his backside onto the log but as far to the other end as possible.

He removed his hat and worked the brim of it into a curl.

Such a waste of a mighty fine hat.

Why, Pa would skin her and her brothers alive if one of them ever treated a hat like that. But she wasn't here to talk about that. "Michael, I don't know what the problem is, but I want you to know that I told Aimee to tell you that I had no book learnin' and that I couldn't read nor write because I had to help my pa raise the youngins after my ma took sick and died."

"What do you mean you can't read or write?" His shocked face made her want to find a rock to crawl under. She dropped her head in shame. "And who's Aimee?" he asked.

"You don't know?"

"No. Why should I?"

"Aimee's my friend who wrote them letters for me."

"I'm confused."

"I can see that. I'm a mite confused myself because Aimee was supposed to tell you that she was writin' for me. Must have slipped her mind." At least Selina hoped that was why Aimee hadn't told him.

"Well, she didn't."

"What did she tell you then?"

"The letters said that your father was dying and that was why you answered my advertisement. When I mentioned that I didn't want someone to marry me because they needed a place, you... Aimee...suggested we correspond a time in order to get to know each other. Then after a couple of months if neither one of us cared for the other, we would find someone else. But the more I wrote, the more I fell in love with…"

"Finish what you were fixin' to say, Michael. You fell in love with who? Me or Aimee?"

"I—I don't know. The woman in the letters?" He placed his elbows on his knees and his head in his hands. "Only now I don't know who that person is."

"Me, neither." She hated having to admit that. "There's only one way to find out. You got them letters with you?"

"Yes."

"Would you mind fetchin' them?"

He stood. "They're in the wagon. I'll be right back."

Selina had a sick feeling as he walked away. If her doubts were right, Aimee hadn't told Michael everything Selina had asked her to. And if Aimee hadn't, then her best friend had done not only Selina wrong, but also Michael.

But surely Aimee wouldn't have done such a wicked thing. Her friend loved her and had always treated her kindly. Unlike those other rich folks she'd worked for who had treated her worse than an unwanted critter. Her friend had even rescued Selina when Aimee's brothers had tried to drown Selina in the river. If Aimee hadn't shown up when she had, she wasn't at all certain she would be here today.

Still, she couldn't help but wonder if Aimee had tricked them. If so, did that mean Selina had up and hitched herself to a man who loved someone else? Namely her beautiful friend Aimee?

Michael took his time walking to the wagon. He needed to get his thoughts together. He had a hard time believing the woman sitting on the log was his bride. The word *bride* stuck in his throat like a chicken bone.

For years, Michael had prayed for God to send him someone like Rainee, his first real crush, but Selina was nothing like Rainee. His sister-in-law was a woman he admired and respected. She was the epitome of femininity, a Southern belle who was educated and smart, beautiful inside and out, genteel yet strong, feisty but sweet, able to hold her own when need be and a real survivor. Everything he wanted in a wife.

Tired of living alone at the age of twenty-seven, with women still scarce in the Idaho Territory, he had decided to take out an advertisement. After all, it had worked for Rainee and Haydon.

If only it would have worked for him.

If only he would have taken the time to get on that train and head out to Kentucky to meet Selina before actually marrying her by proxy. But he couldn't be spared.

The coming of the railroad had made getting feed and supplies much easier. Because of that, he and his family had purchased more property and livestock.

Even with the extra hired help, Michael was needed to tend the cattle and hogs, the apple, plum and pear orchards, the hay, wheat, oat and barley fields. His absence would have put too much burden on his family, and he had refused to let that happen.

He thought his heart had been in the right place at the time, but now he was stuck with the consequences of that decision and had no one to blame but himself. With a heavy sigh, he retrieved the letters from behind the seat of the wagon and headed back to Selina.

Her cowboy hat now rested against her back. Sunshine glistened down on her head, exposing rivers of copper and blond streaks flowing throughout her molasses-colored hair.

Her skin was flawless.

Her teeth were even and white and her striking, rich, coffee-colored eyes held a million questions. Questions he didn't know the answers to.

No denying the woman was beautiful, but none of that mattered. She wasn't what he had wanted or prayed for. Of that he was certain.

He lowered himself at the opposite end of the log from Selina. Without looking at her, he tugged at the string around the parcel and opened the first letter he'd received from her. He practically had it memorized. Neat penmanship and feminine curves looked back at him, mocking him with their precise, dainty script. Script filled with lies and deception.

"This is the first letter I got from you. 'Dear Mr. Bowen. My name is Selina Farleigh. I'm twenty-five years old, five-foot-three inches tall with brown hair and brown eyes. I am responding to your advertisement because my father has taken ill. You see, the man my father works for provides our lodging. Once my father passes on, I will have to leave as I will no longer have a home.'"

"That's not true," Selina interrupted him.

He glanced at her.

"It's true about my pa taking ill but not that other stuff. No wonder you said you didn't want someone to marry you because they needed a home. Well, I didn't need a home, and Aimee knew that. My pa owned a place in the hills. Wasn't much, but my brothers own it now. I could've stayed there with my brother and his wife."

"Why did you answer my advertisement?"

"I let Aimee talk me into it. My pa's dying wish was to see me hitched to a good man. Pa said he could die in peace knowin' I was happily married and far away from Bart."

"Who's Bart?"

"A fella back home who wanted me to marry him." She scrunched her face. "No way would I have married Bart even iffen he was the last man on earth. Somethin' about him gave me the willies. Pa didn't much care for him none either. Said he drank too much moonshine. So when Pa found out about the ad and how Aimee was encouragin' me to write to you and all, he agreed. Said he wanted me to have a better life."

She looked away. "'Course, when he found out you were a pig farmer, he said it wouldn't be much of a better life but at least I'd be far away from the likes of Bart and would always have food to eat. That made Pa feel a whole heap better. Plus, he knew I never wanted to marry a rich man."

Michael's attention snagged on that last comment. Why didn't she want to marry someone rich? What was she going to say when she found out she already had? Did he even care?

"Then again, Aimee was supposed to tell you all a that."

Well, she hadn't. And Michael couldn't help but wonder who the real villainess was here and if all of this was some elaborate scheme to snag a husband. He had no way of knowing the truth. What he did know was, he felt the deception through every inch of his body and the largest portion of that deception settled into his heart.

From the way she was looking at him, he knew she was waiting for his response, but instead of responding, he raised the letter and continued to read.

"'Your advertisement states that you cannot travel as the work on your ranch needs your attention. I am willing to travel, but my father will not let me leave without first being married.'" Michael glanced over at her. "Is that true? Your father would not allow you to leave until you were married first?"

"Yes, sir. And neither would my brothers."

He nodded, then continued to read. From the corner of his eye, he could see Selina pulling the bead up and down on her stampede string.

The more he read, the faster she raised and lowered the bead. And if he wasn't mistaken, a shiny wet spot covered her cheek.

As he read one letter after another and Selina refuted one thing after another, anger replaced any love he felt toward the person who penned them.

"I've heard enough. Please stop."

She'd heard enough? He'd heard plenty. Plenty enough to know he'd been lied to and tricked.

His gaze fell to the stack of letters in his lap that at one time had brought him more love and joy than he'd ever known before. He had loved the sense of humor in them, the wit, the charm, the way the person saw beauty in the smallest things, the feistiness and confidence the person in them possessed. Only that woman no longer existed.

Or did she?

He didn't know anymore.

Didn't know what to believe or who to believe.

This whole thing was making him crazy.

Who could do such a wicked thing? And why? What could their motive be? He folded the letter he'd been reading, stacked it on top of the rest and tied the string around them. What he really wanted to do was burn them and his marriage certificate.

"I'm so sorry, Michael." Selina's voice cracked. "Everything I told her to say, she twisted or made it bigger than it was. She even wrote things I never did say." She shook her head, looking lost, alone, terrified even.

He couldn't help but wonder if it was all an act. He hated thinking like that, but he didn't know the truth or how to find it.

"Can't believe Aimee did that. I don't understand *why* she did this to me. To us." Her gaze dropped, along with her voice. "I—I don't rightly know what to say except…" Her chest rose and fell. "What do we do now?"

Her whisper, broken by tears, tugged at his heart. He hated seeing a woman cry, no matter how angry he was.

What did they do now?

Vows had been spoken, and the Bible made it clear about the wrongness of breaking vows. Like it or not, he and Selina were legally married. There was only one answer to that question. "I guess we head home."

Her gaze flew up to his and the color in her face fled.

Michael understood exactly how she felt. But they had no other choice. He hoisted his body off the log and offered Selina a helping hand up. "We made our vows before God and we need to honor those vows. Let's go home."

Selina picked up her rifle and slung the sling around her neck.

They shuffled their way back toward the train depot.

"Where's your luggage?" he asked without looking at her, his mind and body numb. Dead, even.

"I only have the one bag." She headed toward a patched-up gunnysack, picked it up and faced him.

He stared at the bag, shocked by her obvious poverty. "Here, let me take that for you." His focus trailed to her face.

She raised her head and jutted her chin before shifting her bag away from his reach. "Thank you kindly, but I can carry it myself."

He didn't mean to hurt her pride. He nodded, then pointed to his wagon, the only one left at the station now.

She slipped her hat back on, strode to the back of the buckboard, laid her rifle and sack down, then leaped onto the tail of the wagon, leaving her legs dangling.

That wasn't what he had in mind when he pictured taking his bride home. And what if his family was around when he got back to the ranch? What would they think if they saw her sitting back there and not up front with him?

Indecision tugged him in several directions as he debated what to do. Embarrassed by her appearance, he preferred she stay back there. But then again, if she did, his family would wonder what was wrong and he certainly didn't want to tell them he'd made the biggest mistake of his life. They already thought he was crazy because of some of the poor choices he'd made in the past.

Like the goats he'd bought on a whim.

The little brats had destroyed his mother's garden, chewed up some of the laundry and had even wreaked havoc at some of their neighbors' places. It had taken him a long time to make amends and to get rid of them. No one wanted the goats. He finally had to give them away. His family still gave him a hard time for that one. They'd have a field day with this one.

"Selina." He scuffed at the dirt with his boot. "Would you mind sitting up front with me?"

She frowned. "Why?"

"Because… Whether we like it or not, we *are* man and wife, and I think it would be best if we acted like it."

She tilted her head and studied him. "I see what you're sayin', and I won't shame ya by not sittin' next to you." Before he had a chance to help her, she hopped down and seated herself up front, leaving the sweet scent of field flowers in her wake.

He stared, shaking his head. He wasn't sure he would ever get used to a woman who acted and dressed like a man. And yet, what choice did he have? For better or worse, she was now his wife. And he had a bad feeling it was going to be for the worse.

Chapter Two

Selina scooted as close to the side of the wagon seat as possible. Touching Michael was something she didn't want to do. Her heart ached something fierce knowing Michael didn't love her and that she'd pretty much come all this way for nothing.

If only she'd known all of this back home, she would've never gotten hitched then. She'd seen the ugliness of what a marriage without love could do to folks, to the whole family, and it wasn't a pretty sight.

Long ago she had made a promise to herself to never get married unless the man truly loved her and she loved him. When she'd said yes to Michael's proposal, she believed she was honoring that promise.

Why did she ever let Aimee talk her into answering that stupid ad? If she hadn't, then neither she nor Michael would be in this mess.

Poor Michael. What he must be going through. "Michael."

"Yes?"

"I'm really sorry for what my friend did. I had no

idea she wrote those things and lied to you. Iffen I'd known, I would never have come."

"What's done is done, Selina. We'll just make the best of it."

He sure seemed to be taking it a lot easier than she was. Either that or he was mighty good at hiding it.

Silence followed them the rest of the way home. That was fine with Selina. Gave her time to take in the scenery.

Layers of green rolling hills stretched before her, ending at the base of a mountain covered with trees. Well, if a body could call these here mountains. They weren't nearly as big as the ones back home. In Kentucky, these mountains would be called nothing more than hills.

One thing for certain, this place was nothing like where she'd come from. But then again, nowhere on God's green earth ever would be to her. Born and raised in the Appalachian Mountains, she loved Kentucky and all its beauty. Before she left, she had fastened every little detail of them and her home into her memory so she'd never forget what they looked like.

The sun bore down on her back, heating her body something awful. She sure could use a drink. She licked her lips.

Michael twisted in the seat and reached for something behind him. He handed a canteen to her.

"How'd you know I was thirsty?"

His only response was a hike of his shoulder.

Wasn't long before they rounded a bend in the trees.

"Whoa, girls." Michael pulled the horses to a halt in front of a house five times bigger than the shack she grew up in.

Selina turned to Michael. "Why we stoppin' here?" She gawked at the large two-story house with rocking chairs, small tables and a big wooden swing on the porch that went clear around the place.

"I live here."

"This is yours?"

"Yes. It is."

"Well, I'll be hanged. You told me you were a pig farmer. Or did Aimee lie about that, too?"

"No. She didn't. I am a pig farmer. But I said that I also raise cattle."

"Oh, no," she groaned. "I can't believe I up and married myself a rich man."

Michael turned his head her direction. "You sound like that's a bad thing."

"It is. Iffen I'd a known you was rich, I'd never have answered that ad."

"What do you have against rich people?"

"Lots of things. Folks who have money think they're better than poor folk. Treatin' us like we're lower than dirt. Like we have no feelin's at all."

"Hey, now just you wait a minute. You can't go judging all rich people by the ones where you come from. My family and I do not turn up our noses at poor folks or treat them like dirt, either. Nor are we mean. I resent you clumping us into some category when you don't even know us."

"You might resent it, but the truth is you're just like them rich folks back home. Back at the train station I saw you turn your nose down at me and how I look. My whole life people been judgin' me by the way I dress. All I can say is, I'm mighty glad the good Lord looks at the heart and not the outside like some folks do."

His cheeks turned the color of a rusty-pink sunset.

"Aimee was rich, too. And look what she did to us." Selina spoke under her breath, still in shock at what her friend had done. She didn't want to think about that right now though. It hurt too much.

She hopped down from the wagon and grabbed her bag. Good thing she'd found a flour sack and put it to rights the best way she could, or she wouldn't have had anything to put her few belongings in.

Her eyes trailed to the huge house again and she wondered how many people lived here.

Michael was waiting for her at the end of the steps, looking uncomfortable.

Well, he wasn't the only one who felt that way. *C'mon, Selina. You can do this.* She met him and followed him up the stairs.

Michael opened the door and waited for her to go in first. One thing about the man, he was a gentleman. She stepped inside and stopped. Never in all of her born days had she seen anything so fancy.

The place was filled with more furniture than she'd ever laid eyes on. Her focus slid to the rich brown kitchen table and the six matching chairs with fancy carved legs and arms. Fresh flowers flowed from a large vase in the center of the table, which was covered with a lacy tablecloth.

And the cook stove, why, it was mighty fine. Unlike the old potbelly stove back home. That thing was harder than the dickens to keep burning and the door barely hung on.

Selina stepped farther inside, taking in the whole room. Two cream-colored rockers with gold squiggly lines running through the fancy curved tops and arms sat on one side of the fireplace, facing a matching sofa with blue, gold and cream-colored pillows on it. Betwixt them was a long table. A large oval blue-and-cream rug had been placed underneath the table. Sure was pretty.

Heavy drapes held back by a braided rope covered six tall living room windows.

On the mantel of the large stone fireplace sat a clock, with three different-sized brass candlestick holders on each side of it.

Selina strode toward the fireplace and crouched down, peering past the metal screen.

Why, the thing went plumb through to the other side into a bedroom with a cherry-colored dresser topped with a long mirror, another dresser that was taller and a four-poster bed, and all of them were done in the same fancy carved wood as the rest of the place. On top of the bed was a white quilt with light and dark blue circles and dark blue pillow covers. Pale blue drapes swagged the windows.

She loved blue. A tear slipped from her eye. She thumbed it away and wouldn't allow any more to escape. Knowing Aimee had told Michael that Selina loved blue made her wonder if the blue bed quilt and house curtains were done on purpose. Well, even if they had been, who were they done for? Her or Aimee?

Selina turned to see Michael standing in the doorway with his hat in his hands, watching her. Never before had she felt so out of place or uncomfortable. And she didn't like it. Not one little bit. She pressed her shoulders back, determined to not let it show. "Your home is beautiful, Michael. Whoever took the time of it did a right fine job."

When he said nothing, she played with the bead on her hat string. No longer able to stand the silence, she said, "Well, I reckon you must be hungry. Let me get my rifle and I'll hunt us up some grub."

His head bobbed forward like a rooster. "Grub? Are you serious?"

She raised her chin, not liking how he made her feel with his tone. "Yes, sir, I am serious. You wanna eat, don't ya?"

"Well, yes, but you don't have to hunt for any *grub,*" he said the word *grub* as if he hadn't ever heard it before. "I'm assuming grub refers to food."

Sure enough, he hadn't.

"I have a cellar and a pantry full of meat and anything else you might need. Here. I'll show you." Michael walked over to a small room off the kitchen, opened the door and stepped to the side.

Selina came up beside him at the doorway entry and peered inside. Her eyeballs nearly popped out of their sockets. The room was filled with canned goods, a large bag of flour and sugar, eggs, coffee, cornmeal and just about anything a body would need to fix a meal. Except she didn't see any meat.

"That door at the end of the pantry leads into the cellar," he said from behind her. A little too close behind her as far as she was concerned. She squirmed forward, but his broad-shouldered body took up most of the small space. Thing was, it didn't seem that small before he stepped into it.

Wood, soap and peppermint scents drifted from him. He sure smelled nice.

Swallowing to stop the thoughts, she moved farther into the room, putting even more space between them.

"You'll find whatever meat you need down there along with fresh vegetables and canned fruit."

Selina opened the door and squatted, trying to see in the dark hole but couldn't. It was coal black. When she stood, Michael picked up a lantern and matches from one of the shelves and lit it.

"Here. Take this."

She took it from him and made her way slowly down the steep, narrow stairs, expecting one of them to give way any time, but they never did. They were nothing like the rickety steps back home. These were nice and sturdy.

At the bottom of the steps, she held the lantern up. *Jumpin' crickets!* she thought, unable to believe her eyes. One whole side of the room was filled with hanging meat. All sorts of canned goods lined two of the walls. Barrels of taters, carrots, dehydrated apples, turnips and onions lined the other wall. More food than a body could eat in a year.

Michael stepped into the cavelike room, filling it with his presence. She struggled to keep her wits about her as she continued to take in what was before her. "How many will I be feedin'?"

"Just you and me."

Selina whirled. "All a this food is just for the two of us?"

"Yes. I wanted to make sure there was plenty when you got here. We butchered a few head of cows and some pigs and divided the meat. Mother, Rainee, Hannah and Leah canned all the fruits and vegetables and the fish and chicken, you see."

"There sure is a lot of it. Must've taken them a long

time to put up so much. Well, from now on, I can do ours so they won't have to."

"You know how to can?"

"Sure do. I told you so in my letters." Her heart dropped to the dirt floor of the cellar with that slip of the tongue. Now why'd she have to go and bring up them letters for? All that did was remind her that she wasn't the woman her husband was expecting, that she wasn't loved and that this wasn't a real marriage and probably never would be.

"Well, I need to go and finish my chores." He turned and headed toward the steps.

She followed him, hoping to do something to reclaim her pride. "I'll help you."

He stopped on the stair and looked down at her. The man sure had pretty blue eyes.

"Help me? You don't have to help me. Chores are man's work."

"Not where I come from they're not. Besides, I aim to do my part to earn my keep and to help out around here."

He raised his hat and forked his fingers through his hair, then put his hat back on. "Selina, you don't have to *earn* your keep. You're my wife."

A wife you don't want.

"And no wife of mine is going to do chores."

Did she just hear what she thought she'd heard?

She planted her hands on her hips. "And no man is ever gonna tell me what to do."

Not even her husband—no, make that especially not her husband. She'd never let him bully or boss her around or tell her what she could and couldn't do like her cousin Mary's husband had done. Mary had always been a cheerful and happy sort until she'd gotten hitched. Her husband stripped the life out of her with his controlling, bullying ways. He'd broken Mary's spirit until she was walking and acting like some dead person. Even worse, Mary had let him.

Well, not this gal.

Michael came back down the stairs and looked her right in the eyes. "I'll say it again. Chores are man's work and no wife of mine is going to do men's chores."

Just who did this sidewinder think he was, bossing her around like that? She stepped even closer, coming toe-to-toe with him. "And I'll say it again. No man is ever gonna tell me what I can or can't do." Selina refused to be beholden to anybody. She'd seen the ugliness of that, too.

He closed the distance between them until they were almost nose-to-nose. "You're not doing chores and that's final." With one more hard look he whirled and stomped up the stairs.

Well, she could stomp just as hard as he could and she did, too, until she met up with him. Then, she bolted past him and was out the door and in the buckboard before he even made it to the wagon.

He climbed aboard and glanced at her. "You're incorrigible. You know that?" He snatched up the reins and slapped his horses on the behind. The wagon lurched forward.

She didn't know what that word meant, but she had a feeling it wasn't good.

Michael rounded the trees by the main ranch. *Oh, no.* He should have known his family would do something like this. Neighbors, family and friends filled the ranch yard, along with benches, tables loaded with food and two large signs.

One read: Congratulations Mr. & Mrs. Michael Bowen.

The other: Welcome to our family and community, Selina.

The first thought that struck him was his wife's attire; the second was he hoped she wouldn't open her mouth. He wanted to turn the horses around and head back home before anyone caught sight of them.

"Here they come," his sister-in-law Rainee hollered. Rainee waddled toward them as fast as her pregnant belly would allow. Before he could think of a good way to get them out of there, she stepped up to Selina's side of the wagon and offered her a big welcoming smile. "Selina. Welcome to the family."

With no grace whatsoever, Selina hopped down. "Thank you kindly, ma'am."

Immediately Michael detected suspicion in Selina's voice. One look at her face confirmed it. He figured it stemmed from her earlier comments about rich folks. Well, she'd just have to put her prejudice aside and learn that not all folks who had wealth treated poor folks badly. Sure, he had turned his nose up at her when he first saw her, but she needed to understand it was the shock of seeing her dressed like a man and not a woman. Like a tomboy. An outlaw even.

The sad fact was, rich and poor alike would find her attire inappropriate. He knew many a poor woman and they didn't dress like her, so wealth had nothing to do with people judging her. Her lack of propriety did.

Before he had a chance to introduce her, Rainee said, "I am Rainelle Victoria Bowen." She curtsied. "But, please, call me, Rainee." Rainee looped arms with Selina and led her to the crowd of people.

This whole thing was a nightmare come true.

Seeing no way out of it, Michael hopped down from the wagon and followed them. When he caught sight of the surprised look on the men's faces and the horror on some of the women's as their gazes traveled over her, anger surged through him. He didn't like her appearance, either, but how dare they openly show disrespect for the woman who was, after all, his wife.

He strode to Selina's side and placed his hand at the base of her back.

Selina looked up at him, at his arm and then back at his face, a question lingering in her untrusting wide brown eyes.

His gaze remained fixed on her, taking in her face, her high cheekbones and perfectly shaped lips. The woman was beautiful. Why did she hide it under that hat? Perhaps she didn't know she was beautiful.

Leah and Abby rushed up to meet her.

"Selina, these are my sisters, Leah and Abigail."

"Pleased to meet you." Leah gave her a quick hug.

"It's Abby, not Abigail. That sounds so stuffy. Just like you, Michael." Abby wrinkled her nose at him and then turned her focus onto Selina. "I love your outfit." His sixteen-year-old sister smiled, beaming as her gaze raked over Selina's clothing.

Dear Lord, don't let Abby start wanting to wear pants, too.

His sister-in-law Hannah looked up from wiping baby Rebecca's mouth. She handed the baby to her oldest son, Thomas, who took her willingly. He'd make a fine father some day. Just like his father, Jesse.

"Selina!" Hannah rushed over and gave her a hug. "Welcome to the family. We're so happy to have you here."

"Selina, this is my sister-in-law, Hannah."

"Pleasure to meet ya, ma'am," Selina said.

"Mama, where's my drink? I'm thirsty." William, Michael's five-year-old nephew and Hannah and Jesse's middle child, tugged on his mother's skirt.

Hannah rolled her eyes. "Sorry—I need to get my son something to drink. We'll talk later. You must come and see me. I live over there." She pointed to her and Jesse's house, then swung William into her arms and like a whirlwind she was gone.

Michael's mother scurried up to them. "Selina, I'm Katherine. Michael's mother."

"Pleased to meet you, ma'am."

"Welcome to the family, Selina. You must come by the house tomorrow so we can get better acquainted."

"That's right neighborly of you." Skepticism shrouded Selina's face once again.

"Hi, son." His mother barely glanced at him. "You don't mind if I borrow your wife, do you? There's someone I'd like her to meet."

"Hi to you, too, Mother." He smiled. "No, I don't mind at all."

"Good. Because even if you did, I was going to steal her anyway." Mother reached up and kissed his cheek before she looped arms with Selina and scampered her over to the same group of ladies he'd seen scowling. He watched, waiting and ready in case Selina needed his intervention.

"She isn't what you expected, is she?"

Michael turned toward his brother Jesse. With those

seven words, Michael knew his acting hadn't worked. Making sure no one was within hearing distance he said, "No, she sure isn't. I'm so angry and confused, Jess, I don't know what to do. I married the wrong woman."

Jesse frowned. "What do you mean 'the wrong woman'?"

With a shake of his head, Michael beat back the awful truth. "Selina didn't write the letters—her friend Aimee did."

"I don't understand."

There was no reason to hide the truth. Jesse had been with him through this whole thing from the beginning. In short detail, Michael explained everything to his brother. How the woman he fell in love with didn't really exist. Or if she did, she existed in two different people. One of whom he married. The other of whom he might have actually loved.

Jesse's concern was written all over his face. "Now that's a tough one. But remember, you did pray about it."

"I didn't pray for this, Jess. You know what I prayed for. Why would God do this to me?"

"God didn't do anything *to* you. He did it *for* you. He has a plan, Michael. We talked about this, remember?"

"A plan? What? To humiliate me? And how could you say God did it for me? What could God possibly have in mind? I mean, look at her, Jess. She's…" He couldn't even finish.

Jesse slid his gaze toward Selina. "She's um…different, but she seems friendly enough and she's very beautiful."

"She's different all right. She might be beautiful,

too, but she's nothing like what I had my heart set on marrying."

"Look, I know you wanted someone like Rainee. But there's only one Rainee and she's married to our brother."

"I know that. It's just… Well, every time I prayed for a wife, I asked God to send me someone just like her."

"Maybe He did."

Michael's brows spiked. "I don't think so. I don't mean to sound cruel, but look at the way she's dressed. And the way she talks." He rubbed the back of his neck. "I think the woman who wrote the letters comes closer to what I was wanting in a wife than Selina ever could."

"You don't know that. From what you told me, the person in the letters is a mixture of Selina and Aimee and a lot of things were exaggerated. So you have no idea what Aimee is really like except that she's the kind of woman—"

Michael finished Jesse's sentence. "Who would send her friend out West knowing she had lied, that she had deceived not only her, but also the man she had married. Leaving Selina to deal with the consequences." That thought alone secured his compassion toward Selina.

Nobody deserved to be treated that way. Especially by a friend she trusted. Indignation roiled through his gut. If Aimee were here right now he'd tell her exactly what he thought of her.

"Why did I have to come up with that ridiculous plan to say my vows of marriage in front of Reverend James and sign the marriage certificate and send it to her so she could do the same in front of her minister? If I hadn't, then neither one of us would be in this miserable situation." He caught his brother's gaze. "What am I going to do, Jess? I'm in love with a dream woman who doesn't exist. And even worse… I don't love my wife. She's a complete stranger to me."

All of a sudden, his stomach churned and he thought he might be sick as unbidden flashbacks of another loveless marriage came rushing in on him.

Unbeknownst to anyone, as a young boy Michael had witnessed time and again his brother Haydon's first wife Melanie's rage toward Haydon.

From afar Michael heard Melanie's cruel and spiteful remarks about what a poor excuse of a man she thought Haydon was. How she resented him for bringing her to this desolate place. How she hated him and wished she had never married him. How she had never loved him and had only married him for his money and his position in society.

To this day the memory of the pain on Haydon's face still haunted Michael. His brother's unhappiness had crushed Michael's young heart. His brother changed after Melanie. He was no longer his confident self until years after Melanie's death when God had sent Rainee into Haydon's life. Because of her, Michael now had his brother back, and Haydon was happier than Michael had ever seen him.

Michael wanted the special kind of love Haydon had found with Rainee. With all his heart, Michael believed he had—until a few hours ago. But it was fully clear to him now that his marriage to Selina was nothing but a farce and that his worst nightmare of being stuck in a loveless marriage had now come true. How had he let this happen?

Jesse squeezed his shoulder, yanking Michael from the cave of darkness his thoughts had taken him to.

"I know this is hard, Michael."

You have no idea how hard this thing is. No one does.

"But I have faith in you that you'll do what's right. Keep in mind that when Rainee first came, Haydon didn't want anything to do with her, either. He didn't believe God was in that whole situation, yet look how it turned out. They have two beautiful children and one on the way. Listen, I've got to run. Hannah is waving me down. If you need to talk, you know I'm here."

"Thanks, Jess." Michael pulled his brother into a quick hug then watched him head toward Hannah.

"Hey, buddy." Michael stiffened. The town heckler, Jake Lure, stepped alongside him and slapped him on the back. "Well, I guess we know who wears the pants in your family." Jake cackled and twitched his thick blond eyebrows in a mocking gesture.

Michael clenched his fists at his sides.

Jake looked around and then leaned closer to Michael. "You know, I think I've seen that beautiful face somewhere before. On one of the wanted posters at the jail." He cackled again.

Even though the man was a few inches taller than Michael's six-foot, broad-shouldered frame, Michael found himself wanting to punch Jake. But, he refused to stoop to this man's lower-than-dirt level.

Yet, hadn't he already done that by judging Selina's outward appearance, too? He had even justified his actions by reminding himself that she was not what he was expecting and it was the shock of seeing her dressed in trousers that had made him act so unbecomingly.

Thinking about how despicable his ungodly thoughts had been, he repented immediately. In that second, he decided no man or woman was ever going to get away with talking about his wife like that again.

"I'll thank you not to insult my wife ever again. Now, if you'll excuse me, I need to find my bride." Michael turned to leave.

"Just look for the lady in trousers." Jake's hooting laughter grated on Michael's nerves, but he refused to give into the temptation to pummel the guy.

Instead, he pushed his shoulders back and headed toward Selina. "I will." He tossed the words over his shoulder.

All the way to Selina, Michael fumed. Just who did Jake think he was, anyway? How dare he or anyone disrespect his wife like that? He may not like the way she dressed, either, but maybe that was all she could afford or had or grew up with. So who was he or anyone else to judge her?

He walked up next to Selina, standing amid a group of women who were laughing at something his wife had said. These were the very same people who when they had first laid eyes on her had shown disgust.

He slipped his arm around her shoulder. "Excuse me, ladies. You won't mind if I steal my wife away, will you?"

"We do, but we'll let you," said Sadie Elder, who came out West four years before to marry Tom Elder, a widower with nine boys. She took Selina's hands in hers. "You're just what we needed around here, Selina. It's a real pleasure meeting you. When you get settled, you must come by for a visit. Michael can show you where we live." Sadie looked at Michael seeking his permission.

He nodded.

"Oh, yes, you must come by my house for a visit, too," Mrs. Hawkins chimed in, and the other married ladies put in their requests, too.

Selina had obviously made a good impression on them. They not only seemed to accept her, outfit and all, but liked her well enough to invite her to their homes. That was a good sign. Wasn't it?

"It's right neighborly of y'all to invite me to y'alls homes. Iffen any of you need help, you let me know, and I'll be there quicker than a frog snatchin' a fly."

They all laughed.

"Oh, Selina. You say the funniest things," Sadie said through a chuckle.

Selina looked surprised by Sadie's comment, then she wagged her finger at Sadie and said, "Don't you go hurtin' yourself liftin' that cannin' kettle. I'll come by in a couple days and do it for you." Selina glanced up at Michael and smiled. Her teeth were as white as freshly fallen snow and not a crooked one to be found. The woman really was beautiful. Judging from the way she was willing to help everyone, she must be beautiful on the inside, too. Only time would tell.

"And when that baby is ready to be birthed, I can help you. Iffen you want me to, that is. Like I told you, I helped birth many a baby."

"Thank you so much, Selina. I feel better just knowing you're here. I'll see you soon then." Sadie turned and waddled toward her husband.

Sadie, who was twenty years younger than her husband, was carrying Tom's tenth child. Michael wondered if it would be another boy. For Sadie's sake, he hoped it was a girl.

The loud ringing of the dinner bell jarred his attention.

"Everyone, it's time to eat," his mother hollered.

Each woman took a turn shaking Selina's hand before they left in search of their husbands. Not one of them seemed to mind how heartily she returned their handshakes.

When the crowd quieted down, his mother turned her attention to him and Selina. "Michael and Selina, you get your plates first."

Michael glanced down at his wife. "You ready?"

"Yes, sir. Ain't had nothin' to eat since last night. I'm so hungry I could eat a herd of lizards—skin and all."

Lizards? The thought of eating lizards turned his stomach inside out. He hoped she was kidding. "Why haven't you had anything to eat since last night?" He placed his hand on her back and led her toward the long food table.

"I ran outta money. Couldn't afford none."

Michael instantly felt horrible. "I'm sorry, Selina. I thought I sent you plenty of money to take care of everything."

"Oh, you did. You did. But I couldn't sit by and watch that poor widow woman strugglin' to feed her three youngins."

"What poor widow woman?"

"Mrs. Morrow. Her husband died and she was comin' out West to marry up with a Mr. Clemens. From the way she tells it, he has four youngins himself. His wife died two years ago and he couldn't keep up with them and his chores, so he placed an ad and she answered it. Mr. Clemens sent her enough money for the trip, but some polecat stole it from her. Can you believe some snake would do such an evil thing? And to a widow woman with three youngins no less. Why, iffen I'd caught him, I would have put a load of buckshot into his sorry hide to make sure he never did it again. I'm just so glad you sent me plenty enough that I was able to help poor Mrs. Morrow."

She stopped and looked at him. Concern dotted her eyes. "Don't worry. I'll find some way to repay you. But I ain't sorry I did it. Ain't no way I was gonna sit by and listen to them youngins beg their mama for somethin' to eat when I had plenty."

What an unselfish thing she had done. To go without food so that another woman, a complete stranger and her children, could eat.

Maybe getting to know her wouldn't be such a bad thing after all.

Chapter Three

Back at the house, Selina picked up her bag to ready herself for bed. She had a good time meeting all her new neighbors. Some of them were friendly, too. But all that visiting had tuckered her out. All she wanted to do was find some place to curl up and go to sleep. She wasn't sure where that place was, though. The barn would suit her just fine, but she knew if someone saw her there, Michael would be shamed and she didn't want that for him.

She hoped to one day share her bed with Michael just like her mama and pa had. But that wasn't likely to happen with the way things were. Still, she wouldn't give up hope. Later on, during her evening prayers, she'd tell God's ears that if there was any way for Michael to love her one day, she sure would appreciate it.

Michael. This being her wedding night and all, just thinking about him sent shivers through her. She sighed. No sense pondering on him and making herself feel even worse than she already did. She needed to place her mind somewhere other than him. And she'd start with looking for a blanket or something to cover up with.

She searched a trunk and found one. While Michael was out at the privy, she put on her patched-up nightgown, tossed herself onto the living room sofa and pulled the blanket over her chest. Surprised at how soft the sofa was, she wiggled her way down into it.

The door clicked open.

Michael stepped one foot in and stopped to stare at her.

Selina yanked the cover up under her neck. "I hope you don't mind me helpin' myself to a blanket."

He shut the door behind him. "Selina, this is your home now, too, and I want you to make yourself comfortable here. And you don't have to sleep on the sofa, my bedroom is—"

"I ain't gonna share your bed," she blurted. *Until I know for sure you're in love with me and not Aimee,* but she didn't voice the last part. Thinking about what she'd said, white-hot flames licked their way up her neck and into her cheeks.

With a sigh he took another step in. "What I was going to say was, my bedroom is over there." He pointed to the door off of the living room. "If you'd like to sleep in there, I can move my stuff into one of the upstairs bedrooms. Or, if you would like more privacy, you can take one of them. Whatever you decide is fine with me."

What? No argument? No fight about his husbandly rights? She didn't know whether to be relieved or insulted. Considering their situation, she was definitely relieved. "I'll take one of the upstairs bedrooms. Ain't no sense in you movin' all your belongings."

He looked down at her flour sack, then back up at her. "Tomorrow, I'll see if Leah can take you into town to purchase you some women's shoes and material to make yourself some women's clothing."

It didn't get past her none that he stressed the word *women's* louder and longer than the rest of his words.

"I'm sure Mother and Leah would be more than happy to help you make a few dresses and bonnets and nightgowns and whatever else you may need."

She sprung into a sitting position. The blanket fell from around her shoulders.

Michael's eyes widened. He swung his attention away, looking everywhere but at her.

She snatched the cover up and tucked it back under her neck. "Just you back up your horses, cowboy. I don't need dresses, and there ain't a thing wrong with my clothes. Why, they've still got plenty of wear left in them. Besides, I don't cotton to wearin' dresses. They're just too confinin' and troublesome. You can't even hunt in them."

Michael's attention flew back to her. He crossed his arms over his chest and spread his legs. His stare went clean through her, but she wouldn't let him see that he unsettled her.

"That might be so. But no wife of mine is going to wear men's clothing."

"Listen here, Michael. I've been wearin' them most of my life and I ain't stoppin' now. Men's trousers are more practical."

"They might be more practical, but in case it's slipped your notice, the women around here do not wear pants. They wear dresses."

"I ain't other women. I'm me. And I won't be puttin' on airs for you or anyone else."

His eyes slammed shut for only a moment before bouncing open. "You're a stubborn little thing, aren't you?"

"Ain't tryin' to be stubborn." She wrapped the blanket around her and stood. "But I won't be bullied into being somethin' I ain't, neither." Michael wanted her to be something she wasn't and never would be. A lady. Tomboy was more her style. She'd been one all her life and loved it. Maybe she was stubborn. But some things were worth being stubborn about—and wearing trousers was one of them.

Before Michael could give her the wherefores about propriety and proper attire, his mouth spread into a wide yawn he couldn't stop. After the trying day he'd had, a soft bed and sleep sounded good. So, for right now, he'd let the subject drop, but he would definitely pick it up again in the morning. "It's been a long day, and I'm ready to go to bed. I'll show you to your room first."

He motioned for her to precede him up the stairs, which she did after picking up her sack. At the top of the landing, he stopped and faced her. "There are three rooms. Take your pick."

She peeked inside the first bedroom, then the second and then the third. "Iffen you don't mind, I'll take this one here."

"That's fine." He managed to keep his head from shaking in frustration. "Whatever you want." Somehow he had a feeling she would take the sparsest bedroom. The smallest room with the iron-framed bed, light blue quilt and matching curtains. Only a single dresser, a night stand with a lantern, a wash bowl and basin, three paintings on the wall, and one small closet occupied the room. The other two, which were larger and decorated as nicely as the rest of the house, didn't seem to fit her. One thing for certain, she was a simple woman who liked simple things.

"Well, good night, Selina. I'll see you in the morning."

"Night, Michael," she spoke softly in that melodic voice of hers, the one that in no way, shape or form matched her masculine attire or attitude.

Trying not to think about any of it, he headed to his bedroom, undressed and slid between the new cotton sheets. He rolled onto his side and stared at the blank pillow next to him. Tonight was the night he was supposed to be sharing with the woman of his dreams. Yet he'd felt nothing but relief when Selina said she wasn't going to share his bed.

But he couldn't bear the idea of spending his wedding night alone, without the woman he had dreamed about for five long months. A phantom woman who now only existed in his heart and his imagination. Grief barreled through him as the death of his dream came crashing in on him. Though he was exhausted, he dragged his weary body out of bed, threw on his pants and headed out onto the porch, where he leaned against one of the posts and stared up at the stars and the quarter moon.

Mosquitoes and gnats buzzed around his head. He waved them away as he watched the fading and returning lights of the stars dancing in the darkness above him.

Wind blew through the leaves of the trees and across

his face, whispering a mournful sound that reflected the sad state he now found himself in.

He had no idea how to deal with his swirl of feelings.

Minutes ticked by while Michael berated himself for placing that ad in the first place. For not going out to meet her. For falling in love with a fantasy. If he hadn't done that, then none of this would have happened. "Lord, I know I did this to myself, but what am I going to do about Selina? She's a woman who is the complete opposite of everything I ever dreamed of. Imagined. Prayed for. She's a woman—" He stopped and sighed.

Selina *was* a woman. That much was obvious when the blanket had fallen from her shoulders. Through her thin nightgown, he could see the outline of her womanly curves, curves that would be the envy of most women. Yet the way she dressed did nothing to show her femininity.

He sighed heavily and scratched his neck.

"Lord, You know I've been talking to You for eleven years, asking You for a woman like Rainee. Why would You send me someone like Selina? Why? Please, help me to understand."

He listened for that still, small voice, but the only sounds he heard were coyotes howling in the distance, frogs calling out into the darkness and an owl hooting somewhere off in the trees.

Selina stepped up to the door in time to hear Michael ask why God had sent him someone like her. Her heart broke knowing she was causing Michael so much pain and heartbreak. But there was nothing she could do about it. Still, it hurt something fierce that he didn't want her. Her dreams of them becoming truly hitched disappeared like smoke in the wind.

Careful not to make a sound, she backed away from the screen door and hightailed it back upstairs and into her bed. Not one normally given to crying, she buried her head into her pillow, soaking it with her tears. Something akin to bear claws tore at her heart, shredding it to pieces.

Being in love with a man who didn't love her back hurt something fierce. Living with him every day was going to be the hardest thing she'd ever come up against. "Lord, give me the grace I need to survive. And I'd be right beholden to You, iffen You'd ease this awful pain in my heart and in Michael's, too."

After a few hours of fitful sleep, Selina lit the lantern next to her bed and slid into her garments. She grabbed the lantern in one hand and her boots and stockings in the other and crept down the steps and into the kitchen.

Careful not to make any noise, she made her way down the cellar ladder and cut off a slab of bacon and fetched a couple of eggs before she commenced to fixing breakfast. Coffee, bacon, eggs and fresh flapjack scents made her stomach growl.

Selina stood in front of the dish cabinet. Back home, she had a handmade breadboard counter to hold her dishes. It sort of reminded her of this piece of furniture, but her breadboard counter had a flour bin and several drawers and it didn't have glass doors like this fancy piece did. Plus, hers was covered with oil cloth and this one had a shiny finish to it. Made her afraid to touch it, it was so fancy. But she didn't have any choice. Not if she wanted to serve Michael his breakfast.

She opened the door, pulled out a couple of plates

and froze at the sight of the dainty blue flowers and leaves. They were blue, not yellow, not pink and not any other color but blue.

Her favorite color.

Sure seemed like someone went to an awful lot of trouble to get dishes with blue in them. But, she sighed, they weren't meant for her. She set the table and then sat down with a hot cup of coffee. Bowing her head and closing her eyes, she clasped her hands together and said her morning prayers.

"Good morning, Selina."

Selina yanked her head upward to find Michael standing in front of her with a look of a man who didn't know what to do.

Bags sagged under his bloodshot eyes. His hair was all muffed up, and his clothes looked as if he'd slept in them.

"Did you sleep well?" *Jumpin' crickets, Selina. That was a stupid question. Anyone could see he ain't slept but a wink.*

His gaze slid over her face. "About as well as you, apparently."

Selina wished she had stopped in front of the looking glass before she came down. She had no idea what she looked like. Slowly raking a finger through her hair, she stood and put her back to him. Having him study her like that made her skittish. "Can I get you some coffee?" she asked, even though she had already grabbed him a cup and started to fill it.

"Yes, thank you. That would be nice."

"You just sit yourself down and I'll fetch ya some vittles."

Selina placed a plate with four pieces of bacon on it,

six biscuits and a small mound of scrambled eggs onto the center of the table.

He looked up at her. "Aren't you going to have any?"

Selina glanced at the food and frowned. "Yes, sir." Confused by his question, she lowered herself onto the chair.

Before she could ask more, Michael reached over and clasped her hand in his.

Her attention flew right to him. Warmth spread up her arms and into her body as she yanked her hand away. "Wha—whatcha doin'?"

"Getting ready to pray." His eyes softened.

"Oh." She nodded, feeling dumber than a fence post for asking. She slid her hand back across to his.

His eyes drifted shut.

She knew she ought to close her eyes and concentrate on his prayer but her mind took a turn in another direction. While he prayed, she studied his face, wondering if those full lips were as soft as they looked.

Strength flowed through his rough hand even though he held hers with the softest of touch. Having her hand in his felt right nice, a little too nice considering their circumstances.

Her eyes trailed up his arms. Arms with muscles that were so big they pulled at the seams of his shirt sleeves. What would it be like to have him slip them around her and pull her close? Would she ever be close enough to his heart to hear it beating?

Her attention slid up to his eyes. Heat barreled up her neck and her cheeks felt hotter than the red coals in the cook stove over yonder. Just when had Michael stopped praying and caught her stealing her fill of him?

She looked at their hands, jerked hers from his and

all but shoved the plate of food in front of him. "You—you'd best start eatin' before—before it gets cold."

Eating was the last thing Michael thought about doing right now. When he'd reached for Selina's hand, the instant he'd made the connection, warmth spread up his arm and slipped into his heart. He had no idea what that was all about nor did he want to know. Confused over what had just happened, he struggled to pull himself together so he could pray.

When he opened his eyes and saw Selina studying his arms and chest, saw the longing on her face, something stirred inside him. That foreign feeling made him vastly uncomfortable.

He rammed his fingers through his hair, but they snagged on some tangles. What had he been thinking coming to the breakfast table without combing his hair first? Even when he lived alone, he groomed himself before sitting down to eat. This whole situation had him so upset and confused he was no longer thinking or acting rationally.

To get his mind off the situation, he looked at the paltry plate of food she had placed on the table. Selina said she hadn't eaten yet. If they shared what little food was there, that amount wouldn't hold him long at all. He normally required twice as much as that just to make it until lunchtime.

He didn't understand why, when he had a cellar full of food, she had made so little. His gaze snagged on the numerous patches scattered on her sleeves. Obviously, Selina had come from poverty. Could that be why she had made so little breakfast? Because that was all she had been able to fix back home?

If that was the case, he didn't know what to do or how to handle the situation with delicacy. How could he let her know that it was okay to fix plenty here without hurting her feelings or acting like some rich boy throwing his wealth around?

Michael sighed inwardly. He silently prayed and asked God for wisdom concerning this situation. No answer came immediately, so in the meantime, he made do. He piled half of the eggs, three small biscuits and two pieces of bacon on his plate, then he moved the plate in front of her.

"Somethin' wrong with my cookin'?" She glanced at the center plate and then at his.

"I don't know. I haven't tried anything yet. But everything looks and smells real good. Why do you ask?"

"'Cause you only took half of what I fixed."

"Didn't you tell me you hadn't eaten yet?"

"Yeah. So?"

"Well, that's why I only took half."

Her forehead wrinkled, and her brown eyes narrowed.

Michael had no idea why she appeared so confused. Women. Who could figure out what they were thinking? No man, that's for sure.

He picked up his fork, scooped up a mound of eggs and shoved them into his mouth. Flavor, unlike any he had ever tasted before, burst through his mouth. "Umm. These are delicious, Selina. What did you do to them?" He spoke around the eggs, then gathered up another rounded forkful.

She smiled. "Fried them in butter and bacon fat. And added the tops of those things I found down yonder."

She pointed to the cellar. "They looked like the ramps back home, so I took a chance."

"What's a ramp?"

"An onion or a leek," she said as she added one piece of bacon, one biscuit and a small spoonful of the scrambled eggs onto her plate. "Come springtime, you can find them all over the Appalachian Mountains."

"I see. I'm sure it's beautiful there."

"Sure is." Her face brightened. The woman was definitely easy on the eyes.

"Do you miss home?"

Selina shrugged. "Don't know. Can't rightly say. I ain't been gone long enough to tell." With only a few bites, Selina finished her meager portion, hoping Michael had gotten enough.

"Have some more." Michael pushed the rest of the servings toward her.

"Thank you kindly, but I'm done," she said even though her stomach was pinched with hunger pain and wasn't near full enough. Then again, it never had been before. Now should be no different.

His eyes, soft and questioning, held hers as strong as a foot stuck in a mud hole. "Are you sure?"

Selina had made the decision, and she wasn't backing out now. "Yeah. I'm sure."

Michael's attention stayed on her face a spell before he heaped the rest of the food onto his plate and devoured it within minutes. He looked over at the stove with something akin to longing in his eyes before he averted his attention onto his coffee cup.

"Somethin' wrong?"

"Well, I was just wondering something. Before I

took the rest of the food you said I only took half of what you'd made. Does that include biscuits, too?"

"Yeah. I wasn't sure how many to make. I wanted to stretch the food so we'd have plenty to eat. I'm sorry iffen I didn't make enough." She looked down at her hands, fiddling with the patch on her pants leg. She'd wanted to be such a good wife, and already she felt the pain of his disappointment.

Michael's finger rested under her chin, tugging it upward. "Selina, look at me." With the gentlest touch, he raised her head, forcing her to look at him, even though she wanted to look everywhere but at him for fear he would see the love she had for him in her eyes.

"I'm a big eater. I want you to know that we have more than enough food. So you can make plenty all the time. And…"

She watched him swallow and draw a breath.

"I want you to eat more, too. What you ate this morning wouldn't keep a baby chick alive."

She pulled her eyes away from his intense stare. It hurt to be so close to him, to feel he might care and yet know he didn't.

His finger dropped from her chin and rested in front her.

She wanted to snatch back his hand and cradle it against her cheek.

To hold it.

To feel its strength.

To enjoy the small pleasures a married woman like her ma had enjoyed.

But that would likely never happen, except in her dreams. And dream she would. No one could steal them from her. So when her head hit the pillow tonight, she'd dream of holding his hand.

Of him wrapping his arms about her and kissing her.

But until then, he was waiting for her answer. "Don't rightly know iffen I'd be able to. Food was mighty scarce back home. Always made sure my brothers and Pa had enough to eat first. Then I ate what was left. Which was never much. So, I'm used to not eatin' much. Even with you sayin' we have plenty, I still can't help but be scared that iffen I do eat too much more we might not have enough come winter time."

His eyes trailed over her face, her arms and her body. Well, what he could see of it with her sitting in a chair. Still, his studying her like that made her uncomfortable.

His attention ended on her eyes, and if she weren't mistaken, pity filled his. And she didn't like it. Not one little bit. She didn't want him feeling sorry for her and she'd let him know that. But before she had a chance to tell him so, he hitched his chair back and headed to the pantry.

When he came back he had a copper container with him, sat the thing down in front of her and raised the lid. He reached inside the jar and pulled out a handful of cookies and laid them on her plate and his.

He filled their coffee cups, something she should have thought to do, and then sat down. "Eat," he ordered with a smile. His face turned serious as he looked at her. "I don't want you ever worrying about food again, okay, Selina? We have ten dairy cows, a large herd of cattle and hogs, and plenty of chickens and eggs. We grow our own wheat so flour isn't a shortage, either. Plus, Mother, my sisters, and sisters-in-law all grow large gardens every year. And if something happens to any of the food or gardens, we can go to town and buy some. If worse comes to worst, we'll have it shipped in by train if necessary. Money is not an object."

Selina didn't know what to think. She'd never had such a mess of food before. She glanced at her plate and stared at the sandwiched cookies with the preserves in the middle. They looked mighty good and mighty tempting, too. Putting her fears aside, she decided that for once in her life her belly would take its fill.

Michael took a bite of one of his mother's syltkakor cookies. He thought about Selina not having enough to eat and how she had given her food to her brothers and her father first and then to some stranger on the train. A woman she'd just met. The very idea of that stirred something deep inside him. He wanted to provide for her and protect her from ever going hungry again.

As she continued to enjoy her cookie Michael used the opportunity to study her. Dark-brown eyelashes, long and full, almost touched the top of her high cheekbones. Her nose had a slight bump in the middle, and her lips were pink, with a few cookie crumbs sprinkled on them.

He reached over to wipe them off. The moment his thumb made contact with her lips, her eyes flew open and she jumped back. "What ya doin'?"

"You had crumbs on your lips." He flashed her a sheepish smile. "I was just wiping them off for you."

She swiped her mouth with her hands and then with her sleeve. With one eye slit, she tilted to the side. "Much obliged, I'm sure." She sat as far back into her kitchen chair as possible as if to get away from him.

"What kind a cookies are them anyways? They sure are good."

"They're syltkakors."

"Silt a whats?"

"Swedish sandwich cookies."

"Oh." That was all she said before taking another bite.

Watching her enjoy every morsel made him realize just how much he had taken for granted. He had always had plenty to eat, a roof over his head and an abundance of clothes. Never had he lacked for anything. But Selina had. And yet she didn't seem bitter, nor did she complain about her lack. He wondered just how many times in her life she had gone without so another would not. Knowing how poor she was, he was surprised by her generosity. And if he was willing to admit it even to himself, that generosity endeared her to him. Just how he felt about that, he wasn't sure. But he was sure about one thing. He would definitely find out. That thought both frightened and intrigued him.

Chapter Four

Five cookies later, Selina laid her hand against her gut. This was the first time she'd had a belly full of anything and it felt mighty nice. And scary. Her fears of running out of food stuck to her like caked-on mud. Would she ever get over that fear even after all Michael had said about having plenty?

Michael's eyes trailed to her mouth. Last time he'd touched her lips her belly and heart fluttered as if someone had released a thousand fireflies into them. So before he could brush the crumbs from off her lips again, she hurried up and did it herself.

"Well, I'd better go." He stood. "Thank you for breakfast, Selina." He headed to the front door and put on his jacket and hat.

Knowing he was heading out to do chores, she swigged down the last of her coffee and rushed to where he stood. She pushed her arms into her jacket and shoved her hat onto her head.

With his hand on the doorknob, Michael asked, "Where are you going?" He glanced at the breakfast mess on the table and stove.

"I'm goin' to help you with chores."

"Selina, we've been over this already. I know you want to help and I appreciate it, but it would help me a great deal for you to keep the house clean and have meals ready for me when I come in."

"I can do both. After I help you with the chores, I'll come back here and clean up this mess and get lunch ready for ya, too."

Michael rolled his eyes, swung the door open and stepped outside. His boots clunked on the steps as he tromped down them. That noise was meant to discourage her, but it wasn't going to work. Regardless of what he'd said about her being his wife and not having to earn her keep, she didn't want to be beholden to anyone, especially a man who didn't want her. She'd feel differently if Michael did want her, if he loved her, but he didn't. So, to her way of thinking that meant she was nothing more than a hired hand and a maid.

Selina struggled to stay alongside Michael, even though he paid her no mind. They rounded the bend that hid their house from the rest of the houses, into the main yard where the party had been the night before, and ended up at the barn.

Horses whinnied when they stepped inside. She breathed deeply the scent of horse and fresh-cut hay. Dust twirled in the sunlight and danced its way up her nose, tickling it. She sneezed loud and hard, not once but twice.

The horses snorted.

Michael whirled toward her.

"You sure you didn't blow your insides out, woman? Those are the loudest sneezes I've ever heard. Who would have thought something that noisy could come from someone as tiny as you."

She giggled. "Pa always told me I had the loudest sneezes ever. Said he never had to worry about my whereabouts 'cause my sneezes could be heard all over the mountain. And as long as he heard them, he knew right where I was at."

"I believe it." Michael chuckled.

She looked over at him. That was the first time she'd heard him laugh and she found it mighty pleasant. Something she could get used to.

She even got a glimpse of a little dip near one side of his mouth. Something she'd always been a sucker for.

Michael turned his back to her. He grabbed a pitchfork off of a nearby hook, rammed the fork into a mound of hay under the loft and tossed it into the first stall.

"I'm glad I caught you."

Selina twisted toward the voice and saw Abby.

"Mother saw you heading into the barn, Selina. She asked me to see if you would like to stop by this morning." Abby was a beautiful girl with her blond hair and blue eyes. She looked a lot like her handsome brother.

"That's mighty nice of her, but will you tell her I'm gonna help Michael with chores first, and that I'll stop by sometime today?"

"Sure will." Abby skittered off.

"You don't have to do chores. You can go visit with my mother."

"We done had this discussion. After chores I will." Selina searched for another hay fork and saw one hanging on a peg near the haystack. She filled it with hay and carried it to one of the stalls. The pretty chestnut mare with the white forehead and spotted rump dipped her head and swung it back and forth before diving into the pile.

"That's Macy's way of saying thanks," Michael spoke over Selina's shoulder.

"She sure is purty. Is she yours?" She tilted her head back so she could see his face.

He looked down at her and she forgot all about breathing.

He stared into Selina's eyes. He couldn't pull his attention away from them and the long lashes that framed them. Her irises were large, surrounded by a black ring. Their color was nothing like the solid brown he'd thought they were when he'd first met her. Instead they resembled a reddish-brown sorrel horse he once had.

All of a sudden she ripped her gaze away from him and onto something behind him.

"Why, hello there." Selina scurried over to Miss Piggy and scooped the gray-and-white barn cat into her arms. "Aren't you the purtiest little thing ever?" She stroked the feline's fur and stopped, then examined her hand. "Oh, no. You're bleedin'. You poor baby. Selina'll take care of you and make it all better."

Her words were long and drawn out in the same type of Southern drawl Rainee had. He had loved listening to Rainee talk and he had to admit, he enjoyed the Southern accent in Selina, too. And that surprised him.

Selina helped Michael feed and water the animals then gathered up Miss Piggy and headed for home. Did she really think of the Idaho Territory as her home? Not yet, but hopefully someday she would. Inside the house, she searched everywhere until she found what she needed. When she finished doctoring the cat, she placed the exhausted critter on Michael's bed and headed back into the kitchen.

With one glance at the breakfast mess, she rolled up her sleeves and washed the dishes and set things to right. Michael would have the chores done by now, so she decided to go visit Katherine. She stepped out onto the porch and stopped.

"Good morning, Selina." The very pregnant Rainee stood only a few yards away from her. Other than her belly, she was a tiny thing. Beautiful, too, with her honey-colored hair and matching eyes.

"Mornin', Rainee."

"I brought you some bread and cookies."

"Well, that's right neighborly of you." Selina rushed down the steps and took the basket from Rainee. "You didn't need to do that."

"I know. I wanted to." Rainee smiled.

"Can you come in and sit a spell?"

"I would love to."

As they made their way into the house, Selina said, "Would you like some tea or coffee?"

"Tea would be lovely. Thank you."

"Why don't you take a load off while I fetch ya some?"

"If you do not mind, I believe I shall." Rainee sat down while Selina commenced to making tea.

"Who would have ever thought having a baby would take so much out of a person?" Rainee spoke from the living room.

"Is this your first?"

"No. I have a nine-year-old daughter, Emilia, who we

call Emily, and a seven-year-old daughter, Rosella, who we call Rosie. They are visiting their grandmother."

"When's your baby due?" Selina asked as she came into the living room.

"In a few weeks." Concern skipped across the woman's face. "I hope and pray this baby survives."

Startled, Selina handed her a cup of tea and a small plate with a couple of cookies on the side, then sat down across from her. "What do ya mean?"

"In the eleven years Haydon and I have been married, I have been with child five times. The girls came along just fine, but after them, I lost the next two." Sadness filled her eyes.

Selina laid her hand on Rainee's. "I'm so sorry to hear that. Do you know why they didn't make it?"

"No. And neither did Doctor Berg." She took a sip of her tea. "Since I am being so honest with you I will also tell you I am quite scared to have this one. When Rosie was born, she almost did not make it."

"How come?" Selina hoped Rainee didn't mind her asking so many questions.

"I do not know. Haydon would never tell me. He did not want me worrying."

"I see. Well, don't you be worrin' none about this baby. I can help. I've birthed many a youngin'. Even troublesome ones. You just let me know when your time comes and I'll be there. Iffen you want me to, that is."

Rainee's eyes, the color of a fawn, brightened. "I would love to have you there. Thank you, Selina. I must admit, when I heard you telling our neighbors that you helped many a child into the world, I was quite relieved. Doctor Berg is our local doctor, but he is always so busy that I feared he would not be available when my time came."

"Well, I'll be here. You just let me know."

They sipped their tea, ate their cookies and visited as if they were old friends.

Rainee glanced at the clock. "Where did the time go? I have bread to bake and desserts to make to get lunch ready for Haydon and my girls."

She rose and put her tea cup and empty plate in the sink. "Thank you, Selina. I had a lovely time."

"I did, too. Come back again anytime."

Rainee grabbed Selina's hands. "You must come see me, too. I get quite bored sitting all day. Haydon will not let me do anything. I had to beg him to let me help with the cooking and care for my girls."

Selina's eyes widened. "What do ya mean, he won't *let* you?"

"Can you believe he hired me a maid?" Rainee rolled her eyes and sighed. "I sent her packing straightaway. But my husband brought her right back. I feel quite ill at ease with a maid. No one else has one and they have survived and I can, as well. But Haydon would hear nothing of it, so we finally came to an understanding. She could stay, but I would be allowed to help her some."

"Why'd ya let him tell you what you could or couldn't do?"

"Oh, I assure you, I do not. I just let him think he does." Rainee winked.

Selina smiled. "I knew I liked you." In the very next second a plan worked through Selina's mind. "Rainee, could I ask you somethin'?"

"Yes, you may."

"Do you think…" Selina looked down at the floor. "Do you think you could…" She pulled in her bottom lip and chewed on it. This was a might harder than she'd thought it would be.

"Selina, do not make yourself uneasy. Just ask."

Selina slowly raised her head. Seeing the sincerity in Rainee's eyes, she plucked up her courage. "I was wonderin' iffen you could teach me to talk good. And to read and to write. Iffen you have the time, that is."

"Sure I have time. But I see nothing wrong with the way you talk. I rather like it. Why do you want to change?"

"I have my reasons." Never before had she wanted to change for anyone, but now that she was married to Michael and loved him, she wanted to make him proud. If somehow she could do that, maybe he would come to love her, too.

"Please forgive me for asking, but if you cannot read nor write, how did you answer Michael's advertisement?"

"My friend Aimee did it for me." Boy did she ever. Selina still couldn't believe what Aimee had done to her and Michael. She had thought Aimee was different than the rest of those rich folks. Turned out she was just like them after all.

"I see."

No, she didn't see, but Selina didn't want to talk about that.

"I would be happy to help you. If you want to, come by after lunch, and we will start then."

"I'll be there." Selina walked her visitor to the door. "Thank you kindly, Rainee. That's mighty nice of you."

"You are most welcome. I am looking forward to it."

"Iffen you don't mind, I'll walk with you. Katherine invited me for a visit."

"I do not mind at all. I would love it."

They headed down the stairs. Rainee looped arms with Selina as they disappeared down the path in the trees.

In two shakes of a squirrel's tail, Selina climbed the steps to Michael's ma's house. Her ma now, too. That put a smile on her face. She raised her hand to knock on the door just before it swung open.

"Selina, I'm so happy you came. Please, come on in." For having money, everyone around here was sure friendly. Maybe Michael was right. She shouldn't clump all rich folks together.

Katherine stepped back and motioned Selina inside.

Two girls stood next to the kitchen table staring at her.

"Girls, stop that staring."

"Sorry, Grandmother," they both said.

The taller girl had blue eyes and blond hair and looked just like her pa. The shortest one had doe-colored hair and eyes like her ma. She glanced up at Selina. "You sure are pretty."

Selina squatted down to her eye level and smiled. "So are you. Anyone ever tell you ya look just like your mama?"

She tilted her head and lowered her eyelids. "Yes, ma'am, they have. Thank you."

Selina rose and turned her attention to the older one. "You look like your papa. And you're every bit as purty as your sister."

"Thank you." Her face brightened like the morning sun.

Katherine went and stood between the girls and faced Selina. "Selina, this is my granddaughter Emily." The oldest one squatted and rose. "And this one is Rosie."

The younger girl squatted like the older had. Selina wondered what that was all about.

"Nice to meet y'all."

"Nice to meet you, too," Emily said. Her sister repeated it.

"Okay, girls. Why don't you go back to working on your quilts now."

As the girls headed into the living room, Katherine asked, "Can I get you something to drink?"

"No, ma'am. But thank you anyway."

"Very well. Let's head to the living room where we can get comfortable."

Selina followed Katherine and sat down in one of the chairs.

"Don't mind the mess. I'm keeping the girls occupied by teaching them how to quilt."

Selina looked down at the girls sitting on the floor and the squares of material between them.

"I've never made a quilt before. Always wanted to learn, though."

"How come you didn't?" Rosie asked.

"My ma took sick when I was a youngin, and she died when I was ten, so I never got a chance."

"We'll teach you." Emily looked up at her grandma. "Won't we, Grandmother?"

"We sure will." Katherine smiled at Selina.

"Really? You'd do that?"

"Sure will. In fact," Katherine rose, "I'll be right back." She left the room.

"Are you making quilts for your beds?" Selina asked the girls.

"No, we're making them for our dollies," Rosie, the bubbly one of the two answered.

"What color you gonna make them?"

"Mine's going to be pink and yellow." Rosie puffed out her little chest.

"I'm making mine in two different shades of blue." Emily picked up the squares and showed them to Selina.

"Blue is my favorite color." Selina ran her fingers over the dark and light blue squares.

"I could make mine blue, too." The sad look on Rosie's face made Selina wonder what that was all about until she realized she'd made a big to-do over blue and Rosie's was pink.

Selina placed herself in a circle on the floor with them and looked at Rosie. "Rosie, I like pink and yellow right fine, too. Purple, orange, red—you name it and I like it. So don't you be changin' your mind 'cause someone else likes somethin' different. You just be yourself because the good Lord made you just the way you are. Perfect and just right."

With a big smile Rosie picked up the pink and yellow squares and got right back to work on her quilt.

Sitting with the girls, watching their faces, settled a longing deep inside her to have children of her own.

Katherine came into the room, carrying tied stacks of squared material. Selina leaped up and took part of them from her.

Her mother-in-law set her stack down. "Here you go, Selina. Take your pick of colors."

"Thank you kindly, Katherine."

"Please, I'd be honored if you would call me Mother."

Selina smiled. "I'd be right honored, too… Mother." It felt strange being all formal and calling her mother, but no one else called Katherine Ma, and neither would she. Selina whipped her attention away from Katherine so she wouldn't see the tears building in her eyes. No one could take her ma's place, but it felt nice to have a ma again.

She studied the stacks of squares. Each one had a different pattern. They were all so pretty, and not wanting to make the girls feel badly by choosing blue, she asked, "What's Michael's favorite color?"

"He doesn't have one. Says he likes them all," Katherine answered.

That made it easy. Selina chose a variety of colors. Then, Katherine, with the help of the girls, showed Selina how to sew the blocks together, something called piecing. Having Katherine show her how to do this made her miss her mama. Well, she wouldn't think about that now. She'd just enjoy her time with the girls and Katherine.

Two hours later, Selina excused herself so she could hurry home and fix lunch for Michael. She flew around the kitchen fixing lunch and had just finished when Michael came in the door holding his arm, blood staining his shirt sleeve and handkerchief. Selina's attention shot to him. She tossed the dish towel onto the table and bolted toward him. "Michael! What happened?"

Michael's arm throbbed. "I snagged it on a nail." Now he wished he would have gone ahead and fixed that stupid nail sticking out of the fence yesterday, but no, he'd been so excited about picking up his bride, he had forgotten all about it. Seemed he'd been doing a lot of things he regretted lately.

"Well, let me take a look at it." She unwrapped the blood-soaked handkerchief from around his arm. "This thing sure is deep. You're gonna need stitches. Got any thread and a needle?"

Needle and thread? You've got to be kidding. He yanked his arm back to his chest. No way would he let someone other than a doctor sew him up. "Yes. But I just dropped by to grab a bite and to let you know that I was heading into town to have Doc Berg take a look at it."

"Ain't no need to bother the doctor when I can take care of it for you."

Of course she could. "I'm sure you can, but after lunch I'll head into town just the same. Thank you."

Selina planted her hands on her small waist. "Nonsense. I been sewin' up cuts for as long as I can remember. I'm good at it, too. Fetch me that thread and needle or I'll find it myself. Got any clean rags? And some moonshine?"

"Moonshine? What's that?"

"Homemade corn liquor."

"The only alcohol I have is some whiskey for medicinal purposes."

"That'll work just fine. Fetch it, too."

"Bossy," he murmured under his breath as he headed to do her bidding.

"I heard that."

"Good." He grabbed the whiskey from the pantry and the needle and thread he used to sew up his tack.

He watched her burn the end of the needle with a match then pour whiskey over it. Using warm water, she sloshed a clean rag around the water then irrigated his wound by squeezing the water out of the rag. Gently, she dabbed the excess water and dirt from the laceration. He had to admit she was doing a nice job. She held a clean rag under his arm, tilted the whiskey jug above it and poured it into his cut.

"Ahhhh!" He yanked his arm from her. Whiskey ran onto his pant leg. "What did you do that for?"

"To kill any germs that might be in it."

"That stuff stings." The strong smell of whiskey singed his nose and made his eyes water.

"Oh, you big baby. Come here." She clasped his hand, raised it and started blowing on his cut, cooling the pain.

The contact did funny things to his insides and made him forget all about the stinging.

He stared at her, unable to peel his attention away from her beautiful face and puckered lips. What would it be like to caress those shapely lips with his own? Would they be warm or cool to the touch? Realizing where his thoughts were taking him, he yanked his focus and his mind back to reality. "Aren't you adding germs to it by blowing on it?"

"Oh, for pity's sake." She grabbed the whiskey jug and placed another clean rag under his arm and poured even more alcohol onto the wound. "There. Iffen any of my germs got in there, they're dead now. You happy?"

"No. It hurts. If I would have gone to the doctor, it wouldn't have hurt as much."

"Well, iffen you think that hurt, then you'd best be for backing up your horses, cowboy, and bear down on this." She all but shoved a piece of wood between his teeth and in the next breath she poked the needle through his skin.

He wanted to yell out in pain. Never was he one to handle needles very well. He bit into the wood, almost breaking it in half. What he really wanted to do was jump up and head straight into town to Doc Berg's office.

Pressure applied on his arm took his mind off of the needle. Minutes later, after a few more quick pokes and knots, she announced she was finished. While she made a bandage for it, he studied her work and found her stitches to be as good as any doctor's. Michael had to admit, he was impressed.

She bandaged his arm. "There. All done. Now that wasn't so bad, was it?"

"I hate to admit it, but no. It wasn't too bad. The alcohol was the worst part." He looked up at her and smiled. "Thank you, Selina."

"You're welcome. Now, let me get you some vittles." She put away the supplies she'd used and then set food on the table.

He smiled. This time she'd made plenty. After eating a big lunch, although there were still plenty of chores that needed tending to, having had very little sleep the night before, Michael decided to take a short nap to refresh himself. "Selina, I'm going to take a nap. Can you wake me up in about fifteen minutes?"

Her cheeks turned pink. He wondered what that was all about, but all she did was nod.

He stepped into his room and stopped. Sprawled across his pillows was Miss Piggy, the barn cat. "What are you doing in here, Miss Piggy?"

The cat raised her head, gazed at him a mere second, then laid her head back down.

"She needed a place to sleep," Selina said from behind him.

"There's a barn for that, you know. Animals do not belong in the house."

"This one does."

"No, she doesn't." He strode over to where Miss Piggy lay and stooped to pick her up. But before he had a chance to reach the cat, Selina grabbed his hand on his good arm, surprising him with how strong a grip she had for such a tiny woman.

"Don't you be disruptin' her. She needs to sleep so that cut can heal."

He stood to his full height, crossed his arms over his chest and spread his legs. "This is my bed, Selina, and I won't have animals sleeping on it or anywhere near it. Do I make myself clear?"

"Sure do. But you're forgettin' one thing. This here's my home now, too. You said so."

He did and it was. But there was no way he was allowing animals into his…their…house. He had worked his backside off to provide his wife with nice furniture and he'd be hanged if he'd let some animal that spent all day down at the barn rolling in only who knows what, come in and soil everything he'd worked so hard for. "That's true, but as your husband, I am the head of this house and what I say goes." He sounded like a bully even to his own ears, but he didn't know what else to say to keep Selina from bringing any more animals into the house.

"You may be the head over this house, but I ain't

never let a man boss me around or tell me what to do and I ain't aimin' to start now."

He had only himself to blame for not going to Kentucky and meeting Selina before getting married. Now he was stuck with the consequences of a headstrong woman. If he wasn't so frustrated over the whole mess, he would laugh. She couldn't be more than five-foot-three inches tall, yet here she stood, mere inches from him, glaring up at him and daring him to refute her.

And refute her he would. "That cat better be out of here by the time I get home, or I'll put her out myself." He whirled, changed his torn, bloody shirt, then stormed out of the house.

Chapter Five

The next morning, Michael was already gone when Selina woke up. The cookie jar sat on the table along with an empty milk glass. Selina wondered why he didn't wait for her. Surely he wasn't still upset with her. Yesterday, whenever the cat had woken from her nap and wanted outside, Selina had obliged her. So the animal wasn't in the house when Michael got home. Maybe she'd gotten up too late. She walked to the window and peeked outside. The sun wasn't even up yet and neither were the roosters, it was so early.

It bugged her that he hadn't woken her up to fix him some breakfast. Maybe with his arm hurt he wanted to get an early start, knowing it would take longer. Who knew. Either way, Selina wanted to help her husband with whatever chores needed to be done.

She grabbed a biscuit and gulped it down before heading out to the barn. Inside the barn, she found a lantern and lit it. Once the horses were fed and watered, the barn was mucked clean and the lantern was snuffed, she stepped outside just in time to watch the sunrise.

A long yellow streak outlined in orange rose above

the mountain. Shadowed puffs of clouds dotted the blue sky. "Mighty fine job Ya done there, Lord. Sure is purty." She watched it for a few more minutes, then turned toward the outbuildings in search of Michael.

Little things around her snagged her attention, though, and she forgot all about looking for Michael. God's creation was something to behold. She wandered around the ranch yard, stopping often to enjoy the good Lord's many pleasures. Like the smell of sweet apples filling the fresh air. Dew drops sparkling on the leaves of bushes, birds singing their morning song, squirrels chattering, probably telling something or someone that they were in their territory or taking their food. Yellow, fluffy baby chicks peeped, and chickens pecked away at the feed she'd just tossed them.

Time passed until she realized the sun had fully risen and had driven the morning chill from her body.

Standing near the woodshed, she turned when she heard footsteps brushing the grasses.

Leah came bustling toward her. "Hi, Selina. I've been looking all over for you. Michael asked me to take you into town to buy some material and some new boots. It sounds like so much fun, and I'm looking so forward to getting to know you better," the young woman said excitedly.

Selina looked down where Leah had linked arms with her as if they were old friends. To her delight, so far, everyone here was friendly. Made her feel welcome. She smiled at the pretty young lady whose blond hair shone like a halo. Field flowers surrounded the air about her. "You sure smell nice."

"Thank you." Leah smiled.

"Where is Michael anyways?" She allowed Leah

to lead her toward the barn. Leah's skirt swished as she walked.

"He's out doctoring and checking the cows."

"Maybe I should go help him. Can you show me what direction he went?"

Leah's voice and face fell. "He went up north. I could show you, but I was so looking forward to taking you shopping."

Selina could tell how much it meant to her, and she didn't want to disappoint Leah. "I can help him another day."

"Are you sure?" Her face lit up.

"I'm sure." Selina wanted to earn her keep, but Michael had asked his sister, her sister now, too, to take her, so she reckoned it was okay.

"Oh, goody. Let's go, then. I have the buggy all hitched and ready."

Leah led Selina to a fancy buggy with a half top. A black horse with a spotted rump was hitched to it. "That's a right purty horse. Ain't never seen horses like the ones y'all have before."

"They're palouse ponies. They are beautiful, aren't they?"

"Sure are."

They climbed into the buggy. Leah picked up the reins and gave the horse a light slap on the rump. "Giddyup, Lambie."

Lambie? As in lamb, the animal? That was a mighty strange name for a horse.

Hooves clip-clopped on the hard ground, and tack rattled like chains as they headed down the road toward town.

"You're going to love Marcel Mercantile. They have a nice selection of fabrics and shoes."

Selina was sure she would. She hadn't ever spent much time in a store before. No need to. Never had any money to buy anything. *Jumpin' crickets.* How was she going to pay for the material and shoes? Michael had to know she didn't have any money. Well, she wouldn't fret about that now. She'd wait until she got to the store, then she'd know what to do or what not to do.

"Michael said to tell you he set up an account for you to get whatever you wanted or needed and not to worry about how much it cost. Wasn't that sweet of him?"

Shock ran through her. "Sure is."

About a quarter mile up the road from the ranch, Selina spotted a large herd of cows on one side of the road and a large herd of pigs on the other. Michael and three other men were riding through the cows. She twisted in her seat, longing to join him, but that wasn't going to happen today. She was on her way into town to get new shoes and material to make new clothes.

Things she'd never had before.

Her and her brothers' clothes were made from other folk's hand-me-downs, and they never could afford new shoes. New shoes. Something she needed desperately. The ones on her feet were worn thinner than a moth's wings and about as fragile, too.

Up the road a ways, about two miles, she noticed a sawmill in the trees with several large stacks of wood and logs. And even farther up the road was a field filled with red poppies. "Can we stop a minute?"

Leah looked at her with surprise. "Um. Sure. Whoa, Lambie." She pulled the reins and the buggy came to a stop.

Selina hopped down and ran over to the red poppies. She stooped to take a look at them.

A few minutes later, Leah came up behind her.

"Ain't these purty? The edges of the petals look like the wrinkled skin of an old person. Just as beautiful, too." A bee buzzed around her, landing in the black center of the flower beside her. She watched, amazed at God's creation and how the bee's wings kept that little varmint in one spot while it worked on that flower. Selina turned to say something about it to Leah, but she was back in the buggy.

Selina gently held a flower in her hand and leaned over, breathing in deeply. Sweet honey was the only way to describe the wonderful scent. Not wanting to keep Leah any longer, she made her way back to the wagon, running her fingers lightly over a few of the petals along the way.

She climbed into the buggy. "Sorry to keep you waitin'."

"You weren't keeping me waiting. I hurried back here because I'm scared to death of bees."

"How come?"

"Well, one time, I got stung by a whole bunch of them all at once. Since then I've been deathly afraid of them."

"That's too bad. They're right pleasurable to watch."

"I'll just have to take your word for it." Leah laughed and Selina joined her.

The buggy shifted as it moved forward.

"Them poppies sure were purty." She looked around. "This place is a lot different from back home."

"You're from Kentucky, right?"

"Yes."

"Think you'll like living out here?"

"I reckon I will well enough."

"Were you scared to move so far from home? To marry a complete stranger?"

"Well, I never felt I was marryin' a stranger. Me and Michael had written so much, I felt as iffen I knew him already." She wouldn't tell Leah that things had gotten messed up in that area. She'd keep that information to herself.

"I'm thinking about placing an advertisement in some of the larger newspapers back east," Leah said, keeping her eyes straight ahead.

That shocked Selina. "Why would a purty gal like you need to place an ad?"

"Same reason as you." Leah smiled. "I'm looking for a nice man to marry. I'm not getting any younger."

"How old are ya?"

"Twenty-three. I'll be twenty-four in December. If you don't mind me asking, how old are you, Selina?"

"Just turned twenty-five." She shifted in her seat. "I know it ain't none a my business, but I was told there ain't many women out here even with the comin' of the train. So why would someone as purty and sweet as you have to place an ad? Ain't none of the men here tickled your fancy?"

"There's a few good men who have 'tickled my fancy,' as you say. But, I don't want to stay here. I want to move back to New York to live in the big city again. Years ago, when my father announced that he wanted to leave New York and move out west to the Idaho Territory, I asked Mother why. She said Father had an adventurous spirit. I can relate. I do, too. Just not for this place. The winters are just too long here and I really don't like living on a ranch." Leah sighed. "Even though I was young when we moved, I still remember wearing party dresses and going to balls. I know it sounds silly, but I want to do that again."

"Ain't never been to a ball myself before."

"Oh, you would love it." Leah brightened.

Selina glanced down at her dust-covered and patched clothes.

Leah's eyes followed.

"Don't reckon I'd fit in at a ball." Selina giggled. So did Leah.

"No, probably not. But you sure fit in with our family. Everybody already loves you."

Everybody except my husband.

"Are you sorry you came, Selina?"

"No. Not really."

"I can't wait to place an ad for a husband." The young woman's face brightened at the prospect of the dream.

Hope things work out better for her than they have for me. "Does your family know how ya feel?"

"No. I've been trying to figure out how to break it to them." The dream drained from Leah's eyes. Selina knew just exactly how the girl felt.

"Well, make sure you pray about it first, Leah. Things don't always turn out the way a person thinks they should." Realizing what she said, she quickly looked away and added, "Sure are a lot of wheat fields out here."

Leah looked at her, then at the wheat fields. "There sure are. Selina, what did you mean when you said things don't always turn out the way a person thinks they should?"

Ah, puppy's feet. She was hoping she'd leave that comment alone. Maybe she should tell Leah the truth so she wouldn't make the same mistake she had.

"Just make sure you meet the man you plan on marryin' in person first. That you spend time with him and get to know him real good. A person can only learn so much about someone from letters. The real thing might be a huge shock and a disappointment. Can be mighty hurtful."

"Is Michael different than what you were expecting?"

"No. I am."

Leah's brows rose, then creased with worry. Questions lingered in her eyes, but thank the good Lord she didn't ask them. How could she ever explain what she herself didn't understand?

Selina turned her face the other direction from Leah. They rode the rest of the short way in silence.

When they pulled into town, people gawked at Selina, whispering behind their hands. She didn't pay them any mind, though.

Leah reined the horse in front of a large building with a sign. They hopped down and stepped onto the boardwalk.

"Disgraceful. That's what it is. Disgraceful." A woman eyed Selina up and down, frowning.

"Good morning, Ethel. I'd like to present to you my sister-in-law, Selina Bowen."

"This person is your sister-in-law?"

Leah raised her chin. "Yes, ma'am. She is. This is Michael's wife."

"Michael's?" The woman turned pale. "This is Michael's wife?"

"Yes, ma'am, she is. Now, if you will excuse us, we're here to get some material to make some new clothes for my new sister."

Ethel bobbed her head. Even though she'd said mean things about Selina, Selina looked for the beauty in her.

"You sure have a nice smile, ma'am. And your dress is right purty, too."

"I—I," she stuttered. "I do? It—it is?" The woman Leah called Ethel looked down at her dress.

"Yes, ma'am." Selina smiled at her and Ethel's lips slowly curled upward.

"Thank you." She dropped her head and all but crawled away.

Leah looped arms with Selina and leaned close. "That was nice of you to say such sweet things to Ethel. Whatever you do, don't let what Ethel said bother you. She's just embarrassed because she had gone around town telling everyone that her daughter, Marybeth, had won Michael's affection and that it was only a matter of time before they got married."

"Did he want to marry her?"

"No. She's only fourteen."

"Fourteen?" Selina said loudly, then quickly glanced around, hoping no one heard her.

Leah nodded and they both belted with laughter. When they finally stopped, they stepped inside the store. Selina knew her eyes were bulging, but she couldn't help herself. She'd never seen such a large selection of stuff before in her life.

Just looking at all the different colored bolts of fabrics alone had her mind swimming. She ran her fingers over each one, enjoying the feel of new material. It took her forever to decide on the colors she wanted.

"Michael told me to make sure you got plenty," Leah said beside her. "He figured you'd purchase barely enough to get by and he didn't want you to do that. He said to tell you that he wanted you to have fun and not to think about the money. To get whatever you wanted in the entire store. Knowing my brother like I do, if you don't come home with a bunch of stuff he'll be disappointed."

Selina didn't know how to feel about this whole thing. Didn't quite know how to act, either. Finally, she chose a mixture of muslin and cotton materials in blue, pink and yellow. And enough blue, brown and black denim to make several pairs of trousers not only for herself but Michael, too. She also picked out matching thread and a package of needles.

Leah looped arms with her and led her to the shoe section. She picked up a pair of black lace-up shoes with small heels. "How about these? These are darling."

Selina glanced down at her cowboy boots and then over at the shelf next to the women's shoes. "I'd rather have a pair of those." She picked up a brand-new pair of brown cowboy boots that looked to be her size. New leather filled the air. She looked around to make sure no one would see her. The lady at the counter was busy helping the only other customer in the store, so Selina slipped her boots off and tried the new ones on. They fit perfectly. Felt right nice, too. "I'll take these." She smiled at Leah.

They laid all of her purchases on the counter where the other customer had been.

"Hi, Mrs. Marcel."

"Good morning, Leah. How are you?"

"I'm doing great. How about you?"

"If I were any better, the Lord would have to take me home because I wouldn't be able to handle so much joy." She smiled and more lines filled her beautiful skin.

The gray-haired woman looked over at Selina. Selina waited for the usual look of disgust, but none came. Instead, the lady's lips curled upward into a warm, welcoming smile as she extended her wrinkled hand toward Selina. "I'm Bertie. Bertie Marcel. And you are?"

Selina took her hand and shook it gently. "Selina Bowen, ma'am."

"Bowen?" Her gray brows rose. She looked over at Leah then back at Selina.

"This is my new sister-in-law, Mrs. Marcel. Michael's wife."

"Well, I'll be. That boy finally up and got married. About time. And to such a beauty, too. It's a pleasure to meet you, Selina. And please call me Bertie."

"Thank you kindly, ma'am. It's a pleasure to meet you, too." Selina had to fight back the tears burning the back of her eyes. These people here were sure different. Folks who owned the mercantile back home wouldn't even look at Selina, let alone be nice to her. The only thing they ever did was turn their noses down at her and ignore her as if she didn't exist. Money sure had a way of making people act un-Christian-like.

"Oh. Leah, some letters arrived for you yesterday. My, you sure have become popular lately." She chuckled. "I'll get them for you." Bertie went to a room with metal bars.

"Here, try this." Leah handed her a square piece of something brown.

"What is it?"

"Just try it. You'll love it." Leah bit into a piece and chewed slowly.

Selina turned the piece around in her hand and looked it over before taking a bite. Yum. Sweet and creamy. "What is this? It sure is mighty tasty."

"Chocolate."

"Ain't never heard of it before."

Leah offered her some more, but Selina didn't want to be greedy so she turned down the offer even though she sure did want another piece. She liked chocolate a whole lot.

Bertie returned and handed Leah a stack of letters held together with a string. Seeing all those letters reminded her of Michael and the stack he'd read her at the train station. Letters that had changed both of their lives forever. And not in a good way, either. Poor Michael. Well, she didn't want to think about that now. It was too depressing.

Selina finished getting what she needed, and then they headed home, laughing and talking a sow's ear off all the way back to the ranch.

They arrived home shortly before noon. Selina set her purchases down on the sofa. She noticed Michael had already eaten again. She'd have to talk to him about why he hadn't waited for her to fix him something. Until then, she had work to do. So she ate a biscuit with strawberry jam and a slice of ham on it, put on a pot of stew, then she got right to work sewing herself some new clothes.

Hours later, she held the trousers and shirt she'd made against her body.

"Where did you get those?"

Selina whirled at the sound of Michael's voice and

the banging of the door. She'd been concentrating so hard, she hadn't even heard his footsteps echo on the porch, or the door squeak. It was nice seeing his handsome face again, warmed her like sunshine. She held the new outfit up proudly. "I made them." She smiled, knowing she had gotten all the money's worth possible out of the cloth.

But Michael didn't smile back. Instead, he looked over at the material sitting in a basket next to the rocking chair by the fireplace. "Is that all you made?"

She frowned. "For now. Ain't had time to make nothing else yet."

"But you plan on making some dresses, right?"

That was less of a question and more like an order. One she didn't take kindly to. "Michael Bowen, I told you, I ain't worn a dress since my ma died. A person can't hunt or do chores properlike in a dress. Iffen you think a body can, then you put one on and see for yourself that they can't."

He ran his hand over his face. Something he seemed to do a lot around her. "Selina, you know how I feel about you wearing pants. You're a woman, not a man. When are you going to get that through your thick head?"

She slammed her hands on her hips. "We've already been through this. Ain't no man or no woman gonna tell me what I can and can't wear. So when are *you* gonna get that through *your* thick skull? Just 'cause the good Lord made me a woman don't mean I have to wear a dress."

"I don't care what you say, woman. No wife of mine is going to wear pants in my house. It's neither proper nor comely."

"Accordin' to who?" She crossed her arms in front of her. "Besides, you forget. This is my house now, too. *You* told me that, and I aim to take you at your word."

Michael closed his eyes and dropped his head back, blowing out a long breath at the same time. *Why me, Lord?* "We'll discuss this later. I'm famished. What's for supper?"

"Even iffen we discuss it later, my mind won't be changin'."

With a shake of his head, he went to the sink and pumped the handle harder than he needed to, taking his frustration out on it. When the wash bowl in the sink was full to the brim, he washed his hands, face and neck. The grime from the day ran down the drain. If only he could wash his problems away that easily and watch them all disappear down the drain, too. He grabbed a towel and dried himself off.

"I made stew for supper." She looked over at him as she stirred the pot. "Oh. I just remembered somethin'. How come you left so early this mornin' without lettin' me fix you some vittles? Same with lunch."

"I'm sorry. I forgot to tell you that me, Jess, Haydon, Smokey and the hired hands were going to get an early start. We had lots to do. As for lunch, couldn't wait till you got home. I was famished so I went ahead and ate. Oh, by the way. Thanks for taking care of the horses and chickens this morning and for cleaning out the stalls. That was a huge help." For a man who didn't want his wife doing chores, he had to admit he truly was grateful.

"You're welcome. Glad I could help." Her face beamed under his praise, making her pretty features even prettier. If only she'd learn to control her tongue. "Now sit down while I put supper on."

He obeyed like a good husband and sat down at the kitchen table. Selina flew around rattling dishes and silverware and clinking glasses as she set the table. Grabbing a couple of the crocheted potholders his mother had made, she picked up the stew pot and set it on the table, along with a pan of biscuits and some butter and jam, then poured milk into the glasses. He'd never seen anyone set pans on a table before.

His family always used serving dishes and put the biscuits in a covered basket. One more reminder of the huge gap in their lives to this point.

She raised the lid off the kettle and the savory smell of rich beef gravy reached his nose. His stomach growled. "Smells good, Selina."

"Tastes mighty good, too."

"Been sampling supper already, huh?" He laughed.

"Sure enough have. How else am I supposed to know iffen it tastes good?" A twinkle filled her eyes.

"You got a point there."

She grabbed his bowl, put a large portion of stew into it and handed it to him. He watched as she scooped one small ladle into her own bowl.

"Selina, do you remember what we talked about earlier?"

She looked over at him with a frown. "Not sure what you're referrin' to."

Reaching over, he dipped a full ladle of stew and put it into her bowl.

Surprise jumped to her face. "What did you do that for?"

"Because you won't."

She dropped her gaze and picked it back up, settling it on him. "Don't know iffen I'll ever get used to being able to take as much as I want."

His heart broke for her then. She might be a wildcat, but she was his wife. And for some reason God had brought them together, so he'd try his best to take care of her. Even if she didn't want him to. And even if it killed him. And even if it was sure to drive him crazy. Which it just very well might.

This time he was careful not to grab her hand for prayers, and in a strange way he kind of missed it. So he laid it there for her to take.

She glanced down at his hand, then up at his face. He scooted his hand closer to her, offering it to her.

She inched her hand toward his until she finally rested her small one in his. They bowed their heads.

With prayers finished, he reached over and grabbed two biscuits, slathered them in butter, placed them on a small plate and set it in front of her. "Eat. That's an order."

"I told you, no man will ever tell me what to—"

Nonchalantly, he grabbed a buttery biscuit and shoved it into her mouth. "Hush up and eat."

Her eyes widened, then narrowed. She glared at him and bit down hard on the soft biscuit and chewed. He watched as she swallowed. "You think that's gonna shut me up, well you—"

Again, he shoved the biscuit into her mouth, leaving her no choice but to bite into it. "That's better." His chair moaned when he settled back into it.

Her eyes bore into him the whole time she chewed. At least the woman was mannerly enough to not talk with her mouth full. He was grateful to God for that much, anyway.

Crumbs stuck to her lips, but this time he wasn't about to wipe them off. If he did, she'd probably bite his fingers. Those flames shooting from her big brown eyes as she chewed the massive chunk he'd shoved into her mouth sent him a warning. One he was going to heed.

He scooped a spoonful of stew and put it into his mouth. While he chewed the best stew he'd ever tasted, he buttered several fresh-baked biscuits. The aroma of them reached his nose on the waves of steam. It was hard to enjoy it, though, with Selina staring him down while she ate. A keg of gunpowder ready to explode would have looked less dangerous. She tried to look mean, but she looked kind of cute, and he fought not to laugh.

He picked up a biscuit and brought it to his lips.

Quicker than a flash, Selina's hand shot out, mashing the biscuit against his mouth. She sat back with a smug look on her face, acting as if nothing had happened.

Michael wiped the butter from his face. "So you wanna play, huh?" He grabbed one of the biscuits and headed toward her face with it.

Selina's chair scraped across the wooden floor as she bolted upward and out the front door.

Michael flew after her, chased her through the woods, dodging pine trees and their prickly needles. Syringa bushes slapped his legs. Pine needles and broken branches crunched under his feet on the uneven ground as he pursued Selina through the woods.

Around the curve, he lost sight of her. It was as if she had disappeared into thin air.

Where could she have gone?

He stopped and panned the area but still caught no sight of her.

Stealthily he made his way through the pine and cottonwood trees and the thick underbrush. He held up the biscuit like a weapon, armed and ready. Each tree he approached with caution, quickly looking behind it before trudging onward.

He leaned forward to look behind another tree.

The next thing he knew, his body slammed on the grassy forest floor, mashing the biscuit he held into the side of his face. Selina's body straddled his shoulders, then bolted upward.

He shot out his hand, grabbed her pant leg and yanked on it.

She tugged and jerked to free herself, but he tossed his body onto his back and pulled her down on top of him.

Holding her tight with one hand he scraped some of the biscuits and butter from his face, pulled her down closer to him and raised his hand to smear it onto hers.

"No!" She yanked her head from one side to the other, giggling.

Her laugher was melodious, like a running brook.

He pulled her even closer. Their faces inches apart.

Their eyes connected, peering deeply into the other's.

Neither moved, as if they were frozen in that position.

His attention slid to her mouth. The temptation to kiss her lured him in, but he knew kissing her would be a huge mistake. He blinked, breaking the contact, and slowly released his hold on her shirt. "Yes, well—"

he cleared his throat "—I guess we'd better get back to supper before it gets cold."

She leaned back, sitting on his belly, having no clue of the urges raging inside him. "You give then?"

"I give." Boy did he ever.

She crossed her arms. "I knew you would." Her smile spoke of her untamed spirit.

"Oh, yeah?" No way would he let her think he was that easy. He pressed his fingers around her waist and started tickling her.

"Ahh. No, no." She squirmed, giggling as she tried to get away. But she was no match for his firm grip. He tickled her more insistently, careful to keep his touch from hurting her.

"How's about we call it even?" she said between bouts of laughter and drawing in breaths.

"Will you behave?"

"I'll behave as best as I can." She smiled, then broke free of his grasp and darted back to the house.

He sat up and brushed the leaves and pine cones off of him. One thing he had to give Selina credit for: he never knew what she would do next. And that both frightened and excited him.

Selina rose before the sun and the roosters again. After a breakfast of flapjacks, fried taters and ham slices, she followed Michael from the hog pen as he headed toward the barn. Something butted her knee, almost knocking it out from under her. "What do you think—" She whirled and looked down, smiling. "Why, you little cutie. You wantin' some attention?" She knelt down on one knee and scratched the pink pig behind the ear with a small chunk out of it.

"That's Kitty," Michael said.

"Kitty?"

"Don't ask. Abby named her years ago."

"Y'all got a lotta animals with weird names. A cat named Miss Piggy. A pig named Kitty, and a horse named Lambie. Abby name them, too?" She played with the tip of Kitty's nose.

"Yes. None of us had the heart to say anything so we let her name them. But we were sure glad when she outgrew that stage. Having a horse named Raven and a bull named Taxt were…" He left the sentence hanging.

"Taxt? What's that?" She shifted her attention from Kitty onto Michael.

"A taxt is a mule deer fawn."

"Abby gave a bull a cute critter's name like that?" She stood, and Kitty leaned into her leg.

"Remind me to tell you a few of her other names sometime. Right now I need to go and check on the orchards."

"What kind of orchards?"

"Apple, plums and pears."

"Oh. I'd love to see them. Would ya mind iffen I tagged along? And after I've seen them, would you mind directin' me toward Sadie's house? I told her I'd come in a couple a days to help do her cannin'."

"Sadie lives on the other side of our orchards so that'll be fine. I'll saddle up Macy for you."

"That's mighty nice of you, but I don't use a saddle. And I can get Macy ready myself. All you have to do is show me which bridle to use."

"You don't use a saddle?" His eyebrows shifted above his blue eyes.

"No. Ain't never had one before. Never could afford

one. We were lucky to have a horse. It was given to us by Mr. Clark. He couldn't take her with him when he moved so Pa ended up with her. Was right neighborly of Mr. Clark to think of us."

They stepped inside the barn and Kitty scooted on past the door.

Michael grabbed two halters from a room filled with tack. "I'll get the horses."

"No need to get mine. I can do it."

He looked at her as if questioning whether he should let her or not, then he nodded and handed her a halter.

He led Selina to one of the stalls. She stepped inside and closed the door. "Mornin', Macy. You wanna break outta this here cell and go for a ride?"

Michael stopped on his way to fetch his horse. "You act like she's in jail."

"She is. How would you like to be holed up here day after day?"

"Well, it's not like she can't go outside when she wants."

"Yeah, but it ain't the same. She can't up and leave whenever she wants to."

"Most horses can't."

"I know. I sure am glad I ain't a horse. Couldn't stand bein' cooped up all day. I gotta get out and go for a walk and enjoy all of God's creation. Why, did you know that there are a million different types of bugs alone? Some of them even prettier than a coon's face."

"A coon's face?"

"I guess y'all call them *rac*coons here."

That dip in his cheek made an appearance again even though his smile wasn't any bigger than a minute. "Never thought about all the different kind of bugs there are." Humor trickled through his voice and sparked his eyes.

"My mama used to say that beauty could be found anywhere and that the most beautiful things were often hidden. A person just had to look for them." She glanced over at Michael. "Ain't you never taken the time to notice how many different type of bugs there are? Or how the mornin' dew drops on flowers twinkle in the sun like night stars? Or how the stripes in the hundreds of kind of leaves are different? Why, there's a whole world out there with all kinds of beauty in it to see."

"Can't say that I have. I've usually got too much going on to take time for things like that."

She tsked. "That's a right shame, ya know. You don't know what you're missin'."

"That might be so, but right now what I'm missing is checking on our orchards. I'd better hurry and get to it."

"Mighty shame that you have to rush around here, there and yonder all the time."

"I'm sure it is. But I'll just have to take your word for it."

They readied their horses and led them out of the barn into the warm sun. A light breeze brushed across Michael's face.

He turned to help Selina mount but never got the chance. She grabbed a hunk of mane and swung her small form onto the horse's back. How she did it as small as she was, he wasn't quite sure, and he would have never believed it if he hadn't witnessed it for himself.

He shook his head, amazed, then mounted his own horse.

They rode through willows, white pine, cottonwood and fir trees. One thing was for sure—she hadn't been kidding him when she said she took time to enjoy God's creation.

Although he thought it was cute how her face lit up and her eyes sparkled when she stopped to study yellow buttercup flowers, white daisies, wild pink roses and even a few syringa bushes that weren't even blooming, did she have to do it now? At the pace they were going he would have to work twice as hard and twice as fast to get his work finished.

Not only did she point out every little detail, she had to stop and smell them all, too, closing her eyes as she did. Even placed a few under his nose. It had been a long time since he'd enjoyed the pleasant scent of roses or the sweet smell of a syringa bush. Someday he'd have to take the time to do it again, but right now he really needed to get back to work.

And yet, isn't that what had gotten him into this mess in the first place? Not taking time from work to check things out? Even now though, he still couldn't. There was too much to do and too little time to get it all done. So as much as he wanted to enjoy the things she was enjoying, he couldn't. He needed to hurry her along.

Finally, they reached the orchards. To his dismay, she did the same thing there. He gave up trying to hurry her and resigned himself to having to work late again. Riding to one of the pear trees, he plucked a nice ripe one, reined his horse close to Selina's and handed the fruit to her. "Ever had a pear right from the tree?"

"No, can't say that I have. Don't know that I've ever had a pear before at all."

"Never?" That shocked him. "Well, you don't know what you've been missing. Here, try one."

She took it from him and studied it first. He should have known she would. She closed her eyes, her chest expanding as she breathed in its scent, and then she took a small, hesitant bite and chewed. Her eyes darted open. Her mouth parted and a big chunk disappeared out of the pear. Juice ran down her chin.

He reached over to wipe it away. When his fingers touched her, he noticed how smooth and soft and warm her skin felt under his fingers.

Their gazes connected, then hers dropped to where his fingers still lingered. He yanked his hand away, wishing he didn't have to, wishing he could run his finger over her cheeks and neck to see if they were as soft as the rest of her skin. A quick frown from her and he cast his urge aside and sat back straight in the saddle. "Well, this is where we part ways. Enjoy your pear. Eat as many as you'd like."

"What do ya mean 'this is where we part ways'?" From the fear that flashed through her eyes, he wondered if she had taken it the wrong way and forgotten she had asked him to point her toward Tom and Sadie's house.

He shifted in his saddle, and leather creaked under him. "Remember you wanted me to show you the way to Sadie's?"

Her mouth formed an O and the fear dissipated. He'd been right. She had misconstrued what he had said. Relieved to put her fears at rest, he pointed the direction she needed to go and said, "You need to follow the dirt path over the hill and through the trees. It'll take you straight to their house. But be careful. Out there in Idaho Territory, you may run into wild animals." His sisters traveled alone all the time, but they were skilled in dealing with wild animals. He battled with what to do.

"What kind of wild animals?"

"Bears, coyotes, wolves."

Her eyes brightened. Not a trace of fear showed on her face. In fact, intrigue fluttered across it and that made him nervous. The woman had no idea what dangers lurked out there.

"I wish I would have thought to tell you to bring your rifle." This was one time he was glad the woman had one and knew how to use it.

"You think I'll need it?" Still no fear.

"Probably not. But it's always good to take one with you when you're traveling through the forest. Just be careful, okay?"

She nodded.

"Think you can find your way back home?"

"Yep. I can find my way back from just about anywhere. Now my brother, Jacob, he gets lost worse than a goose in a fog."

He chuckled at her analogy. "You're sure?" What if she didn't? Would he regret not taking her to Sadie's? He seemed to have a lot of those kinds of regrets lately.

Her deep sigh reached his ears. "Wouldn't have said so iffen I couldn't."

"What time you think you'll be home?"

"I reckon not till supper time. I didn't forget about your lunch iffen that's what you're worried about. I sliced some ham and put a fresh loaf of bread on the table for you."

"I wasn't worried about that. But thank you."

She waved him away. "You're welcome. Well, I'd better get iffen I'm going help Sadie with her cannin'. See you later, Michael. And thanks for showing me the orchards and for this here pear." She heeled Macy's sides and the mare started walking away.

Poor-decision regret snuck up on him again. The idea of her going alone tore at his conscience, making him rethink his plans for the day. He wanted, no *needed* to know that she got there and back safely. After all, he was the one who had brought her here to be his wife. She was his responsibility now. "Selina, wait!" He spurred his horse forward and caught up with her. "I'm going with you."

She reined her horse to a stop. "Michael, I know what you're thinkin'. But I really can take care of myself. Been doin' it all my life. I ain't scared of wild animals."

"I know. That's what worries me."

Her lips curled into a smile. "Well, it's sweet of you to worry about me, but I'll be just fine. You go tend to them orchards of yours, and I'll see you later." She kicked Macy into a trot. Her braid swished like a horse's tail as she headed up the hill and out of sight.

Hearing the confidence in her voice, he felt better about letting her go. "Lord, watch over Selina and keep her safe." The woman was starting to grow on him, and that made him nervous.

Toward dark, Michael's stomach growled. The sun was setting, leaving behind a sky painted orange with a few streaks of yellow. At the barn he unsaddled his horse and pitched him some hay, then walked toward his house.

Exhausted from a hard day of work, he couldn't wait to get home, clean up, eat and sit down on the sofa and read first his Bible, then start on *A Tale of Two Cities* by Charles Dickens.

The steps groaned under his weight as he climbed them. He opened the door and stopped short. His eyes all but popped out of their sockets at the sight. Curled up next to Selina on the sofa was a wolf pup.

"Selina! What are you doing?" he barked.

Selina bolted upward. Her eyes blinked rapidly and her gaze darted about the room wildly before landing on him. The pup stirred next to her.

"What are you thinking bringing a wolf into this house?"

"Jumpin' crickets. That's what all the hollerin's about? The pup?"

"That just isn't any pup. That's a wolf."

"I know that. But there ain't no way I was gonna just leave the little varmint there."

"Leave it where? What are you talking about, woman?"

"Poor little thing had its paw caught in a small animal trap. Ain't no way I was gonna leave it there to fend for itself and to keep on sufferin' like it was so I brought it home and doctored it."

"Se-li-na." He drew out her name and scrubbed his hand over his face. "Don't you know how dangerous that is?"

"'Course I do. I ain't stupid, but I was born and raised in the hills of Kentucky and we got all sorta wild animals there, and I ain't never left one to die yet, and I ain't gonna start now. I've been tendin' to them

ever since I was eight and found that baby coon without a mama."

"That—" he pointed to the pup still asleep on the
sofa "—isn't a raccoon. Those things are dangerous.
You're lucky its mama didn't attack you."

"I looked around for its mama. Besides, don't you
know nothin'? Iffen I were in danger Macy would have
warned me by gettin' all antsy, and the hair on the back
of my head never rose so I knew I was safe."

"You can't go by Macy or the hair on your head rising."

"Sure I can. Been doin' it all my life and it's worked
so far. I trust my instincts and the good Lord to keep
me safe."

"You can't go by instincts, Selina. You have to use
common sense. And saying you trust God to protect
you when you're doing something ludicrous is ridiculous. It wouldn't be any different than me jumping out
of a fifty-foot tree and saying that God will keep me
safe because I trust Him. I'm either going to end up
hurt really badly or killed. And most likely it will be
the latter."

"Someone would have to be gone in the head to do
somethin' that stupid."

He tilted his head and hiked a brow.

She slammed her hands on her hips. "You callin'
me stupid?"

"No, I'm not calling you stupid, but what you did
was stupid."

"You know, Michael, the way I see it is, the good
Lord put me on this earth to help save them poor critters. Iffen He didn't, then He wouldn't have given me
the knack for doctorin' them or the desire to."

"So now you're saying God is in this?"

"Yes, sir, I am."

"You're unbelievable, you know that?"

"Don't rightly know what you mean by unbelievable, but I know what's in my heart." She pressed her hand to her chest.

"There's no talking to you. No getting through to you, is there?"

She frowned. "Don't understand. Ain't that what we've been a doin' the last ten minutes? Talking? At least where I come from it is."

He sighed and shook his head. "I want that pup out of here tomorrow. I'll ride with you to put it back where you got it. And from now on, I don't want you bringing any more animals into this house. You understand me?" He kept his voice firm and hard, hoping she would get the message.

She stepped right up to him, leaving mere inches between them. Her head tilted back and she hooked his gaze and held it. "I understand you, but it don't mean I'm gonna do it. I'd rather move outta this here house than have someone tryin' to change who I am. What I live for. And that's doctorin' animals and helpin' people. Aside from all of that, I can't return it." She turned and sat down on the sofa and pulled the sleeping pup onto her lap and started stroking its fur. "I think her mama is dead."

"What makes you think that?"

"'Cause this pup raised an awful ruckus when I was helpin' it, and the mama never did show up. Iffen she were alive, she would have protected that pup of hers."

Selina had a point. About a few things anyway. He was trying to change her. But he didn't see that as a bad thing. Someone had to protect this stubborn, head-strong woman from herself. Still, he glanced at the pup and back at her. Determination and compassion drifted from her.

What was he going to do?

He couldn't keep the wolf.

And he didn't want his wife moving out. That surprised him.

"I'll be gettin' my things now." She put the pup down and walked past him toward the stairs.

He caught up with her and grasped her arm, stopping her. "You don't have to do that, Selina."

"Yes, I do. I won't live where I can't be myself. For whatever reason the good Lord made me the way I am, and I won't be a changin' for you or anyone else. Iffen you're worried about me breakin' the vows we made before the Lord, don't be. I'll just bed down in the barn from now on." She shook off his arm and darted up the stairs, taking them two at a time with her short legs.

He hurried up the stairs after her. "You don't have to sleep in the barn. There's an old cage down in one of the sheds. I'll run and get it. The pup can sleep in it. But just for tonight. Do I make myself clear?"

She gave him that look. One he was coming to know well. That pup wasn't going anywhere.

"I'll be back. I'm going to get that cage now."

He hurried downstairs, lit a lantern, then headed down to the shed, mumbling all the way that the woman was going to be the death of him.

Chapter Six

$\sim\!\!\!\!\!\!\!\!\sim$

Selina bolted up in bed to the sound of a man's scream. She tossed the covers aside, flew down the stairs into Michael's room and stopped. She pressed her hand over her mouth to hold in her laugh at the sight of Michael shoved up against the wall, staring at the wolf pup as if it was something to be feared. The pup's backside stood higher than its front and its tail was tucked between its legs. Selina hurried to the pup and gained its trust before picking it up and cradling it to her chest. "Poor baby. Did Michael scare you?"

"Me? Scare her? How would you like to open your eyes and see that face just inches from yours?"

"This face?" Using what little light there was in the dark room, she studied the gray wolf's features. "Nothing scary about it. Why it's as cute as two baby bunnies leapin' in the air at one another."

"How did it get out anyway?"

"I don't rightly know." Pup in hand, she scurried to the door.

"Where you going?"

"Iffen you must know, to put some clothes on." She

was wearing her thin nightgown. She still hadn't gotten around to making a new one yet.

She whirled and found herself face-to-face with Michael's chest. Tucking the pup closer to her, she covered her threadbare gown best as she could.

"Selina, we are married. You don't have to be embarrassed." His eyes held only kindness.

She didn't know what to say to that. They weren't like a real married couple. Her ma and pa shared the same bed. She and Michael didn't. The way he felt about her, she wasn't sure they ever would, neither.

"I know we don't share the same bed and all…"

Her attention flew to his face. Was the man a mind reader?

"But we do live in the same house. We're bound to see each other in, um, precarious situations now and then."

"Pre-care-ee-ous. What's that mean?"

"Delicate. Perplexing. Problematic."

"Probli what? Purple-lex-en what? You're confusin' me. Can't you just tell me what you're tryin' to say without all them big words?"

"Fine. Just remember you asked for it. So…brace yourself. There are bound to be times we're going to find one another not fully dressed and see things we are not used to seeing. But, we are married so it's perfectly proper and acceptable."

She glanced toward the ceiling and sighed, grateful he'd slept in his pants and not his britches. "I had to ask. Now. Iffen you'll excuse me, I'm gonna get myself out of this pre-care-ee-an situation." She raised her chin and headed toward the stairs, feeling Michael's eyes on her and hearing his deep chuckle.

* * *

Once again Michael had to admit, even to himself, that having Selina help with chores lightened the load for everyone. He stepped into the barn while Selina fed the chickens and collected the eggs. Horses crunched on grain and shuffled their hooves.

Jesse turned from saddling his horse and did a double take. "You look terrible. Like you haven't slept in a week."

"I haven't."

"How come?"

"Selina."

"What do you mean?"

"She's going to be the death of me yet."

"What did she do now?" His brother pulled the cinch tight and removed the stirrup from the top of the saddle, letting it drop to the horse's side before he faced Michael.

"You won't believe what she brought home."

"What?" Jesse's lips quivered and his nostrils flared as he struggled to hold back his smile as Michael had seen him do so many times before.

Michael glowered at him. "You're loving this, aren't you?"

Jesse held up his hands. "No, honest. From the few things you've told me, there seems to never be a dull moment at your house, and Selina is very unique."

"She's unique, all right."

"How do you feel about that?"

"I'm not sure. Sometimes she has me laughing at her backward ways and antics. Other times I want to find the nearest cave at Coeur d'Alene and hide out there the rest of my life." Michael raised his hat, plowed his hand through his hair and replaced his hat. "Yesterday, on her way home from Sadie's, she found a wolf pup and brought it home."

"A wolf? You're kidding."

"No. In fact, when I woke up this morning, the wolf's face was only inches from mine. It about scared the life out of me."

His brother laughed.

"Glad you find this amusing. That thing scared ten years off of my life."

"I'm sure."

"I told her I didn't want her bringing any more critters home but she told me the good Lord made her that way and she would rather bed down here in the barn than stop doing that. I have no idea what to expect next. Or any idea what she might bring home next."

"Don't you think you're exaggerating a little bit, Michael? She only brought a cat and a wolf to your house."

"Only?" He dipped his head and hiked one brow toward Jesse. "The cat I could deal with. But the wolf?" He shook his head. "You know they can't be fully trusted. I wonder what she plans on doing with it once it's healed. She can't take it back because she says its mama is dead, and I refuse to share my house with a wolf, no matter what my wife says. That woman is as unpredictable and stubborn as a mule."

"Hmm. Just like someone else I know who's maybe not unpredictable but definitely stubborn." Jesse laid his hand on Michael's shoulder. "Look, Michael, what's done is done. You can't go back and change the past. The way I see it, you have two choices here. You can start embracing Selina and her uniqueness and pay attention to her good qualities, or you can continue to be miserable. The choice is yours."

"How can I embrace her when she's so different?"

"Different isn't always a bad thing. It can make for an interesting life."

"Interesting? That's one way to put it. But I'm not sure I want my life *that* interesting."

Jesse looked like he was about to laugh again. Michael felt his own laughter rising up in him. He let it out and Jesse joined him.

"Michael, have fun with it. See the humor in what she does. You're always too serious. You need to lighten up. Maybe that's why God sent Selina to you. To teach you to not take things so seriously all the time. To stop and enjoy life once in a while."

"That's what Selina said. Only she said it was a shame I was too busy to stop and enjoy the dew drops on flowers or something like that."

"Maybe you should listen to her." Jesse untied his horse. Dust motes kicked up from his horse's hooves as his brother led the animal toward the barn door.

"Whose side are you on, anyway?" Michael hollered after him. "Traitor."

The only response he got was laughter.

He was glad his brother found it funny. He didn't. Didn't Jesse know how hard this was on him? How he beat himself up on a regular basis for being so stupid? How hard it was for him to have all his dreams ripped from him in one moment?

That the person he had fallen in love with didn't exist.

Spotting a rock on the dirt floor of the barn, he took

his frustration out by kicking it with all his might. It crashed into the wall and echoed throughout the barn.

"You havin' a fit this mornin' or somethin'?"

He closed his eyes and pulled himself together before turning around and facing Selina. "Something like that."

"Anythin' I can help you with?"

"No. You've done enough already." Still put out with her over the pup and lack of sleep, he brushed past her and left the barn before he did or said something else he'd regret.

Selina watched Michael walk away. That man was strung tighter than a clothesline. He needed to learn to relax.

She looked around the barn. Chores were done here, so she decided to head over to Rainee's.

As she made her way across the large ranch yard, calves bawled for their mamas, hens balked and horses whinnied.

Under her booted feet, the boards echoed her arrival at Rainee and Haydon's. Selina knocked on the door.

Wasn't long before the door swung open. Rainee's wide smile made Selina feel welcome.

"Selina, I am so happy to see you."

"I ain't botherin' you or keepin' you from anything, am I?"

"No. Not at all. I was just knitting a blanket for the baby. Please, come in." Rainee stepped aside of the doorway and Selina walked inside.

She had expected to see fancy furniture and fine things, but there was no putting on airs here. Although the furnishings were nice, more than anything else they were downright homey.

"Would you like some tea?"

"Yes. That'd be mighty nice of you. Can I help?"

"No, no. I just finished brewing some." Rainee arranged five small plates on a wooden tray. She picked up a sugar bowl, pitcher and something that held cream in it that matched the rest of her well-used dishes. They sure were pretty with their pink and white roses, gold-colored handles, lids and spout. Chips and all.

Rainee opened a drawer and added spoons and cloth napkins on the tray, too.

Selina watched, wondering how she would ever fit in with these rich folks and their highfalutin ways. But Rainee wasn't anything like she thought she'd be. From the way the woman talked and carried herself, Rainee had come from money, too. Yet she was as friendly as Selina's neighbors back home.

"How have you been, Selina?" Rainee raised the cloth off a basket sitting on a cabinet in the corner. She added four triangle-shaped biscuits and placed them onto the biggest plate.

"Been fine as frog's hair. Yourself?"

"Quite well. Thank you." She smiled. "Shall we head into the living room?"

Selina took the tray and followed Rainee over to two wingback chairs with a small square table in between them. She set the tray on the table in front of the glass lamp and watched as Rainee picked up a small plate and placed a cup on it.

"Do you take it plain, or would you like cream and sugar with it?"

"Ain't never had cream nor sugar in it before. I reckon I'll just take it plain."

Rainee handed her a cup and started to put a biscuit on another plate.

"No need to dirty another dish. I can put it right here." She took it from Rainee and before she set it on the side of her cup, she took a bite. "This is right tasty. What is it?"

"A strawberry scone. Would you like some cream on it?"

"Thank you kindly, but it tastes mighty fine the way it is. Real buttery-like."

"Do you miss home?" Rainee asked.

"I sure do. I miss my family and the easy way of life back home. Here everythin' is rush, rush, rush. Why, you'd think a person was on fire with all that scurryin' about."

"They do keep rather busy, do they not?" If Selina wasn't mistaken that was sadness she saw in her sister-in-law's eyes.

"Do ya ever get lonely out here?" Steam rose toward Selina's nose as she raised the cup and took a sip of the strong brew and another bite of the scone.

"Only for my husband. He takes his leave early in the morning and does not arrive home until after the sun has set. So I scarcely see him. Before I became pregnant, the children and I went with him a lot, but as soon as he found I was with child again, he would not allow me to go with him anymore." Rainee set her cup back in the saucer and turned toward her. "Have you met Kitty yet?"

"I sure have. She introduced herself by buttin' the back of my legs."

Rainee laughed. "That sounds like Kitty. She was a bridesmaid at my wedding, you know."

"Did I just hear you say you had a pig as your bridesmaid?"

"Yes, you did."

Selina slapped her knee and guffawed. "I knew I liked you. I love animals, too. Why, Michael thinks I'm stubborn as an old mountain goat 'cause I'm always bringin' critters home. Last night I was fixin' to bed down in the barn 'cause…"

"The barn?" Rainee interrupted her.

"I brought home an injured wolf and you'd have thought it was a grizzly bear or somethin' worse with the way Michael carried on."

"A wolf." Rainee's delicate brows rose. "You brought home a wolf?"

"Yeah."

"May I see it?"

Selina smiled. The woman didn't make her feel crazy at all because she'd brought the animal home. She reckoned not everyone here was as set in their ways as Michael.

"If you do not have any plans for today, perhaps we could have a lesson and then go see that wolf of yours."

"I'd like that. Thank you kindly, Rainee."

"No, thank you. You have quite rescued me from boredom. Haydon has Abby take the children to the neighbors with her so they do not overtax me. I assure you they do not, but he thinks they do. I rather enjoy them and miss them when they are gone." Love for her children lit up her eyes. "Sometimes I feel as if I shall go mad cooped up inside all the time. I am used to keeping busy and not sitting around knitting all day."

"I ain't one for sittin' myself. Let's get that lesson done then I'll break ya outta here and take you to my place." Her place. Sure didn't feel like her place and she wondered if it ever would.

Exhausted, sore and ready to fall into bed, Michael dragged his body home, terrified at what he might come home to this time. Another animal? Or something worse? He really didn't want to find out, but he had no choice unless he wanted to sleep in the barn. Therefore, he forced one leg in front of the other and climbed the steps. Something smelled good. He opened the door and stepped inside.

Selina stood in front of the stove, flipping something over in the large black skillet. She turned and smiled. "Evenin', Michael."

"Good evening." Now, if this had been a real marriage, he would have stepped up behind his wife, turned her around, wrapped his arms around her and kissed her thoroughly.

But this wasn't a real marriage. Legally it was, but not emotionally. Disappointment sighed through him.

"Sit yourself down and I'll fetch you some vittles."

Michael removed his hat and hung it on a peg. "Thank you. I'll wash up."

Selina buzzed around, smiling and humming, a real bundle of energy. Did the woman ever tire?

He finished washing and sat down. As usual, Selina set the pans on the table, except for the one she'd fried the meat in. She put its contents on a platter.

She sat down and settled her hand close to his plate. He no longer had to ask for her hand—she now offered it. That small gesture pleased him. Why, he had no idea, but it did.

He clasped her hand in his. Warmth radiated through him as it did every time he touched her. "Selina, would you pray tonight? I'm tired."

"I'd be honored." She closed her eyes. "Dear Lord, thank You for a husband who works hard to put a roof over our heads, clothes on our bodies and food on the table. Thank You for Your provision. I pray that these here vittles provide what our bodies need so we might better serve You in all we do. And, Lord. Thank You for Michael. Amen."

To know that all his hard work and efforts were not taken for granted and that she appreciated all he had done to provide her with a nice home and plenty of food warmed him like hot coals on a cold winter's day. "Thank you, Selina."

She stopped dishing his plate and looked at him. "For what?"

"For your thoughtful and kind prayer."

She nodded, then went back to filling his plate.

"So, what did you do after chores today?" Michael took a long gulp of his milk.

She pushed his overfilled plate in front of him.

"Paid a visit to Rainee."

"How's she feeling?"

"Bored."

"I don't doubt it, being cooped up inside all the time like that. She's used to getting out and riding and helping Haydon."

"Before she got pregnant, did he ever mind her helpin'?" She raised the spoon from the bean pot.

"No, not at all."

Selina settled the spoon back into the pot of beans. "How come you do then?"

"I see things differently than Haydon. I believe a woman's place is in the home."

"In some ways you're just like most of the menfolk back home," she said on a sigh.

"What do you mean?"

"Well, they're always orderin' women about like big bullies. Showin' them very little respect. Don't let their wives have a mind a their own. The women that do speak up, they pay dearly for it with a whippin'. Years ago, I made up my mind that no man would ever boss me around like that."

"I know, I know. Boy do I know." He picked up the fried meat and bit into it, trying to discern what it was. Sort of tasted like chicken but wasn't shaped like chicken. It was rounder and the bones were closer together. Strange, he didn't remember anything that looked quite like this in the cellar. He took another bite, still unable to tell what it was. "What is this?" he finally asked around the bite.

"Snake."

"Snake!" Michael grabbed for a napkin and spit the lump of chewed up meat into it. He downed the rest of his milk, barely able to contain his revulsion as he did. "Selina, what were you thinking? People don't eat snake."

She looked like nothing in the world was amiss. "Sure they do. Why, back home we ate it all the time. And plenty of other critters, too."

"What do you mean?" He bore down on his teeth until they ached, waiting for her answer and dreading it at the same time.

"Oh, you know, squirrel, possum, groundhog, bear…"

"Squirrel? Possum?" He swallowed hard. The more she named, the more the snake shifted from his stomach into his throat. He waved his hands in the air in complete surrender. "Stop. I've heard enough."

He shoved his plate away from him, caught her gaze and held it firmly with a sternness she would not be able to misconstrue, "Listen to me. I don't *ever* want to eat any of the things you've just mentioned. There is no reason or need to. We have plenty of beef, pork and chicken." He emphasized each word to get his point across, then waited for her to tell him how she wouldn't let any man tell her what to do. Well, this was one area where *he* would not back down. She could go right ahead and sleep in the barn over that one.

He waited for anger to blow out from her like steam from a locomotive. Instead she put her head down. "I'm sorry, Michael. Where I come from, food is scarce. A body eats whatever it can find. I just couldn't throw the meat away." She spoke so softly that remorse darted through him.

He'd never been poor, so he had no idea what it was like to be hungry enough to eat snake, or possum, or squirrel. He shuddered just thinking about it. But she had, and he needed to remember that.

He reached for her hand. It felt so small in his. "I'm sorry for being so harsh, Selina. There was no way you could have known I don't eat things like snake. But next time, it's okay to leave it. It won't go to waste. Some animal who needs a meal will find it and eat it."

She yanked her gaze up to his and her eyes brightened. "I never thought of it that-a-way. You're right." Selina scraped her chair across the floor and stood.

"Where you going?"

"To fix you somethin' else."

"No need to do that. There's plenty of fried potatoes and biscuits and beans. I'll just eat them tonight." At least she had started making larger portions. For that he was grateful.

"You sure? I can cut you off a piece of ham."

"No, this is fine. Thanks. Now sit down and eat before your food gets cold." He smiled, and her lips tentatively curled upward as she lowered her small frame onto the chair.

She removed the snake from his plate and heaped more of everything else onto it.

"Thank you, Selina. I really am sorry if I hurt your feelings about the snake. Like I said, I'm just not used to things like that."

"I reckon you ain't used to a lot of things I do," she said while putting food onto her plate. Her portions were still small, but each day they were growing. "I know I'm different, Michael. And I know I ain't what you're used to and I understand."

"You're right. I'm not used to your ways. But that doesn't mean I can't learn." Did he just say that? He shoved a bite of potatoes into his mouth to keep it from saying anything else equally as stupid.

"You mean that?" Hope sparked in her beautiful brown eyes.

Knowing he'd put that sparkle there made his heart smile. Maybe he needed to open his mouth more often, after all. "I do." And he found he really meant it, too.

"I'll try and learn to do things the way you like them. But—" she held up her finger "—some things I ain't changin'." She glanced over toward the sofa at the wolf curled up in the old cage Michael had found in one of the sheds.

Her looking over at the pup had him working his jaw. For his sanity's sake, he hoped bringing strange, dangerous animals into the house was something she would try to change, too, but he had his doubts.

As they finished eating in silence, he was glad he hadn't given in to the thoughts of sending her back. For her sake, he would do whatever it took to make this work so she would never have to go back to the unimaginable poverty she had endured.

Selina stood. Dishes clanked and silverware rattled as she started clearing the table. He picked up his dishes and was getting ready to take them to the sink but Selina stopped him. "I can get these. You need to go lie down and rest a spell."

"Thank you, Selina."

"You're welcome. Now scoot." She gave him a light shove toward the living room.

He laid down onto his stomach on the sofa and within minutes felt himself drifting off to the sound of rustling soapy water and dishes quietly clinking.

In his slumbering state, he felt small but strong and gentle hands pressing against his shoulders and up and down his back, working in a circular motion. "Um. That feels nice," he slurred. The hands worked their way up his neck and massaged his scalp. Warmth spread through him. His eyes darted open and he rolled over onto his side with a start.

"What's wrong? Did I hurt you?"

"No. No. Not at all." A piece of her slipped into his soul. He bolted off the sofa with the need to put distance between them. "Listen, I'm tired. If you don't mind, I'm going to bed now."

Hurt flashed through her eyes, and again he felt instant remorse. She had no idea what had been running through his mind, and he had hurt her with his rash actions.

"Thank you, Selina, for working the kinks out of my muscles. They feel much better now."

She nodded.

"Good night."

"Night."

Leaving her standing there, he hurried to his room and closed the door, bracing his back against it. Not only was he starting to respond to Selina emotionally, but now even his heart had responded to her physical touch. Even though the woman was his wife, the whole idea of being connected to her scared him to the core.

Selina took the pup out of her cage and hugged the animal to her chest. She flopped on the sofa and stared at the closed door to Michael's bedroom. It stung that he had run from her like that.

Rubbing Michael's broad shoulders and back, running her fingers through his soft hair, had felt right and yet it had been all wrong. She had made her husband afraid of her. And just when they were starting to talk like normal married folk, too.

All she had wanted to do was draw the ache out of his muscles. But that had obviously been a mistake. In the future she'd be careful to keep her hands to herself. That was going to be mighty hard to do. She loved him. Loved how she felt when she touched him, when she was with him. Felt like she belonged to him, and she did, too. But in name only.

Lord, I want a real marriage. I'd be much obliged to You iffen You would work that out. Thank You kindly, Lord.

When she finished tending to the pup's needs, she pressed her ear against Michael's door, listening for any noise. Not hearing any, she went to the pantry and removed the books, the writing slate and the chalk from behind the canned food. She sat in one of the living room chairs and lit the lantern that was on the table between the chairs. She pulled her sewing basket closer so she could hide her learning stuff down in the material if Michael got up.

For a long time, she practiced writing her letters and silently pronouncing them.

Wood squeaking and feet padding across the floor snagged her attention. She shoved her things to the bottom of her sewing basket, picked up the nightgown she'd been making and commenced to sewing.

Michael stepped into the living room with his hair all rumpled, with nothing on his feet and wearing only a nightshirt that came just past his knees.

"You still up?"

"Nah. You're just dreamin'." She sent him a silly grin.

"It's kind of late for you to still be up, isn't it?"

She glanced over at the tall pendulum clock. A grandfather clock, Michael had called it. "I can't believe it's ten after midnight already." Telling time was one thing she had learned to do. She laid her sewing in her basket and rose. "I'd best get to bed so I can get up in the mornin'." She stopped in front of him. "How come you're up? Can I get you somethin'?"

"No. I just got up to get a drink and then I'm going right back to bed."

"Oh. All righty then." Selina turned to leave, but his arm reached out and snagged hers.

"Selina, thank you for getting the kinks out earlier. I wouldn't have been able to sleep at all if it hadn't been for you."

"You're welcome." Him saying that made her insides feel good.

Neither one moved.

His eyes roamed her face, stopping at her lips. She pulled in her bottom lip with her teeth.

The pup gave a short howl, yanking her attention away from Michael. She stepped past him and retrieved the pup from his pen. "I'd better take her outside for a spell."

From across the dimly lit room, Michael was still staring at her. She pulled the pup closer to her chest and made her way to the door. "G'night, Michael."

"Good night, Selina." His voice sounded deeper, broken even.

When she stepped outside out of earshot of Michael, she whispered, *I love you, Michael. And I'm praying that one day I'll be deservin' of you and that you'll love me back.*

Chapter Seven

Michael woke to banging on his door. He jumped up, pulled on his pants and headed to the front door, swinging it open. Dan, Tom Elder's seventeen-year-old son, stood there looking skittish. His shirt was untucked in several places and his red hair stood straight up.

"Dan, what are you doing here? What's all the ruckus about?"

"Ma's having her baby," Dan said between gasping breaths. "I went to Doc's house first, but he wasn't home. Ma told me to fetch your wife. Hurry. She said it won't be long now."

"I'll get her. Come in." Michael turned and almost bumped into Selina.

"Sadie havin' that baby now?"

"Yes, ma'am. She asked me to come fetch you."

"I'll get dressed and be right there."

"If you don't mind, ma'am, I'll wait. You can ride on the back of my horse."

"No need." Michael jumped in, not about to let his wife run all over the country in the dark with Dan, a boy who was known to get into mischief. "I'll get a couple horses ready and have them here by the time Selina gets dressed."

Selina laid her hand on his arm. "No need for you to do that, Michael. You need your rest. I'll be fine. Just go back to bed and I'll be back as soon as I can."

"No." He gently removed her hand. "I'm going with you."

She shrugged. "Suit yourself."

"I'll help," Dan said to Michael. The two of them ran to the barn and readied the horses.

Michael's intent had been to go back and get her, but Selina met them halfway. They mounted the horses and raced into the night.

When they arrived at Tom's place, Selina jumped down and ran to the house. Michael followed. Neither bothered to knock.

"Selina, am I glad to see you." Sadie stood in the main room with one hand on her stomach and the other on her back.

Tom paced the floor and stopped when he saw them. He rushed to Selina. "Do something, please."

"Calm yourself down, Tom. Everythin' will be just fine. Fetch me some hot water, clean sheets..." Selina continued to give orders.

Michael stood back and watched Selina take charge, calmly and with authority.

Pans clanked on the stove as Tom put water on to heat. When it was hot enough, he took it and everything else Selina asked for into the bedroom where she now had Sadie.

With the bedroom door closed, Michael watched Tom pace, then sit, then stand and pace some more.

This went on for more than two hours until a baby's cry reached their ears.

Tom burst into his bedroom while Michael stood back and listened.

"That's a mighty fine girl you have there, Tom."

A loud crash echoed through the small room.

"Tom!" Sadie's frail voice was soaked in fear.

Michael rushed inside to see what the commotion was all about. Tom lay on the floor next to a broken vase and a toppled table.

Selina knelt by him. "Got any smellin' salts, Sadie?"

"Yes, on the shelf above the wash basin."

"Michael, fetch me the salts, please."

He whirled, found the bottle, and rushed it back to Selina. She waved it under Tom's nose.

Tom moved his head from side to side and shoved Selina's hand away. "Get that stinky stuff away from me."

Michael wanted to step in and tell Tom not to treat his wife like that, and he would have until he reminded himself that the man was reeling from shock. With good reason, too. After nine boys, this was his first girl.

He offered Tom a hand up and shook his hand. "Congratulations, Tom. Can you believe it? You finally got yourself a girl."

Tom's face paled and he swayed, but Michael held him up.

Selina stuck the smelling salts under his nose again and Tom bolted alert. "I'm fine. I'm fine. I don't need any more of that stuff burning my nose hairs and lungs."

Selina moved it and chuckled. "Ain't the best smellin' stuff, is it?"

"That's for sure." Then, as if he remembered his wife, Tom dashed over to Sadie and dropped to his knees next to her on their bed. He reached for her hand. "Are you okay, Sadie? You don't feel dizzy or sick or anything, do you?" Panic rang through every word.

Selina looked up at Michael with a question in her eyes.

He leaned over and whispered. "Tom's first wife died giving birth to their last son. Tom didn't want any more children for fear of losing Sadie, too."

Selina left Michael's side, walked over to Tom and placed her hand on his shoulder. "Sadie's gonna be just fine, Tom. She's as healthy as a horse. Easiest delivery I ever done."

Tom looked up at her, and hope danced through his eyes. "You mean it?"

"Sure do. Now why don't you go fix some coffee or somethin' and let me clean up this mess?"

Tom looked at his wife. Sadie gave a weak nod.

"Thank you, Selina." After he righted the table, the two men headed toward the door. "That's some special wife you got there, Michael. I was so afraid when Dan said he couldn't find Doctor Berg, but Selina handled everything just fine."

"Including you." Michael grinned.

"Including me." Tom smiled. "Can't believe I fainted."

"Well, I'd have fainted too if I found out my wife just gave birth to a girl after all those boys." Michael had hoped someday to have a whole houseful of children. He didn't know if that would happen now. Unless he and Selina could find common ground, he refused to bring children into a world where neither mother nor father loved the other.

Tom fixed coffee and the two of them had just sat down at the table when Selina came into the room with her arms loaded with soiled sheets and bed clothes, looking more worn out than Michael had ever seen her before. Strands of hair stuck out of her long braid and brown circles hung under her eyes. Michael knew he needed to get her home so she could get some sleep.

Selina stood in front of the wash tub, filling it with soap and hot water from the stove.

"Those need to soak," he said, standing over her shoulder. "I need to get you home so you can get some rest."

Selina looked up at him. "I'll be fine. Ain't no way I'm leavin' Sadie to wash these and to fix breakfast for her family. You don't mind, do ya?"

"Has that ever stopped you before?" He couldn't hold back the grin.

She smiled, too, although it was weak. "Nope."

"Listen, I'm going to head home, then. Don't wear yourself out, okay?"

"I won't. Thank you for carin'." She reached up and kissed his cheek. Her eyes bolted open, then her attention swung behind him.

He turned and found they were alone. Tom must have slipped away to Sadie.

"I—I'm sorry, Michael. I shouldn't have done that. It was only—"

Without thinking it through, Michael pulled her to him and shut her words up with his mouth. Sweet honeysuckle and spring met his advance, and in one second he was falling through time and space into her arms and charms.

A knock sounded at the Elder's front door. "Tom, it's me, Doctor Berg."

Michael jerked his head up and quickly released her, nearly sending her crashing to the floor with his suddenness. He should have never kissed her. He whirled and headed to the door, taking with him the memory of her soft lips, lips that had never even responded to his kiss.

Dead tired, Selina headed for home. Cleaning Sadie's house, along with washing her clothes and fixing enough food to last Sadie's family for a couple of days, had plumb worn her out.

Head hung low, she shifted and swayed with her mare's movement. Her head gave a yank, then she raised it and tried to hold it upright. Struggling to stay awake so she wouldn't fall off the horse and break her neck, she turned her mind to her surroundings and back to Michael's kiss. When he had grabbed her and kissed her like that, she'd been so shocked all she could do was stand there.

Her fingers found their way to her lips. She wished Michael would kiss her like that again, but that wasn't likely to happen. From the way he tore out of the house, he must have regretted kissing her. Had it been that awful for him? It sure hadn't been for her. When his lips had touched hers, it was as if the heat of the noon sun had found its way into her body, warming it through with liquid love.

The breeze lifted the strands of hair from around her face and swung them across her cheeks. It took what little energy she had left to brush them away. She wished she could brush the broken pieces of her heart away as easily and let the breeze carry them far away so it wouldn't hurt so bad.

Selina rode into the ranch yard and up to the barn door. She closed her eyes for a moment, then swung her leg over the horse's back.

Before she so much as saw him there, Michael's spicy musk scent surrounded her and his hands went about her waist. She tilted her head backward, and her back brushed against Michael's chest as he lowered her. Her feet touched the ground, but because she was worn out, her legs wilted and she swayed.

Michael's arm wrapped around her, holding her strong and steady. "Thank you, Michael," she whispered through a yawn. She took a half step away from him. Her eyelids felt like someone had tied rocks to them and was pulling them downward.

"I'll take care of Macy. You need to get her home." Jesse's voice reached her ears.

Selina wobbled her attention onto Jesse and offered him a smile.

The next thing she knew, strong arms were scooping her up.

Michael's body shifted underneath her with each step he took. "I'm carrying you home and no arguing with me, you hear?"

She heard, and she wanted to protest but was too tired.

So just this once she'd let him have his way.

And just this once she laid her head into his chest.

And just this once she pretended they were man and wife in every way.

Tomorrow, things would be back to normal.

Tomorrow she would remember that he didn't love her and that he was only doing his duty by her, but tonight she didn't care to remember.

Michael's peppermint breath drifted around her as his breathing increased with each step toward home. His soothing heartbeat swept through his arms and against her back where he held her. Her eyes slid shut and sweet dreams of Michael carrying her floated through her mind.

Selina felt herself being lowered and her eyes bobbed open. "We home?"

"We're home." Michael's voice was as soothing as the birds singing in the trees and the river waters back home.

She pulled up from the couch and dragged her body toward the stove.

"What are you doing?" Michael asked from behind her.

"You ask me that a lot, don't ya?" She tried to laugh but couldn't find enough get-up-and-go to do so. "I'm gonna fix you some vittles then head to bed."

Michael laid his large hands on her shoulders. He turned her around and gently nudged her toward the sofa. "You don't have to do that. Mother made dinner for us tonight. All we have to do is eat."

Relief pushed through her. "That was mighty sweet of her."

"She figured you'd be exhausted after being up all night and gone all day so she made extra and sent it over."

She stopped resisting him and allowed Michael to lead her into the living room.

He gently pressed on her shoulders, forcing her to sit. Her eyes followed him as he walked back into the kitchen. The man sure came from some mighty fine stock.

Michael brought her a plate full of food and a glass of warm buttermilk. She thanked him, then picked up a piece of fried chicken and tore off a chunk. Chewing took more strength than she had, so she put it back down and set the plate aside. She curled into a ball on the sofa and closed her eyes.

Michael filled his plate and headed over to join Selina. His heart melted seeing her curled on the sofa and her food barely touched.

He set his plate next to hers, slid his arms under her shoulders and legs and carried her up the stairs. The woman weighed next to nothing. Selina might act tough, but she felt fragile in his arms, and he could feel her ribs she was so thin. She was eating more than when she had arrived, but not much more. On top of not eating enough, she worked harder than their draft horses during wheat harvest.

He laid her small, sleeping frame on the bed. Poor thing was so tired she didn't even arouse. He looked at her trousers, her belt and her boots, wishing he could put her into something more comfortable. But even though they were married, he wouldn't feel right changing her clothes. Instead, he removed her boots and laid a blanket over her.

Tendrils of hair feathered against her pillow. Her lips parted. He wondered what it would be like to kiss her as often as he liked without restraint.

To hold her in his arms whenever he wanted.
To have a real marriage with her.
To love her.

Chapter Eight

Michael headed downstairs. He picked up his plate and sat down at the table, alone. His attention trailed upstairs to where Selina was sleeping. He'd gotten used to eating with her and it felt weird not to. Funny how the woman was starting to grow on him.

He finished his dinner and cleaned up so Selina wouldn't have to. When he finally headed to his bedroom the wolf howled from his cage near the sofa, making the hair on Michael's neck and arms rise. Before the thing woke up Selina, he hurried and snatched it out of its cage, rushed it outside and set it down on the ground.

The second he let it go, he realized his mistake. The pup took off running into the thick woods. Michael ran after it, dodging trees and branches. He struggled to keep his eyes on where it was heading, but before long the pup had disappeared from his line of vision.

If it were a dog, he would holler its name, but it wasn't, and the animal had no name. Pushing back thick brush, he searched frantically for the wolf, but it was too dark to see. He knew by the time he got back to the house and grabbed a lantern, the thing would be long gone, if it wasn't already. As much as he didn't want the wolf around, he felt like a louse that it was his fault the animal was gone. He should have paid more attention to what he was doing.

How was he going to tell Selina what he had done?

And would she believe him after all the fuss he'd made about having the wolf in the first place?

Selina squinted and placed her hand over her face to block out the light coming in through her bedroom window.

Light?

She bolted up and looked around. What time was it, anyway? She threw the covers back and, since she was already dressed, flew down the stairs and glanced at the grandfather clock. Fifteen minutes after eight. *Jumpin' crickets*. She had way overslept.

The house was quiet. Michael had already gone to work, and that poor wolf pup hadn't been fed or tended to since last night. Her attention drifted to the empty cage.

Empty? Her heart flew to her toes. She ran through the house in search of the pup, but he was nowhere to be found.

She rushed outside, checking all around the house, under the porch, through the trees, under every bush, all the way down to the barn, and still no sign of the young critter.

She bridled Macy and then rode off, widening her search. A rider headed her way. Relieved to see it was Michael, she galloped to him and leaped off her horse. So did Michael. "Have you seen the wolf pup, Michael? He's gone. I can't find him anywhere."

Michael's eyelids dropped.

Oh, no. "Where is he?"

Michael raised his head but wouldn't look at her. "Last night when you were sleeping he started howling, so I took him outside. When I set him down, he darted off into the woods. I tried to find him, but it was too dark to see where he went. I'm really sorry, Selina."

Anger bit through her. Was he? The man never did like the idea of her having the wolf pup in the house. Had he let him go on purpose?

"I know what you're thinking, Selina. I can see it in your eyes, but I didn't do it on purpose. I wasn't thinking. I was so concerned he'd wake you up that I forgot to put the rope on him."

She looked into his eyes. There was truth there. She glanced away, toward the place where she'd found the pup, and sadness drizzled over her heart. She hadn't realized she'd gotten so attached to the little critter.

"Did you get some rest?"

She pulled her attention back onto Michael and the concern in his voice. "Sure did. I slept like a bear in hibernation. Much obliged to you for lettin' me sleep. I'll hurry back home now and get cleaned up so I can come back and help with the chores."

"The chores are all finished. Why don't you go home and rest, sew or do something that isn't too tiring for you?"

"I'm fine. But I think I'll go check on Sadie. See iffen she needs any more help."

"Mother and Leah went to help her today."

"Well, that was right nice of them. What are you fixin' to do now?"

"Head back to the barn to get ready to start harvesting the wheat tomorrow."

"Oh. Anything I can do to help?"

"No. But, I'll tell you what. Why don't we head over to Jake Lure's first? He had a litter of pups he's trying to get rid of."

Her eyes shot up toward him. "You mean it, Michael? You don't mind? I thought you didn't want animals in the house."

He held his hand up. "Wait a minute. Wait a minute. I didn't say anything about it coming into the house. The dog will have to say outside."

The instant the words left his mouth, Michael knew that pup wasn't going to live outside. What had he done? Why had he offered to get her a puppy? Who was he kidding? He knew the answer to that question. When he'd told her about the runaway wolf pup, the heartbreak that had dashed across her face crushed him. To ease her hurt, he was willing to go over to Jake's house. Jake. The man who jeered people by insulting them and had heckled Michael about Selina's trousers. Maybe going over there wasn't such a good idea.

Then he made the mistake of looking at Selina again. Seeing the joy on her face, he knew he would have to follow through with the puppy idea. "Before we go and look at the puppies, you have to promise me it will stay outside."

She weaved her head back and forth. "Sorry. Can't do that. 'Cause once I give my word, I keep it, and I can't promise I won't feel sorry for the little critter whenever it looks up at me outside the door all sadlike."

The woman was honest if nothing else. And she really did love animals.

Now what should he do?

He hated the idea of animals in the house he had spent months building and furnishing—with expensive, quality furniture—so everything would be perfect for his new wife. Whether he liked it or not, Selina was that wife, and it was her home now, too.

All he could do was hope and pray the puppy didn't tear up the place the same way Jesse's puppy had chewed up Michael's favorite toy when he was younger. Or soil anything like when Abby had let one of the barn cats loose in the house and it had a litter of kittens on his father's shirt folded on a shelf in the closet. As a young boy, whenever Michael wore that shirt it was like having his father with him wherever he went, and made him less lonely for him. An animal in the house had ruined that for Michael. But, he wasn't a boy anymore. It was time to let that go. "Okay. You win. Let's go see if Jake has any more pups left."

Selina threw her arms around his waist and pressed her head against his chest. "Thank you, Michael. I'm so happy I could kiss you." She yanked from his arms and looked up at him like a frightened fawn. "I didn't mean I would up and kiss you or nothin'. I just meant that I was so happy I could. But no need to fret, I won't," she prattled on.

Michael placed his fingertips gently over her mouth. "I know what you meant, Selina."

She nodded. "Can we go get that puppy now?"

He moved his hand away and laughed. "Yes. Let's go."

Standing next to Selina's horse, Michael bent one

knee, intertwined his fingers and laid them on top of his knee. Selina placed her foot in his hands and, using it like a stirrup, swung herself onto Macy's back. A breeze of soap stirred in the air as Selina moved.

"You must be excited. You actually let me help you up this time."

She laughed and it sounded like soft thunder and a misty rainfall combined. He mounted his horse and they headed toward Jake's.

When they rode through the bunchgrass, a rabbit skittered out of its hiding place, startling not only them but also their horses. Their mounts snorted and side-stepped.

Selina hung on and calmed Macy down.

Very impressive. Bareback, anyone else would have been thrown.

"Oh, iffen only I'd a had my rifle with me. I'd have shot that little critter and made us some rabbit stew."

Leather creaked as Michael shifted in his saddle. "I don't understand you, Selina. You love animals. You're always doctoring them and here you are wanting to shoot something as cute as a rabbit."

"Oh, I don't enjoy it iffen that's what you're thinkin'. It's a matter of survival, and I know the good Lord put certain things on this earth to provide food for our bellies. I could never shoot somethin' just to be shootin' it. And, it does bother me. But when you see your brothers hungry, you'll shoot just about anything to provide for them."

Michael couldn't even imagine what the woman and her family had gone through. Couldn't imagine what it was like to go hungry, and he prayed he never would. Hearing her comments hurt enough. "Did everyone in your family go hunting?" Side by side, they followed the wide trail through the trees.

"Not when they were younger. When my ma took sick and died, my pa loved her so much he plumb gave up. Forgot all about us youngins. But I didn't. I couldn't bear seein' them beg for somethin' to eat. So, I taught myself how to shoot and hunt and look for plants and other things that were edible."

"How old were you when your ma died?"

"Ten."

"Ten?" Michael felt the shock clear to his toes. What kind of a father let his ten-year-old daughter hunt? He couldn't fathom letting his sixteen-year-old sister Abby go hungry or hunt for food. "How old was your brother?"

"Seven. Ma lost two babies after she had me."

"How many brothers and sisters do you have?"

"Ain't got no sisters. Only six brothers."

"How old were they when your mother died?"

"Jacob was seven. Peter and Eli were five, Matthew was three, and Zeke and Zachary were almost two. Jacob, Peter and Eli are married now. And Doc's payin' for Matthew to go to school to become a doctor so he can take over his practice one day. Zeke and Zachary live with Jacob and his wife, Sarah. Even though they're seventeen now, I could a never let myself get hitched iffen I thought they wasn't being taken care of."

His admiration toward her went up another notch, although he wondered how someone so young could raise a family, especially two sets of twins. "So you basically raised them by yourself then." It was a statement, not a question.

"Had to. My brothers helped when they got older, but it still took a lot of work to gather food and all."

"Why didn't your father help?"

"Like I told you, Pa gave up when Ma died. He just sat around, starin' into the air most of the time until his muscles no longer worked. It got to where we had to carry him everywhere. Sure hurt watchin' him suffer like that."

"What about the suffering you and your siblings endured because he gave up? Didn't you ever resent him for basically dying then, too?"

Even though his own father's death was an accident, Michael had felt that way when the man had died. But, Selina's pa, well, he had just given up and that wasn't right.

His horse shook his head, trying to rid its neck of a pesky horsefly. Michael leaned over and took care of it for him.

"No, I never did resent my pa for that, Michael. He loved my ma something fierce. And before my ma died, Pa used to read to us, tell us stories, hugged us a lot and told us how much he loved us. Pa was a good provider up until then. But his heart broke when Ma died. He said it was as iffen he'd died that day, too. And in a way, I reckon he had."

"My father died a long time ago." Michael still felt his father's death as if it had just happened instead of eons ago.

"What was your pa like?"

"He was a strong man who loved the Lord and loved to spend time with his family. That's one of the reasons why he moved us out here, to spend more time with us. Business took too much of his time back in New York.

And even though he worked hard, long hours out here, we were all together and could go with him anytime."

"How'd your pa die?"

"A tree fell on him. Crushed his chest. He died instantly. I never got to say goodbye."

"You still can, you know."

Michael glanced over at Selina, frowning. "What do you mean? He's gone."

"Well, I never got a chance to say goodbye to my ma. Always felt like somethin' was left undone, iffen you know what I mean."

He understood exactly what she meant.

"So, before I came here, I went to Ma's grave and had myself a long chat with her. Told her I was sorry I never got a chance to say a proper goodbye and all. Told her I loved her. And that I'd see her again whenever I went to meet my maker. I had me a right fine talk with her and all that weight I'd been carryin' with me all them years plumb lifted."

Michael wondered if it would work for him, too. He'd give it a try when no one was around. After all, he didn't want anyone to think he'd lost his mind by talking to the deceased.

Suddenly Selina stopped her horse and jumped off.

"What are you doing?"

"Oh! Did you ever see anythin' so beautiful before in your life?"

He strained to see what she'd found so beautiful, but he didn't see a thing.

Selina squatted and when she stood, a caterpillar crawled up the length of her forefinger.

That's what she'd found so beautiful?

"Can you believe the good Lord took the time to

make each of these here caterpillars different? And iffen that weren't enough, He turns them into beautiful butterflies, makin' them even purtier."

Michael looked at the black hair on the caterpillar. Why hadn't he ever noticed the fuzzy hair before? Or, for that matter, a caterpillar before? Seeing them through Selina's eyes, the thing really was almost beautiful.

"Wanna hold it?" She turned toward him and raised her finger upward.

"Sure. Why not?"

Selina pressed her fingertip to his.

The insect inched onto his finger and onto the back of his hand, tickling Michael's skin. He had to admit, it really was something to see. He glanced to where she'd found it and then to Selina. "How did you ever see this minuscule thing from on top of your horse?"

"Mini school?"

"Sorry. Minuscule—small thing."

She gave a quick nod. "When you're lookin' for it, it's easy."

"You were looking for a caterpillar?" Incredulousness filled his voice.

"No." She gazed upward into the tree. Michael's gaze followed hers.

"See that bird nest?"

He strained, peering through the branches until he finally saw the small nest.

"A long time ago, I learned there's hidden treasures everywhere. You just gotta look for them. See that web?"

"What web?"

She pointed to it. Sunlight captured it in its spell,

making the spider web glisten, revealing the intricate pattern. Why had he never noticed how uniform the web was? How silky it looked?

He glanced around, wondering what other "treasures" he had missed because he'd never taken the time to look. A rush of excitement skittered through him. Maybe someday Selina could show him even more of the things he'd missed. Right now, though, he needed to hurry up and get a puppy so he could get back to work. "We'd better go." He glanced at the insect still exploring his hand. "What do I do with this?"

"You can let it loose on one of them leaves."

Michael leaned over and waited as it left his hand and crawled onto a large leaf.

They mounted their horses and hurried to Jake's house.

Everything was quiet when they pulled into Jake's yard. No dogs came to greet them.

"Somethin' wrong?" Selina stopped her horse next to his.

"Shh." He placed his finger to his lips. "Do you hear that?"

Selina tilted her head. "The only thing I hear is a dog barkin'. Sounds mighty upset."

"Wait here. I'll go see what's going on."

"I'm comin' with you."

Michael stopped Selina's horse by grabbing a rein near the bit. "No. I want you to stay here. Until I know how bad it is, I want you to stay."

"I'm used to seein' all kind of bad stuff. Nothin' bothers me."

"You really are a stubborn little thing, you know

that?" He let go of her horse. "Don't say I didn't warn you."

"I won't."

They wove their way through the fir trees.

The barking got louder. At the top of the hill they looked down. Banjo, Jake's dog, was next to his master's body, which was lying face down at the bottom of the hill. The thin, loose rock was too dangerous to take the horses down, so Michael looked around for a safe place. "Let's go around that way."

They followed the hill until they found a spot where they could safely go down. As they neared Jake, Banjo bared her teeth, growling low and menacing, placing herself between Jake and them.

"It's okay, Banjo. We're here to help."

The dog stopped growling and tilted her head sideways.

"You remember me, don't you, girl?"

Banjo dipped her head the opposite direction.

Michael dismounted and so did Selina.

He loosely wrapped the reins around a bush and took two steps toward Jake and stopped. "Wait here." He glanced back at her. "Please?"

She looked at the dog and nodded.

Michael was grateful she listened to him this time. Unsure what Banjo would do, he didn't want her getting hurt.

He extended his hand toward the dog and slowly approached him, talking to her in a calm voice. When he reached Banjo, he let the dog sniff his hand. "I'm here to help him, girl."

Keeping his eye on the dog, which still looked uncertain, he slowly knelt beside Jake and laid a hand on him. His body was warm—he was alive. Michael eased Jake over onto his back.

Blood and dirt covered one side of his face and forehead where a nasty cut oozed. "Jake, can you hear me?" Michael looked over at Selina standing near the horses. "Grab my water canteen from off my saddle."

Selina tied Macy's reins to the same bush as Michael's horse and grabbed his canteen. Michael turned his attention back onto Jake and continued to call the man's name.

She handed him the open canteen, then squatted on the opposite side of Michael.

"That's a mighty nasty cut he's got there. I reckon he's got a concussion."

Hearing her say the word concussion, he wondered how she'd ever learned such a big word.

"We need to take him to his house so I can clean that up." She examined the cut. "It's deep. He's gonna need stitches."

"I think what he needs is a doctor. Would you mind riding into town and getting Doctor Berg?"

"No need for that. I can fix him up just fine."

"I know you can. What I'm concerned about is his unconscious state." Michael laid his canteen against Jake's lips and let the water run into the man's mouth.

Jake stirred and groaned.

"Can you hear me, Jake?" Under his closed eyelids Michael could see Jake's eyes shifting and rolling before they fluttered open.

"Michael? What are you doing here?" he rasped. Jake started to sit up but stopped. He clutched his head and lay back onto the uneven ground.

"I'm going to take you to your house, Jake. Do you think you can handle riding my horse?"

Jake managed a nod. "Nice to see you again, Selina," he slurred, then turned mocking eyes up at Michael. Remembering Jake's jeering comments about Selina when he'd first met her, Michael darted a warning glance at the man.

Jake turned a slow but cocky grin toward Michael. Even injured, he never stopped his jesting, only this time he'd done it with his eyes and his smirk-laden grin.

Michael had half a mind to leave the man here.

"We'd better get you to the house so I can clean that up."

"You ain't touching me," Jake groused.

"I ain't gonna leave you like this." Selina stared at Jake.

Michael knew that look well. It meant she was going to do what she was going to do and nothing or no one would stop her.

Look out, Jake, he thought, then he remembered Jake telling him that he knew who would be wearing the pants in his family.

Was Jake right?

"Help me get him up, Michael."

Jake again sent him a smirk.

"No. I say we just leave him here. I'm sure some bear or coyote needs something to eat for dinner tonight." Michael stood and looked down at him.

Jake's eyes widened with fear. He glanced up at Selina, then back at Michael. "You heard the lady," Jake said, and no smirk covered his face this time.

Selina and Michael helped put Jake atop Michael's

horse. Up the hill and to the house they went, Michael leading the way.

Inside Jake's house, they settled him onto his mattress.

"What happened anyway?" Michael asked.

"I heard the dogs barking and wolves howling. Figured the wolves were after Banjo's pups, so I thought I'd take my shotgun and scare them off. Never got a chance, though. Went looking for Banjo's puppies. Slipped on a piece of rock and tumbled down the hill. Last thing I remember was hitting my head on something hard." His words were strained.

"When was that?"

"Before sunrise." He rubbed his wound, staining his fingers with blood and dirt. "Don't know what would have happened if you hadn't come along. I'd still be down there." He frowned, then flinched, then reached to touch the wound again, but Selina moved his hand away and placed it at his side. "Why did you two come over here anyway?"

"To see if you had any more pups left."

"Oh. Had two females but they're gone. I think the wolves got them or they're running with them. Not even sure if that sort of thing happens, all I know is they're gone."

Selina looked over at Michael. He was certain she was remembering the wolf pup. Again, he wanted to ease her heartbreak by getting her a puppy, but it looked like that wasn't going to happen. Not today anyway. But he'd keep his ears open.

Selina went about heating water, cleaning, stitching and bandaging Jake's wound. "Want me to fetch

Doc on account of that concussion?" she asked when she was done.

"No. I'll be fine. Had one before. He'll just tell me to rest and to make sure someone wakes me up every so often." Jake smiled, then grimaced.

"Well, who's gonna wake you and take care of you?" Her concern didn't slip past Michael. He saw it in her eyes.

"Could you stop by Tom's on your way and see if he'll let Dan come stay with me a couple of days?" he asked Michael.

"Sure. If we're going to do that, though, we'd better leave now," he added to Selina.

"I ain't leavin' here until I fix him some vittles first."

Michael's gaze flew to Jake. He waited for the smirk, but it never came. In fact, Jake's face was blank from shock, no doubt.

"Thank you, Selina, for helping me." He looked back at Michael. "That's one fine woman you've got yourself there, buddy."

He knew Jake meant it, too.

Through the green and gold clusters of tall, thin-bladed grass they headed for home. Mosquitoes buzzed and hovered around them, landing on their arms and faces. Selina kept swatting at them, trying to keep them away from her, but the little varmints were not to be stopped.

Their horses swished their tails hard and fast, shifted their pointy ears and shook their heads trying to rid themselves of the pests, too, but they wouldn't leave. "This sure is interestin' grass. Has to be almost three feet tall. Does it have a name?"

"It's bunchgrass."

The stuff grew in bunches, but Selina wasn't sure if Michael was teasing her or not. Judging from the serious look on his face, she reckoned he wasn't.

"Sorry about the puppy."

"Wasn't meant to be I reckon."

"I'll see if I can find you one somewhere else."

"Okay." Her legs dangled as she rocked with the rhythm of the horse. Macy's tail brushed against her pant leg as she continued to swat at not only the mosquitoes but also a huge fly that kept hanging round. "When we get back home, do you need help gettin' things ready for tomorrow?"

"Tomorrow?"

"Yeah. Earlier you said you had to get things ready for harvestin' the wheat."

"Yes, I do. But there isn't anything you can do to help."

"Oh. Well, I reckon I'll rid the garden of weeds before I go see Rainee, then."

"Do you go there often?"

"I do. I like Rainee. She's good folk."

"She sure is."

"Rainee's from the South, too, so how did she meet Haydon?"

"She placed an advertisement for a husband and Jesse answered it."

"Jesse answered it? He's been married to Hannah a long time. Why would he go and answer an ad for a wife?"

"For Haydon."

"Huh? That don't make a lick of sense."

"It's a long story."

"Well, we got time before we get back to the ranch." She watched his chest rise and fall.

"Rainee's brother wanted to sell her to the neighbor man next door. A man who had murdered his wife."

Selina gasped. "That's horrible. Why?"

"He needed money. Anyway, Rainee found out and so she placed an ad and Jesse sent for her to be Haydon's wife."

"Haydon know about it?"

"No. Boy was he angry when he did find out. Haydon didn't want anything to do with her, but then she rescued him and he fell in love with her. Now they're happily married with another child on the way."

Leave it to a man to give the short version. She wanted to hear more, but she'd ask Rainee sometime instead.

As they rode home in silence, one thing kept buzzing through Selina's mind like the pesky mosquitoes around them. She knew for certain Michael really didn't want anything to do with her, either, but he was stuck with her because they were married.

If only their situation would turn out as well as Rainee and Haydon's. She doubted it ever would, though. And that ripped the heart right out of her. Each day she spent with him, she loved him more and more. In fact, she'd fallen in love with him round about the fourth or fifth letter he'd sent her, and even coming here hadn't changed that.

They rode through the Bowen's ranch yard to the barn. After taking care of her horse, Selina turned to Michael. "You want me to bring you some lunch out here or you wanna come home and eat?"

"It would be great if you brought it here today. I have lots to do."

"I can do that. I'll be back quicker than it takes to cook frog legs."

"Frog legs? You eat frog legs?" Michael's eyes were wider than a purple ironweed bloom.

She wondered if they had any ironweed around here. Sure helped a lot of stomach ailments and the pain after birthing a baby. "Sure do. They're mighty tasty. Ain't you had any before?"

Michael's hand shot up. "No. And I don't ever plan on it, either. So don't get any ideas about ever fixing me any, okay? Promise."

Selina giggled.

"I don't like the sound of that laugh."

He really looked worried now. She giggled harder.

"Se-li-na. You said once you promised you wouldn't go back on your word, so I'm pleading with you to promise me you won't ever fix me frog legs." He scrunched his handsome face as if that was the worst thing that could happen to him.

Selina burst out laughing while Michael continued to look like a coon caught in a live trap.

"I need to get busy. When you're done laughing, would you bring me something to eat, please? And no frog legs, either." He whirled, mumbling something about eating at his mother's house from now on.

She chuckled all the way to the house.

While she threw together two roast beef sandwiches, she imagined what Michael's face would look like if she really did serve him a helping of frog legs. For pure orneriness, she'd do it just to see. Nah. That would be too cruel.

She wondered if he liked crawdad tails. Were there even any around here? She'd have to find out and fix him a plate of those. After all, he didn't say anything about crawdad tails.

Chapter Nine

Selina stood on Rainee's porch and knocked on the door.

Footsteps drew nearer and it swung open. Selina blinked. A woman with red hair answered the door.

"Is Rainee home?"

"Yes, ma'am, she is. Won't you please come in?"

Selina stepped inside and looked around.

"Excuse me. I'll be right back." The tall woman who looked to be in her early twenties disappeared through the back door.

The woman must be the maid Haydon had hired to help Rainee. She didn't need a maid. Selina would be glad to help her.

Voices drifted from the direction the woman had gone.

Within minutes Rainee appeared, hair all sweaty, her calico sleeves rolled up and the front of her white apron soaked. "Hi, Selina." Rainee waddled up to her and gave her a hug but was careful not to get too close. "Forgive my appearance. I have been helping Esther with the laundry." Rainee pressed her finger to her lips. "Shhh. Must not tell Haydon, okay?" She giggled.

"Should you be a doin' that in your condition?"

Rainee waved her off. "I feel fine. Truth is, I feel better when I am working than when I am not. Sometimes it is most vexing having a husband who will not allow me to do these things myself. But—" she sighed "—he loves me and is worried about me."

"You're mighty lucky."

Rainee frowned, then turned toward Esther. "Esther, would you please fix us some tea and bring a few of the cookies we baked this morning?"

"Yes, ma'am."

"And, Esther. There are only a few pieces of laundry left. Would you mind finishing them? And while you are outside hanging them, would you please keep an eye on the children? When you finish, please send the girls in and then you may go home, and I will pay you for the whole day." Rainee smiled.

The pretty woman's big green eyes lit up. "Thank you, ma'am."

"You are most welcome. And thank you, Esther, for all your hard work."

Esther's face glowed. She turned and headed into the kitchen.

Rainee motioned for them to head into the living room. As they sat across from each other, Rainee lowered her voice. "Is something wrong between you and Michael?"

Selina didn't know what to say. She didn't want to disgrace her husband, but it sure would be nice to have someone to talk to about it. Then Michael's words from earlier came to mind. "Michael told me when you got here Haydon didn't want you. Do you mind iffen I ask why?"

Esther brought their drinks and cookies. It felt strange being waited on.

As Esther left, they both took a drink of their tea. Rainee set her small plate with the cup on it on her lap so Selina did the same.

"Michael is right. When I first arrived here, Haydon did not want anything to do with me. I was so hurt and confused I did not know what to do. I had no money and no place to go. I could not go home, either, because my brother had beaten me until I could no longer bear it. That is when I placed the advertisement. I thought I was coming here to a man who really wanted me. Was I ever shocked to discover that not only did he not send for me, but he did not want me, either."

"I know the feelin'," Selina whispered, staring at the cup in her lap.

"What do you mean?"

Selina drew in a deep breath. Gathering up as much courage as she could, she caught Rainee's eye. "I need someone to talk to about this. Promise me you won't say anythin' to anybody about what I'm fixin' to tell you, okay?"

"It will not leave this room. I assure you."

Did Selina dare trust her? The last person she trusted had done her dirty and now she and Michael were paying for it.

Then again, Rainee hadn't told anyone about their reading and writing lessons, so maybe she could trust her about this, too. Besides, the woman knew what it was like not to be wanted by the man she'd come to marry.

"Remember when I told you that my friend Aimee wrote those letters to Michael for me?"

"Yes."

"Well, Aimee didn't write what I'd told her to. But I didn't know that until after I got here and had Michael read the letters to me that Aimee sent him. Aimee had stretched the truth about some things. Plus, most things were what she'd say and do, not me. And she left out a lot of things, too. Michael was mighty shocked when he saw me." Selina tore her eyes away from Rainee. "Aimee never did tell him I couldn't read or write and that I carried a rifle and hunted. Or that I wore a cowboy hat and boots and trousers."

Rainee giggled.

Selina yanked her eyes toward her sister-in-law, frowning and wondering if she was making fun of her.

Rainee stopped laughing. "I am sorry, Selina. I am not laughing at you. It is just that I have always wanted to dress like you."

Selina's mouth dropped open. "You did? Are you joshin' me?"

Rainee shook her head. "No, no. I always have."

"Well, I'll be. Ain't never heard anyone like you say somethin' like that before. They usually make fun of me."

"What do you mean 'like me'?"

"Someone who's got money. I ain't had the best of luck with rich folks."

"Neither have I."

Again, Selina's jaw fell open. "What do you mean?"

"Most people who come from wealth are such snobs and can be quite hateful."

Selina didn't know what to say to that.

"I really do envy you, Selina. I would love to wear a pair of trousers. Dresses are so binding. I would love to be like you. Free. A breath of fresh air."

The back of Selina's eyes stung. "Thank you kindly, Rainee. Nobody's ever said anythin' like that to me before, either."

Rainee laid her hand on top of Selina's. "I really do mean it, Selina." She sat back. "The closest thing I ever got to wearing pants was my riding skirt."

"What's that?"

"Basically a pair of pants that look like a skirt."

"Would you show me how to make some?"

"Sure will."

Then Selina glanced at her lap. "Rainee, I know you said ya envy me and all, but could you help me to become a lady like you?" She looked up at Rainee, hoping with all her might her friend would say yes.

"Why do you want to change who you are, Selina? Everyone loves you just the way you are."

"Not everyone."

"Michael?" Rainee asked softly.

Selina nodded.

"I am so sorry, Selina. Of course I will help you. But, I wish you would reconsider."

Oh, how Selina wanted to. She loved who she was and didn't want to change for anyone. But she loved Michael. And if he wanted someone like Rainee and Aimee, then that's what she'd give him. Her gut ached just thinking about being someone she wasn't, though.

"Selina."

Selina shifted her attention back onto Rainee.

"Please pray about this first, okay? I can see this is truly vexing you. But God did not make you to be like someone else. He made you the way you are for a reason. Did you ever think that perhaps God wants to use who you are to do something in Michael?"

The weight in her gut lifted. "I never thought of that before. Maybe you're right. I'll pray about it first." She smiled, feeling much better.

"Selina!" Emily and Rosie ran over to her.

Selina jumped up and gave the girls a hug. She pulled back and looked at the wet spot on the front of her dress and smiled. "Looks like you two have been helpin' with the laundry."

"Yes, we have," Emily said.

Rosie hung her head.

"What's the matter, Rosie?" Selina asked.

"I didn't get to help because I dropped the clean pieces on the ground and Miss Esther had to rewash them."

"Oh, sugarplum. I'm sure you didn't mean to." Selina wanted to make the girl feel better.

"She didn't." Emily stood up for her sister. "She was just trying to help."

Selina wished she'd had a sister to stand up for her growing up. Even more so, she wished she had girls of her own. At bedtime, she'd have another long talk with the Lord about that among other things, too.

She visited with the girls a spell, finished her tea and the gingersnap cookies, then hurried home. After spending a few hours sewing clothes for her and Michael, she went in search of something that would work as a net for catching fish—and maybe some crawdad tails. She smiled. Being herself felt mighty nice.

* * *

Close to home, the strong smell of food reached Michael's stomach. Hungry enough to eat the side of a barn, he hurried up the steps, slung the door open and froze in the doorway. "What is she doing in here? Get that pig out of here right now!"

Sitting next to his wife at the kitchen table was Kitty.

"Well, hello to you, too. She followed me home so I let her in to visit with me." Selina patted the pig's head.

"To visit with you?" Michael stepped inside, letting the door slam shut behind him. Was this woman for real? "Just look at her. She's covered in mud and who knows what else."

Selina glanced down at Kitty. "It's dry. Besides, don't worry. She ain't hurtin' your fancy furniture."

"My fancy…" He expelled a long breath of frustration. "I don't know how to get through to you. What is wrong with you, woman?"

"Ain't a thing wrong with me. Rainee said so."

He'd never seen Selina look so smug before. "Rainee? What does she have to do with this?"

"She likes me just the way I am."

"Yes, well, she doesn't have to live with you. I do."

"Ain't you lucky?" She smiled.

"Lucky?"

"Yes. God is teachin' you somethin', Michael. And any time the good Lord teaches us somethin', it's always an adventure."

"Living with you is an adventure. I never know what I'm going to come home to."

"Well, at least I ain't borin'."

"That's for sure." He could do with some boredom.

"See."

Michael's chest heaved as he let out another heavy sigh. There was no winning with this woman. "Please. Just put Kitty outside and please, please don't bring her in here again. I'm going to clean up for supper." He turned and headed toward the sink. With his back to Selina, he asked, "What are we having?"

"Fried taters and onions, greens cooked in bacon fat and salt pork, fried fish and crawdad tails."

Michael froze. Did she just say crawdad tails? He wrinkled his nose and shook his head. Nah. She couldn't have. Crawdad tails were only used as fish bait. He must have misunderstood. He finished washing his face and hands while Selina set the table.

He sat down at the end of the table. A table loaded with a covered Dutch oven pan, two cast iron skillets, a covered bowl, a plate of butter, a jar of strawberry preserves and a pie pan with a few pieces of apples slices sticking out of the lattice top crust. His mouth watered just looking at it.

Selina filled their milk glasses and sat down in the chair on his left. As was their ritual, he reached for her hand, ignoring the usual warmth that spread up his arm.

They bowed their heads. "Father, we thank You for this day and for all that we got accomplished. Thank You for sending us to Jake's today and for using Selina to help him. We thank You for Your bountiful provisions, in Christ's name, Amen."

"Amen." Selina reached for his bowl, raised the lid on the Dutch oven kettle and spooned some green, wilted-looking vegetables with chunks of bacon into it. That must be the greens she was talking about. He had to admit, they looked good. He forked a bite and ate it. Salt exploded into his mouth, along with the taste of bacon. Aside from the shock of how salty they were, they were really delicious. "These are really good."

"Thanks."

"What are they?"

"Mustard greens and mountain sorrel."

Mountain sorrel? Wasn't that a weed? And what were mustard greens anyway? He didn't dare ask what they were. He was better off not knowing.

She grabbed his plate and raised a lid off one of the frying pans.

The fried potatoes and onions looked delicious.

She spooned a large mound onto his plate. Then she raised the lid on another skillet and scooped out a large fish, trout if he wasn't mistaken, and laid it next to the potatoes.

"Where did you get the fish?"

"I caught them down at the crick this afternoon."

"*You* caught them? Down at the *what?*"

She held the covered plate midair and looked at him with a confused frown. "That's what I said, didn't I? I caught them down at the crick. Crick, as in, you know, a small stream a runnin' water."

"Oh, you mean *creek.*"

She set the lid down on the table and looked over at him. "That's what I said. Crick."

"No, you're saying crick, not creek."

"Crick, creek, who cares? I caught us a mess a fish to eat for supper and they're gettin' cold with you sittin' there arguin'."

"I can't believe you went fishing. Did you clean them, too?"

"Well, who else woulda done it, Michael? Ain't you ever heard of a woman fishin' before?"

"Only one. Rainee. But—" he shook his head "—a lot of the things you do, I've never heard of any other woman doing. In fact, I've never met anyone like you before."

"That's 'cause there ain't no one like me. God made me one of a kind. Just like He does everyone. There's no two people alike."

For that, Michael was grateful. He couldn't handle another one like Selina.

She pulled the cloth off of the covered plate. Small mounds of deep-fried something was on them. She placed a pile on his plate and then fixed her own plate.

Michael tried everything except for the little fried bits. That was next. Using his fingers, he picked one up and put it in his mouth and bit down. The texture was a little tough, the flavor different. Good, actually. He popped another one into his mouth, and then another. "These are really good. What are they?"

"I told you we were having crawdad tails."

Michael froze. He'd forgotten all about her saying that because he was certain he hadn't heard her correctly. But he had and now he wished he hadn't. Suddenly the piece in his mouth grew and his stomach roiled.

Weeds and fish bait? The woman was trying to kill him. Against his better judgment, he allowed his manners to take over and swallowed the ball of fish bait. He leaned back in his chair and eyed Selina. "Selina, we've had this discussion before, but it bears repeating. We have plenty of food. You do not need to go hunting for it. If you wanted fish, you only had to ask me, and I would have gotten you some. Do not—I repeat, do not—ever feed me fish bait again."

"Fish bait? You callin' my cookin' fish bait?" Her chair scraped against the hardwood floor as she leaped up. Flames shot from her big brown eyes as she mashed her hands onto her hips.

Michael held up his hands. "Sit down, Selina. That's not what I meant."

"Then just what did you mean?" She plopped onto her chair, never taking her fiery eyes off of him.

"We use crawdad tails for fish bait. We don't eat them."

"Back home we do both." She crossed her arms over her chest and made no motion to go back to eating.

Michael rested his arms on the table. "Look, I understand that you were poor and had to hunt and fish for your food. But you don't have to do that here. Trust me. We have plenty of food."

"I know that, Michael." Her voice softened. "Did ya ever think I might like to fish and that I might like to eat some of them foods I grew up with?"

Knives of understanding ripped into him. No, he hadn't. Not even for a half second. Right then he suddenly realized that she actually enjoyed eating those things. She wasn't trying to be obstinate. She was trying to bring a little of her old home here.

"Truth is I miss home." Her eyes fell downcast. "And sometimes when I find things that remind me of Kentucky, it helps me to be less lonely for my family." She roughly wiped away a tear that trailed down her cheek, and sniffed.

Now he'd done it. He'd made her cry with his insensitivity. Wishing he could take it all back, he reached over and laid his hand on top of hers.

Her gaze slowly slid to where his hand rested.

"I'm sorry, Selina. Of course you miss your home. Oh, speaking of your home, I almost forgot. Some letters came for you today." Maybe that would help ease her homesickness.

Homesickness. Fear tore into him at that one word.

When Haydon and Melanie had moved here, it wasn't long before Melanie had become restless and the vicious fighting began, destroying Haydon, Melanie and those who loved them. Before Michael would allow himself and Selina to go through something like that, he would get their marriage annulled. But not until he did everything he possibly could to make this marriage work, and to make Selina happy and to help ease her homesickness.

"Letters? For me?" Her eyes brightened.

He pulled them out of his vest pocket and handed them to her.

Sadness replaced the joy he'd seen only seconds ago.

"I can't read, remember?"

How could he have been so foolish? "I'm sorry, I forgot. I can read them to you, if you'd like."

"I'd like that very much. But can we do it after supper? I'm mighty hungry."

"Sure."

"Thank you kindly, Michael. And I'm sorry about the crawdad tails. You made me promise not to fix frog legs but you didn't say anything about these so I figured it was okay. From now on, I'll just fix enough for myself and make you somethin' else. Is that all right with you?"

"That's fine. Thank you for understanding."

"Didn't say I understood." She smiled and winked at him.

That playful wink felt as if one of those fried fish had come to life and was flopping around inside his stomach. To get his mind off the effect she had on him, an effect he wasn't ready to deal with, he picked up his fork and shoved a bite of potatoes into his mouth. They really were good the way she fixed them. The craw-dads, however...

Chapter Ten

Selina finished the dishes. She couldn't wait to see who had written her from back home. Home. She missed her brothers and the Appalachian Mountains. There, she could be herself and no one thought anything of it. No one cared if she fixed frog legs, crawdad tails or greens. In fact, they loved and appreciated all her hard work.

Here, nothing she did was ever right, and she sure didn't feel needed or wanted.

Back home, she had a sense of belonging, too. Well, with the exception of rich folks. But the only time she had to be around them was when she went to pick up their mending and laundry.

The last pan clinked when she hung it on the nail off to the side of the cook stove. She draped the towels on a peg above the sink and turned toward the fireplace and to Michael, who was watching her as she made her way toward him. She sat in the chair next to his.

"You ready?"

"Sure am. Can't wait to see who wrote me." She

watched eagerly as Michael opened the first envelope and pulled out a piece of paper.

Selina,
We sure do miss you around here, but we's awful glad you found yourself a good man. Things is the same round here. Well, except for no pa. Still hard to believe he's gone. But he's with ma now, and that's what he was wanting all along. Everyone here is a doing good. The boys are growing like weeds and stronger than oxes. Afore long they'll be able to beat me at arm wrestling. They all send their love. Sarah too. She's gonna have a baby come first part of the year. We're sure excited about it. Can you imagine me a pa? I kinda like the idea. How bout you? You fixin to have any youngins anytime soon?

Selina's face burned hotter than the coals in the fireplace.

Michael looked at her from the corner of his eye.

Logs popped and crackled, filling in the quietness. If only it would fill in the awkwardness, too. But nothing could. The way things were betwixt them right now, there wasn't much chance for her and Michael to have any children. They were just two people living under the same roof, pretending to be married.

"Selina, I don't want to offend you or anything so please don't take this the wrong way, but how come your brother knows how to read and write and you don't?"

"None taken. Weren't any teachers around when I was younger. Two years after Ma died, one came to the mountains from some big city back east. I was too busy providin' for my brothers and pa to go to school, but I made sure they went. Jacob didn't wanna go. He wanted to help. But I made him go." She leaned closer to Michael, anxious to hear more. "Now, is that all he said?"

Michael's eyes dropped to the paper.

We sure would appreciate hearing from you. So, Michael, if you are reading this, would you drop a line, letting us know how our sister is doin? We'd be mighty grateful. Thank you kindly.

Zeke and Zach said to tell you hi and that they love you and miss you.

We love you too, Selina, and miss you heaps. Come for a visit whenever you can.
Love,
Jacob and Sarah and the boys

"Do you want to reply to it now?" Michael asked.

"No. I want you to read me the others first."

She listened as he read the letter from Eli and his wife, Bobby Sue, and now from Peter and his wife, Bella.

Dear Selina,
I just wanted to let you know that Pastor Hickens and I were thinking about you and praying that all is well with you. Mrs. Jenkins and Mrs. Albin send their love. Just so you know, you can stop worrying about both of them now because they are being taken care of almost as well as when you were taking care of them. Aimee has been helping them. She…

At the mention of Aimee's name, she jerked her attention onto Michael to see his reaction. Wrinkles lined his forehead but he kept right on a reading. Only Selina didn't hear another word, she was too busy wondering what he was feeling.

There was one letter left. She watched as Michael ran his finger under the seal and removed the letter from its envelope. The muscle in his jaw worked back and forth and his brows furrowed. Whoever it was from had him mighty worked up. Only she couldn't tell if it was anger or something else. He excused himself to get some firewood and was gone for almost an hour. She could hardly wait to see who the letter was from.

Ever since Selina had arrived, Michael had shoveled his anger at himself and her friend into a deep hole, burying and hiding it as well as he could. But seeing the signature on the letter he held, all the bitterness, resentment and anger resurfaced.

He sucked in a deep breath and willed none of those things to show while he read to Selina. Selina felt bad enough about the whole situation and he didn't want her feeling worse. Living with her had proved she wasn't capable of the deception that had led to their ill-begotten marriage.

To deal with the anger he had toward himself and Aimee, he had taken it out on the firewood when he split it, pounded harder than necessary on the nails when he repaired the corrals, and shoveled the muck in the barn with a vengeance. The stench of it was as bad as the stench of his anger, anger that needed to be purged like the dung in the barn. When none of those things worked, and actually exacerbated things, he had finally turned to prayer. That was the only thing that helped him deal with it enough to go back inside the house. He offered up a quick prayer and then turned to the letter.

My dearest friend,
I hope you and Michael are settled into your new life together. I'm so happy for you, Selina. I only wish I could find someone as wonderful as your Michael seems to be. You are so blessed to have someone like him, as is he to have someone like you. Both you and he deserve the best, and I wish you both all the happiness in the world.

Michael continued to read, his voice monotone even though a gamut of emotions stirred inside him. Emotions he couldn't quite put his finger on.

Things are not the same around here without you. Rather boring, actually. Father is planning another party. I so hate those things. Everyone here is so phony. Unlike you, Selina. You are the one and only genuine person I know. Don't ever change. For anyone. You hear me. Oh, before I forget, Bosley had her puppies. Seven of them. I think of you every time I look at them. They're so sweet and loving and accepting. Just like you, my dear friend. You are truly one of a kind. I am planning a visit real soon as I cannot wait to see you again. I love you and miss you terribly.
Give Michael my love.

No thanks. He wanted no part of the deceptive woman.

Your forever friend,
Aimee

Michael folded the letter and put it back into the envelope. Though the room was quiet, the ticking of the grandfather clock and Selina's breathing roared like a violent stampede.

Selina set the rocking chair into motion. "I sure don't understand her." He barely heard her, her voice was so soft.

"You don't understand what?" he asked equally as quiet.

"She acts like she ain't done nothin' wrong."

That's what he was thinking, too. Aimee seemed to think that he and Selina deserved each other. Why would the woman think he would like Selina? He'd told her what type of woman he was looking for. And Selina was far from it.

Would he ever be able to truly forgive Aimee for deceiving them?

And would he ever be able to love Selina the way he had loved who he'd thought she was?

Selina struggled with Aimee's letter. It surprised Selina that Aimee acted like Michael and Selina belonged together. If only she had kept Michael's letters, then she'd have asked Rainee to read them to her. To find out what they really said. But she hadn't kept them because she couldn't read them herself anyway.

Aimee said she was coming for a visit. Truth was,

Selina didn't want her to come. The very thought of it tied her stomach into knots. Especially after all those words about how wonderful Aimee thought Michael was. Sounded as if Aimee loved him, too.

Like a flung rock to the head, reality smacked her. *Dear Lord. She is, isn't she? Aimee's in love with Michael.*

Selina pondered how Aimee was more Michael's type than she was. Aimee was unmarried and a real looker, too. Would Michael fall for her once he laid eyes on her and saw how sweet and kind she acted?

With Michael and her being married in name only, would Michael get their marriage annulled so he could marry Aimee? That thought frightened her more than anything ever had in her life before. Well, there was no way she would let that happen. She had to figure out a way to win Michael's heart—and fast. She'd have to work harder to learn how to write so she could write Aimee and tell her she wasn't welcome here. If not, she feared she would lose Michael forever.

That night Selina wrestled with her sheets. Long before the sun peeked over the mountain, she got up, flew through breakfast and chores and then hurried over to Rainee's.

A surprised Rainee greeted her at the door.

"What am I gonna do, Rainee?" Selina blurted before she even stepped inside. "I can't have her show up now…"

Rainee opened the door to let her in.

Emily and Rosie looked up from the table and their puzzle, then rushed over to Selina and hugged her.

"You want to help us put our puzzle together?" Rosie asked.

Selina glanced at the wooden puzzle pieces scattered on the kitchen table. Normally she would love to spend time with the girls, but today she had too much on her mind and really wanted to talk to Rainee.

"Not today, girls," Rainee said. "I want you to go find Esther and stay with her until I tell you it is okay to come back inside, okay?"

"Yes, Mother," they both said with disappointment.

Selina hated disappointing them like that, but she'd make it up to them later.

When the girls were out of sight, Rainee looped arms with Selina and led her to the living room. A tray with a pot of tea, cups, the small plates she learned were called saucers, and all the fixings for tea were set on the round table between them.

Rainee fixed them both a cup of the dark brew. "Now, tell me what this is all about. Who is coming to see you?" She held the cup to her lips.

"Aimee. She says she's comin' for a visit. She's real purty, Rainee. And Michael fell in love with the woman in them letters. The letters were more her than me. I'm so afraid when he meets her and gets to know her, he'll send my hide packin'."

"Michael would never do that, Selina. He is a man of his word."

"Maybe so, but I ain't takin' any chances."

Rainee seemed to be studying Selina for a moment. Her tea cup tinkled when she set it down. "I have an idea. Come with me."

Selina followed Rainee into one of the rooms. There stood the same kind of treadle sewing machine that Selina had at her house but didn't know how to use.

Rainee showed her how to use the machine. Selina

caught on fast, and the two of them commenced to sewing.

That evening, Selina couldn't wait until Michael got home. With supper on the stove, she sat on the sofa, watching the door.

The boards on the steps creaked.

Selina hurried to stand in front of the fireplace.

Footsteps sounded on the porch, then stopped at the door.

Selina held her breath.

The door squeaked opened.

Michael stepped inside and stopped when his attention landed on her. His eyes almost popped out of their sockets. "Se-Selina? Is that—is that you?"

Michael was certain his heart had stopped beating. The vision in front of him could not be his wife. "What happened?"

She frowned. "What do you mean, what happened? Ya told me you wanted me to make dresses, so I did. Well, one at least anyways."

"That was days ago, and you made it clear you weren't going to wear dresses."

"A woman can change her mind, can't she?"

"Guess so. But, you said you weren't changing for anyone."

"Ain't changin' *who* I am, just what I'm wearin'."

Boy was he ever glad she did. She looked great in a dress. He ran his eyes down the length of her. Her molasses, copper-and-honey-colored hair hung to her waist in waves. The woman really did have a shape to be envied by any woman.

The vision of loveliness standing in front of the fireplace was more of what he had in mind when he pictured the woman he had married.

His heart picked up its pace as she glided toward him, looking and walking every bit the lady. Her pink skirt swished with each step she took, and he found he couldn't peel his eyes away from her.

Only a foot separated them now.

He got a whiff of something sweet.

Her brown eyes sparkled as she looked up at him. "What do you think?"

"I think I like it. You—you look beautiful. I could get used to coming home to this."

"Could you?"

He slid his attention to her hopeful, beautiful eyes.

Eyes that suddenly seemed to be pulling him into their depths.

He inched his body closer to her.

She took a small step toward him.

His heart beat faster, and his body trembled.

She looked up at him, blinking.

His arms reached out to her, pulling her to him.

His gaze lowered to her slightly parted lips, lips that invited his to join them.

But just to make sure he wasn't mistaken, when he leaned his head down, he searched her face for permission.

Her eyes slid shut. That was all the permission he needed. He covered her lips with his, drinking in their softness, enjoying the feel of her. His heart yearned to draw her even closer, so he did.

"Anybody home?"

Michael whipped his head toward the door, letting Selina go. "Jake? What are you doing here?" Michael's insides groaned. Of all the times Jake had to stop by, why did he have to pick now?

"I was on my way home from town and thought I'd stop by and tell Selina thanks again for saving my life."

"Come on in," Michael said, even though he really wanted to ask him to come back another time.

The screen door squeaked as it opened and closed. Jake stepped inside and his eyes bulged. "Woo wee. You sure look beautiful this evening, Selina."

"Thank you kindly." Selina glowed under his praise.

The look of approval on Jake's face bothered Michael, so he tucked Selina under his arm. "She sure does."

"Would ya like to stay for supper?"

Please, please say no.

"I'd love to."

Michael inwardly groaned again.

"Well, have a seat and I'll fetch another plate."

Jake sat in the chair across from Selina's. Michael noticed Jake was well-groomed and smelled of soap and shaving cream. Even his clothes were pressed, not very well, but they were pressed nonetheless. Just who was he trying to impress? Selina?

Selina brought an extra plate and glass and set it in front of Jake. He followed her with his eyes as she headed to the stove. "She sure looks nice, Michael," Jake whispered. "I'm sorry about what I said about her when she first came. I was wrong."

Those words meant a lot coming from the one person who never seemed to speak a kind word about anyone.

Selina's shiny mane shifted from side to side at her waist as she headed back to the cook stove. He'd never seen her hair down before and it was definitely a sight to see. She was a sight to see. He only hoped she would wear her hair down more often and start wearing dresses all the time.

She brought a covered basket, a plate covered with a towel, a saucepan, and the Dutch oven kettle and set them down.

His heart stopped, fearful of what was in the pan. Some bizarre food?

He held his breath when she removed a lid exposing creamy mashed potatoes.

Michael breathed a sigh of relief. So far so good.

She filled both men's plate with a generous portion and a small portion for herself.

Anxiously he watched as she raised the lid on the saucepan. Steam and the smell of gravy rose.

Whew. Thank You, Lord. Michael kept his smile hidden.

She filled a ladle and made a hole in their mounds of potatoes and filled it with the smooth, rich, brown gravy.

He glanced at the towel-covered basket—he wasn't worried about that one. It either had biscuits or bread. As for the covered plate, that one had him worried. Who knew what was under that cloth? Just so it wasn't crawdad tails, fried snake or some other crazy food.

She raised the cloth to reveal something fried.

His breath held. It sort of looked like chicken, but he wasn't sure.

"What piece of quail would you like, Jake?"

"Quail? That's quail?" Michael asked somewhat relieved.

"Sure is."

"Where did you get quail?" Michael asked.

"Killed it myself."

"You hunt?" Admiration filled Jake's eyes.

"Been huntin' most of my life."

"I'm impressed." Jake seemed to be impressed with a lot of the things Selina did. And that bothered Michael.

Selina tilted her head and looked surprised. A piece of hair fell across her cheek. Michael longed to move it out of the way just so he could feel her soft skin underneath.

She loaded their plates with quail. "Y'all want regular biscuits or cornbread ones?"

"I love cornbread," Michael said. "I'll take three of them and two of the regular biscuits."

"Me, too," Jake added eagerly.

After she handed them out, they bowed their heads and prayed.

"What else can you do?" Jake scooped a large forkful of mashed potatoes and shoved it into his mouth, then put a slab of butter on his biscuit.

"The same stuff everyone else does, I reckon."

"No, not everyone. I don't know anyone other than Doc who can sew cuts like you. And this food is delicious. As delicious as the meal you cooked for me. That was the best meal I'd had in a long time." He looked at Michael. "Your wife is one fine cook."

"She sure is." *That is, if a person didn't count the fried snake and crawdad tails,* but Michael kept that thought to himself.

"Thank you for your kind words about my vittles. How's the head doing?"

Jake smiled. "I'm doing well, thanks to you."

Hey, I was there, too. If it weren't for me taking her over to get a puppy, she wouldn't have even seen you to help you. Just where did that come from? It wasn't like him to be jealous. Especially over Selina.

"Iffen you want me to, I can check it and change your bandage before you go."

"That'd be great. Thanks." Jake drank half a glass of milk and wiped his mouth. "I was wondering something. Out here, you need to be a strong woman to survive. You got any friends back home just like you?"

Michael sucked in a piece of quail, completely blocking off his air supply. He grabbed his throat. Selina jumped up and shoved his head to his knees. Air whooshed from his lungs and a piece of quail flew from his throat and landed on the floor.

He rasped and wheezed, "Thank you, Selina."

"You're welcome." Her eyes raked over him with fear. "You all right now?"

He took a generous drink of his milk. "Yes. Thanks to you." Hadn't he just heard those same words from Jake?

Michael couldn't believe that the man, whose main goal in life was to taunt people, actually wanted someone just like Selina.

They went back to eating and Jake and Selina talked the whole time, leaving Michael to wonder why he and Selina didn't have conversations like that.

Jake hung on Selina's every word as she talked about Kentucky and the Appalachian Mountains.

Michael watched her eyes light up, heard the sweetness in her melodic voice. His gaze fell to her lips as she talked.

Those same lips he had enjoyed kissing earlier.

Seeing how easily she and Jake carried on a conversation, he wondered if he could ever enjoy talking to her like that. If he could ever love her.

Jesse said love was a choice. Michael had willingly made that choice once and look where it had gotten him. He had married a woman he thought he knew extremely well. A woman he loved and had given his heart to. Yet, here he was married to a complete stranger he did not love. Just like Haydon had done.

Thoughts of the horror of his older brother's first marriage stormed over him. The image of Haydon carrying Melanie back to the ranch that last, fateful day when she had fallen to her death, memories of his brother—silent, sorrowful, angry, inconsolable.

There were rumors afterward. Michael had heard Melanie was unfaithful, that Haydon blamed himself for not being attentive enough, for keeping her here when she so wanted to leave. And now she was dead.

But those were only ghosts in his memory now, the bits and pieces a young man gathers as his family struggles to live through a crisis. Try as he may, he couldn't shake any of them as he listened to Selina talk to Jake. Was he stepping right into the trap he had sworn he would never go near?

All he knew was his heart was in his throat and his mind was spinning around so fast he couldn't catch it. Everywhere he looked was the possibility of ending up just like his brother, and he had no idea how to avoid the fate that seemed to lie in wait to swallow him whole.

Selina dried the dishes and put them away. Over and over she pondered Michael's kiss. She wanted more. But until she was certain it was her he was thinking of and not Aimee or some woman who didn't exist, she wouldn't share his bed no matter how much she wanted to. It was a good thing Jake showed up when he did. She wasn't sure what would've happened if he hadn't. And that would not have been good.

Tomorrow she'd get busy and make herself a few more dresses and she'd wear her hair down more often, just because Michael liked it that way.

She still couldn't believe she was wearing a dress just to please a man. But Michael was worth it, so she would do whatever it took to win his heart and to hold on to him. She wasn't going to let Aimee steal her man.

Finished with cleaning up the kitchen, she wiped her hands on the towel and hung it on the peg above the sink, then headed over to where Michael was sitting in the living room with his Bible.

She sat down.

"Why didn't you tell me you could draw?"

Selina yanked her head toward him.

"The first I heard of it was when you told Jake. What else should I know about you?"

"Ain't much else to tell."

"Where did you learn to doctor people?"

"Doc taught me." Selina chuckled. "With six brothers who always had cuts and broken bones, Doc said it would save him a heap of trouble iffen I learned. When the boys got older, every free chance I got I went with either Doc or Josephine, the midwife back home, to learn not only how to doctor, but how to birth babies. I just wished I would have learned before it was too late."

"Too late for what?"

"My cousin Lou Ellen. She died givin' birth. Wouldn't have happened iffen there had been someone there to help her."

"Earlier you said you miss your home. What do you miss about it?"

"My family mostly."

"Would you mind drawing me something?"

"Now?"

"Yes. Now."

"I ain't got no paper or pencil."

"I do." Michael walked over to his desk, and when he came back, he handed her a thin square board with a stack of papers on it and two sharpened pencils.

"What do you want me to draw?"

"Something about Kentucky that means something to you."

She nodded.

Michael read his Bible while she drew.

The picture in her mind slowly came to life on the paper. When it was just the way she wanted it, she smiled, then looked over at Michael. "I'm done."

Michael stood behind her. "Selina, it's beautiful."

"That's the house I grew up in. On the porch are the rockers my pa made before my ma died. Hangin' from the tree over yonder is a swing he'd made for all of us. It's ratty now, but I drew it as I recollected it when it was new. All them trees—" she pointed to the ones in the drawing "—they're hickory nut trees. And that's the river we drew water from and caught fish from. It's a whole lot bigger than the ones y'all have here."

She continued to describe the boulders nearby, the different kinds of bushes and flowers. "Well, that's it. That's my home. Old home, anyways."

"It's very pretty. You are one talented, gifted lady."

"Gifted? I ain't gifted. Talents and gifts come from the Lord. The Holy Spirit does the drawin'. I just sit down and let Him use my fingers. Speakin' of gifts and the Holy Spirit, would you read to me outta the Good Book? It's been a long time since anyone has."

"Of course. I'd love to. What would you like to hear?"

"Didn't get much Bible readin' back home, so I'd be mighty thankful for anythin' you read." She set her drawing, the rest of the paper and her pencils on the coffee table.

Paper rustled as he turned the Bible pages. "I'll start in the book of James. 'James, a servant of God and of the Lord Jesus Christ, to the twelve tribes which are scattered abroad, greeting. My brethren, count it all joy when ye fall into diverse temptations, knowing this, that the trying of your faith worketh patience.'"

"What's that mean? Diverse?"

"It means a great deal of variety. Or in this verse, many temptations."

She nodded. "I see."

"'But let patience have her perfect work, that ye may be perfect and entire, wanting nothing.'"

"I sure do struggle with patience sometimes."

"Me, too. Actually, I think we all do—otherwise the Lord wouldn't have bothered putting it in His Word."

"So what's it say we're to do when we're tempted?"

"Well…" The pages rustled as he turned them some more. He ran his finger down the page. "Here it is. It says here in James 4:7, 'Submit yourselves, then, to God. Resist the devil and he will flee.'"

"Submit? What does that mean?"

"Well, the way I understand it is, when we're tempted, we're supposed to turn to God. In doing that, we set ourselves up to receive His transforming, saving power. If we simply try to resist the devil without turning to God, then we're depending on our own strength and our own willpower. And our strength and willpower are in no way sufficient."

She frowned and tilted her head.

"Not sufficient means it isn't enough."

He must be getting to know the look she gave because he'd explained that word without her even asking.

"We need God's grace and His mercy to help us resist the devil and flee temptation."

"I see. I'll have to ponder on that. Thank you, Michael."

"You're welcome." He covered his mouth when he yawned.

"It's gettin' late. You'd better get to bed."

"Yes. I'd better. It's going to be a long day tomorrow. Actually, for the next few weeks, too. I want to warn you, you won't be seeing much of me during that time. We'll be doing our best to get the wheat in."

"I understand. Iffen there's anything I can do to help, let me know, okay?"

"The best thing you can do to help is to take care of things around here. Laundry, mending, meals, stuff like that. If I don't have to deal with any of that, it makes a huge difference."

"I can do that. I'm gonna do of heap a sewin', too. And I'll make sure you have plenty of vittles and water to take with you."

"Sounds good." He rose, then looked down at her. "Just don't send me any crawdad tails or frog legs, okay?" His eyes had a twinkle when he said it.

She giggled. "I won't." She stood. "Michael? Could we pray together before you go to bed?"

"Sure." He reached for her hands and bowed his head. He started to pray and when he got to the part about thanking God for her wearing a dress, she couldn't help but laugh.

Michael opened his eyes and looked at her, his expression serious.

"Sorry. I just found it funny."

"I mean it, Selina. You wearing a dress means a lot to me." His blue eyes roamed over her face.

She tilted her head. "How come?"

"I don't know. I just know that it does." He still held her hands. That meant a lot to her. She was grateful for any touch or any affection he gave her. And as much as she wanted to share a bed with him, she was grateful he wasn't forcing his husbandly rights on her, instead giving them time to get to know each other before they did. If they ever did, that is.

Suddenly she felt the need to ask, "What did you want in a wife, Michael?"

Selina's question sent Michael backward. "You really want to know?"

"Wouldn't have asked iffen I didn't."

He dropped her hands and stepped to the fireplace. With one hand on the mantel, he stared into the dwindling fire, deciding what he would say. The truth was always best. "I wanted someone like Rainee. *Not* Rainee, but someone *like* her," he hastened to add lest Selina get the wrong idea that he was in love with his sister-in-law. Yes, he loved Rainee, but like a sister now.

"And…" Selina interjected.

"Someone who's confident, genteel, educated. A real Southern lady, who could hold her own in any type of

situation whether it be here on the ranch, or at a dinner theater, or entertaining prospective business clients.
I wanted someone to take care of my home and children. Someone who supports me in what I do. Someone who isn't afraid of jumping in and helping, even
getting dirty when the need arises. Someone with spit
and fire. Who challenges me. Who's willing to fight
for what she believes."

As soon as the words left his mouth, he realized Selina fit that part of his dream wife perfectly. And today,
she was dressed every bit a lady. A beautiful lady at
that. One who had walked with dignity and grace. The
other missing attributes he could learn to deal with. The
one he couldn't was love.

"Go on," she whispered.

"Someone to come home to. But most of all someone I can love with all my heart and who loves me
back the same."

"I love you, Michael," she whispered.

Michael stopped breathing and his heart stopped
beating.

The air in the room suddenly vanished.

He had no idea how to respond to that because he
didn't love her back.

"You don't gotta say nothin', Michael. I know you
don't love me. I just wanted you to know that someone
does love you. And that someone is me." She didn't
look at him.

If she was the woman he'd fallen in love with, those
words would have thrilled him. With a little hope and
a lot of prayer, perhaps someday they would. "Thank
you, Selina, for letting me know." He kissed her on the
cheek. Her skin felt soft against his lips. Before he got

carried away again, he stepped back. "And now, I really must get to bed, or in the morning I'll regret it." He brushed past her and headed to the bedroom. Without looking back he said, "Good night, Selina," and stepped through the door and shut it.

He propped his back against the solid wood and closed his eyes. When he opened them, they landed on the empty bed. A bed he longed to fill with love.

Shoving away from the door, he removed his clothes and climbed into bed. "God, I know You don't make mistakes and that there's a reason You put Selina and me together. Therefore, I'm asking You, Lord, to fill both of our hearts and home with love. Selina deserves no less."

Selina sank into the chair. The things he wanted in a wife trailed through her mind.

She pondered each one.

Confusion coiled in her mind. Wasn't she everything he'd said he wanted? Well, except for the genteel part. Nothing genteel about her. As for the lady part, she could work a little harder on that. She could wear dresses more often to please her husband, and she'd keep reminding herself to walk like Rainee had showed her, with something she'd called poise. Nothing more than walking slower with your head up straight and your shoulders back.

As for the rest of his list, it definitely described her. No. No it didn't. He said he wanted someone to entertain potential business clients and who could handle themselves at a theater. Could Rainee teach her how to do that? After all, he wanted someone like her. Selina didn't blame him—Rainee was wonderful.

He said he wanted someone who could educate his children, too. That wasn't her yet. But it could be. She'd work harder to learn to read and write. With that thought in mind, she pulled out her lessons and got to work. As for the rest of Michael's list, well, he wanted a fighter. *Well, sugah, you got one.*

Chapter Eleven

For almost three weeks Selina worked hard at keeping the house clean, making Michael's favorite foods and sewing shirts and pants for him and new dresses for herself. She'd finished making her first quilt, too.

Every time she saw Michael's smile and the approval on his face when she wore a dress and left her hair down, it pushed her to work harder at changing. She was even trying to learn to talk better, too, but that part wasn't going too well. Rainee thought it unnecessary anyway, but she still helped and understood.

No kisses had been shared between Selina and Michael since the last one, but Selina felt it was only a matter of time before he came around again. After all, he'd been dogged tired every night when he came home from the fields.

Today was the last day of harvesting. Michael's footsteps on their porch didn't have their normal spring. He walked like a man in his nineties, shuffling as he came in the door, more tired than she'd ever seen him before. "Evenin', Michael."

He nodded.

Selina grabbed the lunch bucket and water jug from him and set them on the round table next to the door.

His smile barely curled his lips.

"You okay?"

"I'm fine."

"Sure you are," she said mockingly as she pressed her hand against his forehead. "You're burnin' up. Why don't you clean up and head to bed, and I'll bring dinner to you there?"

"I'll be fine." His voice sounded weak.

She slammed her hands on her hips. "You ain't fine, Michael. Your skin feels hotter than white flames." She stepped behind him, placed her hands on his shoulders and gave him a push toward his bedroom.

He didn't fight her but shuffled his way slowly to his room. Inside, he flopped on the bed and sat there, staring at the wall.

"You need help gettin' undressed?" When she realized what she had asked him, her face flooded with heat. She hadn't thought before she spoke. For years she'd helped her pa undress down to his underclothes. But this was different.

Michael slowly raised his head toward her. "I could use some help."

Selina swallowed. The man really was sick. He never let her help him. And this time he was going to let her undress him. She wasn't sure how she felt about that now that he'd said yes. But she reckoned it was fitting because, after all, he was her husband.

She stepped in front of him and slipped his suspenders over his shoulders, then undid his buttons and tugged the shirttail out of his trousers. She climbed on the bed behind him and pulled his shirt off.

His broad-shouldered body was a sight to behold. God had really outdone himself on Michael. She wanted to run her hands over his smooth back to feel the hard muscles underneath her fingers. But now was not that time.

She removed his shirtsleeves by running her hands down his arms. Arms that bulged, that were as solid as rocks, only warm. She needed to hurry and get him cooled down. Hopping off the bed, she came around to the front of him.

A blond lock of hair fell across his forehead, touching his eyebrows and almost his eye.

Without thinking, she reached out and brushed it away. Halfway through, her attention snagged onto Michael's blue eyes.

He was watching her.

She should move away but she was as stiff and unmovable as a frozen pond.

Her mouth turned dry as hard bread.

Michael watched her every move.

She wondered if he was going to kiss her again.

"You're so beautiful, Selina," he whispered.

"So are you," she whispered back. Then catching her slip-up, she said, "I meant you're mighty handsome yourself."

He raised his hand and slid it behind her neck, tugging gently on it until her lips touched his. She melted into them, wanted to melt into him, but his lips were hot under hers. Even though she wanted more of his tender kisses, that would have to wait. Michael had a fever, and she needed to doctor him back to health. There would be time for kissing later. She hoped. Reluctantly, she raised her head.

"What's wrong?" His eyes looked droopy, tired.

"Nothin's wrong. It's just that you're hotter than the sun in July. You need to rest, Michael. Why don't you finish undressin' while I fetch you some vittles?" Her eyes wandered to his bare chest. "I'll—I'll be right back." She fled the room.

Seeing his bare chest, she had a yearning to press her head against it, to hear Michael's heartbeat in her ear, to be held next to it. To him. "Dear Lord, help me," she prayed on the way to the kitchen. "Temptation is a mighty powerful thing. And right now, I'm being mighty tempted."

Michael sat on the edge of the bed, dazed. The gentle feel of her hands as she ministered to him touched him deeply. He wanted to pull her into his arms and kiss her until he had no breath left. But he wouldn't. Only deep, abiding love would induce him to go further. So if and when that happened, he wanted the moment to be special. For both of them.

It took every ounce of energy he had to remove his pants, climb into bed and bury himself under the covers. Selina said he had a fever, but a chill drove clear down into his bones.

Selina stepped into his bedroom holding a tray. She set it on the stand next to him before reaching over and grabbing the extra pillow. The one meant for his wife.

"Sit up a minute."

He raised himself up.

As she placed the pillow behind him, Selina was mere inches from him. The verse he had read about temptation and fleeing it flashed through his mind. He closed his eyes to blot out the temptation before him.

The bed dipped. He opened his eyes.

"Here, sip some of this."

"What is it?"

"Just drink it, Michael. I promise it will help break that fever of yours. Trust me."

He took a sip and pushed it away, frowning. "Does this have alcohol in it?"

"Whiskey. Didn't have moonshine or I'd have used it instead. Whiskey'll have to do."

Not being a drinking man, he hated the taste of whiskey, but she asked him to trust her, so he decided he would. He'd seen enough of her doctoring skills to believe she knew what she was doing.

"What else is in it?" He took another sip, cringing inside at the bittersweet taste.

"Tea, ginger and honey."

Michael finished drinking the tea, feeling the warmth of it spreading into his body. Exhausted, he let his head flop back against the pillow.

"Ready to eat now?"

He didn't have the strength to raise his arms, but he needed to eat to get his energy back. "Yes."

"Tell you what. Why don't ya let me feed you so you can save your strength."

It had been a long time since someone had pampered him when he was sick, so he lay back and thanked God for the help and compassion Selina showered on him.

Selina reached for the bowl and spoon on the tray and settled the bowl under his chin before she laid the spoon to his lips. He opened his mouth and let her feed him.

Delicious was the only way he could think to describe the food. "What is that?"

"Chicken 'n' dumplins. Looks like I picked a right fine day to fix it, too. It'll help ya heal."

She fed him one spoonful at a time. It didn't take him long to fill up. Now all he wanted to do was sleep. His eyes drifted shut.

The bed shifted. His eyes opened to a slit.

Selina tucked the blanket around him and under his chin. "Sleep well, Michael." She leaned down and kissed his cheek. Her lips felt cool next to his hot skin. "Iffen you need anything, you holler. Don't you be gettin' up, you hear?"

He nodded and closed his eyes.

Hours later, Michael woke up. His blanket was damp and he no longer felt hot. He let his eyes adjust to the dark room, wondering what time it was.

In a rocking chair next to his bed, Selina sat sound asleep. How long had she been there?

He took the opportunity to study her.

Her hair, gathered to one side, flowed down the chair, revealing a sleek neck, a graceful, feminine one.

His gaze slid to her heart-shaped face, her high cheekbones and her nice lips. The woman was not only beautiful, she was compassionate, nurturing and unselfish, as well.

"Michael? You okay?" Selina asked through a sleepy voice.

"I'm fine. I actually feel pretty good."

She sat up in the chair.

"You were right. That stuff you gave me broke my fever. And now I need to get out of these wet nightclothes and sheets. They're soaked."

"I'll get you some dry clothes." She lit the lantern next to his bed and then rummaged through his bureau and then the trunk at the end of the bed. She came back with a clean nightshirt, sheets and blankets.

Michael tossed the blankets off. Selina whirled, turning her back to him.

He stood, and she put her arm behind her back, offering him the shirt. "Soon as you get that other one off and this one on, I'll make up your bed."

He smiled. Last night she had seen his bare chest and run her hands slowly over his arms. Now, she was bashful. He found it rather endearing.

Michael slid the damp nightshirt off and put the dry one on. "I'm finished. You can turn around now."

She turned, reached for a pitcher and glass sitting on his night stand, filled it with water and handed it to him. "Why don't you sit over yonder—" she pointed to the rocking chair she'd been sleeping in just minutes before "—while I make your bed up?"

He did as he was told and watched as she hurried to change his bedding. She really was a sweet little thing. He pulled his pocket watch out of his vest pocket and looked at it. Three in the morning. "Selina, why don't you head on up to bed now? I'll be fine."

"You sure? I hate leavin' you to yourself."

"I'll be fine. I feel a lot better. Go on and get some sleep."

She nodded. "Iffen you need me, don't you hesitate to call me, okay?"

"I won't. Good night. Or should I say good morning?"

She smiled and headed out of his room.

Michael woke to the smell of bacon and coffee. Sunlight peeked through the windows. He checked his watch again. Eight-thirty. He groaned, unable to believe he'd overslept. Chores needed to be done. He dressed, then hurried out into the kitchen.

Selina stood at the stove wearing her trousers again. He refused to let his disappointment show. "Morning."

She kept her back to him but turned her head. "Mornin'. Sit yourself down. I'm almost finished heatin' things up. How you feelin' this mornin'?"

"Good. Just a little tired from working the last few weeks from sunup to sundown."

"I'm sure you are. I know I would be." She poured him a steaming cup of coffee and handed him a plate filled with pancakes, bacon strips and scrambled eggs.

"Aren't you having any?"

"Already ate."

"How long you been up?"

"Long enough to do chores and fix you breakfast. I told Jess you probably wouldn't work today 'cause you had a fever last night. He was mighty worried about you, but I told him you were doin' all right. He said to tell you to stay home, that he would do chores today. I told him I took care of most of them and I would finish after I checked on you. He put up a mighty big fuss about that. But I didn't let him stop me."

"I can believe that," he whispered.

"I heard that."

Michael smiled. "Just what time did you get up?"

"Never went to bed after I left your room. I came in here and fixed me some vittles, then headed to the barn."

Michael was speechless. She spent all night sleeping in a chair, making sure she was there if he woke up and needed anything, and then she did all of his chores so he could sleep. "You're something else, you know that?"

Spoon in hand, she turned and looked at him, frowning. "What do you mean, 'I'm somethin' else'?"

"Just what I said."

"Is being 'somethin' else' a good thing or a bad thing?"

"Depends."

"On what?"

"On what the circumstances are. In this case being something else is a good thing."

"Oh, I see." She nodded and smiled. "Then I'm glad I'm somethin' else."

Michael chuckled. One thing for sure, there was never a dull moment with Selina around.

He picked up his fork and started eating. "What are you doing anyway?"

"Making you chicken soup for lunch in case I ain't home."

He stopped his fork midway to his mouth. "Where you going?"

"To Rainee's. Yesterday she wasn't feelin' so good. I think that baby's fixin' to enter the world anytime now. I want to see iffen she needs my help."

"You think she's going to have it today?"

"I do. I feel it in my gut." She faced him again. "You don't mind that I go there and leave you alone for a spell today, do you? Iffen I thought you needed me, I'd stay. But, you said you were feelin' better, so…"

"No, no. You go ahead. I'm going down to the barn to help clean up the harvester and stuff."

"You don't need to do that. Jess said him and the

boys would handle it. I really think you should rest. Give your body a chance to recover completely."

"We'll see. I might just go down and help for a bit and then maybe I'll meet you at Rainee's and see how she's doing."

Selina placed the lid on the pot she was stirring and set it off to the side. "Well, I'd better change my clothes and head on over there."

She was going to change her clothes. That meant she'd only worn the trousers to do chores in. He knew what she was up to. She was wearing dresses because she knew how much it meant to him. Well, if she could give up her stubborn ways, so could he. From now on, he'd try a lot harder to be a better, more understanding husband. He remembered the gift he had for her in his vest pocket. "Wait, before you go. I have something for you."

She stopped and watched him as he headed over to her. "Hold out your hand."

He placed the rock on her palm, wondering why he was so nervous all of a sudden.

When she looked down at it, her eyes widened. "Oh, Michael. That's so purty. What kind of rock is this?"

"An opal. When I saw it, I thought of you and the hidden beauties you spoke of."

As she examined the pearly white rock her eyes grew wider and her smile broadened. "Just look at them shiny pinks and blues and greens. They sparkle like broken glass in the sun." She looked up at him and hugged the rock to her chest. "Thank you, Michael. I'll treasure this for the rest of my life."

She reached up, kissed his cheek and smiled before heading up the stairs.

Seeing the pleasure that small gesture had given her brought a smile to his face. Sure didn't take much to please her. And for some reason, that pleased him.

Selina knocked on Rainee's door and Esther answered it. "I came to see how Rainee is today," Selina said.

Concern wrinkled the corners of Esther's eyes. "Somethin' the matter?"

"She's in bed. Says she's not feeling very well."

"Is that Selina?" Rainee's voice sounded from her bedroom. "Send her in, please."

Selina followed Esther to Rainee's bedroom and the rich brownish-red four-poster bed with spindly posts and light purple bedding.

"How you feelin' today. Any better?"

"No. I believe my time is here." Rainee rubbed her hand over her rounded belly. "I am so glad you are here. I feel much better already."

"Well, don't you fret none. Back home I helped Doc birth over a hundred babies."

Haydon stepped into the room, looking all nervous and worried. "I sent Smokey to get Doc. Do you need anything? Can I do something? Do you need another pillow? Something to drink?"

Selina smiled to herself, knowing things were the same everywhere.

Two hours and lots of contractions later, Selina shooed Haydon out of the room. Doc still hadn't shown up, but this baby wasn't waiting for him any longer.

She checked and saw the baby's head crowning. "Okay, Rainee, push." The second Selina saw the cord wrapped around the baby's neck she ordered Rainee to stop pushing. Her cousin had died because of the very same thing. Well, she wouldn't let Rainee or this baby die. She'd helped Doc back home enough to know what to do now.

"I am not sure I can stop," Rainee lamented.

"Rainee, you have to," Selina said calmly. "Draw in a deep breath and listen to me. You *have* to stop pushin'."

"What is the matter?" Rainee asked, fear running through her voice.

As much as Selina didn't want to tell Rainee what the matter was, Rainee needed to know how important it was for her to stop pushing. "The cord is wrapped around the baby's neck."

"Dear God, no."

"Don't panic. I can unwrap it, but you have to stop pushin', okay?" She had to get it unwrapped as fast as she could to save not only the baby's life, but Rainee's, too.

"Okay. I shall try." Rainee stopped pushing, her breathing came hard and uneven.

"You're doin' good, Rainee. Now, be ready to push as soon as I tell you to, and don't stop until I say it's okay, ya hear?"

"Y-yes." Rainee gasped for air.

Holding on to the slippery head as best she could, Selina ran her hand under the cord and carefully slid it over the baby's head. Selina silently praised God that the cord had stayed attached and in one piece. If it had broken, Rainee could have bled to death. "Okay, now push, Rainee. And don't stop until I tell you to."

Rainee pushed and pushed and in moments the baby was in Selina's hands.

The doctor burst into the room and without asking took the baby from Selina. Within seconds, the baby howled. Selina went to Rainee's side and dipped a cloth into the cool water and blotted the moisture from her face and neck.

"Thank you, Selina." Rainee reached for her hand and gave it a weak squeeze.

"You're welcome."

Knowing Rainee was in good hands with Doc Berg, Selina washed up and then slipped out of the room. Her nerves were plumb worn out just thinking about what could have happened to Rainee if that cord had broken. That thought set her body to shaking again.

Michael sat on his mother's porch swing with his niece Rosie. Yards away from them, Emily visited with her grandmother, who was watching the girls while Rainee had her baby.

Michael wondered how things were going with Rainee. In a few minutes he'd go and see, but for now he was just enjoying the sunshine and spending time with the bubbly child sitting next to him.

"Did you see what I made, Uncle Michael?"

He glanced down at his niece and the doll she held up for him to see, all wrapped in a handmade, large-stitched and slightly crooked quilt.

"You sure did a nice job on it, Rosie. It's very pretty."

"It sure is." She toyed with the quilt around her doll for several long moments before she looked up at him. "Aunty Selina's favorite color is blue, you know."

"Yes, I know it is." Did he ever. That was why he had ordered blue-patterned china, and had their…his… bedroom decorated in blue.

"Mine's pink. And that's okay. 'Cause Aunty Selina said it was."

"What do you mean Aunty Selina said it was?" Michael couldn't wait to hear this one.

"Well, when she came to visit Grandmother, she really liked the blue squares Emily had picked. Made me feel a little sad. Like I didn't choose a pretty color or something. But then Aunty told me God made all different kinds of colors for us so we could each have our favorite. That He made each of us different, too. And that I was perfect and just right like I am." Rosie's little chest puffed out.

"You sure are, munchkin." He kissed her on top of the head.

"Know what else she said?"

"No. What else did she say?"

"She said that it was okay to like different things and to be different. I like that." The smile beamed like the bright sunshine around them. "You wanna know why, Uncle Michael?"

"Yes, I do."

"'Cause, I always wanted to be like Emily, that's why. She's so smart and pretty. Always does things just right and I don't. But after Aunty Selina told me that, I know it's okay to not do things the same way Emily does. Doesn't mean I'm not as good as Emily, just different. And that's okay."

Out of the mouths of babes. "It sure is." This was a lesson he needed to learn, too. It was okay if Selina was different. He just needed to learn how to live with those differences.

Sitting here, listening to his niece chatter on, the desire to have children of his own overpowered his emotions. He glanced over at Haydon's house. He couldn't sit there any longer, wondering how things were going.

He excused himself and went to Haydon's. When he stepped inside, Selina was closing Rainee and Haydon's bedroom door. One look at the worry lines on his wife's face and her tired eyes sent concern rushing through Michael. Concern not only for his wife, but also for Rainee. He went to her side. "You're trembling. Is everything okay in there?"

Selina nodded. "Everythin's fine now. It was a good thing I was here, Michael, or things could've been really bad for Rainee. Doc Berg only just arrived a minute ago."

"What do you mean? What happened?"

"The cord was wrapped around the baby's neck."

Michael gasped.

"Iffen that cord had broke, Rainee could've bled to death, just like my cousin." She shuddered.

"Thank God you were here to help." Michael opened his arms and Selina sank against him. "Thank you for saving them." He hugged her to his chest.

"No. Thank the Good Lord. All I did was what He told me to do." She stepped back from his arms, and he wondered why.

"I think you need to go home and get some rest, Selina. You've had a long night and day."

"I'm fine." She slumped in a nearby chair.

"You don't look fine. Your eyes are barely open and you look like you could fall asleep any second. I'm taking you home. Now."

She yanked herself up straight in the chair. "I ain't going home just yet. I need to be here to help Rainee."

"Yes, you are going home. Rainee's fine, the baby's

fine. But you're not. Besides, Doc Berg is with her now. There's nothing else to be done here."

"I said I was fine. Just tired is all."

"All the more reason for you to go home and get some rest."

"Michael's right." Haydon stepped into the living room. His hair was rumpled and he looked like he'd aged ten years. "Doc Berg is finished. He said Rainee and the baby are doing well and that you did a very good job." Haydon stepped up to Selina and clasped her hands. "Rainee told him the cord was around the baby's neck. Doc said you saved my wife and son's lives. How can I ever thank you enough, Selina?"

"You just did. Besides, I was glad I could help."

"I'm so glad Michael brought you into our lives, Selina." He gave Selina a quick hug. "Now, go do what your husband says. Go home and get some sleep."

"Yes. You heard the man. Do what your husband says," Michael ordered, winking at her.

She pursed her lips and narrowed her gaze at him. Michael stood and took her arm. "Come on, sweetheart. It's time to go home." Had he just called her sweetheart? He glanced down at her. Judging by the way her eyebrows were raised, he must have. Well, what was done was done. He turned his attention to his brother. "Congratulations on your new son, Haydon."

Haydon stood up straighter. "I have a son. Can you believe it?"

"Did you name him yet?" Michael asked.

"Yes. We sure did. His name's Haydon. Haydon Junior."

Michael didn't think it was possible, but his brother's chest puffed out even further.

They headed to the door and stopped.

"Tell Rainee I'll check in on her tomorrow. Unless she needs somethin' tonight. Iffen she does, you come get me, you hear?"

"Will do. Thanks again, Selina."

"Take care of little Haydon Junior," Michael told his brother.

"You can count on it."

They slipped outside into the darkness and headed for home. All the way, Michael's heart ached with envy. Would he ever know what it felt like to be a father? To hold a son or a daughter in his arms. To watch them grow up. Take their first step. Call him Father.

He darted a sideways glance at Selina. Over the past several weeks his affection toward her had been growing. There was more to his wife than her strange attire, her lack of education and her different way of talking. And it was time to find out even more about her. Maybe it was time to start courting his wife.

Chapter Twelve

Selina stretched in her bed. Sunlight lit her room. She wondered what time it was, so she tossed the covers aside to check.

"Oh, no you don't. Stay right where you are."

Selina froze with her hand holding the blanket mid-air.

Michael stepped into her bedroom carrying a tray and smiling. His blue eyes sparkled and so did his teeth. No stubble dotted his manly chin. He wore one of the new blue shirts she'd made and pressed for him.

He set the tray on the nightstand close to her bed. "I brought you breakfast. So sit up, okay?"

She eyed him warily.

He folded the blue blanket down around her lap.

He grabbed the extra pillow on her bed, gently shifted her shoulders forward and slid it behind her back. "There. That's better."

He set the tray on her lap and turned. With a single yank, he spun the chair around, set it down by her bed and sat. "I hope you like them. It's about the only thing I know how to make." His eyes held hope.

Selina glanced at the huge pile of flapjacks. "Where's your plate?"

"I already ate. Those are yours. The coffee's a little on the strong side. Isn't as good as yours, but it isn't bad."

Selina kept watching him, shifting one eyebrow and then the other. "Okay, Michael. What are you up to?"

"Up to? What do you mean? Can't a husband bring his wife breakfast in bed? You did it for me yesterday."

"Ain't the same. You were sick. I ain't."

"Do you have to be sick for me to do something nice for you?"

She dipped her head sideways, but her eyes stayed on him.

"Look, I know you're wondering what I'm up to, but please, just eat your breakfast. See, I even heated the syrup." He lifted the small pitcher and poured it over the stack of flapjacks with a large chunk of butter melting in the center. He cut a triangle out of the hot cakes, and brought it to her lips.

She opened her mouth, keeping her eyes on Michael.

His eyes slid to hers. She ate, staring into his beautiful blue eyes. "These are right tasty." She took the fork from him and dove into the stack.

Michael chuckled. "That good, huh?"

"Sure are."

"When you're done eating, get dressed. You can even wear your trousers if you want."

Her eyes darted open. She slammed her fork down on the tray. The dishes rattled and coffee sloshed over the side of her cup. "Okay, what's goin' on? You can't stand my trousers."

"I know. But I thought we'd go for a ride today and

I figured you'd probably be more comfortable wearing pants instead of a dress."

"Goin' for a ride? Where?"

"It's a surprise. Now finish eating and get dressed. I'll see you downstairs." He pushed the chair back near the window and headed out the door.

Selina watched him disappear.

He was acting mighty strange. She'd better hurry and eat and get dressed so she could find out what that polecat of a husband of hers was up to.

Michael whistled while he tossed two apples, a chunk of cheese, leftover biscuits, ham slices and gingersnap cookies into a flour sack. He had just finished filling the canteens with water when Selina glided down the stairs. Shock barreled through him. The woman wasn't wearing trousers, but a lavender skirt, a yellow blouse and cowboy boots. Cowboy boots. He shook his head and chuckled. Now that was what he was used to seeing.

He met her at the bottom of the stairs and took her hand.

Just like she had when he served her breakfast in bed, she eyed him suspiciously. Well, let her be suspicious. She had every right to be because he was up to something. But he wasn't telling her what—he'd show her instead.

"Sure you don't want to wear your pants? We'll be doing a lot of riding today."

"Nope. See." She pulled one side of her skirt off to the side, revealing the split down the middle. "They're as good as britches. Rainee told me about them. Showed me hers. She even helped me make them."

Michael laughed. He should have known. "Well, they look very nice on you, Selina."

"Thank you. That's mighty nice of you to say so."

"Well, I have everything ready. So let's go."

"Don't you have chores to do?"

"Nope. I already did them. Sound familiar?"

She frowned. "Oh, so that's why you're doin' this. To pay me back. Well, I don't want to be paid back. I did it 'cause I love you." She gasped and slammed her hand over her mouth. "Um, we'd better go iffen we're a goin'." She darted away from him, slapped her cowboy hat on her head and grabbed her rifle, which was leaning against the bench near the door. Then she was out of the house before he could even pick up the canteens and flour sack filled with their lunches.

When he neared the door, he heard her mumbling. "Can't believe I up and said that. The man doesn't love you, so why're you tellin' him you love him, Selina girl? Ain't you got no pride left? Or did you throw it all away on that man?"

While Michael smiled at her antics, at the same time he felt bad that he did not reciprocate her sentiment. All he could do was keep praying someday he would. He walked up beside her. "I didn't get the horses ready yet. We'll have to do that first."

"Where we goin'?"

"Now, what did I read the other day about patience and letting it have its perfect work?"

"And what did I say about not havin' any?" she shot back.

Was she ever fast at those comebacks. "You got me there. Come on. Let's hurry."

"Michael." She laid her small hand on his arm and

warmth spread through it, landing in his heart. "Can we check on Rainee first?"

"Already did. Haydon said she was resting and that she was doing very well. We'll go by and see her later, okay?"

"Okay."

He could tell she was disappointed, but he didn't want to wake Rainee.

They hustled down to the barn. The familiar smell of horse, grain, hay and dust greeted his nose.

"Hi there, Abbers."

Abby whirled and tossed her hip-length braid behind her. "Selina! Hi."

His little sister hugged Selina.

"What about me?"

"Oh. Hi, Michael." Abby hugged him with less enthusiasm than she did Selina.

"Hi yourself. I see how I rate." He winked at Abby and she wrinkled her nose up at him.

Leah stepped out of the stall, leading her horse.

"Hi, Selina. Boy don't you look nice."

"Thank you kindly. So do you."

"Hi to you, too, sis."

Leah gave him a quick wave.

"Where are you two heading off to?" Michael asked.

"We're going into town. You want to come with us, Selina?"

Michael blurted, "No!"

Leah lips curled upward. "I see. And just where are you two going?" She waggled her eyebrows.

"That's none of your business." He smiled.

"A surprise," Abby chimed in. "Ooo, I love surprises." She walked over to him and cupped her ear with her hand. "Whisper to me what it is. I won't tell."

Michael leaned down near her ear. "No."

Abby yanked her head back. "Oh, you. You're so mean."

He tweaked her on the nose. "And don't you forget it."

"Come on, Abby," Leah said. "Help me get Lambie ready so we can go. I don't want to miss..." She stopped and yanked her gaze over at Michael.

"You don't want to miss what?"

"Nothing."

"Le-ah. Who is he?"

Leah shook her head. "No one, Michael. I'm teasing you. Do you think I would take my little sister with me if I were going to see someone?"

"Yes."

Leah blushed.

Something wasn't right. He wanted to follow her to see what she was up to, but Abby was going with her, so the thought of her meeting someone did seem pretty far-fetched. Still.

"We goin' ridin' or what?" Selina tossed him a halter.

They readied their horses and rode off, making their way down the Palouse River into the deep woods. Michael followed the tracks until they came to a grove of trees. There they were, just as he had hoped.

He dismounted and held up his arms to her, waiting for her to refuse his help and jump down by herself like she always did. This time, however, she accepted his help, which pleased and surprised him. She swung her right leg over the horse's withers and placed her arms on his shoulders.

He held on to her even when her feet touched the green grass below their boots.

She gazed up at him, and his lips curled upward. "You smell nice, Selina."

"It's that lavender water Rainee give me."

He smelled her neck, letting his breath brush the hollow of her throat.

She swallowed. "What—what'cha doin'?"

"Enjoying my wife's perfume." He breathed deeply, his senses coming to full alert.

"I—I see."

He raised his head, and when their eyes connected, the sun suddenly seemed brighter in spite of the clouds covering most of it.

Selina stared up at him.

He leaned and lightly touched his mouth to hers, whispering, "Your lips are so soft."

She said nothing.

He pulled back and stars sparkled through her eyes. The urge to kiss her floated over him like the clouds above, but he wanted to take things slowly with her. "I brought you here because there's something I want to show you."

"O-Okay."

Leaving her nearly speechless was something that rarely happened.

From out of his saddle bag he grabbed his spy glass and gazed through the trees with it. "Look." He handed it to Selina and stood behind her. "Hold it up to your eye and look over there." He reached his arm around her and pointed to a place in the midst of the trees. The scent of lavender and soap swirled around him like the air from a crisp spring day. He needed to concentrate on showing her what he'd found. *Focus, Michael, focus. And not on Selina and how nice she smells and how good she feels in your arms.*

Selina held the spy glass against her right eye and shifted her head one way and then the other. Michael knew the exact moment she spotted it. "Is that—is that who I think it is?"

"Yes. It's your wolf pup."

She turned to glance up at him. The surprised innocence of a child on Christmas morning clothed her features. "How—how did you find her?"

Those lips of hers so close to his were tempting.

Slow, Michael, slow, remember?

He forced his gaze from her mouth and onto the woods where the pup was. "I noticed the wolf pack the other day. I wondered if the pup you doctored was among them, so I kept track of their whereabouts until I could show you that she's back with her family and doing well."

"You—you did that for me?" She blinked.

"Yes."

"Thank you, Michael. That was mighty nice of you. I'm much obliged." She walked in the direction of the pack of wolves.

Michael caught up to her and clasped her upper arm, halting her. "Stay here. It's too dangerous. We're taking a chance by being this close as it is." Although his voice was but a whisper, he kept it stern along with the look he sent her.

"I just want to see if her leg is healed."

"It is. If you want to see for yourself, then take a look through the glass."

She held it up to her eye again. "Can't see it. The others are in the way."

"Just wait."

"There's that ole patience thing again." She sighed.

"Sure is." He chuckled. "They're starting to get restless. We'd better go."

She nodded. "Thank you, Michael, for bringin' me here. It means a lot to me."

"I know. That's why I did it."

"You sure can be sweet when you wanna be, you know that?"

"When I want to be, huh?" Mirth inched his lips into an upward curl.

"Didn't mean it like that."

"I know what you meant. It's okay. You can be pretty sweet yourself…when you want to be." He winked. "Now let's go."

They mounted their horses and rode through the woods. Wind foraged through the trees, rustling through the branches and finding its way to them.

Michael gazed up at the sky, wondering when it had turned so dark. Being in Selina's presence and seeing her joy and surprise had him shutting out everything else around him.

Lightning flashed in the distance. Thunder rumbled above them within seconds.

"We'd better hurry and take cover. That storm's moving in here fast. We'll never make it home in time. Follow me."

Branches and pine needles crunched under the

horses' hooves as they rode swiftly through the trees, bushes and foliage. She followed the path he cut.

The wind blew harder, lifting Selina's hair, tangling the strands with its rising fury.

"Hurry, Selina." The coolness of the storm descended on them. Lightning struck again and again and each clap of thunder grew louder and quicker.

The sky opened and rain pelted down on them, soaking their clothing.

Michael led Selina through the trees to a hidden cave he'd discovered deep in the hillside when he and his family had first arrived in the Idaho Territory. It had been dug years ago by an old prospector looking for gold.

They stopped at the large cavern's opening and dismounted. Both Macy and Michael's horse Bobcat were used to being in closed-in spaces, so he grabbed the reins from Selina and led them inside the dimly lit cave. Just inside the opening, he dropped their reins, knowing they would stand still as long as their restraints were in that position. Haydon had trained them well.

Wet horse and leather and a hint of sulfur filled the damp interior of the cave.

Chills rippled through Michael's body.

Selina loosened the stampede string on her hat and let it fall against her back. She stood, rubbing her arms. He removed the blanket from one side of his saddle bags and draped it around her shoulders, closing it snug against her neck.

"Thank you kindly."

He nodded.

"Aren't you cold?"

"A little."

"Well, here." She moved one arm out in a gesture for him to join her under the blanket.

He nodded and she removed the blanket, draped it around him, tucked herself under his arm and pulled the ends of the blanket together.

"This is rather cozy, don't you think?" Michael gazed down at her.

"Sure is." She smiled up at him.

They stood there, staring outside.

Thunder rumbled above them.

Wind whistled through the trees.

But the sound Michael heard most was his own heartbeat pulsating in his ears. What was it about being so close to her that set his heart racing? Was this what love felt like, or was this just some physical attraction because of Selina's beauty? Isn't that what had lured Haydon to Melanie? *Lord, help me to not make the same mistake. Guide me where Selina's concerned, Father.*

He continued to silently pray about the situation and for his wife until peace filled his soul.

Selina laid her head against Michael's chest. His soothing heartbeat drew her soul further into his. She wanted him to kiss her again. She loved the feel of his lips on hers. And every time he kissed her, her toes curled and her knees turned to mush. Each day she was around him, she loved him more. If she wasn't mistaken, he seemed to be caring for her more and more, too—and trying to make this marriage work. She sure hoped so, hoped it wasn't just some fancy on her part.

The hankering to kiss him settled into her chilled bones. His body heat warmed her outsides, but his kisses would warm her insides. Of that she was certain. *Wonder what he'd think if I kissed him.* Only one way to find out.

Selina slid her head up his chest and raised it to meet his eyes. Smiling eyes that pulled her in faster than quicksand, only not nearly as dangerous. Or maybe they were. A heap of courage was what she needed to follow through with her plan to kiss him. Willing some into herself, she pushed forward, "Michael, would you mind kissin' me again?"

His lips slowly curved into a smile, and his eyes sparkled like sun on water. "Don't mind if I do."

He shifted her body around until she faced him. Strong arms wrapped around her, cocooning her with them and the blanket.

His face leaned toward hers at the same time hers raised upward. Lips soft, yet firm, took hold of hers in the gentlest way.

Being wrapped in his arms felt right and good.

After what seemed like forever, he raised his head. "Somethin' wrong?"

"No. Nothing's wrong." He smiled and his voice sounded breathless and croaky. "It's stopped raining. We'd better head for home."

She wasn't ready to leave, though. "What about the lunch you packed? I'm mighty hungry."

"I am, too," he whispered, his eyes swirled with emotion. "Let's eat, first."

Could it be that Michael was falling in love with her? For the first time since she got here, she had hope for just that. And that hope set her stomach and heart to fluttering as much as it did when Michael kissed her. *Lord, have my prayers been answered?*

Chapter Thirteen

The next day, Selina went to check on Rainee. Afterward, she went home, changed from her dress into some trousers, grabbed her rifle, placed the sling around her neck and went for a long walk through the trees.

She took in a deep breath, enjoying every little aroma that mid-September in the Idaho Territory brought her way—moist leaves, pine, forest dirt and a hint of rain.

Stems of light filtered down through the trees from the bright afternoon sun. She walked higher and higher up the mountain. She stopped between two cedar trees and slowly followed their trunks upward with her eyes. Those giants sure made a person feel small. They were so tall that it looked like they could reach up with their branches and touch the few clouds speckling the sky.

"God, You sure outdone Yourself with these. They're mighty pretty to behold. Thank You, Lord, for allowin' me to be a part of somethin' so wonderful. I just love it here, Lord. And Lord, iffen there's any way, could You help me and Michael to become a real family someday? I'd sure be beholden to You. Thank You kindly, Lord."

She continued walking. Every once in a while, she

stopped to smell and to feel the softness of the wild pink rose petals, to admire the brown center in wild daisies, the fine bright yellow color of buttercup flowers and the different kinds of bush berries. Some berries she hadn't seen before. She wondered if they were something she could eat. But not knowing for sure, it was best to leave them alone.

She walked through fields of grass that almost reached her waist. Her eyes took in the green-and-gold rolling hills of Paradise Haven. A name most fitting.

Birds entertained her with their happy songs as she continued to take in the area Michael had called the Palouse.

Snuggled against a hillside with dirt patches, grass and bushes stood an old broken-down house and a barn. Curiosity got the best of her.

She headed toward the buildings, running her hands over the top of the tall grass blades and enjoying the soft yet stiff feel of them against her fingertips.

Off to the right of the house stood a large cottonwood tree and on its left a grove of green bushes.

No glass filled the windows or doors. Part of the roof had caved in and the chimney was in mighty poor shape, broken into all kinds of pieces.

She stepped up to the door and peeked inside. A broken drop-leaf table lay on the floor along with a heap of broken boards.

She strained to see everything from the doorway but couldn't, so she placed one foot on the wooden floor to make sure it was safe before she placed the other one, too. The planked floor was solid as a rock, so she took a look around, imagining what the place had been like before being deserted.

In one bedroom sat a rusty bed frame and an old broken-down dresser with only one drawer that hung as if it were fixing to fall at any minute.

She looked at the staircase, wondering what was up there. Should she go see? Was it safe? She tested the first step. It creaked under her weight but felt pretty solid to her.

Careful not to get in too big a rush, she tested each step as she made her way up.

At the third step from the top she could see what was in the open space. Besides busted-up chimney bricks and broken boards, the only other thing here was a wooden box in the corner. From what she could tell, it looked like it wasn't in too bad of shape. She wondered what might be in it.

The boards groaned as she slowly made her way toward it.

Holding her rifle back out of the way with one hand, she leaned over and raised the lid.

A mouse darted out from behind it, startling her.

Selina screamed and jumped back.

The crunching sound of splintering wood echoed loudly in the empty space.

The floor disappeared under Selina's feet, dropping her through it hard and fast.

Her legs buckled when they hit a pile of broken boards below, and her head slammed against the iron bed frame.

Then everything went black.

Dragging from exhaustion, Michael lugged his body up the darkened steps to his house. No lights shone through the windows and no food aromas greeted him.

"That's strange." His words floated into the black pitch of night. The only sounds he heard were the squeaks of the screen door and front door as he stepped inside.

No food waited on the stove or the table. No lit lanterns. And no Selina in sight. "Selina!" he hollered.

Silence.

"Now where could she be?" He searched the house, checking each room, including the pantry and cellar, calling her name as he did. By the time he reached the last room, he was starting to panic.

His attention trailed to where her rifle usually rested, but it wasn't there. He quickly lit a lantern and flew outside, yelling her name and listening for a response.

Coyotes yapped in the distance.

Crickets chirped.

He rounded the house, searching for her. When he couldn't find her, he hurried to his brother's house and knocked on the door. He hated to bother Haydon, having a new baby and all, but Jesse and his family were having dinner with some of the neighbors.

The door swung open. "Michael? What's the matter?" Haydon asked as Rainee walked over.

"I can't find Selina." Michael stepped inside. "Did she come by and see you today, Rainee?"

"Yes, she did. But that was hours ago." Wrinkles lined her forehead.

"She's not home and I can't find her anywhere. Did she say where she was going after she left here?"

"She said it was such a lovely day that she wanted to go for a walk and explore the ranch. You think she got lost?" Rainee turned fearful eyes on him and then up at Haydon.

Haydon slipped his arm around Rainee and pulled

her to his side. "I'm sure she's fine, darling." He smiled, but even Michael could tell it was forced.

"I'm going looking for her." Michael whirled around.

"Wait. I'll go with you." Haydon looked behind him at their maid, Esther. "Esther, will you throw together some food and water in case we're gone all night?"

"Yes, sir."

"I'll go saddle up the horses. Will you run and get Smokey?" Michael asked. "If anyone can find her, he can."

"That's right. He found Rainee." Haydon lovingly looked down at Rainee and gave her a quick kiss.

He sure had. Their family would be lost without the man who was more like a father to them than a long time friend and employee.

"Meet you at the barn," Michael said.

"Be careful," he heard Rainee say to Haydon, and his gut twisted.

"I will." Haydon sprinted toward Smokey's small cabin, and Michael ran to the barn, the lantern swinging in front of him.

Worry had now escalated into panic.

In the short six weeks Selina had been there, he realized only now how much she had come to mean to him. He admired her free spirit. How she took the time to enjoy the little things in life. How she helped anyone who had need and asked for nothing in return. He admired her spunk and her love for animals. Well, except when she brought them into the house. So far, he'd come home to a cat, a wolf and a pig, and during wheat harvest, a raccoon, a bird and a squirrel, which he immediately shooed out despite Selina's protests.

He stepped inside the barn. His shadow danced

against the wall as he lit another lantern and hung them on the hooks on the wall.

Michael finished saddling the last horse, then tied a couple of rolled blankets onto each one. Smokey stepped inside the barn with his bloodhound, Skeeter, a gift from Haydon. Haydon had brought Skeeter back from his trip to Rainee's place in Little Rock, Arkansas. Said it was the perfect gift for the man who eleven years ago had used his tracking skills to help find Rainee when she'd fled into the woods to escape her evil brother's plans to sell her to a murderer.

"Thanks for coming, Smokey."

Gray completely covered his head and more wrinkles lined his tanned, leathery face, but the man could just about outdo all of them when it came to working. "Anytime, boss."

"How many times have we told you to stop calling us boss? You're family, remember?"

"No, he doesn't," Haydon said, stepping into the barn. He had three canteens in one hand and an overstuffed sack of food in the other. Michael's brother handed each of them a canteen, then tied the bag of food onto his horse's saddle. Haydon's horse, Rebel, danced, ready to go. So was Michael.

"Thanks, Smokey. Haydon." Michael eyed each one. "Let's go."

They blew out the lanterns and led their horses from the barn.

"You have anything of Selina's with you for Skeeter to track?" Smokey asked.

"No. But I need to stop at the house and get a jacket. I'll grab something then."

Smokey gave a quick nod. "A hairbrush or anything will do."

They mounted their horses and headed to his house. Michael ran inside and up the stairs. His attention fell to Selina's hairbrush. What was left of the old thing, anyway. Instantly he felt horrible. Why hadn't he made sure all of her needs were met? As he ran down the stairs he wondered what else she needed that he didn't know about. He made a mental note to find out.

Michael grabbed his jacket, shoved a few candles and a box of matches in his pockets and raced out the door.

Smokey and his dog stood next to his horse. The older man stepped forward and took the brush from Michael and placed it under Skeeter's nose. "Find her, Skeeter."

The bloodhound bayed and headed into the trees. Michael and Smokey quickly mounted and took off after Skeeter and Haydon, who was right behind the dog.

An hour later they topped a hill and saw McCreedy's abandoned house. Skeeter bayed, ran down the hill and disappeared inside the house.

"Heeya!" Michael tucked his legs tight into Bobcat's sides. He leaned back as the horse jarred his way down the hill.

The hound continued to bay.

Michael reached the house first. Before his horse even stopped, Michael dismounted and rushed inside the broken-down house. "Selina!" He followed Skeeter's bark. It was only when he got closer that he noticed a small form lying on the floor on a heap of splintered wood. "Selina." He rushed to her side and dropped to his knees.

"Don't move her, Michael." Smokey's silhouette filled the doorway. "Let me check her over first," he cautioned as he headed toward Michael.

Michael nodded, even though he knew Smokey couldn't possibly see him. He reached in his pocket, pulled out the candles and matches and lit them. Candlelight flickered across his wife's pale face. He wanted to pull her into his arms and cradle her, to make everything okay.

Haydon stepped up next to them, holding a canteen. He took one of the candles from Michael. "Is—is she all right?" His words were rough and broken and mingled with fear.

Michael looked at Smokey, praying about what the next words would be.

Smokey didn't answer. Instead, he took the opened canteen from Haydon, raised Selina's head, put the canteen to her lips and tilted it. Water ran down Selina's chin and neck.

She didn't stir.

Michael struggled to remain calm, but panic was taking over. "Smokey?"

The elderly man cleared his throat. "Doesn't seem to be any broken bones or anything." His eyes slowly trailed upward at the gaping hole in the ceiling. "She's one lucky woman to be alive."

Michael drew in a long breath of relief.

After a moment of pause, Smokey tried to give Selina another drink.

She still didn't stir. His friend stood.

"Smokey?" Michael looked up at him from his squatting position. "Why isn't she responding?"

Smokey shook his head. "She has a huge knot on her head."

"I'm taking her to Doc Berg's." Michael scooped her up into his arms and stood.

"That's a good idea." Haydon's voice sounded off-pitch and strained and his eyes had a blank stare. Instantly, Michael knew why.

He wanted to comfort his brother, to ease the memories, but before he had a chance to say anything, Haydon spun on his heel and headed outside.

Smokey and Michael exchanged a knowing look. "He'll be all right, boss." Smokey's words were full of assurance, and Michael knew he was right. Haydon was a survivor. His brother would deal with his feelings and move on like he always did. Still, his heart hurt for the pain his brother had suffered. But nothing could be done about that now. Besides, Selina needed his undivided attention.

They stepped outside the old house and strode up to their horses.

"Give her to me," Haydon said.

Michael looked over at him with questioning eyes.

"I know what you're thinking, Michael, and yes, it's hard seeing her like this. But you have a chance to help Selina. I didn't with Melanie. Hand her to me until you can get on your horse. Then go. Take care of your wife."

His brother was right. He did have a chance to help Selina. With a heavy heart, Michael handed his wife over to Haydon, then swung into the saddle. His brother placed Selina's limp form into his arms and gave him the reins.

"Thanks for helping me, Haydon. I'm really sorry you had to see this." He glanced down at his wife and then back at Haydon.

"I'll be fine," Haydon assured him with sad yet sturdy eyes. "Now go on."

Michael gave a quick nod to his brother, then to Smokey. He reined his horse toward town. All the way there, he prayed, holding her close, willing her to stay alive and thanking God they had even found her.

Voices. Selina heard voices. But they sounded far away. Where was she and why couldn't she open her eyes?

"Selina? Can you hear me?"

Michael? She struggled to open her eyes. Finally, she could see through a small slit.

Michael's face blurred and pitched and swayed before her.

She concentrated on opening her eyes wider. Michael's face was no longer fuzzy or drifting.

Words tried to leave her mouth, but they never did. It was as if they were stuck in her throat.

"Here." A cool hard surface touched her lips. "Drink this?"

The liquid pooled into her mouth. She coughed, then swallowed. More liquid. "What happened?" she asked like a croaking frog.

"You fell and hit your head, love."

Love? Did he just call her love? She must have hit her head a lot harder than she thought. Now her mind was playing tricks on her. She tried to sit up, but pain shot through the back of her head. She reached toward that spot, but Michael's calloused hand clutched hers.

"Don't. You have a bump the size of an egg back there."

Another round of pain sliced through her head like the sharp blade of a hunting knife.

"How's our patient doing?"

Selina's attention wobbled over to the door. Doc Berg came walking toward her.

"Hi, Doc."

"How you feeling, Miss?"

"Like someone took a moonshine jug and smashed it against the back of my head."

Michael moved so the doctor could sit in the chair he'd been sitting in.

"You're one lucky young lady. From what Michael here tells me, you fell through the upstairs floor. You'll be sore for some time, but I didn't find any broken bones, only a few scrapes and bruises. You would have ended up with a whole lot more if you hadn't been wearing those pants."

She looked over at Michael and gave him a look that said, *see, pants ain't always a bad thing.*

He offered her a half grin.

"I'm going to keep you here overnight so I can keep an eye on you and make sure that bump doesn't get any bigger and that you don't get a fever."

"I can do that," Michael said, shocking Selina plumb down to her toes.

"I thought everyone at your place was busy harvesting the wheat."

"No, we're all done with that."

Doc Berg stood and faced Michael. "I'll be honest with you. I don't like the looks of that bump on her head, Michael. Someone needs to stay with her around the clock for at least a couple of days."

"I can."

"How can you do that and get your chores done, too, Michael?" Selina asked. "Haydon will probably stay home a couple more days with Rainee. So that leaves Jesse, Smokey and your hired hands to do the rest. I can't do that to them. So I think Doc's right. It's best iffen I just stay here."

"I'd feel a whole lot better if she stayed here, too, Michael. Me and the missus can take turns keeping an eye on her. We know what to look for, where you wouldn't."

Michael didn't say a word, but finally he nodded. "Okay. Well, I'm going to head on home, then. I'll be by sometime tomorrow to check on you." He leaned over and gave her a kiss on her cheek. "Do what Doc says and don't be giving him a hard time, okay?"

"Me? I never do stuff like that."

Michael narrowed one eye and hiked a brow before turning to the doctor. "You have to watch her, Doc. She's a feisty one who doesn't take kindly to being told what to do."

She saw a look pass between the two men along with a smile.

"Okay, y'all. I promise I'll behave and do what Doc says."

Michael flashed her a satisfied grin. "I'll see you later, love." And he was out the door.

Love. So her mind hadn't been playing tricks on her after all. She really had heard him call her *love* earlier. She liked the sound of it. Things were finally looking up between them. The two of them just might have a chance at a real marriage after all. That thought curled her lips and toes and warmed her heart.

Michael hated riding off, leaving Selina behind. Seeing her lying on the floor of that old house made him realize how important she had become to him. Who would have thought he would ever even think of her in a romantic, loving way? After all, to him she was the lady in trousers. And when he first saw her in those trousers, *lady* wasn't really the word that came to mind.

Today, the thick denim trousers had actually protected her legs from getting shredded with lacerations. He was glad she didn't listen and do everything he liked or wanted and that she stayed true to her real self. Because if she hadn't, she could have ended up... He didn't, no, couldn't, think about that.

Tack rattling, leather creaking, branches breaking and leaves rustling filled the silence, along with wolves howling in the distance. Their low mournful sounds made him lonely.

More lonely than he'd been even back when having a wife was just a nice idea. Strange how life kept bringing him around to how nice it was to have Selina as his wife.

Chapter Fourteen

Outside Doc Berg's house, Michael checked his pocket watch for the tenth time. 7:00 in the morning. The lights had been on for more than an hour, and Michael couldn't stand the wait any longer. He hurried up the porch and rang the bell.

Through the glass he could see Doc Berg walking down the hall toward the door. When Doc opened the door, he said, "I figured you'd be early. Only I figured you would have gotten here long before now." He stepped aside to let Michael in. "Are those for me?" Doc grinned, looking at the bunch of goldenrods and asters in Michael's hands.

"Sorry, Doc, but they're for Selina. And I've been here since six. I just didn't think you'd appreciate me waking you up."

"I've been up most of the night."

Concern squeezed Michael's heart. "Is Selina okay?"

Doc removed the spectacles off his nose and eyed Michael. "She had a rough night."

"Is she okay now? May I see her? I promise not to wake her."

Doc paused, then nodded. "Let me take those. I'll have the missus put them in some water."

"Thanks." Michael handed him the wildflowers then quietly opened the door to where Selina was. The shades were drawn and the lantern in the corner was turned down low. Michael sat in the chair beside her bed.

Even in the dim light, her cheeks looked pale against the white blanket. She might act tough, but seeing her like this showed him that wasn't the whole truth. Just like she had in the old house, she once again looked frail and helpless. But now she had him to take care of her. And take care of her he would.

Michael bowed his head and closed his eyes. He clasped his hands, rested his elbows on his knees and prayed silently. "Lord, I pray for a complete recovery for Selina. Help me to love her the way she deserves to be loved." That familiar fear shrouded him like a suffocating cloak.

Would he ever be free to trust in their relationship? To trust in love?

Michael shifted his gaze to her and watched her sleep. Minutes dragged by. He stood and paced the room, then watched her sleep some more. He kept the vigil for almost two hours.

Worn out from worry, he sat back down in the chair.

Still sleeping, Selina turned her face toward him and a strand of hair fell across her cheek.

Careful not to wake her, he brushed it aside, letting his finger linger on her soft skin. He longed for her to wake up, even if it meant eating crawdad tails and possum stew. He shook off that thought, knowing he must be completely losing it to even think such a thing. But no matter how far he pushed those thoughts away, he couldn't shake the feeling of what it would be like to lose her. "Please, God, just let her be okay. Please."

"Michael." Mrs. Berg rested her hand on his shoulder.

Startled, he stood.

Doc's wife set the flowers on the stand near Selina's bed and motioned for him to follow her.

"You've been here more than two hours now. There's no reason for you to stay. She's heavily sedated and will probably be asleep for a few more hours. Why don't you go on home?"

Michael's heart yanked him back and forth, stay or go, stay or go. He hated leaving his wife. But sitting here, watching her like this was driving him nuts. "You're right. I don't want to risk waking her, especially after Doc said she had a rough night. Would you please tell her I was here and that I'll be back later?"

Mrs. Berg nodded.

Michael turned his attention toward Selina. Needing the connection to her, he wanted to lean down and kiss her cheek but he was afraid he would wake her, so he didn't.

As hard as it was to do, he headed toward the door.

Selina sat up in bed. Her head pounded and her stomach felt queasy. All night her head had ached something fierce and she'd thrown up every time the doctor fed her broth. Fresh-cut flowers on the nightstand caught her attention. She lay back down and stared at the clusters of tiny yellow and light purple flowers in a jar.

Mrs. Berg, the sweet brown-haired lady who carried

herself with poise and grace, entered the room. "You still feeling sick?"

"Yes, ma'am. I am."

"How's your head?"

"Feels like someone took a sling shot and slung a rock at it."

Mrs. Berg leaned over and peered at the back of her head. When she moved back in front of Selina, her gray eyes were comforting.

"That was so sweet of your husband to bring you those goldenrods and asters," Mrs. Berg said.

Selina glanced at them again. So that's what they were…goldenrods and asters. "Michael was here? When?"

"Early this morning. He stayed quite a while. You were sleeping so soundly he didn't want to wake you, especially after the night you had. He asked me to tell you that he was here and that he'd be back later."

Disappointed she has missed him, she wanted to pick up the flowers and smell them, but her stomach hadn't settled. "You got any ginger?"

"Ginger? No. Why?"

"'Cause nothin' works better for an upset belly than ginger."

"I'm sorry. We don't have any. Would you like me to bring you more broth?"

"No. No." She waved her hand. That was the last thing she wanted. "What I would like is to go home."

"I can't let you do that. My husband wants to make sure you're better before he lets you leave here."

"But I have to go. We're havin' an end-of-harvestin' party at the ranch, and I wanna help."

"Well, even if you could go home, you're going to have to take it easy for a few days anyway."

Selina hated sitting around, wasn't used to it. She liked to keep busy. Normally no aching head would stop her, but she'd promised Michael, and she wouldn't go back on her word.

"Do you have any mendin' that needs doin'? I've gotta have somethin' to do."

"I do. But I'm not bringing it to you, dear. You need to rest."

"Can't rest. I don't want to. I want to—"

"Are you giving Mrs. Berg a hard time?" Michael strode into the room looking more handsome than anyone had a right to. He looked at Selina with raised eyebrows then at Mrs. Berg. "Hello again, Mrs. Berg. I'm sorry. I can't leave my wife alone for a minute without her giving someone a hard time. She's one stubborn, determined woman."

Selina crossed her arms. "I ain't stubborn. Just don't like bein' stuck in bed is all."

"Well, like it or not, doctor's orders."

"Hmmpft. Don't you got chores to do or somethin'?"

"Nope. Finished them so I could come here and bother you."

"I'm sick, remember?"

"I'll leave you two alone." Mrs. Berg looked from one to the other with a smile on her face. She turned and headed toward the door. "Young lovers are so cute."

Selina felt the blush from the tip of her toes plumb up to tip of her head. Lovers? If only the woman knew. "Thank you kindly for the flowers, Michael."

"I knew you would enjoy them. You enjoy everything."

Not everything. She didn't enjoy knowing Michael didn't love her. Oh, he was trying to and all, but love didn't shine through his eyes. Not the way it did betwixt her ma and pa and her friends who had married for love.

"What are you thinking about?"

"You." Again heat fired up her cheeks.

"What about me?" He took her hand in his.

"Was mighty thoughtful of you to bring me flowers. When did you find time to do that?"

"Early this morning. On the way here, I picked them."

"I was sure sorry I didn't get to see you earlier."

"I didn't want to wake you. Doc Berg said you were up sick all night. How are you feeling now?"

"Not too good. I'd feel a whole lot better iffen I was at home in my own bed."

"Now, Selina. You know what Doc said."

"I know, I know. But I don't have to like it."

He sat on the bed and pulled her into his arms. "I hate seeing you like this."

"I hate bein' like this."

He held her and gently rocked her and she let him.

Michael held her in his arms until she fell sound asleep.

Doc Berg stepped into the room.

Michael held a finger to his lips and pointed to her.

"She sleeping?" Doc Berg whispered. "That's good. You should go and let her get some rest."

He didn't want to go. He'd just gotten here. Besides, it was lonely around the house without her. Boring even. As much as he hated to admit it, he was getting used to her antics, her high-spirited ways, even to having critters in the house and strange foods on the table. Truth was, it just felt odd being there by himself.

But he couldn't very well expect her to listen to the doctor if he didn't. Careful not to wake her, he laid her back on the bed and stood. He gazed down at the woman who was beautiful inside and out.

He felt a tug on his shirtsleeve.

Doc Berg motioned for him to step outside the room and into his office.

"Have a seat." Doc sat behind a mahogany desk covered with papers and sprinkled with medicine bottles.

Michael sat in the cushioned chair across from the desk.

Doc Berg rested his arms on the desk and leaned toward Michael. "I'm worried about Selina, Michael. That lump on her head hasn't gone down. In fact, it's gotten a little bigger. I'm concerned there may be some bleeding on the brain. Sometimes bleeding comes slow or fast. If that spot doesn't go down or get any smaller by this evening, I'm afraid I may have to operate."

Michael listened in horror as Doc explained in detail exactly what he had to do to relieve the pressure. His stomach roiled as he thought of the drilling procedure. "Sounds dangerous." He swallowed hard.

"It is. That's why I'd like your consent to do it if I need to."

How could Michael give his consent to do something that was so dangerous? "I need to talk to Selina about this first and see what she says."

"No. I don't want to worry her about this. Her getting upset could cause more problems." He stood and so did Michael. "Think about it and give me your decision. Don't wait too long. Her life may depend on it."

Hearing those words was like a stab to the heart. Michael watched Doc's back as he headed down the hallway, rounded the corner and disappeared. How could Doc ask him to make such a decision?

He needed guidance. Michael hurried down the stairs, stopping only long enough to tell Doc he would be back later.

On the way home, he prayed for wisdom. None came. In the field, he saw Jesse riding in the midst of the cows. Michael coaxed his horse to go faster, slowing only when he neared the herd.

"What's wrong?" Jesse rode out to meet him. "Is Selina all right?"

"I'm not sure." He told him what Doc said.

"Sounds to me like you have no choice."

That's what he was afraid of. Worry and fear crawled inside him, and he closed his eyes to block them out.

"You love her, don't you?" Jesse asked with gentleness.

Did he? He didn't even know anymore. "I've been trying to."

"That's part of your problem. *You're* trying to do it under your own strength. Jesus said, 'Apart from me, you can do nothing.' But God didn't leave it there, Michael. The Bible says, 'I can do all things through Christ who strengthens me.'" Jesse draped his arm over the saddle horn. "Any time we try to do things under our own strength or our own power, we are setting ourselves up for failure.

"The Lord wants His children to depend on Him, Michael. You may not be able to love Selina on your own, but God can do it through Christ as you submit to Him. Ask God to give you a deep, lasting love for your wife, Michael, and He will."

"I'm so confused, Jess. I thought I loved her when she was like Rainee. Then when she got here and wasn't, I didn't think there was any way I could love her. Now part of me can't imagine life without her and part of me thinks I'm crazy for even thinking that."

"Oh, I get it. You thought you married a fantasy woman."

"No, that's not what I did."

"Yeah you did. You thought if you married the perfect woman you dreamed of, then everything would always be perfect and you'd never get hurt. Well, I hate to tell you brother, but that's not reality. Real love ain't no fantasy—it's messy, and sometimes it's downright hard. And with real love there's no guarantee you'll never get hurt. You can't love somebody with one foot out of the door. If you love her, it's got to be all the way, no matter what happens. That's real love—not this straddling the fence thing you've got going on."

Michael put his head down as every fear he ever had attacked him. Jesse was right. That's exactly what he had wanted—the perfect woman who would never hurt him. But that woman didn't exist. Never did and never would. And now love looked even scarier than it had before.

Jesse's words applied to letting go of his fears, too. To be free to love Selina, he needed to keep on giving his fears to Christ every time they came knocking on the door of his heart and mind. "Will you pray with me, Jess?"

"Sure."

They bowed their heads and prayed not only that he

would make the right decision about Selina's medical condition but also about the state of his heart. When Jesse was done, Michael had hope and a renewed vigor to continue courting his wife. But first he needed to decide what to do about the consent to operate.

He thanked his brother and headed back into town, racking his brains about what to do. "Michael, what did Jess just get through telling you not even ten minutes ago? God wants you to depend on Him—not yourself." Michael's voice echoed through the trees, bounced back at him and whipped him upside the head. "Didn't you just read the other night about if you needed wisdom to ask God?"

Over the green rolling hills, he rode. He closed his eyes. "Lord. I need wisdom. You said if I asked for it, You'd give it to me. Well, Lord, I'm asking. Show me what to do about Selina. Give me wisdom beyond my own understanding because I sure need it right now."

He opened his eyes and raised his head. "Even better, I'm asking for Your mercy and Your grace to heal Selina. I pray these things in Your Son's name. Amen." Peace unlike any he'd ever known before nested inside him.

Selina opened her eyes. The first thing she saw was Michael. "Hi." She smiled.

"Hello yourself." He leaned closer to her. "How are you feeling?"

"Better. My head doesn't smart near as bad as it did."

"Thank the Lord for answer to prayer."

"You prayed for me?"

"Sure did. Does that surprise you?"

"Everything you do lately surprises me."

"Makes life more interesting, right?"

She sat up.

Michael jumped up and propped an extra fluffy pillow behind her back.

"I sure could use somethin' to drink." She moved her tongue around inside her mouth, trying to moisten it.

"I'll get Mrs. Berg." He returned with a glass of water and a bowl of broth and sat down beside her.

Selina took the water from him. Concerned she might not be able to keep it down again, she sipped it. Her stomach was fine. She drank a little more. Still fine. Then a little more. She grinned. No more upset belly. "I'll take that broth now." Her hand reached out to Michael.

"You don't feel sick?" Hope sparked his eyes.

"No. In fact, I'm so hungry I could eat the hide off a grizzly. Ain't they got anything more than broth to eat around here?"

"Yep. You're feeling better." He smiled.

"I sure am. So you'd better watch it, mister. I just may feed you some more crawdad tails. Or better yet, some possum stew."

His blue eyes widened. "You're kidding right? Tell me you're joking."

Selina giggled. "I'm joshin' you. But, just so you know, iffen we were back home in Kentucky, we *would* be eatin' possum stew."

"I'm glad we don't live there." The serious, relieved look on his face tickled Selina. And yet at the same time, she realized once again just how wide the gap was in their worlds. They sure did live differently.

Truth was…in the short time she'd been here, she was getting used to his ways and even liked some of them better. Some she didn't. Like wearing dresses. She wasn't sure she'd ever get used to that. Trousers were a whole heap better and more comfortable, too. Only thing was, trousers didn't put a light in Michael's eyes like dresses did.

His eyes held hers gently. "What you thinking about?"

"Trousers."

Michael laughed. "Trousers? What about them?"

"Oh, I was thinkin' how I'm still tryin' to get used to not wearin' them all the time." She tapped his chest with her finger. "You'd better appreciate it, mister. I ain't ever changed for anybody before. And to be honest with you, I'm not right sure how I feel about that or iffen I can ever learn to talk like y'all do. I'm sure you noticed I ain't doin' too good with that so far."

"I hadn't noticed." His lips held a smirk.

"You'd better be nice to me, or I'll fix you not only possum stew but gopher stew, too."

"It's nice to see you're doing better. Even if I have to put up with your threats." He grinned.

She smiled.

"I see someone is feeling better." Doc Berg entered the room, smiling.

"I sure am. Can I go home now?"

He walked around the other side of the bed and gently pressed the back of her head. His eyebrows rose.

"What's wrong?" Michael asked.

"Nothing's wrong. I'm just surprised."

"About what?"

"The lump is almost gone. This morning it was…and now it's…" He shook his head. "I don't understand."

"I do. It's called the power of prayer, Doc."

"Does this mean I can go home?" Selina asked.

"It sure does," Doc said. "But you need to rest and take it easy for a few days. And gradually introduce solid food as you can tolerate it."

"Will do, Doc." She tossed the covers aside and set her feet on the floor. "Where's my clothes?"

Doc laughed. "They're in here." He walked over to a large cabinet, opened the door and lifted her clothes off a hook. "The wife washed them for you."

"That was mighty nice of her. Please be sure to tell her thank you for me."

"I'll do that. I'll leave and let you get dressed. Don't forget—nothing strenuous for a few days, young lady."

"I'll try."

"I'll see to it." Michael sent her his take-charge look. She sent one of her own back at him. Nothing would stop her from helping with the after-harvesting party. Nothing.

After what seemed like forever, Michael pulled the buggy to a stop in front of the house. "Stay," he ordered.

She rolled her eyes, but wanting to please him, she obeyed.

He came around, swooped her into his arms and carried her onto the porch. "Close your eyes. I have a surprise for you."

Her eyes closed, he carried her inside and put her down. "You can open your eyes now."

"Oh, my." Her hands went to her face. "Oh, Michael." She walked over to the kitchen table and picked up the drawing she had done of her home back in Kentucky.

He stepped up behind her. "Do you like it?"

She turned and clutched her picture in the beautifully handmade frame to her chest. Tears leaked from her eyes but she didn't even care. "Like it? Oh, Michael, I love it. Thank you." She threw her arms around him and pressed her head into his chest.

"I thought we would hang it above the fireplace mantel, if that's okay with you. Then when you get lonesome for home, you could look at it."

"That's the sweetest, most thoughtful thing anyone's ever done for me." She stood on her tiptoes and pulled his head down to hers and kissed him. Every ounce of love she had for him she poured into that kiss. When he responded and didn't push her away, her heart smiled with even more hope.

Chapter Fifteen

"Selina! What are you doing?" Michael wrinkled his nose at the smell of wet pig. "You're not supposed to be doing anything strenuous, remember?"

"I ain't. I'm just givin' Kitty a bath. Besides, it's been four days since Doc told me to take it easy."

"What do I have to do, tie you to the bed?"

"You'd have to catch me first." She kept her eye on Michael while she continued scrubbing the sow.

"That can be arranged." He cocked his head, wiggled his eyebrows and took a step toward her.

Selina tossed the bucket of cold water on him, drenching the whole front side of him.

He sucked in a sharp breath. "Oh, you're going to pay for that one."

Selina tossed the bucket aside and darted off through the trees.

Michael followed her and so did Kitty, oinking all the way.

Last time he had chased Selina, she'd gotten away. This time he was ready. He glanced upward, behind

him and off to the sides, making sure she didn't take
him by surprise again.

Branches rustled nearby.

From the corner of his eye, he spotted her ducked
behind a bush. He stopped and let out a dramatic, disappointed sigh. "Well, Kitty. It looks like we lost her.
We'll just go back to the house and wait for her." Turning on his heel, he walked past Selina, pretending not
to see her.

Kitty waddled behind him.

Suddenly, he whirled and latched on to Selina. "Got
ya." He started tickling her neck and shoulders with
one hand while the other held her tight.

In between giggles, she said, "Remember. I'm not
supposed to do anythin' strenuous."

"If you can wash that pig, you're well enough to get
tickled." His fingers found the spot on her waist that
made her squirm the most.

"Stop, stop," she begged through her laughter.

"Not until you promise you'll rest."

"Kitty, help me!"

Kitty stuck her snout in the air and shifted her head
back and forth between them.

"She can't help you. Now promise me, or I'll keep
it up."

Without warning, her lips latched on to his.

Shock rippled through him so ferociously that he
froze. Then as if his fingers had a mind of their own,
they snaked their way through her hair at the back of
her head. Michael pulled her closer.

She wrapped her arms around his neck and smiled
at him.

"Uh-hmm. Am I interrupting anything?"

They yanked apart. Jake. Michael groaned. The man's timing was terrible.

"Jake, what are you doing here?"

"I heard about Selina's accident and thought I'd stop by to see if she was okay."

Selina fussed with her hair, putting even more distance between them.

"She's better now. Thank you." Michael only glanced at her.

"Glad to hear it. I was sure worried about you."

"Won't you come to the house and sit a spell, Jake? I'll fetch us somethin' to drink."

"I'd like that."

He might, but Michael wouldn't.

Selina and Jake walked side by side toward the house, leaving Michael to walk with Kitty. He wanted to say something, but he didn't want to sound like a jealous, insecure husband.

Jake stopped and turned around. "Michael, did you know that Mr. Drakes is selling out? I was just telling Selina about it."

"No. I hadn't heard that. Why?" He picked up his pace and without being too obvious he stepped between Jake and Selina.

"The missus is tired of the long winters. She wants to go back east and live in the city. Told him if he didn't, she was going without him."

Michael's gut twisted.

Jake looked past Michael to Selina. "Can't picture you ever living in the city."

"Ain't never lived in a city before. Don't plan on it, neither."

His stomach relaxed.

She scurried ahead of them, sprinted up the steps and disappeared inside the house.

Jake turned his attention back to Michael. "I hope you know how lucky you are to have found someone like her."

"I do."

Loneliness covered Jake's eyes.

"Hey, why don't you place an ad? Maybe you can get lucky, too."

"I've been thinking about it. I used to think people who did that were desperate. No offense, buddy."

"None taken."

"But there aren't many women around here who can handle the harsh winters. Even though the town's grown and the train comes through here now, the women still don't seem to stick around. Especially them city women. Good thing you got yourself a good country woman and not some highfalutin city lady."

Michael had never thought about that. What if the woman in the letters had turned out to be one of those who couldn't handle the harsh winters? Without a doubt, his fears really would have come true then.

They stepped inside the house. Selina had coffee and oatmeal cookies ready for them. An hour later, Jake stood. "Well, I'd better get on home. Got chores to do." He faced Selina. "Thanks for the coffee and cookies." Jake turned to Michael. "Thanks for the visit."

"Any time." As soon as he said it, he wanted to snatch back his words. Every time Jake came, Selina and Jake talked while he remained quiet, having nothing at all to add. Those two would have made a great pair. The thought of them together felt like someone had slung a stone into his heart. They might make a good pair, but she was his wife, not Jake's.

Standing outside on the porch, Selina said to Jake, "Are you comin' to the after-harvest party tomorrow afternoon?"

"Nothing could stop me from coming. I'm looking forward to it. I'll see you there. You too, Michael."

"Yeah. See you tomorrow." Just what he wanted to do, watch Jake occupy all of his wife's time.

"He sure is nice. I enjoy talkin' to him."

"You two sure seem to have a lot to talk about."

"We sure do." She smiled. "Do you know he keeps a goat in his house?"

"Yes. I was sitting there when he said that. Remember?"

"Oh, yeah. That's right. I plumb forgot."

That hurt.

"Well, I'd better get supper on."

"No."

"What do you mean, no?" Puzzlement darkened her brown eyes.

"Come on." He clasped her hand in his.

Her steps were like a one-legged turtle. "Where we going?"

"You'll see." He led her upstairs into the east bedroom and stopped just outside the closed door. "Okay, now close your eyes."

She eyed him suspiciously. "Why?"

"Come on, Selina. Just do it."

Her chest heaved and she nodded.

Once her eyes were closed, he waved his hand in front to make sure she wasn't peeking. Then he opened the door and led her inside. "Okay. You can open your eyes now."

Her mouth dropped open and her eyes blinked. "Oh, Michael. Are those for me?"

"Who else would they be for? Of course they're for you."

Selina walked to the bed. She glanced at the silk slippers before picking up the blue silk dress and holding it under her chin. "I ain't, I mean I have never had anythin' this purt...pretty before." She gazed up at him, then frowned. "But where would I ever wear anythin' this fancy?"

"At dinner."

"Dinner?" She looked down at her yellow muslin dress. "What's wrong with what I got on?"

"Nothing. But you'll want to wear that—" he pointed to the dress in her hands "—because I'm taking you to the finest dinner theater in town."

Selina's heart sank. She knew *finest* meant a place where she would never fit in.

"Do you like them? Mother made them."

Selina numbly ran her hand over the soft material and itchy lace. "She sure did a fine job."

He took the dress from her and laid it on the bed, then handed her a blue velvet box.

She had a feeling she knew what was in that box. When she raised the lid, her fears came to life with a punch to her gut. The dress, the shoes, the expensive jewelry, all of it represented the type of woman Michael wanted. Deserved even. And it wasn't her.

"I can't do this, Michael." She handed the box back to him.

"I don't understand. What's wrong?"

"Michael, I can't change my roots, who I am. You deserve a whole heap more than I could ever be." She bolted past him and flew down the stairs and out the door.

The trees swiped her face as she ran through the forest to the hilltop. Tears streamed down her cheeks. She hated treating Michael like that, especially after he went through all that trouble to have a dress made for her.

Tired from running, she sat down against the trunk of a large tree, wrapped her arms around her knees and rested her head on them.

"God," she said, sniffling. "I know I said my vows before You and all, and I promised to stay with Michael until death parted us. But I have to break that promise. I'm right sorry, but I shoulda seen it afore now. We're just too opposite. Michael deserves someone much better than me.

"So, I'm askin' You ahead of time to forgive me for breakin' that promise. I won't get married again and sin against You that way, but I have to set Michael free." At that thought, a thousand knives cut through her heart, shredding it slowly, torturing her soul until breath became hard to catch. Tears flooded her cheeks like a gulley wash.

She leaned her head back against the tree and closed her eyes, letting her heart have a good cry.

Suddenly, the hair on the back of her neck and arms stood.

Her eyes darted open.

She had a feeling she was being watched. By who

or what, she didn't know. But she'd hunted enough to know when she was in danger. And right now, she was in a heap of danger.

Two hours had passed since Selina left. It was dark now, and Michael was starting to get worried. He wished he'd gone after her when she first ran out. He was still nursing his wounds over the rejection of his gifts. He tried to do something nice for her by having his mother make her a beautiful gown and shoes. He'd even had the sapphire and diamond necklace and earrings shipped in from back east to go with them. But she wanted nothing to do with his gifts. It was time to put his hurt feelings aside and go looking for her.

Michael lit a lantern, grabbed his rifle and headed into the woods. "Lord, please show me where she went. And show me what to do to make things right. I'm so confused by everything right now. Please help me."

He climbed the hill, following the path, hoping to see her somewhere along it. Holding the lantern high, he checked the trees. Checked everywhere.

A loud scream pierced the air.

Michael set the lantern down and raced toward the sound.

Moonlight shed its silvery light in the darkened forest.

Dry foliage crunched under his feet.

Another scream.

He ran faster, harder, ignoring the branches slapping against his face.

"Help! Somebody help me!"

That was Selina.

His heart pounded against his ribs.

"Help!" Her voice got louder.

And then he saw her—and it.

A bear standing on its hind legs just yards away from her.

Selina held a stick almost as long as she was tall in front of her like a weapon. But that stick was no match for a hungry bear.

Instinct kicked in and Michael raised his rifle, aimed at the bear and pulled the trigger.

He missed.

The bear turned toward him, dropped on all fours and ran straight toward Michael.

Michael reloaded, aimed again and pulled the trigger.

About seven yards away, the bear dropped to the edge of the path with a crash.

Everything was silent.

Forcing his hands to stop shaking, Michael reloaded and waited, making sure the bear didn't get up. He inched his way to the animal and poked the bear with the barrel of his rifle. It didn't move. Relief poured through him, and his gaze shifted to Selina.

She stood still as a statue, staring in his direction.

He rushed to her and pulled her into his arms.

"Is it—is it dead?" Her voice trembled along with her body.

He glanced back at it, then at her. "It's dead."

Selina sunk against his chest. Her shoulders shook.

"Hey, it's okay." He rubbed her back in what he hoped was a soothing gesture. "Everything's okay."

"No, it isn't. And it ain't never gonna be, neither."

"What do you mean?"

"I'm leavin', Michael. I'm goin' back home."

He yanked his head back and stared down at her. "What? What do you mean?"

"Just what I said." She pulled out of his arms and swiped at her eyes. "I can't stay here anymore."

He wanted to snatch her back, but her look sent him a warning not to.

"You can't go. I don't want you to go. You're my wife."

"I'm sorry, Michael. But my mind is made up." With a shudder and a sigh, she turned to walk away from him.

Michael caught her by her arm and turned her around to face him. "Look, I know this isn't the ideal marriage for either one of us. But we need to work at it."

"I can't never be like Rainee. Or Aimee."

"I'm not asking you to."

"But that's the kind of woman you want. That dress and them slippers told me that. Can you look me in the eye and tell me that I'm wrong—that you don't want a woman who can wear those things and act all proper?"

Michael looked away. As much as he wanted to, he couldn't.

"Just as I thought." She yanked her arm away from him and headed down the mountain.

His head hung low in shame as he followed her. Ever since Rainee had arrived, he'd dreamed of a woman like her. One who could fit into his ranch-style life *and* the elite social life if need be. Knowing he had hurt Selina over his discarded dreams made him feel lower than low.

Selina headed upstairs to pack her meager belongings. She wouldn't be able to leave until morning, but when morning came, she'd be ready. She would ask Rainee to loan her the money for a train ticket and when she got back to Kentucky, she'd take in sewing to pay her back.

She opened the closet door and reached for a dress but stopped. Those weren't hers. She closed the door and sat on the bed.

The stairs creaked. Michael was coming.

Selina sprang up to close the door, but Michael stuck his foot inside and blocked it before she had the chance. "Please move your foot, Michael."

"Not until you let me in."

"We have nothin' more to say to each other."

"Well, maybe you have nothing more to say, but I've got plenty to say." He pushed on the door, and she was no match for his strength. His body filled the doorway.

She stepped back, crossing her arms over her chest.

"Look, Selina," he said, his voice going ragged. "It doesn't matter what I want or don't want. God chose to put you and me together and we need to stay together. We need to try and work this out. I care about you, Selina. I really do." His eyes searched hers.

She blinked. "I can't live like this, Michael. I tried wearin' dresses to please you, to be the type of woman you wanted. But when I saw that fancy ballgown, it reminded me that that was the type of woman you really want. That even with all the changes I made, I still ain't good enough for you. And never will be."

"I'm so sorry you took it that way." He took a step toward her.

She held up her hands. "Please don't come any closer."

"Why, Selina?" He took another step toward her.

"You know how I feel about you, and you comin' closer ain't helpin' things none. I ain't made of stone, you know. I got feelin's."

"So do I." He took another step.

"But they ain't for someone like me." She stepped back.

"How do you know that?" He took another step.

"I just do." She took another back.

"Are you sure?" He stepped closer.

She moved back farther until her back touched her bedroom wall. Against her will, his eyes held hers prisoner, and she was unable to pull her attention from him.

He pulled her to him.

She stiffened, but he tugged harder until she found she couldn't resist him.

His arms went about her, and he pressed her head into his chest, settling his chin atop her head. "Please stay. We need more time."

Being in his arms, breathing in the spicy forest scent that was all Michael, her heart skipped like a stone across the pond, and she found she couldn't say no.

Chapter Sixteen

Clean and refreshed from his dip in the creek, Michael headed to the house and stepped inside. In front of the fireplace, with her back to him, Selina stood wearing a blue dress and matching ribbon in her hair that flowed freely past her waist. He was glad she hadn't left, but things were far from settled between them and he knew he had a lot of ground to make up with her.

"You look beautiful, Selina." He wanted to step toward her but his feet wouldn't move, and that was a good thing because he didn't know what he would do.

"You look mighty fine yourself."

"Shall we go?"

"I'm ready whenever you are."

"What all needs to go?"

"That picnic basket." She pointed to the large basket on the table.

"What's in here?" He picked it up and opened the lid to find cloth-covered platters nestled inside. One peek and he saw his favorite cookies, Swedish oatmeal cookies, Brunscrackers, and his favorite one of all—Swedish tea cookies. The thought of the buttery sandwich cookies with the buttercream frosting in the middle made his mouth water. When he reached to grab one, she slapped him on the hand.

"Those are for the party."

"What if they all get eaten before I have a chance to get any? Can't I have just one of each?"

"I know they're your favorites, so I made plenty of extras for you. They're in the cookie jar." Was there no end to her sweetness? Making his favorite cookies. She really was a thoughtful little thing. He shoved his arm through the picnic basket handles and scooped it up, then offered her his other arm.

She looped her arm through his, and out the door and down the steps they went. "You brung, I mean, you *brought* the buggy?" Surprise fluttered through her eyes, eyes that endeared her to him.

"Can't have my wife walking and getting all dusty, now can I?"

The scent of roses surrounded her.

He set the basket on the floor of the carriage and offered her a hand up. She settled her skirt, and he climbed in next to her. Their shoulders brushed, then melded together.

Michael looked at her and smiled.

Innocent eyes gazed up at him, blinking, and her lips parted.

Like a moth drawn to flames, those sweet lips lured him to her until he found himself leaning into her and capturing her mouth in a brief but pulsating kiss.

Their lips separated and they smiled at each other before he picked up the reins. Maybe things would work after all. "Giddyup." Michael turned his horse toward the ranch yard. A quick glance at his wife and his shoulders straightened. This time he would not be embarrassed to ride in with her. Not because the lady who'd worn trousers when he'd first introduced her to everyone was now wearing a dress and looked prettier than a field of buttercups. No, it was because she was beautiful on the inside and he was proud to call her his wife.

Joining the reins in one hand, he reached over and clasped hers.

Her gaze slid to their adjoined hands, then turned up at him, questioning him with a look only. He answered with one of his own—admiration and pride.

Buggies and wagons nestled against the base of the trees in the ranch yard. Tepid air drifted down the mountain, but the sun balanced it, making it a warm, but not too scorching, day.

"There's Rainee. I can't wait to see Haydon Junior again."

He parked the buggy and helped her down. His eyes scanned the crowd of neighbors. Unlike the last time they'd gathered together, surprised looks were quickly replaced with admiration.

He grabbed the picnic basket with one arm and offered her the other, leading her into the crowd.

Women gathered around Selina, gushing about how beautiful she looked and crowding him away from her. "I'll go put this on the table," he said over the flock of ladies' heads.

She nodded and turned her attention back to the women.

On his way to add their basket, Rainee, carrying Haydon Junior, came walking toward him.

"Hello, Michael," Rainee said passing him by.

"Whoa, just a minute there. Where are you going

in such a hurry that you can't even stop and let Uncle Michael see his nephew?"

"I wanted to see Selina."

"Seems like you and everyone else." He glanced over to where she stood.

"She sure looks lovely."

"She sure does."

"Her reading has improved greatly, too."

Shock slammed into him. "Her reading?"

"Yes, she—" Rainee stopped. Her eyes widened in horror. "Oh, Michael. I was not supposed to say anything. She would be quite displeased if she knew I had. Oh, my. Please, do not tell her I told you. It slipped out."

He rested his hand on her arm. "Relax, Rainee. I won't say anything." Michael darted a glance over toward Selina, then turned his attention back onto Rainee. "How long she been learning to read?"

"Ever since she arrived."

Michael didn't know why, but the thought of her trying to improve herself blessed him.

"Please, do not tell her I let it slip. Promise me you will not."

"I won't, Rainee. I promise. Now let me see that baby."

She handed Haydon Junior over to him. Michael tucked him to his chest, and the hunger to be a father returned. His attention once again slid over to Selina. Maybe there was a chance for them to be a family after all.

"Okay. Give me my son back. I want to go see Selina."

Michael did as he was told and watched Rainee walk away and inch her way into the crowd surrounding his wife. He continued to watch as Selina took his nephew from Rainee. She looked so natural holding a baby in her arms. He visualized her holding their child, and he smiled at the image.

The dinner bell rang. The ladies separated from Selina in search of their spouses. Michael strolled over to Selina and offered her his arm. They gathered around the table with the rest of their neighbors, family and ranch hands.

Haydon's voice boomed as he spoke, "Let's bow our heads." When he finished praying, women bustled about uncovering dishes. Families lined up at the tables, filling their plates with a menagerie of foods.

Once he and Selina had their plates filled, they found seats.

Within seconds, Jake strode up. "Mind if I join you?"

Yes, he minded. What was with Jake coming around so much lately? Michael thought he meant no harm, but now he was beginning to wonder.

Selina nudged him in the side.

"No, no, don't mind at all."

Jake smiled at Selina as he lowered his bulky frame down. "You're looking prettier every time I see you. Is that a new dress?"

"Yes." Selina's cheeks tinted to a light shade of pink. Was she blushing because of Jake's compliment, or was she embarrassed by the attention he had just lavished on her? Michael wasn't sure why Jake's attention to Selina bothered him so much.

This time, however, Michael wasn't going to be left out of the conversation. "Selina."

She pulled her attention away from Jake and onto him.

"Back home, did your neighbors get together after harvest season?"

"Sure did, but we gathered together when the weather changed, any time someone had a baby or when the first frost gathered on the ground. Why, any excuse we could find, us neighbors used it to get together."

"You had parties that often?"

A strand of her molasses-colored hair slipped over her shoulder. He wanted to reach over and slip it back, but not in front of Jake. Touching her always did funny things to him and he was afraid it would show.

"We sure did."

"What were they like?" Michael asked before Jake had a chance to.

"Well…" She set her fork down. "Ain't much different than this one. Except we always set up a wooden floor in the middle of a clearin' or the meadow and had us a dance. Folks brought their fiddles, guitars, banjos. Some folks even made music blowin' into empty moonshine jugs. Others would play spoons. Anythin' that made music, they used it. Always had a heap of contests, too."

"What kind of contests?" Michael found he really wanted to know.

"Contests to see who could toss an ax closest to the center of a circle. Horseshoe toss. Log sawin'. Iron skillet toss. Just about every kind of contest you could think of. Everything from gunnysack races, to berry pickin', to corn shuckin'. Womenfolk entered their pies in the pie tastin' and eatin' contests. Well, one man did, too. Piney Baker. He'd enter his blackberry pie over and over again. And every time he lost on the count of his pie crust had the texture of uncooked grits."

"What's grits?" Jake piped in.

"Y'all ain't never had grits?" Shock sang through her slow melodious voice. A voice he now enjoyed listening to. "You don't know what y'all are missin'."

"What is grits? What does it taste like?" Michael shot up his hand. "Not that I want you to make me any," he added quickly, afraid she'd make him another crazy food he wouldn't like. "I'm just curious what it is and what it's like."

"Well, it's kinda bland. But it's mighty tasty iffen you add lots of butter or cheese or sugar or syrup to it. Some folks mix it in with their eggs. Some pour red-eye gravy on top. I never did that. Don't care much for the taste of that stuff."

"What stuff?" Jake asked, and Michael frowned.

"Redeye gravy."

"Never heard of it. What is it?" Jake tore off a huge chunk of buttered bread slathered with jam and shoved it into his mouth, but his focus never left Selina's face.

"It's made from ham drippings."

"Sounds like you grew up with some unusual foods," Jake said.

Frustrated that once again Jake was occupying Selina's attention, Michael tore off a chunk of Selina's Southern fried chicken. There was nothing unusual about it. She made the best chicken he'd ever eaten.

"Wasn't unusual to us." She looked at Michael, her eyes and lips twinkling. "There was one contest you could've never done, Michael."

"Oh, yeah. What's that?" Michael suddenly felt challenged.

"The crawdad eatin' contest."

She was right. He would have never been able to enter that one. The others sounded fun, though.

"Crawdad tails?" Jake looked shocked. "You eat fish bait?"

"That's what I asked her. She made me some for dinner one night. I hate to admit it, but they weren't too bad. Even though they tasted all right, I still couldn't eat them once I knew what they were. But at least they weren't frog legs. I'm glad for that."

Jake's eyebrows rose toward the sky. "You eat frog legs, too?" He looked horrified.

Michael understood Jake's reaction firsthand. He chuckled.

Selina shot him a scowl. "We sure do," she said proudly. "Y'all don't know you're missin'." Defensiveness stole her voice.

He hadn't meant to hurt her feelings by laughing.

"They're right tasty."

"Did you ever enter your fried chicken?" Michael asked. "If so, I imagine it won."

Her cheeks brightened to a light shade of red. Her gaze fell to her lap. "Sure did. Won first place every time."

"I can believe it." Jake tore off a chunk. His cheeks bulged like a chipmunk.

Conversation continued to flow as they ate. As Michael finished the last bite of his chicken, Jesse headed toward him. "Michael, can you help me a minute?"

"Sure." He stood and looked down at Selina. "Be right back."

She nodded.

Several yards away, he glanced over his shoulder and noticed Jake had moved around to the other side of the bench and was now sitting next to Selina. He hurried and helped Jesse chase Kitty down and put her back into her pen, then strode back over to her. "Excuse me, Jake. But I believe you have my seat." He forced his lips to curl into a smile.

"Oh. Um. Sorry about that, buddy." Jake picked up his plate and hurried back to the other side of the table.

Michael sat next to Selina and faced her. "What would we need to set up a few of those contests you were talking about?"

Her eyes brightened. "You mean it?"

"Yes. I think everyone here would really enjoy them."

She threw her arms around him. "Thank you, Michael." Her breath sent shivers skittering through him. "Okay." She yanked out of his arms and leaped up from the bench. "First we'll need—"

"You need to finish eating first. And no crawdad eating contest. No mention of it, even."

"Oh, you big old teasin' polecat. Ain't time to catch any today and you know it."

"Can I help with the contest?" Jake asked.

"I don't see why not. Let's get to eatin' so we can have some fun."

Michael refused to let his jealousy come between his wife's happiness in sharing a part of her culture here in the Idaho Territory. He would work with Jake and be grateful for his help, too.

They finished eating and cleaned up.

"Okay, let's see." Selina glanced up at Michael standing near the barn. "We need to fetch a couple of cast iron skillets, an ax or two, four horseshoes, somethin' to use as a spike. Need two of them. And as many empty grain sacks and gunnysacks as you can find. I need a few dozen eggs and some clean soup spoons."

"What do you need the spoon and eggs for?"

"Well, you have teams of three. You place an egg in the spoon and carry it to the next person on your team without dropping it. Iffen you drop it, you have to go back to the startin' line. If you don't drop it, you hand off the egg and spoon to the next person. The first one to reach the finish line with a whole unbroken egg wins."

"What do they win?"

Selina pressed her finger to her lip. Just what would they win? Back home there were homemade quilts for the women who won and axes for the men. No time to do that now. Or was there? "Just a minute. I'll be right back." Selina scurried over to Katherine.

"Excuse me, Mrs. Hansen, but I need to ask Mother a question."

"I'll leave."

"No, no. Don't leave." She ducked toward Katherine.

"Mother, you know that quilt we finished?" She still couldn't get used to calling her new ma Mother. Maybe one day she would.

Katherine smiled. "Yes."

"Well, I know I made it for Michael for Christmas, but I was wonderin' iffen I could have it now."

Katherine paused, a confused look on her face.

"Is that all right?"

"Oh, sure, sure. You just took me by surprise is all."

"What do you need the quilt for?" a neighbor standing nearby asked.

"You'll see. It's a surprise."

"Oh, I love surprises," Katherine chirped. "I'll go get it."

"No. Not yet. Iffen it's all the same to you, I'll get it when I'm ready."

"That's fine, Selina."

"Thank you kindly." She gave her a quick hug and raced back to the barn.

Horse flesh, hay and saddle oil swirled up her nose. And so did dust. Oh oh. She felt a sneeze coming on. Achoo! It echoed through the barn.

"Selina's here," she heard Michael say from inside the tack room.

"How do you know it's her?" Jake asked.

"I know her sneeze."

"You two are strange. You know that?"

"Yep. Makes life interesting." Michael stepped out of the tack room with Jake on his heels.

"What you got there?" she asked Michael.

"Prizes."

"Jumpin' crickets! You're giving them away?" Her attention stuck on the brand-new halters in Michael's hand.

"Yep."

"Those sure are mighty nice prizes. Ain't ever gave anythin' that nice before back home."

"What did you give for prizes?"

"Oh, jars of preserves and pies and sometimes a pocket knife iffen it was a good crop year."

"Those sound like nice prizes," Michael said.

"I agree." Jake licked his lips and rubbed his belly.

When they finished gathering and setting everything up, the three of them climbed onto Katherine's porch and Michael rang the bell.

Everyone stopped talking and the kids stopped playing. All attention was on her husband.

"This year, I want to do something different," Michael announced. "Something fun." He pulled Selina to him and tucked her under his arm. "Back in Kentucky, where my wife is from, when the harvesting is over, they have a get-together something like this. Only they hold contests. They even give away prizes."

Selina saw the surprised look on everyone's faces, especially her brothers-and sisters-in-law.

"So that's what we're going to do. First, we're going to start with an ax-throwing contest. Anyone who wants to participate can follow me when I'm finished talking. The other contests will be…" She listened as Michael explained the rest. When he finished talking, there was silence.

Selina's heart sank.

Michael's smile vanished.

Jake looked shocked and angry.

Suddenly, whoops and hollers filled the air.

Selina found herself being picked up and swung around. "Put me down, you ole polecat. We got contests to run." She giggled.

Three hours later, the last contest was the sack race.

"Come on." Michael grabbed Selina's hand and took her over to the table where the empty gunnysacks were lying. He picked one up and tugged on her hand, pulling her to the starting line.

"I can't do that with you, Michael. I'm too short and you're too tall."

"If it gets complicated, I'll carry you."

She hesitated. "I don't know."

"Chicken."

"Polecat. You got yourself a partner."

"Sure do." He winked at her and her heart winked in return. Only he couldn't see her heart, so she flashed him a wink of her own, and he chuckled.

Excitement and anticipation bubbled over her like water over river rocks.

At the starting line, they each put a leg into the gunnysack. A feeling of being protected washed over her. She'd always had to be the protector, and now she had a sense she could give that job to Michael. After all, wasn't that what God intended all along?

"Ready?"

"Sure am."

"Then put your arm around my waist." He smiled down at her. That one dimple peeked at her.

"Oh" was all she could manage. Her arm slipped around him. Being this close to him always turned her mind to mush.

She glanced to the left. Six other teams had joined them. Two couples, whose names she couldn't remember. And Tom and Sadie, which surprised Selina since it hadn't been all that long ago that Sadie had had her baby. But one thing she knew about Sadie, she came from tough stock. Sadie leaned past her husband and smiled at Selina.

Selina smiled back and gave a quick wave.

Abby and her friend Betsy stood next to Sadie. Next to them were Jesse and Hannah. Jake and Leah were teamed up, too. Those two made a mighty fine-looking couple, too. She wondered why the two of them didn't get hitched.

"Ready?" Haydon hollered from the end of the finish

line. "On the count of three." Pistol raised, he counted. "One. Two. Three."

Bang!

Selina struggled to keep up with Michael, but she did. As they got closer to the finish line, only three couples were left. Tom and Sadie, Jake and Leah and Selina and Michael.

Yards away from the finish line, they were lagging behind, so Michael picked her up. Her legs dangled as he rushed toward the rope stretched between Haydon and Smokey.

Tom and Sadie were ahead of Jake and Leah and she and Michael by inches.

From the corner of her eye she watched Leah and Jake tumble to the ground.

Only feet left to go.

Strain and determination wrinkled Tom and Sadie's red faces as they struggled forward, stretching their necks out as far as they could just as she and Michael tumbled to the ground.

"The winners. Tom and Sadie!"

Cheers filled the yard.

Michael stood and reached his hand toward Selina, helping her up. "That was so much fun. Thank you, love." He kissed her cheek, then led her over to where the crowd stood.

"Time to give out the prizes," Michael shouted.

"Be right back." Selina rushed inside Katherine's house, snatched the quilt from the trunk and ran back to Michael's side, puffing.

Michael called out each winner's name. Men who didn't win moaned, saying they wished they'd a won a nice halter, too. "Now for the winners of the gunnysack race... Tom and Sadie." Selina handed Michael the quilt she'd made. Her very first one.

"Oh, Tom. Look. A quilt." Sadie beamed. "We sure needed one," Sadie gushed.

Selina's heart grew to bursting.

It was getting late, so everyone pitched in and cleaned up the yard, putting tables away, loading their wagons and thanking Selina and Michael for providing such a wonderful fun-filled day with the games. Finally, the last wagon pulled out of the yard.

"I don't know about you, love, but I'm ready to head home."

"Could we do somethin' first?"

"What's that?"

"Can we take the buggy up the hill and watch the sun set?"

"Sounds nice." He gazed down at her, smiling.

They said their good-nights to the family, and Michael offered her his hand to help her into the buggy.

Up the trail they headed until they reached the top. Michael reined Bobcat to a stop.

For a few moments, neither said a word.

Michael slipped his arm around her shoulders and pulled her closer to him. Selina rested her head on his shoulder.

They sat back to watch God's masterpiece at work.

Above the shadowed rolling hills an orange sky with yellow clouds outlined the fading sun.

A perfect setting to a perfect day.

"I know why you tripped me."

"What do you mean?" Selina whispered.

"You know what I mean." His soft voice melted her into him further. "You knew Sadie and Tom needed blankets for the winter so you tripped me so they would win."

"Are ya mad?" she whispered again.

"Mad?" He tilted her head. Their eyes connected and held. "How could I be mad at one of the sweetest gestures I've ever seen? Where'd the quilt come from, anyway?"

"From me. It was the first one I ever made."

"You're kidding?"

"I'm not."

"You really are something. You know that?"

"You keep tellin' me that. Still not sure if being somethin' is a good thing or a bad thing."

"Trust me. It's good." With those words, his lips found hers and held them for a long time.

Now, that was an even more perfect ending. The only thing that would make it better was if Michael would whisper those three little words against her lips.

Chapter Seventeen

"Yesterday was great," Michael told Selina over breakfast. "I don't know when I've had a better time."

"Me, too." She refilled his coffee cup.

"What are your plans for today?"

"Well, I need to go to town and pick up some supplies."

"Me, too. You want to go together?"

"Sure. I'd love to."

"Can you be ready in about," he glanced at the clock, "ten minutes?"

"I'm ready now."

Michael looked over her new black trousers. Before he'd gotten to know Selina, it would have bothered him to be seen with her wearing men's trousers, but not anymore. Now that was just Selina.

She followed his gaze. "Oh. I plumb forgot I was wearin' pants. I got up early and fed the chickens and horses."

"What time did you get up?" Michael sipped his coffee. His eyes never strayed from her.

She looked down at her lap. "I never went to bed."

Michael frowned. What did she mean she'd never gone to bed? He'd seen her climb the stairs.

"I tried to sleep but couldn't. So, I got up and read—" Her wide eyes darted to his.

"You can read?" He already knew the answer to that question, but he promised Rainee he wouldn't say anything and he intended to keep his promise.

"Some. I'm still learnin'. Gettin' easier everyday, though. I can write some, too. Now iffen I could just talk better. But—" she sighed heavily "—I talked this way my whole life and the words fall out before I have a chance to correct them."

Michael set his coffee down and pulled Selina's hands into his. "Selina, I think it's great that you're learning to read and write…for your sake. But… I don't want you to change the way you talk. I like it."

"You—you do?"

"Yes."

"But I heard you tell Jess I talked funny."

She heard that? What else had she overheard? "I must admit, it did bother me at first, but now I like it." He kissed her hand. "It's you."

Her face lit up like a candle in a dark room. She smiled. "I'll be right back." She whirled and ran upstairs.

Minutes later, the rustle of skirts drifted over to him. He glanced toward the stairs. His breath hitched and his heart bucked like a wild horse in response to seeing her in a soft pink cotton dress that showed off her feminine curves. He couldn't wait to show *her* off in town.

Twenty minutes later, Michael stopped in front of Marcel Mercantile. The first person he saw was Ethel.

He groaned, knowing how cruel the woman could be and knowing that she had spread rumors about how he had feelings for her daughter.

He helped Selina down from the wagon and draped his arm around her shoulder. "Morning, Ethel."

"Morning, Michael." Ethel turned to Selina. "You sure look nice, Selina. I heard how you helped save Rainee and her son's life. And Sadie, well, she can't say enough good things about you." The woman babbled on and on about all of Selina's attributes. "Next time you're in town, drop in. I live in the green house at the end of this street."

If Michael hadn't heard it for himself, he would have never believed it. Ethel being kind? Inviting Selina to her home? Ethel never invited anyone to her home.

They finished gathering their supplies and headed back to the ranch.

At the house, Michael had just finished unloading the wagon, when Doc Berg came to the door.

"Is Selina home?"

"Yes, she's inside. Why?"

"The Barrison twins' wagon rolled over and I'm headed to their house now. Your place was on the way, and after I saw the great job she did sewing Jake's head, I thought I would see if Selina would be willing to come and help me. That is, if you don't mind."

"I don't mind. But it's up to her. How are Bo and Sam?" Michael asked as they headed into the house.

"Won't know until I get there."

They stepped into the kitchen. Selina was standing at the sink. "Selina, Doc's here. He needs your help."

Selina wiped her hands off on her apron. "What can

I do for you, Doc?" She removed her apron and hung it on a peg near the sink.

He explained the situation.

"You don't mind iffen I go, do you, Michael?"

"Before you decide," Doc interjected, "you need to know she won't be home until way after dark. It takes almost an hour alone to get there."

"No, I don't mind. I have a lot of work to get caught up on this afternoon anyway."

"Thank you, Michael." She kissed his cheek and headed out the door with Doctor Berg.

Hours later, after branding and fixing fences, Michael made his way home. A light was on inside his house. He knew it wasn't Selina—she hadn't gotten back yet and wouldn't be home until later that evening.

Lately, a few shady prospectors looking for gold had started making themselves at home in other people's houses when they were not at home.

Michael pulled his derringer out of his boot and crept up the steps, careful to not make a sound. At the window, he stayed back far enough to not be seen and peeked inside.

What in the...?

Who was that?

He took a minute to study the woman sitting on his sofa.

Starting at her feet, his eyes made their way up.

Pink silk slippers peeked out from under a pink ruffled dress. Her head rested on the back wing of the sofa. Her face was covered by a row of long ringlet curls.

Was the woman hurt or asleep? Only one way to find out.

Because the front door squeaked when it opened,

Michael went around back and slipped inside through the back door, then made his way into the living room.

"Uh-hmm." He cleared his throat.

The woman's head wobbled upward and turned his direction.

Michael's breath hitched in his throat.

Misty gray eyes stared up at him through a haze of sleep. She sat up and pushed the curls off her face. "You. You must be Michael," she said.

Before him was a very beautiful woman.

Who was she?

And what was she doing here?

"Michael?" She rose from the sofa. When she tilted her head a curl fell across her porcelain cheek.

"Yes. I'm Michael. And you are...?"

"Aimee. Aimee Lynn Covington." Her words came out slow and precise and she curtsied just like Rainee had when she first came here.

His eyes widened. "You're Aimee?"

"Yes, sir. I am." She looked behind him. "I hope you don't mind but when your sister, Leah, and I got here no one was home. I asked her if it would be all right if I waited here. I wanted to surprise Selina."

She'll be surprised all right. He knew *he* was.

"Where is she?"

"Who?"

She frowned. "Selina? Your wife. My best friend." Her delicate brows rose.

The woman had done her friend a huge disservice. Aimee was no friend. "What are you doing here?" His teeth ached from biting them so hard. This woman had nerve showing up here like this.

Aimee frowned, and the gray in her eyes darkened

like thunder clouds. "I told Selina I was coming for a visit. Didn't she get my post?"

"Your letter said you would be coming sometime to visit us, but it didn't say when." He knew he should have written back to tell her she wasn't welcome here and never would be.

"Well, I just missed Selina so much, I had to come and see her. Where is she?" She looked around again.

So many emotions were running around in Michael's head that he had a hard time catching up to any of them. He stared at the beautiful, genteel Southern lady in front of him. All those years when he had pictured a wife for himself, he had envisioned someone just like Aimee. But now the only vision to fill his mind and his heart was Selina.

In that instant it dawned on him. He loved Selina. Not only loved her, but he was *in* love with her. Happiness flowed through his veins like warm, liquid sunshine.

"Michael, are you okay?"

"What?" He placed his attention onto Aimee. "I'm fine." He couldn't keep the joy out of his voice or from his face. "I'm better than I've been in a long time."

"You haven't answered my question. Where is Selina? Is she okay?"

"Oh, yes. She's more than okay. She's great." He knew he sounded stupid but he couldn't help that, either. "She's helping Doc Berg."

The woman's rigid shoulders relaxed. "I'm so glad she's okay. I don't know what I would do if something happened to her. She's the most amazing person I know."

"She sure is."

"I'm so glad you feel that way." She looked down at the floor. "Michael, by now you know that I didn't write everything Selina told me to."

That snagged his attention. "Why didn't you?"

"Because if I did, you wouldn't have sent for her."

Anger coiled inside of him. How dare she talk about his wife like that. "Why not?"

"Because most people listen to her talk or they look at her outward appearance and judge her unworthy. They don't get to know the real her. I just knew if someone did, they would love her, like I do. They would see that underneath her rugged exterior is a heart of pure gold. A lovely person who deserves the best. Who deserves the love of a good man." Her gaze came up to his. "I could tell from your letters that you were an honest, decent man. I'm sorry I deceived you, Michael. Are you sorry I did?"

He could see how important his answer was to her. She really did love her friend. He heard it in her words and saw it in her eyes.

"No. At first I was. I'm ashamed to say I did just what you said everyone else does. I judged her by her outward appearance and her speech. But then I got to know her. To know her heart, and you're right. She is a wonderful person." He paused, and all the anger he held toward Aimee and himself relinquished its hold on him. Selina had told him he deserved someone better. She was wrong. "I don't deserve her. But I love her so much I'll do whatever it takes to deserve her."

"Oh, Michael, I'm so happy for you and Selina." Aimee threw her arms around him and hugged him. He hugged her back, happier than he had ever been.

* * *

Selina slid from the buggy, bone tired. All she wanted to do was to head straight to bed.

Lights were on in the house. Michael must still be up.

Anxious to see him in spite of how tired she was, instead of climbing the steps she hopped onto the porch. On her way to the front door, she passed the living room window and glanced inside.

Jumpin' crickets!

She backed away from full view of the window and peeked inside.

Michael and Aimee had their arms around each other. When they separated, Selina right away noticed the joy on her husband's face, and her heart shattered into hundreds of tiny pieces.

She closed her eyes and refused to let the tears stinging the back of her eyes fall. Her fears had come to life. She knew something like this would happen if Michael ever laid eyes on Aimee. Everything he said he wanted in a wife, Aimee was it, and Selina wasn't.

Well, he could have her. They could have each other.

She quietly made her way back across the porch and hopped down. Where she would go this late, she had no idea, but she wouldn't go back into that house ever again. She couldn't. It hurt too much seeing them hugging and seeing the happiness on Michael's face.

Michael paced between the living room and kitchen, peering out the windows occasionally. With Selina gone, he hadn't felt right about having Aimee in the house, so he had taken her to his mother's to see if she could stay the night there.

For the twentieth time, he looked at the grandfather clock. Doc said it would be late, but Michael thought he meant eight or nine, not midnight.

Every time he prayed, deep in his gut he felt something wasn't right. He'd waited as long as he was going to. He grabbed his jacket and rifle and one other thing from his dresser and headed down to the barn.

When he stepped inside, he heard the muffled sound of crying. He strained to listen where it was coming from. Quietly he made his way to the ladder leading up to the loft.

The crying grew louder.

He climbed the ladder only as high as his head so he could peek around to see who it was. Laying on one of the blankets they kept in the barn was Selina, curled in a ball. Michael scurried up the ladder, rushed to her and dropped to his knees beside her. "Selina?"

She curled up tighter, keeping her back to him. "Go away, Michael." She sniffed.

"What's wrong, love?" He laid his hand on her arm.

She shoved it away with one swipe.

Fear clutched his insides. "Selina, what's wrong?"

"You know good and well what's wrong. Now go away."

"No, I don't know. And you're scaring me. What's wrong?" He dropped into a sitting position and pulled Selina onto his lap, cradling her stiff body against his.

She twisted, trying to get away, but he held her securely without hurting her. His wife refused to look at him. "Let go of me," she whimpered before going limp in his arms.

Now he really was scared. Selina's spunk usually rose to the occasion. So whatever had her upset must be huge for her to give up so easily. Whatever it was, he was going to find out. "I'm not letting go until you tell me what's wrong."

She yanked her tearful gaze up to his. Even in the dark shadows of the barn the moisture in and under her eyes sparkled. Seeing her pain, his heart rent into pieces. He laid his thumb under her eye to wipe away the tears, but she brushed it off with a yank, too.

Without warning, fire flashed through her eyes. She stiffened in his arms and tried to sit up, but he held her so she couldn't move. "I'll tell you what's wrong, you no-good polecat."

"No-good polecat? What did I do?"

"Don't think I don't know what's goin' on. I may not be the most learned person in this world, but I ain't stupid, neither."

"I never said you were. What's this all about, Selina?"

"I saw you and Aimee huggin'."

That was what was bothering her? Relief replaced his fear and he laughed with the release of knowing that was it.

"You think that's funny? Well, I don't." Selina jerked upward, but he captured her around the waist and pulled her back onto his lap. She fought him, but he gently restrained her.

"Selina, listen to me. Yes, you saw me and Aimee hugging. Do you want to know why?"

"I already know why." She squirmed some more. "'Cause she's more what you're wantin' in a wife than me, and you couldn't help yourself when you laid eyes on her."

"Oh, my love." Out of pure joy, Michael laughed

again. "You've got it all wrong. It's you I want. When you saw us hugging, I had just told her that I realized I love you. That I'm *in* love with you."

She stopped squirming and looked up at him. "What?"

"I said…" He gazed down at her tenderly, willing his eyes to show the depth of love in his heart for her. "I love you, Selina."

"You—you do?"

"That's what I said." He tossed her own words back at her with a hint of humor and a small smile.

"Oh, Michael, you mean it? You ain't in love with Aimee?" Her eyes searched his.

"Now, how could I be in love with her when I'm so madly and completely in love with my wife?" He held on to her securely with one arm and pulled out a little cloth sack from his vest pocket with the other. He reached for her left hand and slipped the gold band with blue sapphires and diamonds onto her finger.

She gazed down at it. "A wedding ring? For me? It's so beautiful."

"So are you." He cupped her chin and with a voice husky with love, he said, "And now, my love, I'm going to prove to you just how much I really do love you." His lips touched hers. She surrendered her lips to his in the sweetest, most passionate kiss he'd ever received.

Nine months later, Michael paced the floor of their house. From their bedroom a loud cry pierced the air. He rushed inside.

"Here, Michael. Take your son." Doc wrapped a blanket around him and handed the baby to him. "I have to deliver another one."

"Another one?" Michael swallowed hard. Twins? Selina was giving birth to twins? Shocked to the essence of his being, all he could do was stare into the face of his son until he heard another cry. His attention flew to Doc. "Another boy?" he asked.

"No. This one's a girl."

Michael gazed over at Selina. Their eyes joined as their hearts and bodies had so many months before. Contentment wrapped around him like the blankets around his children. Children.

He was a father.

And a husband.

Michael thanked God that He hadn't answered his prayers the way Michael thought He should. That the Lord knew what was best for him and had blessed Michael far beyond any desire he'd ever had the day God sent him a very unlikely wife in trousers.

* * * * *

WE HOPE YOU ENJOYED
THIS BOOK FROM

LOVE INSPIRED
INSPIRATIONAL ROMANCE

Uplifting stories of faith, forgiveness and hope.

Fall in love with stories where faith helps
guide you through life's challenges, and discover
the promise of a new beginning.

6 NEW BOOKS AVAILABLE EVERY MONTH!

"I'm sorry I was distant before. That was just me being foolish."

Samantha didn't ask what he was talking about; she obviously knew. "What was going on?"

Corbin debated finding some intellectual way to say it, but he wasn't thinking straight enough. "I got turned upside down by that kiss."

"Yeah. Me, too." She glanced at him and then turned to put a stack of plates away.

"It was intense."

"Uh-huh."

Now that he had brought up the topic, he wasn't sure where he wanted to go with it. For him to go into the fact that he couldn't get involved with her because she was an alcoholic... Suddenly, that felt judgmental and mean and not how he wanted to talk to her.

Maybe it wasn't how he wanted to be with her, either, but he wasn't ready to make that alteration to his long-held set of values about who he could get involved with. And until he did, he obviously needed to keep a lid on his feelings.

So he talked about something they would probably agree on. "I was never so scared in my life as when Mikey was lost."

"Me, either. It was awful."

He paused, then admitted, "I just don't know if I'm cut out for taking care of a kid."

Her head jerked around to face him. "You're not thinking of sending him back to your mom, are you?"

Was he? He shook his head slowly, letting out a sigh. "No. I feel like I screwed up badly, but I still think he's safer with me than with her."

She let the water out of the sink, not looking at him now. "I think you're doing a great job," she said. "It was just as much my fault as yours. Parenting is a challenge and you can't help but screw up sometimes."

"I guess." He wasn't used to doing things poorly or in a half-baked way. He was used to working at a task until he could become an expert. But it seemed that nobody was an expert when it came to raising kids, not really.

"Mikey can be a handful, just like any other little child," she said.

"He is, but I sure love him," Corbin said. It was the first time he had articulated that, and he realized it was completely true. He loved his little brother as if the boy were his own son.

"I love him, too," she said, almost offhandedly.

She just continued wiping down the counters, not acting like she had said anything momentous, but her words blew Corbin away. She had an amazing ability to love. Mikey wasn't her child, nor her blood, but she felt for him as if he were.

If he loved his little brother despite the boy's issues and whining and toddler misbehavior, could it be that he could love another adult who had issues, too? He was definitely starting to care a lot for Samantha. Was he growing, becoming more flexible and forgiving?

He didn't know if he could change that much. He'd been holding himself—and others—to a strict high standard for a long time. It was how he'd gotten as far as he had after his rough beginning.

Corbin wanted to continue caring for his brother, especially given the alternative, but the fact that Mikey had gotten lost had shaken him. He didn't know if he was good enough to do the job.

Samantha's expression of support soothed his insecurities. He wanted love and acceptance, just like anyone else. And there was a tiny spark inside him that was starting to burn, a spark that wondered if he could maybe be loved and fall in love, even with a certain nanny.

Don't miss
Child on His Doorstep
by Lee Tobin McClain, available August 2020 wherever
Love Inspired books and ebooks are sold.

LoveInspired.com

LIEXP0720

Traces of fog lingered along the East River. Off-duty police officer Vivienne Armstrong paused at the fence bordering the Brooklyn Heights Promenade to gaze across the river at the majestic Manhattan skyline. Her city. Her home.

Slight pressure against her calf reminded her why she was there, and she smiled down at her K-9 partner. "Yes, Hank, I know. You want to run and burn off energy. What a good boy."

The soft brown eyes of the black-and-white border collie made it seem as though he understood every word, and given the extraordinary reputation of his breed, she imagined he might.

"Jake! My baby! Where's my baby?" a woman screeched.

Other passersby froze, making it easy for Vivienne to pick out the frantic young woman darting from person to person. "He has blond hair. Bright green pants. Have you seen him? Please!"

"I'm a police officer," Vivienne told the woman. "Calm down and tell me what happened."

The fair-haired mother was gasping for breath, her eyes wide and filling with tears. "My little boy was right here. Next to me. I just… I just stopped to look at the boats, and when I turned to pick him up and show him, he was gone!"

Vivienne gently touched her shoulder. "I'm a K-9 officer and my dog is trained for search and rescue. Do you have any item of your son's that I can use for scent?"

The woman blinked rapidly. "Yes! In my bag."

Vivienne watched as the mother pulled out a stuffed toy rabbit. "Perfect."

In full professional mode, she straightened, loosened her hold on the dog's leash and commanded, "Seek."

Hank circled, returned to the place at the river fence that the woman had indicated earlier, then sniffed the air and began to run.

The leash tightened. Vivienne followed as hope leaped, then sank. The dog was following air scent. Therefore, the missing child had not left footprints when he'd parted from his mother. Someone had lifted and carried him away. There was only one conclusion that made sense.

The little boy had been kidnapped!

Don't miss
Tracking a Kidnapper *by Valerie Hansen,*
available wherever Love Inspired Suspense books
and ebooks are sold.

LoveInspired.com

Love Harlequin romance?

DISCOVER.

Be the first to find out about promotions,
news and exclusive content!

Facebook.com/HarlequinBooks

Twitter.com/HarlequinBooks

Instagram.com/HarlequinBooks

Pinterest.com/HarlequinBooks

ReaderService.com

EXPLORE.

Sign up for the Harlequin e-newsletter and
download a free book from any series at
TryHarlequin.com

CONNECT.

Join our Harlequin community to
share your thoughts and connect
with other romance readers!
Facebook.com/groups/HarlequinConnection

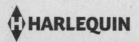

HSOCIAL2020